PENGUIN BOOKS

THE JUDAS HEART

The Judas Heart

INGRID BLACK

PENGUIN BOOKS

PENGUIN BOOKS

Published by the Penguin Group
Penguin Books Ltd, 80 Strand, London WC2R ORL, England
Penguin Group (USA) Inc., 375 Hudson Street, New York, New York 10014, USA
Penguin Group (Canada), 90 Eglinton Avenue East, Suite 700, Toronto, Ontario, Canada M4P 2Y3
(a division of Pearson Penguin Canada Inc.)
Penguin Ireland, 25 St Stephen's Green, Dublin 2, Ireland
(a division of Penguin Books Ltd)
Penguin Group (Australia), 250 Camberwell Road, Camberwell, Victoria 3124, Australia
(a division of Pearson Australia Group Pty Ltd)
Penguin Books India Pvt Ltd, 11 Community Centre, Panchsheel Park, New Delhi – 110 017, India
Penguin Group (NZ), 67 Apollo Drive, Rosedale, North Shore 0632, New Zealand
(a division of Pearson New Zealand Ltd)
Penguin Books (South Africa) (Pty) Ltd, 24 Sturdee Avenue, Rosebank, Johannesburg 2196, South Africa

Penguin Books Ltd, Registered Offices: 80 Strand, London WC2R ORL, England

www.penguin.com

First published in 2007
Published in Penguin Books 2007
1

Set in 13.5/16 pt Monotype Garamond
Typeset by Rowland Phototypesetting Ltd, Bury St Edmunds, Suffolk
Printed in England by Clays Ltd, St Ives plc

ISBN: 978-0-141-02530-8

Dangerous conceits are in their natures poisons
Which at the first are scarce found to distaste
But, with a little act upon the blood,
Burn like the mines of sulphur.

Othello, Act III, Scene iii

Prologue

The last time I'd seen Leon Kaminski, I had almost shot him. It would've been a mistake if I had, but I doubt that would've been much consolation to his family afterwards.

In those days I was a Special Agent with the Federal Bureau of Investigation, working out of upstate New York. I was part of a team hunting a fruit cake known to the press as the White Monk, who'd murdered three women in the woods round Saratoga.

It was my last case as a Special Agent, though I didn't know it at the time.

It was one of those things that become significant only in retrospect.

I don't get along with woods. And I don't get along with mountains or fields. Take me more than ten minutes from the nearest deli and I'm lost. Some people like to sleep within range of the sound of waves washing the shoreline. I like to sleep with the sound of traffic coming in through an open window: the shriek of tyres, howling sirens, raised voices.

I need to be reminded I'm alive.

Consequently I was already freaked out before we even got out of sight of the road. What made it worse was that it was late in the year, dark too early; one of those days when the day barely seems to have roused itself before it's closing down and putting up the shutters.

Soon I got separated from the others.

Great start.

All I could see were shadows, with more shadows behind. Sound was muffled in the trees. Things scurried. Branches snapped. The birds sounded like human voices, mocking.

Then there were no birds either.

That was worse.

I didn't know where I was going. Didn't know what I was doing. All I knew was what I was looking for. That was a local man called Paul Nado who, it was rumoured, knew the geography of these woods better than he knew the layout of his own yard.

He also had priors for indecent assault, and no alibis for the time of the three killings. He fitted the profile. He matched the witness description. The few friends he possessed also said that Nado had been obsessed since he was at school with the original White Monk, the ghost of a monk from way back who was supposed to haunt the area and who had given the killer we were now hunting his ridiculous alter ego. Nado even used to dress up in an old white robe like St Francis and sneak around peering into people's windows after dark.

More to the point, he'd gone AWOL after being questioned by police investigating the three killings. Altogether Nado looked promising – and, as it turned out, he was more than promising. He was indeed the White Monk.

The only problem at that moment was finding him.

How long could a being hide out there in the woods without being caught?

I didn't want to find out.

That's why I was getting ready to throw my hard-won reputation as a hardass to the winds and call for help. Instead I saw a figure through the trees, walking silently.

Nado.

It had to be.

I reached for my gun, cocked the hammer, got ready to call on him to freeze.

And if he didn't, I knew what I had to do.

I didn't intend taking any chances.

Then the figure turned round and looked in my direction, like he could sense the gun trained on him, and I saw that it wasn't Nado.

Wasn't the phantom White Monk either, which in a way was a bigger relief.

It was JJ.

JJ was what we always called Kaminski, though I never did find out why. Nicknames obey strange rules. Sometimes they just stick and then everyone forgets where they came from. Kaminski himself always hated it and begged us to stop using it, but we never did.

Probably because of the begging.

He was part of the same FBI team. In fact, it was his profiling work which had led the way to Paul Nado's door. He'd thrown himself into that case like no other agent I'd ever known. He breathed it. It consumed him. *But where the hell was he going now?*

'JJ?' I whispered.

Then louder.

'Jesus, JJ, are you trying to get yourself killed? What are you –'

Kaminski simply looked at me, smiled and raised his finger to his lips to shush me.

Then he turned and disappeared into the trees.

By the time I'd made my way back to the others, it was completely dark and the search had been called off an hour ago. 'Where's JJ?' they said. And when I told them what I'd seen, some of the other agents thought I was crazy. No change there, then.

He must've got lost, they reckoned, and enjoyed a good laugh at his expense.

It wasn't that cold, after all.

It wasn't like he'd freeze.

Next morning, when Kaminski still hadn't returned, *that*'s when they started to believe me. That's when they stopped laughing.

Not surprisingly, his disappearance caused something of a stir. That's me using deliberate understatement. His disappearance sent the whole unit into turmoil for a time. Some of the other agents even wondered if he'd become Nado's latest victim. Maybe he was following a lead. Maybe he'd heard something and gone after the White Monk by himself.

He'd always craved the credit for closing a case.

Maybe this time he'd just taken his thirst for glory a step too far.

The only problem with that theory was that, at the exact time we were combing the woods, Nado himself was on a Greyhound bus heading toward Michigan, where the big hero later turned himself in after seeing his ugly mush on the TV news in his motel room.

It was a year to the day before the mystery of Kaminski's whereabouts was finally cleared up, when the man himself was discovered hanging out in a trailer park in North Carolina which, if you knew Kaminski, was the last place in the world you'd have expected to find him.

A five-star hotel in Vegas, maybe, but not a trailer park in North Carolina.

Not a trailer park *anywhere*.

What I heard is that he'd had some kind of breakdown, that the strain of working the White Monk case had caused him to crack up; and, looking back, I could see that all the signs had been there. And I say I heard about it because by that time, I'd left the FBI too.

I'd had enough.

I guess that case took its toll on all of us.

The straw that broke the camel's back.

I'd called him personally a few weeks after he was brought back to the city to ask if he was all right, if there was anything I could do to help. The conversation was strained. He was on medication. His voice kept drifting in and out like the stations on a cheap radio. He said he was fine. He said he simply couldn't take it any more. He thought if he just walked and kept walking, he wouldn't have to deal with all the crap that came with being in the FBI and having your head invaded by those dark images and memories.

He just wanted to get away, he said.

To disappear.

To stop thinking.

I could relate to that.

We promised to keep in touch, but of course we never did. I wrote a book about my experiences and moved on. As for him, I never did hear what he was doing, though a couple of years ago I saw a news report from back home about a murder case which quoted a Special Agent Leon Kaminski, so whatever it was that had made him crack up they'd managed to put the pieces back together again. Like Humpty-Dumpty.

Unless there was another Leon Kaminski out there, taking up where the old one had left off. Maybe the FBI makes replicas of us all and stores them in a huge basement in Quantico, ready to take over when the real one's used up.

Nothing would surprise me.

Nothing, that is, except for what happened when, by chance, I caught sight of Kaminski in Dublin one day about ten years after I'd last seen him.

I

Someone once said the best cities are those that a man can walk out of in a morning.

How long it should take a woman to walk out of them, the author of the quotation never got around to explaining. I guess women didn't count in those days. Or maybe he thought women should be too busy preparing a banquet for twelve and dreaming up new ways to please their man when the lights go out to have much time left over for mere walking.

It could be that he even believed encouraging women to take to the road was a dangerous practice because once they started, how could you be sure they'd come back?

If so, he had a point. Sometimes the view is better far from home.

Dublin certainly fits the definition, whoever's doing the walking. There may be more people living here than in Boston, my home town – plenty more, and every year the city grows. But it rarely feels like it. Dublin remains what they call in the guidebooks compact.

That means small.

I don't hold that against it. I've never exactly been a giant myself. And good things, as my mother always used to assure me before I got too old to be reassured by lies, come in small packages. Besides which, there are more than enough places to hide out if that's what you need. As in any city, you could live here a lifetime and still find roads you hadn't noticed before leading to places you hadn't expected. Hidden places. Secret corners.

There are nearly sixty pages in the city's A to Z guide, from Abbey Cottages to Zoo Road and all points in between – and that day, as it passed five o'clock and headed sluggishly to evening, I could have been anywhere in those sixty pages.

I could have taken any turning in that maze of possibilities.

Instead I was making my way up into the heart of the city, away from the river, toward the place where I'd arranged to meet Grace once she finished work, and taking my time about it, because it was summer and the city was stretching out around me as lazily and contentedly as a cat, unselfconsciously itself, and there was no sense in hurrying anywhere when the day was like this, the streets glinting golden from the slowly descending sun, the squares all leafy shadows and silence, the tower blocks turned into cathedrals of glass and chrome, shining like promises, the whole place tingling with life.

The plan was to catch something to eat before heading to the theatre later to watch some hotshot young American actor I'd never cared for in some play I didn't want to see – Shakespeare, of all things. Not my scene at all. And that might've been why I was taking my time as well. The upshot was that at that precise moment when I could have been anywhere I was actually emerging out of the soothing coolness of Crown Alley into the bright glare of Temple Bar. A couple of minutes later, or earlier, and I might never have seen him.

Likewise if I'd take a different route that day.

So call it chance.

Call it a sixth sense.

Whatever you call it, there I was.

It was Sunday, which meant the book market was just winding down for the day. There were stalls laden down with

8

old paperbacks, and more books in rickety cases standing at angles on the cobblestones. First editions. Only editions. People were milling around.

It was a scene I'd witnessed a hundred times before, and there was nothing very extraordinary about this one, except . . . except that something made me look over, and I found myself looking at my own face staring out from the picture on the back of one of my books.

And I was looking good, if I say so myself.

It sure is amazing what they can do with computers these days.

The book was a study I'd written a few years ago on criminal profiling, and I felt a little irritated, as I always do when I see my books for sale in second-hand stores. Not least because it's another book that someone somewhere didn't want. Didn't want it so much that they just had to get it out of the house. What can I say? I'm a delicate flower of innocent maidenhood. Rejection hurts. The other reason it bugs me, of course, is because I don't get a cent on the resale. Your book can go on being sold on for ever, with everyone else getting a cut on it each time, and none of it ever gets back to me. It offends my sense of fair play.

What am I saying? To hell with fair play. It offends my pocket.

So it was the book I noticed first rather than the man leafing idly through it.

He was standing leaning up against the side of the stall, using the shelter of the overhead canopy as a shadow for reading. He had the book in one hand, and with the other he was shielding his eyes from the sunlight. It was a very JJ way of standing.

At first I couldn't say for sure that it was him. I'd spent the day playing poker with Thaddeus Burke and some of his friends down by the quays, and, yes, I'd been drinking a little too. The fog of whiskey had combined with the thicker fog of the heat. I'm not at my best in summer as it is. My brain doesn't function properly once the temperature hits 20 degrees. My head felt simultaneously light and heavy. The two together could easily make me believe I was seeing things, or at the least that I couldn't immediately trust what I saw.

Plus there is something about Dublin itself, I've always thought, that makes misidentification a constant danger. In Dublin I'm constantly half seeing people who look half familiar, and I'm never sure if they really are who I think they are at all.

There was a moment of uncertainty like that when I first saw the figure holding my book. And yet I felt sure it must be him. He looked a little older than I remembered, but then that could be because he *was* older. So was I. So was everyone. He looked a little more crumpled too, a little darker at the edges. Even, I found myself thinking, a little sadder. He'd dyed his hair, but he looked like he didn't much care any more what he looked like, and that wasn't like him at all. All the same, I knew there could be no doubt.

It was him all right.

No one else could be so JJ-like without being JJ.

For a moment I found myself wondering if he was waiting here for me. But that was absurd. *I* hadn't even known I'd be coming this way myself. How could he have known it?

And he soon disproved that theory, anyway, because he looked up and saw me standing on the other side of the square, and there was no mistaking his surprise. He stared as if it was my presence here that was unlikely, not his – and then, in a gesture that made me shiver with the memory, he lifted a finger and placed it flat against his lips.

Ssh.

Then he looked up suddenly at something high up behind my back, and his eyes widened, before taking the same finger that he'd placed against his lips and pointing up with it, urging me to look. And, like the fool I was, I turned my head to see what it was.

All I could see was the grey façade of an old building. A long-haired redhead in a white dress was sitting on the ledge of a window near the top, one leg dangling out, and smoking a roll-up cigarette which, from the abstracted expression on her face, suggested there was possibly more in it than tobacco. What was I supposed to have seen? What had he –

As I turned my head back toward him, I saw what the pointing had been for.

My book now lay discarded on the cobblestones.

Kaminski was gone.

I had no idea which way he'd fled, but there was an alleyway to the left of where he'd been standing which led away from the square, and I took that, running quickly, hardly knowing why or what I would do or say if I caught him. I had no right to do or say anything.

I'd have to figure those little details out later.

It wasn't long before I saw him. *He* wasn't running but he had quickened his pace so that he had now almost reached Dame Street, where the road shimmered hotly with traffic.

'JJ!'

He glanced back, and for a moment looked like he might stop.

But no. He was on the move again, and I saw his hand shoot up above the other heads, like a child in school eager to answer a question from the teacher.

He was hailing a cab.

The crowd seemed to thin out as I got nearer the road, almost as if they were clearing a path for me. It meant I had a good view of him as his cab pulled to the side of the kerb and he slipped smoothly into the back seat, slamming the door.

'*JJ, wait!*'

The cab pulled away, leaving me standing, breathless and uncomfortably hot, watching as it accelerated down Dame Street toward Trinity College.

My first thought was to flag down the next cab, and yell: 'Follow that car!'

I'd waited my whole life to do that. I guess that's what comes of watching too many bad movies.

But there weren't any other cabs around. And, even if there had been, I was too astonished to act fast enough. Of all the reactions I could have imagined to the sight of me, that was the last one I could've expected. I hadn't let myself go that much, had I?

Paralysed by confusion, I stood and watched as the cab got further away.

Any other day it would've been stuck in traffic, but today was Sunday and it was gone in moments. At the lights on College Green, it turned left.

The last sight I had of Kaminski this time was of his face, peering out the back window, watching me watching him, making sure the brief pursuit was over.

Then that sight faded too.

He had melted into the city.

The old magician had pulled a disappearing trick on me for a second time.

2

'There are lots of Americans in Dublin,' said Fitzgerald. 'The place is full of Irish-Americans looking for their roots.'

'JJ isn't Irish,' I said. 'He's Polish. If he wanted to visit the old country, he'd have booked a flight to Warsaw, not Dublin.'

'Maybe he's lost. Or making a connection,' she quipped. Then, when I didn't smile, she continued: 'Then what if he's over seeing relatives? There are plenty of Poles in Dublin right now. They've even set up their own cable TV channel, you know. And don't you remember, I actually arrested a Polish man for murder last month. That's the seventh nationality I've arrested in the past three years. I like to think of it as a sign that we're getting very tolerant and multicultural. We welcome murderers now from all parts of the globe.'

This time, I couldn't help smiling.

'They should put that on the holiday brochures,' I suggested. 'Think of the boost it'd give to tourism. You could even offer a discount for block bookings by psychopaths.'

'There you go,' she added to that. 'Your friend could simply be here on holiday.'

'People like JJ don't take holidays.'

'He could have changed since you knew him.'

'People like JJ don't change either. It'd be too quiet for him here anyway.'

'Dublin's too quiet for you too,' said Fitzgerald, 'but you're still here.'

13

'What can I say? Love makes us all do strange things.'

'That's it. He must be in love.'

We were catching that bite to eat in a tiny Italian place in Wicklow Street. That is, we'd got past ordering and on to the first glass of wine, but not so far as to actually start eating, unless the bread basket that I was quickly making my way through counted.

Fitzgerald was doing what Fitzgerald did best. She was being rational. I needed that sometimes. Counterpart to my craziness. Though it still didn't explain why Leon Kaminski had run from me, as I lost no time reminding her.

'True,' she conceded. 'That's not what you'd call normal behaviour. Not that you're exactly a practitioner of the fine art of behaving normally yourself.'

'I'll ignore that remark.'

I looked across the table at her, and once again my dominant thought as I watched her was how well named she was. She did have grace, a poise and elegance that had always eluded me. I was lucky to have gotten her. There were days when I thought she was way out of my league. I didn't deserve her. She put up with a lot, and she rarely complained.

Grace Fitzgerald was a Detective Chief Superintendent with the Murder Squad of the Dublin Metropolitan Police, and she was the very reason I was in Dublin at all.

I'd met her shortly after coming to the city for the first time. She was a source for a book I was writing at the time about a serial killer called the Night Hunter who had killed five women. Somehow we were still together – and, with my talent for screwing up relationships and getting people hacked off with me, that ought to be considered something of a miracle.

Without Fitzgerald, I doubted I'd still be here at all. Dublin was a great place to hang out, but I would never have stayed here longer than a couple months if it hadn't been for her. Because of her, I'd now been here much longer than I'd ever stayed in one place. Before I knew it, I was living here and I couldn't even recall when I passed the line from passing through to actually living in the place. That was a line you crossed before you knew you'd crossed it, and then sometimes it was too late to get back to the other side.

She was perfectly integrated into the city in a way I'd never been in any place. Boston, maybe, but even there I don't remember ever being entirely comfortable. Maybe I was just uncomfortable in my own skin, and you couldn't change that, couldn't slough and shrug out of it like a snake when the weight of everything became too much.

Fitzgerald wore her own skin like it was a silk gown. It fitted her exactly, and through her it was like a thousand invisible lines radiated out and criss-crossed the whole city, so that she and it became inseparable. I found myself able to get a connection to the city through her; otherwise I'd merely have been drifting, ghost-like, through the streets, rootless, pointless.

Right now, I was trying to explain to her why I felt so unnerved by seeing Kaminski.

I was failing because she still didn't get it.

'How do you know him, anyway?' she said.

'He was in the same FBI field office as me in upstate New York,' I explained. 'He was senior to me, obviously. I'd only just left Quantico, and he was the golden boy, fast-tracked to the top, his path laid out. He was good-looking, always well dressed. His parents came from Poland after the war and settled in New Jersey, and they'd instilled that into him. He had to look the part. He had to blend in. Be anonymous.'

She nodded. 'I know the type.'

'Kaminski played his part to perfection,' I said. 'He'd

effortlessly erased whatever traces remained of his European genes and become the true all-American college kid. You know, teeth so bright you had to wear shades, and so straight you'd think they were put in his mouth with the help of a spirit level. Not a hair out of place. His skin was so perfect you'd swear he must have had the DNA of new-born babies injected into the nape of his neck every morning at seven sharp, and twice a day at weekends for that extra glow. He probably thought he looked like Tom Cruise. He certainly had to wear heels like Tom Cruise, because he wasn't much taller than I am, and *everyone*'s taller than I am. The Seven Dwarfs included.'

'You didn't get along with him?'

'I got along with him fine. Hey,' I said, when I saw her looking at me sceptically across the table, 'don't be so cynical. I get along with people all the time.'

'I'll take your word for it.'

'It surprised a lot of other people too,' I admitted with a shrug. 'They had a system when you were starting out in the FBI. You didn't have a job as such, but fully fledged agents could take whichever younger inexperienced agents they took a shine to along on operations. Hence the new-comers tended to ingratiate themselves with the older ones. Well, you know me. I was never one for ingratiation. Something insolent is encoded in my DNA. Despite that, JJ took me under his wing. I don't know what tricks he thought I brought to the party, but he must've thought I brought some because he was always picking me.'

'He must have seen you as a challenge,' said Fitzgerald.

'That's what I reckoned. I certainly got a lot of experience thanks to him, worked on a lot of cases that would otherwise have passed me by, or which I might've waited years before coming into contact with. I was grateful. It could be tough for women in those days. I thought we were friends. That's why I couldn't understand why he didn't tell me what he was feeling in the run-up to his disappearance. I always felt I could've helped.'

'And afterwards it was too late because by then you'd left the Bureau too?'

'Precisely.'

Left. That makes it sound so simple. In fact, nothing could be further from the truth. I was only in the FBI five years, which is only a quarter of the recommended period before retirement, but I burned out faster than I'd expected. I'd had enough of death. I didn't realize then that death has a habit of following you around, no matter how hard you try to escape it.

Whatever the reason, I ended up resigning my post and writing a book about my experiences in the Bureau. The book did well enough to lead to other books, I got a movie deal, I had real money for the first time in my life, and by a circuitous route I finally found myself here in Dublin, where I continued to write the odd book now and then.

Very odd books, some might say. Crime books, books on profiling, sketches of old cases, unsolved murders, forgotten killers. I had a new life, but people in the FBI had never forgiven me. They felt betrayed. I'd had angry calls from former colleagues demanding why I'd done it. Personally, I think they overreacted. But that's the way it goes.

I didn't hold it against them.

I moved on.

Or I thought I had. Now here he was, back in my sights. Acting suspiciously.

'You should find out where he's staying, go round and say hello,' said Fitzgerald. 'You don't always have to make things more complicated than they really are. There are a million innocent explanations as to why he could be here.'

'I don't think so,' I said confidently.

'You sound pretty confident.'

'That's because', I said, leaning across the table with a smile of triumph, 'I took down the number of the cab JJ got into and managed to track down the driver.'

'And?'

'And it turns out that Leon Kaminski isn't Leon Kaminski at all. Or rather he isn't calling himself that. He's staying at a hotel under an assumed name.'

'That's not a crime. Not technically.'

'You haven't heard the name he's using yet. Want to take a guess what it is?'

'I don't like the odds.'

'Buck Randall III.'

Fitzgerald laughed so hard that diners at the other tables turned to look at her disapprovingly.

'*That* is one great name,' she said, shaking her head.

'Isn't it?' I said. 'Sounds like the hero of some fifties Western series on TV. Now what would JJ be doing creeping round Dublin calling himself Buck Randall III?'

'You got me,' she said. 'I give up. Tell me.'

'I don't know, that's the point. It was a rhetorical question.'

'Is that what you call it?'

'He must be here on FBI business. *That's* why he ran. He didn't want me knowing. He didn't want me interfering.'

'You? Interfere in things that are none of your business? The very thought.'

'I'll ignore that remark too,' I said, and as I spoke I realized there was nothing left in the bread basket but crumbs. I'd probably spoiled my appetite for dinner now.

'Do you want me to make some calls?' said Fitzgerald, taking pity.

'You'd do that?'

'Anything for a quiet life,' she said. 'But you know, if he *is* in Dublin on FBI business, then I'd be the last person to find out about it. You Americans rarely believe in sharing information about what you're up to with we unsophisticated locals.'

I was about to rise to the bait, as I always did when people in Dublin started reeling off their litanies of anti-Americanisms, when Fitzgerald's cellphone went off.

The smile vanished from her lips, and the same diners who had disapproved of her laughing were now openly muttering rebelliously.

'Shit,' she said. 'What now?'

She took it out of her pocket and looked at it.

'It's Healy,' she said. She meant Sean Healy, a fellow detective on the Murder Squad and the one she felt closest to in the whole department. They'd worked together on cases from the first day she joined. 'I'd better go see what he wants. Don't be going anywhere now.'

Fitzgerald pushed back her chair and rose. By the time she reached the lobby, she was already through to Healy. The glass door swung shut and cut off her voice, but I could still see her through the glass, talking quickly. I refilled my glass with wine and swirled it around just for something to do with my hands and tried to suppress the feeling that the evening had come to an abrupt end.

'Duty calls?' I said when she got back.

'A woman's body's been found.'

'Murdered?'

'Would they be calling me on my night off otherwise?' She sighed. 'The City Pathologist's already on his way over. I guess that puts paid to *Othello*.'

'I'll try not to be too disappointed,' I said.

I hadn't even realized it was *Othello* we were going to see.

'Are they sending a car?'

She nodded.

'Five minutes' time. And I've been looking forward to dessert all day. Oh, well, it'll be good for my figure.' She caught my eye. 'I'm sorry for ruining your evening.'

'It can't be helped. Don't go beating yourself up about it.'

'Will you be OK on your own?'

'I think I can manage to find my way home,' I smiled. 'If I get lost, I'll call 999. Don't worry about *me*. There's no point getting hooked up with a garbage man and then complaining when he has to go and take out the trash. That's part of the job description.'

'What a charming way you have with words.'

'You know what I mean.'

'I do. I wish I didn't, but I do.'

3

I made my way home alone through the warm evening streets only to find that the elevator was broken again. That meant I had to climb the seven flights of stairs to my apartment, and by the time I got there I couldn't deny that I'd been in more agreeable moods.

To make matters worse, the door had started getting temperamental lately and I had to kick it a few times before it opened. The woman who lived alone across the hallway from me came out to ask if everything was all right. What she meant was that I should shut up.

I told her everything was fine. What I meant was that she should get back to bed and mind her own business. It wasn't much after ten and the woman was in her pyjamas.

And I thought *my* social life left something to be desired.

I'd spent the last couple of hours since Fitzgerald was summoned to the scene of another death just walking round, idly following a haphazard circuit of streets that were so familiar to me by now that I could have walked them with my eyes blindfolded.

Not that I intended to try.

You never know what you might step in.

Cities in summer always come into their own after the sun goes down. During the day it's too hot to stir, too hot to care, but at night the dark takes the edge off the heat that has gathered in the streets. People come out and experience the city with an immediacy impossible at other times of year. Usually they just regard the streets as passages to connect the places they need to get to. In summer, people become a part of the city instead of intruders in it. Temple Bar tonight had been humming with voices and music and the clatter from the open windows of restaurant kitchens. Tables and chairs had spilled from every doorway, and people were drinking wine and flirting with one another. Without Grace, I felt disconnected from it all. It seemed a waste to be spending the night alone.

Death has no consideration for people's lives.

Once inside my apartment, I put a CD on low without even looking at what it was, then took a beer from the fridge and carried it out to the balcony, sitting with my feet on the balustrade, surveying my kingdom. I lit a cigar to keep the beer company. Cuba's greatest gift to civilization, though since its other contributions included political repression, censorship, and a way of life so wretched that huge numbers of its own citizens would rather risk shark-infested seas to cross to Florida than remain, that's not necessarily saying much.

Far across the river on the Northside, I could see the light at the top of the Dublin Spire glowing, a personal Pole Star for everyone like me who had nothing else of their own to look at that night. The rising smoke from the cigar made the light quiver.

Somewhere out there was Kaminski.

Or should that be Buck Randall III?

Fitzgerald was right, she usually was right. I shouldn't let what Kaminski was doing in Dublin bother me. He had a right to go where he wanted and to call himself whatever he liked. And if he *was* on FBI business, then I had even less right to know.

I'd relinquished the right to be involved in those matters a long time ago.

But it's never been my nature to let things go. That's what gets me into trouble. And it wasn't like I'd asked for this reminder of my past life to barge its way in unceremoniously.

Nor had I asked to be reminded of it in so bizarre a fashion.

All he'd had to do that afternoon was wave a greeting, say: 'Hello, Saxon, how's things?' A couple of moments of polite conversation, then: 'I have to scoot, but you keep in touch now, you hear?' Even if both of us knew it was a lie.

Instead, he'd raised his finger to his lips as if imploring my silence, just like before, and it was like he was mocking me. Though why I should feel mocked by the memory of *his* disintegration was unclear. It wasn't me who'd lost it. Though some of my former colleagues certainly thought otherwise when they read my book – and lost no time telling me.

Sitting here so far from the world where I'd originally known Kaminski, I couldn't help being perplexed at how it had come to this. Why did things have to get so *weird*?

What made it worse was that our dealings with each other had always been so uncomplicated. Most of the time, at any rate. There was one little incident between us that I didn't much care to dwell on which had made the atmosphere awkward for a time, but even that hadn't been allowed to poison what had always been a straightforward relationship.

We'd always been able to laugh too.

Usually at my expense, it's true, but that was fine by me. I'd never made the mistake of taking myself too seriously. Doing what we did every day, you couldn't afford to.

One time, I recalled, we'd been swapping ghost stories, late at night with a beer and a cigar, and I'd make the mistake of telling JJ about something which happened to me as a child. The incident itself had stayed with me since childhood, the kind of thing you find yourself remembering in unexpected moments or revisiting in dreams.

I must have been eight, nine, something like that. I'd been playing hide-and-seek with friends in a broken-down rooming house at the end of the street in Boston where I lived with my mother and brother and sister – my father had never been around much in those days, or any days, come to that, and I can't say I'd ever missed him much – and I'd seen a little girl like myself, dark-eyed and sad, sitting on a chair in an empty room where wallpaper was peeling from the walls and foul water was dripping from a leak in an overhead pipe and making a large pool at her feet. She'd stared at me and smiled and held out her hand, as if for help.

When I walked toward her, she vanished.

I don't think I've ever run so fast.

My friends all laughed and said I was crazy, said I was seeing things. Maybe I was. All I know is that I never dared go back there to play again – and neither did they.

Years later I tried to find out whether anything had ever happened in that house, whether what I'd seen was a trace of something bad that had happened there long ago, but of course there was nothing of the sort. It was just a regular house on a regular street in Boston. I don't know what I expected. To learn that the house had been built on the site of an old Native American burial ground or something, I guess.

Like I say, sometimes I think I've watched too many movies.

The last time I was home briefly, I saw they'd pulled the house down, and nothing had been put up in its place. I saw my mother shuffling to the corner store in her slippers too, though I didn't approach or stop to say hello. I hadn't come to see her.

That was an ordeal I tried to avoid as much as possible.

Kaminski, needless to say, had found the whole incident in the house when I was a kid hilarious. Serves me right for telling him about it. Next day he and another friend of his in the Bureau by the name of Lucas Piper had made up a mock old-style black-and-white Hollywood cinema poster with my picture on it and the words *Saxon is Back as . . . Claire Voyant – The Girl Who Saw Ghosts* written along the bottom like the title of a movie. Then they'd posted it on to the wall of the office above my desk, where I couldn't miss it.

And nor could anyone else.

Boys will be boys.

I smiled now, remembering it, as I made my way to the fridge for another beer. Being in the FBI had taken its toll, but there were happier moments too. I shouldn't forget that.

And then I stopped, feeling foolish.

Of course, why hadn't I thought of it before?

Lucas Piper had been Kaminski's closest friend in the Bureau. Perhaps his only true friend, the only one who penetrated the surface and got to meet the real Kaminski underneath.

I know I certainly never had.

The two men had grown up together in Ohio, though Piper's family was as blue collar as Kaminski's was trying desperately to be white bread. Half of Piper's folks worked in the steel mills. The other half didn't work at all. Despite all that, they were inseparable at high school, went on to the same college, joined the Academy at the same time. They'd double dated, gone on skiing holidays each winter, even shared an apartment together for a while. They were nick-named the Siamese Twins, and some people even used to joke that they should get married and be done with it. If anyone knew what JJ was doing in Dublin, it would be Piper.

Though whether he chose to tell me was another matter. I'd never gotten on as well with Piper as I had with Kam-inski. Never gotten on with Piper much at all.

I'm not saying he had a problem with women, but he was always competitive with me. Like he felt threatened. He once admitted that he thought I'd only gotten where I was because I was a woman, which would've made me laugh if it hadn't been so ridiculous.

Then, as now, the Bureau had certainly been pulling out the stops to get more women to apply, but once they applied it was another matter. There were still more than enough of the old guard at the training academy who considered it a personal failure if they gave a woman an easy time, making a female graduate rarer than a Bigfoot in downtown Manhattan.

You simply didn't get through an intensive course master-ing a range of disciplines from behavioural science to crimi-nal law to firearms tuition on some kind of half-baked politically correct favouritism. So much as even fall short on the two-mile sprint and the push-ups, and you were out. Gender didn't come into it.

Piper's kneejerk hostility had eased over time, but he'd never truly accepted my right to be there. No matter how many cases I worked, he never stopped insinuating behind my back that I was only where I was because I'd gotten *on* my back for the right people at the right time. He made it clear I'd never be an equal in his eyes.

That never bothered me particularly, since I didn't like

the way the world looked from his eyes anyway. But right now it left me with a potential problem.

Would Piper talk to me?

I'd just have to call him and see what happened.

But what was his number? I could remember the old number for his house in New Jersey, but what were the chances he was still living there? No, I knew a better way to contact him. I left the beer perched precariously on top of the fridge and went to the closet at the end of the hall where I kept my junk – or what, for insurance purposes, I called my papers. Basically it was all the crap I'd accumulated from ten years of researching and writing books. And in my case, that's a lot of crap. I accumulate so many bits of paper that I should really open a recycling facility in my apartment.

The cranky woman with no sex life across the hall would love that.

I knew Piper's cellphone number had to be in here somewhere, because I'd written it down a couple of years ago when it had been given to me by a source I'd contacted about a book I was writing on infamous unsolved missing persons cases. He hadn't been able to help – that was his excuse, at any rate – but gave me Piper's number to fob me off.

Either that, or he just didn't like Piper.

Piper was known as an authority on missing persons. It was said, usually by Piper himself, that there wasn't anyone he couldn't track down.

Same as Kaminski, he wasn't short on self-belief.

That might've been what drew them together.

It was Piper who'd found Kaminski in North Carolina, and my source told me there was one particular case Lucas had worked on lately in Pennsylvania which would be perfect for my book. A witness in a mob murder trial had fled in fear of what would happen to him if he testified against his former associates. Piper found him and brought him back within hours of the trial. The prosecution got their conviction.

The man himself got a bullet in the back of the head three weeks later, when he was supposed to be starting a new life on the witness protection programme.

That's showbusiness.

Perfect the case may have been, but I hadn't felt up to calling anyone from the old days at that time, and certainly not Piper, so reluctantly decided the book would have to manage without Piper's input. But I knew his number had to be in here somewhere.

Dig hard enough and I'd probably find the Lost Ark of the Covenant too, not to mention Indiana Jones himself searching for it.

Consequently, by the time I found what I was looking for and returned to the kitchen, it was after midnight, the CD was long finished and the beer was warm.

I poured it down the sink and took a cold one from the fridge, perching on a stool and draining most of the new bottle in one swig. Clearing out my junk was thirsty work. Then I finished off a half packet of potato chips I'd left sitting out last night, before picking up the remote and flicking idly through the channels as I drank.

It was only when I found myself wondering if I should watch a rerun of *Taxi* that I realized I was doing anything I could think of to put off making the call to Piper.

Damn, I hate it when I run out of excuses.

Not giving myself time to dream up another evasion, I snatched up the American cell phone I kept for such purposes and tapped in the number I'd spent so long digging for in a dark hole. I knew I didn't have to worry about the time, since New Jersey was five hours behind Dublin.

The night was still young over there.

I just hoped that, after all this trouble, he hadn't changed his number.

He hadn't. On the fifth ring, Lucas Piper answered. I recognized his deep, rich, slightly sardonic voice at once, though I hadn't been prepared for what he was going to say.

'You're late,' he said.

4

'That's a nice way to greet an old friend, I must say,' I remarked when an awkward pause made it clear that I wasn't exactly who he'd been expecting to hear from.

'I'm sorry, I was waiting for a call from someone else,' he answered eventually, gruffly, pointlessly. I'd figured that much out for myself. 'Who is this, anyway?'

'It's Saxon,' I said.

There was another uncomfortably long silence.

'You remember me, don't you, Piper?'

'Oh, I remember you all right, Saxon. How could anyone forget you?'

'I'm a hard woman to forget.'

'You're a hard woman, period,' Piper said. 'What you calling for? Old times' sake?'

'In a way. How are things at the FBI?'

'You want to know that, you'll have to talk to someone in the FBI.'

'I thought that's what I was doing,' I said.

'Not me, sister. Not any more. You know that old proverb about what to do when you're in a hole? Well, I stopped digging.'

'So what're you at now?'

'I set up my own company. Surveillance. Phone tapping. That kind of thing.'

That fit. Piper had always been a bit of a communications boffin. His house had been like something out of an electronics catalogue. Closed-circuit TV in every room. Switches everywhere. He was obsessed by security. Never felt safe. Some people thought he was paranoid, but then paranoid is arguably a good thing to be when you're a Special Agent. He'd even hooked up some kind of system which meant he could phone home and turn on his lights in New Jersey even if he was in Nebraska, Europe, wherever. Why he'd want to turn his lights on in New Jersey if he was in Nebraska is another matter.

I guess geniuses don't get where they are without thinking outside the box.

'Best decision I ever made,' he said.

'Yeah?'

'I got tired of being passed over for promotion. Every other agent seemed to be going places while I was running faster than ever to stay in the same place.'

'I'm sorry to hear it.'

'It's the curse of service. Besides, you know what the pay's like. Sucks. Now I'm bringing in more money than I know what to do with. Guess that makes two of us, huh?' He laughed, but there was no pleasure in it. It was more like a cough or a sneeze, just a sound his body gave out to release pressure. 'You going to tell me what you want from me?'

He sounded suspicious.

I can't say I blamed him. It had been a long time.

'I'm looking for a number,' I said. 'For Kaminski.'

The silence this third time went on even longer.

'I can't help you,' was the answer that came at last. 'I haven't spoken to Kaminski in over a year. Last time I tried to phone him, he'd changed his number. I don't have his new one. I'm sorry.'

Not as sorry as I was. Piper had been the one person I was sure would know what was happening with Kaminski. Now it turned out he knew as little as I did.

Nevertheless, I pressed on.

'Do you at least know what field office he's working out of these days?'

'Listen, Saxon, you've been out of the loop a long time –'

'I'm only asking for a number, Piper,' I said testily. 'I'm not looking for the lowdown on all the Bureau's secrets. I won't even tell him it came from you if it makes you uncomfortable.'

'It's not that,' Piper said. 'Kaminski's not with the FBI any more either.'

'JJ quit?'

I couldn't have been more astonished if he'd told me Kaminski had taken a vow of celibacy. He'd had FBI sewn into his being the way a kid on his first day in school has his name sewn on the inside of his jacket. He was wedded to the FBI the way the Pope is wedded to the Catholic Church. The idea of his leaving it was like John Paul Getty announcing he'd had enough of being rich and was giving it up for, well, a trailer park in North Carolina.

'What happened?' I said.

'It's a long story. He went a bit, how shall I put this, loco. His wife died.'

'I didn't even know he was married.'

'You do now. She was abducted after visiting some store not far from where they lived. Her body was found later. Strangled. They'd only been married a couple of months.'

Suddenly it didn't look so inexplicable that JJ looked frazzled.

'They ever find who did it?'

'No. That was the problem. Kaminski was convinced he knew who'd killed her. He wanted the Bureau to go after the guy. They thought he was losing it. Getting unstable. It was suggested gently that he take a break from work to help him get over his wife's death. Instead he handed in his shield and walked. That was the last anyone saw of him. I don't know what he's done since. I tried phoning a couple of times, but he never returned my calls.'

'So where'd he go? Where's he now?'

'No idea.'

'You haven't been able to find him?' I said. 'That's not like you. What happened to the man who could find the proverbial needle in any field of haystacks?'

'I didn't *try* to find him,' retorted Piper, bridling at the implied criticism.

'You didn't?'

'I was out of the loop myself by that point. I didn't have the resources. And, in addition,' he sounded more reluctant now, as if he didn't know whether he ought to be saying what he *was* saying at all, 'we'd not been getting along so well before it happened. Things had changed. And *after* it happened . . .'

'Let me guess,' I said. 'You told him the same as the FBI.'

'More or less. I hadn't seen him for months, then out of the blue he calls and wants my help tracking down his wife's killer. I told him he needed to take it easy. That he was heading for a breakdown. Let's just say it wasn't what he wanted to hear.'

'And that was the last you saw of him?'

'That was the last anyone saw of him,' said Piper. 'Soon after, he disappeared.'

'Like last time.'

'Exactly like last time, only this time I don't think he intends coming back. I know Kaminski better than anyone. If he doesn't want to be found, he won't be.'

'You found him in North Carolina.'

'That's my point. The only reason I found him then was

because he was *ready* to be found. This time, it's different. This time I think he's gone for good.' He stopped abruptly, as if the thought had only just occurred to him. 'Why do you want to speak to him anyway?'

I wondered what he'd say if I told him I'd seen JJ that afternoon in Dublin, but decided I'd have to go on wondering because I wasn't going to tell him.

I don't know what held me back. Maybe it was what Piper said about Kaminski wanting to be lost. That afternoon, he had run away. Maybe he didn't want to be found.

'It's nothing,' I said carelessly instead, hoping it wouldn't be obvious to Piper I was lying. He'd always been perceptive when it came to picking up on all those signs a speaker unwittingly gave away when they were being evasive. I trusted in the fact he could only hear my voice, and all the non-verbal clues I was probably giving off right now were only being transmitted to my empty apartment. 'I wanted to ask him about a case we worked on together years ago. There were a few details I'd forgotten that I needed to clear up.'

Piper gave no indication that he thought my answer was incomplete.

'You're not writing another book, are you?' was all he said.

'What else is there to do these days?'

He laughed the same hollow laugh. 'Speak for yourself, Saxon. I have plenty of things to be doing with my time these days. Life is good.'

'You don't miss it?'

'The FBI? Are you kidding me? That's like asking a guy who's just found out his VD's cleared up whether he misses the itch. You saying you do?'

'Every minute of every day,' I said before I could stop myself.

If bafflement could communicate itself down a phone line, Piper's did right then.

'What's to miss?' he said.

'I don't know,' I admitted. 'The feeling that you're making a difference. That you're not just standing by and handing the keys of the world to the bad guys.'

'Last time I looked, there were still bad guys everywhere.'

'All the more reason to stick at it,' I said.

'I stuck at it long enough,' he said. 'I gave the Bureau twenty years. Now all I want is for whatever time I got left on this earth to be mine. That's not much to ask, is it?'

'It isn't.'

'But listen,' he went on unexpectedly, 'since it's you, I'll do you a favour. I'll make some calls, ask about Kaminski, see if anyone's heard from him recently.'

'You will? That'd be great.'

'I'm not promising anything,' said Piper. 'These days I'm nothing but a civilian with a business to run, remember? It may take a little time.'

'Whatever you can get for me,' I said, 'I'd appreciate it. Here, I'd better give you my cellphone number so you know where to reach me. And then I'll get the hell out of your ear. Leave the line free for that other call you're waiting for. I'm probably keeping you from something more interesting.'

'You are, since you mention it.'

'What can I say? My timing always was lousy.'

'At least some things never change,' said Piper, as he took down my number. 'That's almost reassuring. Nothing else stays the same. All it does is get older. But, hey, enough of my problems. I'll talk to you again when I have something. Goodnight.'

'Goodnight,' I said, and felt happier as I replaced the phone. Piper had said: 'I'll talk to you when I have something.' Not if, but when. His self-belief hadn't changed either.

Unless . . . the thought struck me at that exact moment . . . unless he *already* knew where JJ was. Unless they were in this – whatever *this* was – together.

Promising to call me back might've simply been a way of playing for time.

I groaned. It was too late for figuring through all the possible permutations of a situation. Sometimes you had to stop thinking so much and leave things to work themselves out. And with that piece of fortune cookie wisdom, I locked up and made my way to bed.

Lying in the dark, I found my mind coming full circle back to earlier that evening when I'd been sitting at my window, looking out at the city, wondering where JJ was.

Lives unravel so easily. He had everything, and then it comes to pieces in his hands, all for a perversity of fate, and for that, JJ's life turns 180 degrees in an instant and he's looking in an entirely different direction than before.

Instead of looking into the future, he's trapped in the past.

Everything stops.

But I still wanted to know what he was doing here in Dublin, and I had a couple of places where I could start. I was tired but also impatient to begin. I checked the clock. It was after 2 a.m. Piper had been right, without knowing it, when he said: 'You're late.'

I really needed to start getting some early nights.

5

The phone rang early the next morning, waking me up. Still half asleep, I snatched at it, anxious to know if it was Lucas Piper ringing back with information about Kaminski, though I didn't for one moment believe he could've gotten anything for me that quickly. What's more, it would now be the middle of the night in New Jersey. Lucky New Jersey. I'd had a restless sleep. The heat had made me uncomfortable. Even kicking off the sheets hadn't helped.

The caller, though, was Fitzgerald, and I had to suppress a faint disloyal feeling of disappointment as I lay back against the pillow.

'Sorry, did I wake you?'

'No,' I said. 'I mean, yes, but it doesn't matter. You know me, I'm always up with the lark, eager to throw myself into the joy of another Monday morning. How's it going?'

'I've had better nights.'

'You manage to snatch any sleep?'

'Ten minutes in the car.'

'It must be bad.'

'How do you quantify bad?' replied Fitzgerald. 'Sometimes I think that's the worst part of this job. Death no longer surprises you. It's just another night's work.'

For investigator and investigated alike.

Call it the banality of evil.

'She was definitely murdered, then?'

'I think we can safely say it wasn't suicide. But you know Alastair Butler,' she said, meaning the City Pathologist. 'Until he's completed the autopsy, he's not willing to say for certain that it's murder. A victim could've been seen by a roomful of witnesses taking seventeen bullets in the back, but, until he's satisfied himself there's no chance the cause of death could really have been smoke inhalation, he's not going to commit himself.'

'Pathologists are all the same,' I said.

'Tell me about it,' she sighed. 'All the signs are that she was tied naked by the wrists and ankles to the bedposts, mouth taped over, before the bastard put a plastic bag over her head and tightened it with cords until she suffocated. There were some signs of genital bruising too, suggesting a possible sexual assault. He also' – and here she hesitated slightly before continuing softly – 'cut off one of the fingers of her right hand.'

'Post-mortem?'

'Thankfully so.'

'Trophy?'

'Doesn't look like it. He left the finger behind.'

'Then why cut it off in the first place?'

'A friend we spoke to says she always wore a ring on that finger. It belonged to her mother. It was left to the victim after her mother died. It hasn't turned up, so it looks like it was the ring he really wanted.'

'He couldn't just take it off?'

'In this case, apparently not. According to Butler, the victim suffered some sort of cadaveric spasm. Her fingers were clenched tight. He wouldn't have been able to just unfold them to get the ring off. Cutting would have been the only way.'

Now I understood. It usually takes between two and eight hours for rigor mortis to develop in a dead body. In cases of cadaveric spasm, however, rigor mortis sets in immediately, sometimes in all the muscles of the body, but generally in a smaller group of muscles. It's a rare enough phenomenon, but most pathologists were bound to come across it from time to time. The point was that a tightened fist would take considerable effort to open.

Though that didn't mean this killer only cut off the finger because there was no other way of getting the ring. Cutting off the finger may have been what he intended to do all along.

Hence my next question.

'Did he bring the knife with him?'

'I see what you're getting at, but no, he got it from the kitchen.'

'Making himself at home,' I said grimly. 'Did he take it with him?'

'It was left lying on the floor by the bed. He wiped it clean first on the bedsheet.'

'Fingerprints?'

'Gloves,' she said. 'There was also no sign of a break-in. So either he knew the victim and she let him into the house, or he had a key, or knew where to get one. Plus it turns out she had a secret camera hidden at her front door, recording who came and went. The tapes have been taken away. Whoever killed her must have known the camera was there. You can't even tell it's there from the doorway outside. But until Butler finishes his report and makes it official, we're not going to be able to release any further details to the press. That's why they're going crazy. He can't be hurried.'

'You're the one who'd better hurry up and make an arrest, then,' I said. 'Give them something to report. I'm disappointed in you. You must be slowing up in your old age.'

'Give me a chance. We only got a positive ID from her father an hour ago.'

'Are you allowed to tell me her name?'

'She was called Marsha Reed.'

'Reed?'

Fitzgerald must've heard something in my voice.

'You know her?'

For a moment, something had flashed into my head. The trace of a memory, though it was gone as quickly as it arrived.

'Her name sounds familiar,' I answered feebly.

'It would make things a damn sight easier if you could tell us something about her,' Fitzgerald said. 'We don't have that much on her. She only moved into the area about three months ago. The neighbours know nothing about her. Hardly anyone seemed to speak to her. Some of them don't even recognize her picture. And none of them heard a thing, naturally.'

'How long had she been dead?'

'No more than twenty-four hours,' Fitzgerald said. 'We've got a taxi driver who remembers dropping her at the door on Saturday night about ten o'clock. He says she was drunk, kind of giddy, in high spirits, you know. She needed help to the front door. He had to unlock it for her. He says when she opened her bag to get out the key, there was a large amount of cash inside. He couldn't say how much, but a few thousand certainly. It wasn't in the house when the body was found, but he insists he didn't take it.'

'That's what they all say,' I remarked.

'Don't worry, Healy and I are heading over to speak to him as soon as the forensic team are finished here. But his story seems to stack up in all other respects. Unless he's the kind of man who's capable of killing a woman, cutting off her finger and then returning to continue the night shift without any outward signs of stress or disturbance.'

'Stranger things have happened,' I said. 'But look on the bright side. If the house was locked and there are no signs of a forced entry and the tapes from the hidden camera are gone, then at least you're narrowing down the possibilities. It does sounds pretty much like it was someone she knew.'

'That might not necessarily narrow it down,' said Fitzgerald cryptically.

'It doesn't?'

'It's a long story. I'll tell you about it over lunch. Give you something to look forward to.'

'Can't wait. I didn't think you'd be able to get away.'

'I'll be here a few hours yet,' she conceded. 'You know how long the forensic work can take. They're vacuuming the place now, and then the fingerprint section will come in, and they'll have to lift soil and grass samples from the garden, and make shoeprint moulds, and check for tyre marks, and take apart the plumbing to look for traces of blood in the pipes. But I'll have to take a break eventually unless they want a basket case with severe exhaustion heading up this investigation. It'll have to be out at my place, though.'

'Sure. Any reason it has to be there? My apartment's closer.'

'I have to go back and pick up some stuff,' said Fitzgerald. 'I'm meeting the Commissioner later this afternoon, remember? I need to get the right outfit. You can't have Detective Superintendents going into meetings looking like they've spent the night at a crime scene, after all,' she added sarcastically. 'Might give the wrong impression.'

'I forgot about the Commissioner,' I said. 'Your place it is, then. And listen, I'll pick up some food before heading out there.'

'Sounds good. I'll be there around one, OK?'

'One it is,' I said.

I put down the phone, cursing myself for forgetting about Fitzgerald's meeting with the Commissioner. She'd only been given final word of it three days ago, and since then her preoccupation with the impending meeting had been making her unusually distracted.

Unusually, because being distracted had always been *my* job.

The reason for the meeting was the retirement some months previously of Assistant Commissioner Brian Draker, former head of the Murder Squad, the search for whose replacement had dragged on so long now that Fitzgerald had taken to joking how she was almost tempted to ring up Draker and beg him to come back. Yeah, in the same way that people in London might be tempted to ring up the Great Plague and ask it to return because they missed it so much. Now it seemed the DMP had finally found their man, and Fitzgerald was going to be told at the meeting who she'd be working under for the foreseeable future.

I'd tried to persuade her to apply for the job herself. Draker had given her plenty of trouble in his time as Assistant Commissioner, and I resented the thought of her having to go through it all again with the next jerk who felt threatened by a strong, intelligent woman.

But throughout Fitzgerald insisted she'd rather take redundancy and stay home listening to me gripe all day than be stuck behind a desk – or, worse, schmooze her way round Dublin with officials, politicians, civil servants and other wastes of oxygen, assessing budgets, holding meetings, allocating resources, shuffling paper, as any responsible, career-minded Assistant Commissioner was expected to do. Investigations on the ground were all that mattered to her, all that ever *had* mattered, and if I was honest I couldn't have felt the same way about her if her priorities had been any different.

I don't know what that said about the two of us. A therapist would probably conclude that our single-mindedness was a sign of some personal or social dysfunctionality. A masquerade to conceal some inner loss.

That was yet another good reason to stay well clear of therapists.

6

Hugh, the old guy who minded the door of the building and sorted the mail and banged the pipes half-heartedly when something went wrong with the heating, was sitting on his usual chair in the lobby when I got downstairs. He was reading a newspaper. To be exact, he was reading the sports pages at the back of the newspaper which meant I had a clear view of the front-page story: *Girl Brutally Murdered in Inner City Tragedy*.

Reporters didn't hang around like pathologists, waiting for every detail to be meticulously checked out before deciding what had happened.

'That's a bad business,' he murmured with a shake of the head when he saw what I was looking at. He had a vaguely reproachful look in his eyes, like he blamed me in some mysterious way for what had happened. 'If you ask me, the whole town's going downhill. There never used to be things like this when I was younger.'

'There have always been murders,' I pointed out mildly.

'Not like this,' Hugh said, turning the newspaper over and jabbing a bony finger at the front page. 'Says here he sliced her up.' There was a relish in his voice now. Nothing gives people more satisfaction than wallowing in the world's wickedness. 'It makes me glad I'm old. At least I won't have to live to see it getting even worse. And it will, you mark my words. Dublin's getting as bad as that place you come from. What do you call it again?'

'America?' I offered.

'That's the one,' he said. 'You're always killing each other over there, aren't you?'

'Not all of us,' I said. 'A few of us manage to get through each day alive.'

But he wasn't really listening. I hoped I wasn't about to get a lecture from Hugh as well on all the things that were wrong with America.

In my experience, lectures like that were rarely brief.

I stopped him in his tracks by handing him a piece of paper.

'What's this?' he said suspiciously.

'The name of a locksmith,' I told him. 'He's coming over to take a look at my door. I've been having a few problems with it.'

'I could take a look at it, if you like. Save you some money.'

Think fast, girl. Let Hugh near the door and it wouldn't open till the Second Coming.

'That's OK,' I said quickly. 'The locksmith's a friend of mine. I just wanted to make sure you let him in. He'll be here about eleven. You'll be here?'

'I'm always here,' Hugh declared grumpily. 'Nowhere else to go, have I? They'll have to carry me out of here feet first in a box.' And for the second time that morning, it almost sounded like he was relishing the prospect.

'Well, if you could just hang on until you've let in the locksmith, I'd appreciate it.'

'Very amusing,' said Hugh as I headed to the door. 'You should be on TV.'

I waved goodbye as I stepped out into the morning's sharpness, but Hugh had already retreated back into his newspaper. The crossword this time.

He seemed to be coping well enough with the disintegration of Dublin society.

*

Soon as I hit outside, I could tell it was going to be another hot one. The sun hadn't yet blistered the day, but the air was tense with trepidation, waiting, expecting the assault. It was already growing bright. The trees in St Stephen's Green were ablaze with colour. Windows shone like silver on fire. The edge of things was furred with light. I slipped on my sunglasses to dim the world into bearability. Last thing I needed right now was a headache.

I'd woken that morning with a purpose. I knew what I had to do. I was going to head straight round to JJ's hotel and say hello. And if that turned out to be as easy as it sounded, I'd be lucky. But what was the worst that could happen? He could tell me to take a hike. Plenty of people had told me to do that before. He could join the list. Alternatively, he might've been thinking about what happened yesterday, regretting it even. He might be glad to see me.

And that might be a pig I could see coming into land at Dublin Airport . . .

Whatever his reaction, I wasn't going to think about it beforehand, I was going to plough on and let happen whatever was going to happen.

And if he did tell me to take a hike, I'd have gotten him talking at least.

That'd be progress.

I walked down Kildare Street and turned right at the end, following the flow of the traffic round by Lincoln Place and into Westland Row, getting caught up in the tide of passengers streaming out of Pearse Street Station, inexorable as always, sheltering as best they could in the shadows of buildings, relieved at every breath of wind, while workmen hung from the scaffolding like half-wild monkeys, shirtless, wolfwhistling every woman who passed below. The hotel where Kaminski was staying wasn't far beyond the station, hiding down a lattice of neglected and purposeless streets, but at first sight I felt certain that this mean, faded building couldn't be the right one.

The cab driver had said the Caledonian, right?

The building looked like it was waiting for the wrecking ball. There was a jagged crack right down the centre of the outer wall like a stroke of lightning. Metal bars hugged the front as if holding the bricks back from throwing themselves down on to the street below.

Half the letters in the hotel's painted sign had peeled off, and the railings at the front were buckled inward, as if a car had recently mounted the kerb and rammed into them. Or had it happened years ago and it was simply that no one had got around to fixing the damage?

The hotel was a reminder that, however much I might imagine I knew the city, the unexpected was still possible. I don't think I'd ever noticed the place before in all my circuits of the streets. One thing was certain. Either Kaminski had fallen on some seriously hard times, or he was deliberately staying in a place where no one who knew him would ever anticipate finding him. I took a deep breath and walked in through the front door.

The inside of the hotel was even shabbier and dingier than it looked from the outside, and that was some achievement. It never ceased to amaze me what people would put up with when they booked into a hotel. If they wanted to live like pigs in their own homes, I could respect that, that's their choice. But why they wanted to live with the accumulated filth of strangers was a total mystery. The place looked like it hadn't been dusted since the hotel went up over a hundred years ago. The chairs were unpicking themselves with age. The carpets were held together with threads. Come to think of it, the threads were all that was left. Heavy velvet curtains guarded the windows like bouncers, stopping the light from coming in.

A woman at reception looked up as I came in.

She was sitting on a stool behind the desk, smoking a cigarette with one hand and turning the pages of a magazine with the other, though her eyes were actually focused on a TV at the other end of the counter on which some grim morning chat show was playing.

She had large breasts and a floral patterned dress that was way too tight for the strain her chest was asking it to take. She looked flustered and sweaty, and her make-up could have been photographed from space. She had that exaggerated femininity that ends up displaying the opposite effect to the one intended. She was . . . forty? Fifty? Pick a number. Whatever the real age, it was more years than she cared to acknowledge. Her hair hung loose, and blonde as the bottle it came from had made it. Her roots were showing, in more ways than one.

She regarded me suspiciously.

'Yes?' she managed eventually.

'You have a guest staying here by the name of Buck Randall.'

I couldn't bring myself to add the last part of his chosen title.

'I'm afraid Mr Randall left word that he was not to be disturbed,' the woman answered with a look of satisfaction, like she'd won some battle I hadn't even realized was being fought. Maybe she had a soft spot for Kaminski and wanted to keep him to herself. Her voice oozed a fake gentility that people often affect this side of the Atlantic. Though why they bothered was an answer that escaped me every time.

'He won't mind being disturbed by me,' I said.

Like hell he wouldn't.

A look of deflation passed across her features, but she was still reluctant. 'Mr Randall was very specific about not being disturbed.'

'What if it's an emergency?'

'Is it an emergency?'

'It might be.'

She considered the point carefully, before deciding: 'I'll call his room. Wait there.'

She eased herself down from the chair, adjusted her clothes awkwardly around her hips and squeezed through a narrow door into a back room, where I heard the sound of a telephone being picked up, followed by silence. A few moments later she returned.

'Mr Randall must be out,' she said, glancing at the rack of room keys behind the chair where she'd been sitting when I first walked in. She frowned. 'That's funny, he didn't leave his key. I must have missed him. If you want to leave a message for him –'

'I'll call back later,' I said, and I was halfway across the lobby to the door when an idea suddenly occurred to me.

There was another way of finding out what JJ was up to.

Near the door was a stand of leaflets and flyers telling visitors what cultural delights awaited them in the city: shows, exhibitions, museums, stores. The ones that caught my eye were advertising the Shakespeare performance that Grace and I had missed last night.

Othello, starring Zak Kirby as Iago, 8 p.m. at the Liffey Theatre.

I took one, digging out from my pocket the pen that I always carried, in the unlikely event that creative inspiration should strike me on the hoof, and scribbled down the first number that came into my head.

The number didn't matter, what mattered was what the leaflet would show me.

I folded it in two, then walked back to the reception.

She'd been watching me the whole time from the side of her eye and gingerly took the leaflet between her long red fingernails as I handed to her.

'On second thoughts, leave this for Buck,' I said. 'Ask him to call me. I wrote down the number. As long as you're sure it's not breaking the no disturbing rule –'

'I'll leave it in his pigeonhole, madam.'

And she turned round and popped the leaflet into a small space marked with the number thirteen. Thirteen. That was the room where JJ was staying.

'Thanks,' I said and flashed a smile.

It wasn't returned.

Satisfied, I turned round and headed to the door to leave.

Except, of course, I didn't leave.

Thankfully, finding Kaminski's room was a lot more straightforward than getting up the stairs without the female impersonator on reception realizing I hadn't gone.

And, once I found it, getting inside was easier still.

A chambermaid was pushing a cart piled high with towels and clean sheets and boxes of soap along the corridor. I flashed my sweetest, most benign smile and told her I was Buck's wife, that I'd forgotten my key and needed to get back inside.

She looked Malaysian, and I'm not sure she understood much English. But she obviously followed what I was trying to say because she fished for the right key from the string at her waist and unlocked the door without objection. She didn't appear to care either way once she'd established that I was unthreatening. And why should she care? She was one of that international army of foreign workers that keep half the Western world going.

Overlooked, overworked, despised and receiving little for it in return but a total absence of security and a pay cheque that wouldn't keep a dog in comfort – not to mention the same dog's basket of abuse from all and sundry into the bargain. The last few years had seen more of these people arriving in Dublin than in the entirety of the city's history. Generally the traffic of misery had gone the other way.

That didn't mean the city's population was any more willing to be sympathetic to those forced to travel far from home in order to make a meagre living. Instead, as in any city, there were always people who chose to believe that immigrants were coming only to steal their jobs, conveniently forgetting the fact that these were mostly the jobs the natives didn't want to do in the first place because they considered themselves too good for them. That's what they call stealing? If these people were thieves, then they were the kind who broke into your house, before tidying up, cleaning the bathroom, taking out the trash, and putting a roast in the oven to slow cook in time for your arrival back home.

I tried offering the woman some money for opening the door, but she just smiled awkwardly and shook her head, backing off toward the cart, looking a little bemused.

And then I felt ashamed for trying to use money to make myself feel benevolent.

By the time I was inside JJ's room, I could already hear the cart rattling down the corridor, like a miniature version of the trams that now ran below the windows of my apartment, clanging round St Stephen's Green into the night. I stood with my back to the door, just making sure there really was no one in here with me. What if JJ had a woman in the room? That would've been something, stumbling into JJ's love nest uninvited.

Not that it looked much like a love nest, I thought, as I got used to the room and satisfied myself it was empty. The nest of some neglected old eagle who didn't much care where he spent his time, perhaps. The room was dingy and smelled faintly of damp, and the drawn curtains only added to the seedy atmosphere. I tiptoed across the floor to draw them back. Bright light poured through the gap I'd made and instantly lost its power.

Never mind, it was sufficient for my purposes.

Though as I quickly realized, there wasn't much to see.

It had looked better with the curtains pulled over. There was a TV, a chair, a double bed with a table next to it on which sat a kettle, a scattering of tea bags in paper envelopes, cartons of UHT milk, an unopened packet of biscuits and a copy of the *Dublin Street Guide*, essential reading for a stranger in town.

The bed didn't look like it had been slept in.

And I wouldn't have slept in it either. I'd have taken my chances with the armchair.

JJ was a fastidious man. Least he had been when I knew him. I couldn't see him willingly picking a place like this. Was it all he could now afford? Or did he figure this was the kind of place where a man could hide out as long as he wanted without being disturbed?

It was certainly the place for hiding things. There were probably a few tropical diseases which had been hiding out here since the world began. They say there are undiscovered species even now deep in the Amazon jungle, but I'd bet the Amazon had nothing on the species of unmentionable life that were to be found in this room.

That made it all the more important I find out why JJ was putting up with it.

Starting with the wardrobe, I began to hurriedly search

the room, stopping only once as I heard footsteps in the corridor outside. Voices. A laugh. They passed by.

I pulled open a few drawers. Underwear. T-shirts. A couple more pairs of shoes over by the window. Pants and shirts in the wardrobe. Nothing fancy, and he'd always been fussy about how he dressed. There was also a case on the top shelf of the wardrobe, but there was nothing in that either, and shaving stuff in a bag in the bathroom together with an aerosol deodorant and some headache pills. There was nothing under the bed, or in the drawers of the bedside cabinet save for the traditional Gideon Bible left by missionary-minded souls who, for some peculiar reason, had concluded that hotels were the best places to find converts.

In my experience, lonely men left alone in hotel rooms were more likely to switch to the subscription porn channels than open up the Acts of the Apostles.

Apart from that, the room held nothing of interest but a copy of a local listings magazine folded and left in the waste-paper basket. I tried flicking through the pages to see if Kaminski had marked anything, but the pages remained as the printer intended them.

I sat on the bed, defeated.

So much for my plan for searching.

Then I noticed a piece of paper poking out from inside Kaminski's copy of the *Dublin Street Guide* on the bedside table.

Eureka.

What Kaminski had slid inside the book was a scrap torn from a newspaper and folded over so many times that the creases had begun to pull apart. Opening the paper out to lay it flat on the bed was an operation which required patience, care and delicacy.

So naturally I tore the damn thing immediately.

It hardly seemed worth all the effort when the unfolding was done.

On one side of the newspaper was an ad for a sale of discount porn DVDs and videos at a store in Capel Street, north of the river, and another for a closing-down clearout at a wholesale pet supplies outlet on the outskirts of town. Talk about an unlikely combination. I doubted that either had much to command Kaminski's attention, unless he'd developed a taste for porn or poodles since we'd last met. Hopefully not both at the same time.

It must be this on the other side, then – but how?

Woman Killed in Accident – a small news item, undated, though I could tell by the print that it came from the *Dublin Evening Press*, and the pet store ad mentioned something about closing down at Easter, which meant it had to be at least four months old.

> The woman who was knocked down and killed in a south-side suburb of Dublin yesterday evening has been named as 42-year-old Cecelia Corrigan of Priory Crescent, Donnybrook. The unmarried teacher died instantly after being struck by a car in Herbert Road shortly after 7 p.m. and was pronounced dead at the scene. The driver of the car was questioned by police and later released without charge. 'There was nothing he could do to avoid hitting her,' said a witness. 'She just stepped out in front of him.' A front-seat passenger in the car involved in the fatal accident was later treated in hospital for shock but was not kept in overnight. The dead woman's remains will be removed from her home tomorrow evening at 8 p.m. for burial at Glasnevin Cemetery on Friday. Police have asked for any further witnesses to contact them at their nearest Metropolitan Police station.

And that was that.

There wasn't even a photograph of her.

I felt weary all of a sudden. I was more at sea now than I'd been before I tricked my way into Kaminski's room. And that was saying something.

What interest could JJ have in the accidental death of a fortysomething schoolteacher in Dublin months ago? If tracking down the man who killed his wife was the reason he left the FBI, how had he ended up checking out the accidental deaths of spinsters in the suburbs? Had Kaminski known this . . . what was her name again . . . Cecelia Corrigan? How could he? Or was there simply more to her death than met the untrained eye, but which had caught Kaminski's? I scanned the scrap of newspaper again for a hint of anything untoward, but if there was any suggestion of mystery in the text, it was completely lost on me. Was I putting two and two together and getting ninety-nine? It wouldn't be the first time.

Maybe I was losing my touch.

Maybe I never had a touch to lose.

But I folded it up carefully and replaced it all the same. He'd taken the trouble of inserting it there. He must have had his reasons. I just wished I knew what they were.

I checked my watch.

Ten.

Time enough if I hurried.

7

Once outside, I began to feel a touch ashamed of myself for being so inquisitive.

Even if Kaminski was interested in this Cecelia Corrigan's death, what of it? It was someone else's story, someone else's jigsaw, not mine. Things often have private meanings to an individual that shouldn't be communicated to any other human being.

That lost meaning if they *were* communicated.

I should go home, forget I ever saw him, forget I'd ever heard the name of poor dead Cecelia Corrigan in whom Kaminski might or might not have an interest. And yet I couldn't. I had a hunch there was some connection here to what Piper had told me on the phone. Or was I conveniently imagining I had a hunch as a way of legitimizing my curiosity?

Grace had warned me about that before.

All I knew is that I was going to give it one more shot, to try to make sense of things before I gave up. Before I learned to mind my own business.

Next stop was Pearse Street, a short walk from the hotel. The road – once grand, now a shabby, seedy main thoroughfare where no one lingered long if they could help it and certainly not after dark – ran all the way from Trinity College down to the Grand Canal, where it crossed the bridge and broke up into Ringsend and Irishtown. Halfway along the street there was a library, home of the City Archives, some dating back to the twelfth century.

Closer to my own purposes, the battered brown building

also housed the Dublin Collection, incorporating thousands of local, national and international newspapers, some stored bound, most on microfilm. In the past I'd spent hours in these rooms. Now I came here rarely. Soon I was seated at a desk in a corner of the library, near an old man in a threadbare tweed jacket despite the warm, who sat with his eyes closed, obviously asleep, though his head didn't droop once. He was obviously practised in the art of dozing unobtrusively.

I settled down to the tedious business of going back through back issues of the city evening newspaper to see if I could find more details of Cecelia Corrigan's fate.

Local newspapers never cease to astound with the sheer cascading avalanche of pointless details they manage to include about stuff that no one else would surely consider of any importance. Flower shows. Summer fêtes. Lost animals. Things that could be of interest only to people who lived in the city, and not to so many of them either. It was the same everywhere. Each city was a capsule separated from the world and existing in some bubble of its own. Each person who lived there had their own map of the city in their heads, and it warped their vision so that the city was always larger to them than the surrounding country, no matter how huge, no matter how important. It was what happened on each street and in each neighbourhood, rather than in the world beyond, which mattered. We are all solipsists.

Reading them at times could be like trawling for one solitary fish in the ocean.

Without a net.

That morning I was lucky. I found the fish. Cecelia Corrigan had died in March. There was a handful of reports on the accident which killed her, a few days of silence, then fewer reports of her funeral. Nowhere was there the slightest hint of any suspicious circumstance surrounding her death. The driver of the car which killed her had even attended the funeral. There was a blurry picture of him in one of the news reports, standing next to a young woman named in the caption underneath as Cecelia Corrigan's niece, Becky. His name, it seemed, was Mark Hudson. The woman's surviving family obviously bore him no ill-will.

There wasn't much more in the deaths notices. *In loving memory . . . with deepest sympathy . . . fondly remembered . . .* the standard formulae of grief.

As far as I could see, only one item stood out from the printed huddle of mourners. That was a message offering commiserations to Becky Corrigan on the death of her aunt from 'your colleagues at *Dublin Eye* magazine'. That was the same magazine I'd noticed in Kaminski's waste-paper basket at the hotel.

Not that owning a magazine was a crime. Even I had to admit that.

Then I saw it. A couple of weeks after Cecelia Corrigan's funeral, thanks to some overzealous security man, there'd been a brief security alert at Dublin Airport when a parcel had arrived with her name on the front and a return address from the Terrell Unit in Livingston, Texas.

The Terrell Unit was where Death Row prisoners were housed, though it wasn't where they were executed. That happened forty miles away in Huntsville, Walker County, in the east of the state. I'd flown down there once to interview an inmate, and a more unnerving town I'd never known. They called it Prison City because one in four of the population is an inmate, and the Texas Department of Criminal Justice is the town's biggest employer.

Outwardly, everything looks ordinary, unexceptional, quiet.

Inwardly, it feels like the whole place is built on bones.

Don't get me wrong. I've never been some hand-wringing bleeding heart who thinks the state has no right to take life. It's just like all the misery the prisoners have caused has been dragged along there with them and holed up in the walls. Some of it is bound to leak out and poison the air. I couldn't live some place like that. I couldn't breathe.

Cecelia Corrigan evidently saw things differently. She'd been writing to one of the prisoners on Death Row in Texas and campaigning for his conviction to be overturned.

That wasn't so uncommon. There was an unending supply of gullible . . . sorry, compassionate women, usually past their prime and unmarried, who wanted to strike up relationships with men behind bars. Some were simply lonely. Some were looking for romance. For soulmates, God help them. Having gone so long without the real thing in their lives, they were grasping in desperation on to this meagre, obscene, long-distance substitute. Ironically, the fact these men were behind bars made it safer to love them. Nothing would ever come of the romance, so any fantasy could be projected on to it.

Some women went further. They were actually turned on by the thought of what these men had done. They wanted the sordid glamour of a close association with evil.

Others still were motivated by a principled opposition to the taking of life – though why this should manifest itself via an attachment to men who had taken life in far more perverse and brutal ways than any gas chamber ever had was something they'd have to explain. I certainly couldn't do it. The folks who gathered outside prison gates on the night of each execution, lighting candles and sobbing like it was Mahatma Gandhi who was being put down inside, should try visiting some crime scenes. Ask them then if they still want to idealize men for whom murder lies somewhere between a hobby and a vocation.

Cecelia Corrigan's correspondent had been a man by the name of Jenkins Howler.

The name meant nothing to me, but then why should it? There were plenty of prisoners on Death Row and plenty more being added every year.

Murder is a business that never seems to go into recession.

The parcel detained at Dublin Airport purported to be from Howler, though of course it couldn't actually have come from him. Death Row inmates are not even allowed to smoke, let alone send mysterious parcels to their dead penfriends. Inside was a rough, hand-made bouquet of flowers. Howler had obviously found some way of getting the flowers sent in tribute to his late penfriend via a third party. Who it was I had no idea, but that wasn't so important as the fact I had finally found some thread of a story which it made a semblance of sense for Leon Kaminski to pursue. Was Howler the man that JJ suspected of killing his wife?

Had Kaminski come to Dublin looking for evidence to prove it?

Whatever the reason, I had something to work with at last. It was at this point I realized, no matter how guilty I felt about interfering with things that were none of my concern, that it had gone too far now for me to turn back. Kaminski – Cecelia Corrigan – Jenkins Howler – I simply had to keep following the trail to see where it led.

And I knew just who to ask.

Back home, I switched on the radio and weaved in and out of signals along the dial in search of more information on Marsha Reed's death, but there was nothing apart from the usual diet of cheesy pop music for those whose attention span started to struggle after three minutes, and talk radio stations where people were encouraged to drown themselves in whatever sea of complaint was lapping at their personal shore at any particular moment.

That day, like most days, the voices were mainly spitting out the usual diet of bile about the United States. Here we go again. I'd learned soon after coming to Dublin that, though the welcome was friendly enough on the surface, you didn't have to dig down very far to find that the people who passed as the foremost thinkers in Dublin, the ones whose voices whined out of every screen and every radio, considered the United States to be little better than the Third Reich, imperialist overlords imposing their savage and depraved values on the world. Values like, oh, democracy and free speech and respect for women.

Scary stuff, huh?

I'd quickly grown tired of being expected to show humility in the face of my country's alleged litany of sins, or to parrot the carping as some precondition of membership of a club that I didn't want to belong to anyway. There were plenty enough Americans in Dublin willing to do that. We were expected to whisper our nationality apologetically, like it was shameful. Being American and proud of it was the new love that dare not speak its name.

Not that I've ever felt proud of being American either. Being proud of where you're born makes no more sense than being proud of having blue eyes. There's nothing you can do about it either way. But I damn sure wasn't going to be made to be ashamed of it.

Eventually I found a news station, but all they said was what'd been in the newspapers that morning: that a woman's body had been found in a house in Dublin and that police were trying to contact members of her family before naming her.

In the end I snapped off the radio impatiently.

'Is that where the Chief is?' came Boland's voice from over by the door.

Until about a year ago, Niall Boland had been a member of the Murder Squad alongside Fitzgerald, though he'd never really been cut out for murder, if that's the right way of putting it. He knew that himself better than anyone.

There are plenty of fine police officers who should never be allowed near a murder investigation, and Boland was most definitely one of them. The writer Brendan Behan once said that the police in Dublin looked like they'd had to be coaxed down out of the mountains with raw meat, and I guess it was men like Boland he was thinking of. There was a thick-set roughness about his appearance that spoke more of the farms and hills than it did of the city. It sometimes felt like some cosmic joke that he had been born in Dublin at all. Everything about him betrayed a man who ought to have been rising at dawn to inspect his own fields and reclining at night with his feet stretched toward a peat fire.

But that country boy solidity masked a sensitivity that meant he was always going to find working the Murder Squad too damaging. Murder affected everyone, of course, unless they were chiselled out of stone, nursing hearts dead to the business of being human, but it was true that it took a certain sliver of ice in the heart to be able to go on doing it, day after day, murder after murder, and if Boland ever had ice in his heart it had melted long ago.

Eventually he gave up the battle against reality and jumped ship. With his girlfriend, he opened a locksmith's store in the indoor market that ran between South Great George's

Street and Drury Street. It was Boland's name I'd given to Hugh that morning.

I'd gotten back from the library to find him already at work. It said something for how much I trusted him that I didn't mind his being here without me. There weren't many people I could say that about. Like Lucas Piper, I was a little paranoid about security.

'You don't have to call her Chief now,' I pointed out, walking over to the front door where he was kneeling, tightening screws. 'You're a free man.'

'She'll always be Chief to me.'

'Don't tell Cassie.'

'She's Chief No. 2,' he said with a grin.

'A man cannot serve two mistresses. Unless you're one of those men who like being bossed about by big domina-trixes in leather masks and tight lederhosen with whips and chains,' I said. 'I've read about your sort in the Sunday newspapers.'

'My secret is out,' Boland said. 'That must be why I'm so good with locks.'

'Speaking of which,' I said, 'how much longer are you going to be?'

'Didn't you ever hear that old saying about patience being a virtue? I'm nearly done. These are fascinating old locks you have. Seems a pity to replace them.'

'As long as they work,' I shrugged.

'Give me five minutes, then, and I'll be out of your hair.'

'You meeting Cassie for lunch?'

'Not today,' he said. 'I have to stay in and mind the shop.'

'Just imagine,' I said. 'If you hadn't left the Murder Squad, you could be over there now with the rest of the team instead.'

'No thanks,' said Boland firmly.

He was another one, getting on with their lives, like Piper. Another one who'd been able to leave it behind.

'Do they have any idea who did it?' he asked now.

'No,' I said. 'But there doesn't seem to be any sign of a forced entry, and it was a bit late at night for the killer to be posing as the gasman or a courier to get inside, so either it was someone she knew and she let them in, or it was someone with a key.'

'The Chief should check her locks,' said Boland.

I frowned. What did Fitzgerald's locks have to do with this woman's murder?

'The dead girl's locks,' explained Boland when he saw my blank look.

'I'm still lost,' I said.

'You'd be surprised by the things I've learned since starting this job. One thing I've learned is never to trust a locksmith. Apparently, there's a brisk black market trade in keys.'

'There is?'

'Think about it,' he said, warming to the theme. 'A locksmith gets called in to change someone's locks, and when he's in the house he sees a few nice pieces scattered about, maybe he even knows a bit about antiques or collectables and realizes what they're worth. More to the point, he knows other people who might be interested in getting their greedy hands on the stuff. So he makes a couple of extra keys of the place he's just fixed up, and Bob's your uncle. He sells them on and a few weeks later the people come home to find there are considerably fewer things in the house than there were when they went out.'

'This is a bit more serious than a robbery.'

'Same difference, as far as the methodology goes. You never know, her locksmith could've taken a shine to her and cut himself an extra key for when he summoned up the courage to act on it. Locksmiths make spares illicitly all the time, though they don't like to shout about it, for obvious reasons. There was even a case in Japan recently of a writer who was murdered after publishing a book exposing what they were up to.'

'I guess that's how you could afford a new car,' I teased him.

I'd seen the new people carrier parked on the kerb when I got back from the library. It looked impressive, though it wasn't going to look so impressive once the clampers got to it.

'I got that entirely legit,' Boland said. 'Just because I know some of the wicked ways of the trade doesn't mean I take after them. Besides, I don't need to. We're doing so well now we've just taken a young lad on to work with us. Wish I'd done it years ago instead of plodding along, playing at being a real policeman. I hardly do the locks myself now. I just sit in the shop and send the new boy out. I'm only here doing these ones because it's you.'

'I'm honoured,' I said. 'Not to mention relieved. At least I can trust you not to go selling on my keys to the criminal underworld.'

'The bad guys wouldn't stand a chance against you even if I did.'

'I wouldn't say that. My karate's a little rusty these days,' I joked. 'It's an intriguing idea, though. I'll tell Fitzgerald what you said. It might be worth following up. At least it would explain how the killer got in and out without any sign of a break-in.'

'You really think it's worth checking out?'

He looked pleased to have come up with a useful suggestion.

'I wouldn't say it if I didn't. You know, Boland, sometimes I think you'd make a good policeman. You're wasted in your new life.'

8

'Your Ceceilia Corrigan had an interesting taste in friends,' said Burke.

Thaddeus Burke, that is to say: owner of, and sole worker at, Burke and Hare's, a radical (at least that's what he called it) bookstore down by the quays, where the water slapped continually at brown stone, lingering idly on its way to the sea.

Decorated former US marine, lifelong communist, cat lover, whiskey connoisseur, truly execrable poker player – there was something in Burke's overcrowded personality for everyone. And, speaking for myself, it was the terrible poker that I liked best, plus the fact that he seemed to effortlessly gather a whole bunch of equally terrible poker players round him. For a girl who paid her way through college back in Boston playing poker, they made for easy, if not so rich, pickings. Sometimes I truly wished he'd get to know some rich people for a change and invite them along on one of his poker nights. Sadly, Burke was drawn to the marginalized and the penniless, and there's only so much hard cash you can snatch from these people before you start feeling bad about it. Guilt takes all the pleasure out of winning.

Well, some of it.

All the same, I had to admit that playing poker with Burke's inner circle of Dublin's dissolute was less stressful than those far-off days in college when I'd spent my nights in darkened downtown rooms across a table from the kind of men my mother had always warned me to stay away from. And she was right. Those were the days when, if you played poker, you were never really sure if you wanted to win. Losing might've meant poverty, but you didn't know *what* winning might mean. Chances were it wouldn't be pleasant.

No one ever asked any questions about what anyone else there did from nine to five. That was one of the rules. But they didn't need to wear badges to signal that these were men who were less used to handing over their own money than taking other people's money off them. Whether the other people wanted to hand it over or not.

It was inevitable that an exile like me would find my way to Burke eventually, and so it had proved. I counted him now as one of my few genuine friends in the city, and I hoped he could say the same about me. His politics I wasn't so crazy about, but I figure that a man's politics are his own concern. More important than any ideological differences was how he carried himself as a human being, and Burke had a dignity and self-possession in his bearing that you often see in the best soldiers.

I'd never seen him lose his temper, not even when he came down from his room above the store some mornings to find the word *Nigger* painted across the front window.

The continuing suspicion of a black face in some quarters of the city was one of those hidden parts of life in Dublin that they never get around to mentioning in the guide books.

It was Burke I'd asked to check up for me on Jenkins Howler, since he had a computer hooked up to the internet, where he could track the progress of the workers' revolution across the globe (current status: way behind schedule), and I didn't. He also needed it for his business. Half his sales were online now, he'd told me not so long ago when I was complaining at the permanent hum the computer made behind the desk. Most of his customers never even came into the store. My relationship with technology, by contrast, was almost as bad as my relationship with other people. Almost, but not quite.

It's true that logging on to the internet would probably have made researching my books a whole lot more straightforward, but I still didn't want to. I know my personality, my weaknesses. I'm too easily distracted. I wouldn't trust myself with that much opportunity not to do any work. No, I preferred to stay with my usual methods of online research, namely getting Burke to do it. Besides, it gave me an excuse to come round and drink his whiskey.

That clinched any remaining argument.

'She's not my Cecelia Corrigan,' I said now in answer to his earlier remark about the dead woman's choice of friends. 'She wasn't anybody's. That was the problem. Who'd choose to have a guy on Death Row for a friend if there were other available options?'

'What have you got against prisoners on Death Row?' said Burke.

'What have I got against them?' I repeated incredulously. 'You mean, apart from the fact that they're a collection of murderers, rapists, gangsters, armed robbers, cop killers, drug addicts and child molesters?'

'Who says? The Texas Department of Criminal Justice?' said Burke. 'That ain't exactly the testimony of the angels. They make mistakes. Innocent men get strapped to the table too, you know, while the doc injects them with that crap.'

'I know that, Burke, but you –'

'And have you ever looked at those statistics?' he interrupted. 'Only 11 per cent of the population of Texas is black, and you wanna guess what the percentage is of black offenders on Death Row in the state? 40 per cent. 40.

Over 50 per cent of Texas is white, but white prisoners only make up 30 per cent of the inmates on Death Row.'

'That doesn't excuse what they've done.'

'I'm not saying it does. I spent twenty years as a soldier. I don't have any illusions about human nature. But you can't divorce the issue of capital punishment from the social, political and racial context in which it's implemented by the government,' Burke said.

'Shooting dead the cashier so you can take twenty bucks from the cash register isn't making a political statement.'

'No, but giving thirty years to a white guy who shoots a cashier, and a one-way trip to the prisoners' graveyard in Huntsville to a black guy whose does exactly the same, *is* a political statement. The whole system stinks.'

'Look, not even I'm crazy enough to say the system's perfect,' I said. 'I just can't think of an alternative. The dead deserve justice. It's the only thing we've got left to give them. And those men, they carry on spreading evil even when they're behind bars. It's their nature. They *should* be dead.' I paused. 'Is Jenkins Howler black?'

Burke grinned. 'You think I'm fooled by the way you just sidestepped the argument about capital punishment there and tried to switch the talk back to the reason you came round here?'

'Obviously not.'

'You're damn right I'm not. But for your information,' said Burke, 'Jenkins Howler isn't anything any more, black, white, Hopaki Indian or Eskimo. He's dead, and there are no segregated buses in hell.'

'Dead?' I said.

'That's the usual outcome when you're executed.'

Burke placed a sheet in front of me, showing a headline from a three-month-old copy of the *Texas Ranger* which said: *Rapist-Murderer Executed in Huntsville*. It even featured a picture of him. Howler had been a weasely man with a pinched, mean-looking face, scrappy moustache, bad teeth.

And no, he wasn't black.

'Good-looking guy,' I remarked.

'And with a personality to match,' Burke stressed. 'I don't want to give you any more ammunition for your simplistic and unrepentant right-wing views on the American criminal-justice system, but I seriously doubt if this guy's passing is going to be much loss to the world. Not if this stuff is anything to go by, at any rate.'

This stuff turned out to be a pile of press cuttings and write-ups about Howler that Burke had downloaded and printed out for me from the internet.

He laid them down on the table, then sat back, watching the world go by outside his window, as I began to flick through the sheets. Burke, bless him, had even put the collection into chronological order – oh, what it must be like to have a logical mind – starting with a ten-year-old news item about Howler's arrest for the rape and murder of a female hitchhiker whose body had been found in shrubland by the side of the road near Austin three weeks earlier.

The gun which had been used to kill the girl was found in the glove compartment of Howler's pick-up truck. Not exactly a criminal genius, then.

When DNA testing, as a later news report confirmed, also linked Howler to the scene, he soon confessed. Though not to the murder of a young black woman shot dead at a crack house in Tyler two years previously, which tests showed was also carried out by the same gun. His story was that he'd bought the gun in a bar in Galveston, which was possible, I guess. Few guns being passed around on the black market had a clean history. Each one was corrupted by its history and corrupted by those who had held it. Having too little evidence to go on, the prosecutor decided not to pursue that charge. The rape and murder was sufficient for a conviction as it was, especially when DNA tests also matched Howler to three further rapes of students in the university town of Austin some years previously.

There were further reports, growing more intermittent as time passed, of Howler's trial and sentencing, then of the various appeals launched by his attorneys against the capital sentence, all of whom seemed to talk as if it was Howler who was the true victim of all this.

Finally came the execution.

There seemed to have been quite a campaign to have Howler's sentence commuted to life imprisonment. He'd been a particular favourite of the nuns. He'd found Jesus when he was inside – don't they all? – and his new religious friends were gathered outside the night he died, praying, singing hymns, lighting candles, bleating to reporters about the cruelty and injustice of taking human life. Pity Howler hadn't embraced that creed a bit earlier.

'Did he make a last statement?' I said, noticing it wasn't in the pile.

'He did,' said Burke. 'I thought I printed it out for you. Isn't it there?'

I rifled quickly back through the pages.

'I can't see it.'

'I'll print you another one off,' he said. 'It was very touching. He said he was very sorry for all that he'd done, and all the hurt he'd caused, and he asked the family of the dead girl for their forgiveness. He said that he was going home now to the Lord, where he would answer for his sins, and he hoped they'd find some comfort in his death.'

'Your dictionary obviously has a different definition of touching than mine.'

'And your dictionary obviously doesn't acknowledge the existence of the word repentance,' said Burke.

'I believe in the *word*,' I said, 'I just don't know whether it amounts to much.'

'At least he was facing up to what he'd done,' said Burke. 'That's something. Some of these men keep the families of the victim on the rack right to the end. They enjoy it. I guess that's why there was such a campaign around Howler. The sinner repenteth and all that. There was even a documentary about the campaign to save him on one of the public access networks. I could try and get hold of a copy, if you like, but I wouldn't raise your hopes too high.'

'My hopes are never high. That way everything is a pleasant surprise.'

'This is the definitely the guy you wanted to know about, then?'

'It's him all right,' I admitted.

'And you think this is the same guy your old friend JJ has an interest in?'

I'd told him when I called earlier from outside the library on Pearse Street about seeing Kaminski in Temple Bar.

'I not only think it,' I said, 'I know.'

'How do you know?'

'I just know, is all.'

'You just know? So it's that kind of knowing, is it?' he said. 'That's the kind of knowing I think *I'm* better off not knowing too much about. That's the kind of knowing that could get a girl into a lot of trouble.'

'I like being in trouble.'

'You do, don't you?' said Burke. He shook his head with

mock sadness. 'It's a wonder to me you never wound up in the next cell to a guy like Howler.'

'I'd need a sex change first.'

'You know what I mean. Still,' he said, shrugging, 'you know your own business, and I know how to mind mine. Though I must admit I'm curious as to how an ex-Bureau man's presence in Dublin is supposed to be connected to an execution in Texas.'

'I'm curious too,' I said. 'All I know is that this Howler was writing to Cecelia Corrigan and now she's dead too and Kaminski's sniffing around her corpse. It was nothing, an accident, but I can't help feeling there must be some connection.'

'And you thought the key to the code was Howler?'

'That was the idea.'

He was silent a moment, considering.

'Maybe', he suggested in due course, 'Kaminski thinks this Howler might have passed on information to her before he died, and he wants to know what it was.'

'Maybe's a big country.'

'Then take this stuff with you as your guide,' said Burke. 'You haven't had a chance to study it properly yet. Though, if you want my advice, I don't like the way it looks.'

'Explain yourself, soldier.'

Burke shrugged. 'It just feels wrong. You be careful.'

'What could happen?' I said. 'Howler's dead, the woman he was writing to is dead.'

'But the guy who got you interested in this is still very alive and running round the city, and you don't know what the hell he's doing. I don't want anything to happen to you.'

'Nothing can happen to me. I'm indestructible.'

'That's what all the folks in the graveyard thought.'

Burke looked up as the bell on the door jingled and a

74

small fat guy in an ill-fitting T-shirt with a hammer and sickle on the front was framed against the sunlight in the door. I recognized him. He was known as Red Ned, though I doubted that was what it said on his birth certificate. He was one of Burke's poker circle, though far as I knew it wasn't the night for poker. Unless the cowards had started organizing games without me.

'Am I early?' he said as he came in.

'You're early,' confirmed Burke, 'but come in anyway.'

'Saxon,' the newcomer nodded. 'You're the last person I expected to see here.'

'Don't worry,' I said. 'I'm just off. I didn't realize the time. What am I missing?'

'We're having a meeting here later on,' said Burke. 'We get together a couple of times a week to plan the overthrow of the capitalist system.'

'Aren't you boys a little old for all that bullshit?' I teased.

'We're giving capitalism until next Tuesday to crumble, and if it doesn't we're taking up embroidery. You're welcome to join us,' Burke said. 'Having you on board during the revolution might just tip the balance.'

'It's a tempting offer, but I promised Fitzgerald I'd go round and prepare lunch.'

'Listen to you,' said Red Ned with a wink. 'You're starting to sound like a housewife.'

'That's what I hate about you pinkos,' I said with staged offence. 'Soon as you start to lose the argument, you immediately resort to insults.'

'Words are the only weapons we have against the oppressors,' he said solemnly.

'You're breaking my heart. I'd better get out of here before you have me weeping with more hard-luck stories about the workers.'

'It's your loss, comrade.'

'I doubt that, but I'll make you a deal. You start the revolution without me, and if things start going your way I'll make sure to switch sides in time for the victory parade.'

'Spoken like a true mercenary,' said Burke.

9

I picked up some food that could be heated later from a tiny Middle Eastern place I'd discovered once while walking near Fownes Street. It wasn't far out of my way. I didn't know if Healy liked this kind of food, but he'd have to put up with it. Fitzgerald had sent me a message earlier that he'd be coming too. Briefly I considered walking back to my apartment and taking the Jeep out from the underground car park, but by the time I'd gotten up there and taken the car from its place, I'd have wasted another fifteen minutes. By the time I struggled through the traffic to her house, I'd have wasted even longer. I decided to take the train instead.

Tara Street was near. A train rattled over the bridge above as I approached the station, filling the air with its thunderous clang, making the air seem hotter somehow as it disgorged a bellyful of carbon fuels into the atmosphere and melted another iceberg, if you believe all that jazz about global warming. Typical that I'd missed the train. Then I saw with relief that it was going the other way. Trains were fairly regular, but even so I didn't want to be kept hanging around longer than necessary.

It was a relief to turn off the street into the Stygian gloom of the station. It felt like the last remnant of coolness in the city. Oasis in the desert. Inside, I bought a ticket at the booth, and then pushed through the turnstile to take the escalator up to the crowded platform.

I stood with my back to a pillar and lost myself in the buzz of conversation that rose and receded like a tide around me. I avoided catching anyone's eye. I didn't feel like being dragged into conversation. My body might've been in Dublin, but my brain was in Texas. I was with Jenkins Howler, and I have to admit I've enjoyed better company.

To keep focused, I let my eyes fall to the platform.

There, just before the drop on to the tracks, a line had been newly drawn, along which was also painted a warning: *Do Not Cross the Yellow Line.*

I smiled.

Crossing the line was what I was best at. What I'd always done. I had crossed the line this morning again in JJ's room. I shouldn't have intruded on his privacy like that. Another twinge of guilt came, but I suppressed it impatiently. It was important to suppress guilt or you'd never get anything done. Never get anything interesting done, at least.

But there were other lines I'd crossed, throughout my life, and it was only after you crossed them that you realized nothing would ever be the same again. And by then it was always too late. There was no going back. Sometimes it was for the best. Sometimes not.

The biggest line I'd ever crossed was when I joined the FBI. Behind me then was one world, and the new world I entered made me see everything in an entirely different light.

Or perhaps light is the wrong word, since what I saw was so dark.

Those experiences tainted my mind and made it impossible for me to go back to feeling positive or trusting about things again. I lost my faith in human nature. I lost my faith in people doing the right thing or stopping bad things from happening.

Leaving the FBI was another huge step, because now my mind had been battered and changed, but there was nothing I could do with my thoughts any more but brood on them, impotently. There is less that can be done in the FBI than you hope, disappointment is perpetual, a feeling of inadequacy pervades the soul. But at least you can do *something*, even if it is never enough. Once outside, I was permanently barred from that world I had come to know. I'd dwelt there once. Now it was a foreign country. I was across the border.

Perhaps if I'd taken a different path and tried, I mean really tried, to put it behind me, I could have made things work. I could have moved on. But no. With my great talent for screwing up, I had carried on writing about that life and hanging round its edges, even wound up with a woman who still worked in the investigation of murder, which meant that it was constantly within my orbit, though there was nothing I could do about it but look on.

From the other side of the line.

And yes, I had killed a man once. That was another crossing of the line, albeit one I tried to revisit in my memory as little as I could, easier said than done though it was.

Dreams were the worst.

They're beyond rational control.

I was grateful when my melancholy thoughts were interrupted by the snaking arrival of the train around the bend into the station.

That is, I called it a train, but the locals knew it as the DART. The letters stood for Dublin Area Rapid Transport, though there were times when the Rapid part of the acronym sometimes felt more like a vague aspiration than an iron-clad promise. Still, it was a good way to get around certain parts of the city if you didn't feel like driving. I climbed aboard.

No seat, it was too busy, so I simply grabbed a pole that connected floor to ceiling and held on as the carriage jerked forward, trying to concentrate on where I was going, because

I didn't want to start daydreaming and miss my stop. I'd done that before.

Instead I stared out of the window and watched them go by, the names of the stations ticking off in my head like the beat of a metronome.

Pearse.

Grand Canal Dock.

Lansdowne Road.

Sandymount.

Sydney Parade.

It was only as the train pulled out of Sydney Parade that I realized it was where I was supposed to get out. I'd been staring at the station's name written on a metal sign, feeling hollow. Sydney had been my sister's name. She was dead now. Her funeral was the last time I'd been home to Boston, and sometimes I didn't know if I'd ever go back again.

After Sydney died, there was nothing there worth going back *for*.

I stepped off at the next station, which had been saddled with the singularly ugly name of Booterstown, and began walking back along the seafront. The tide was out. A wide expanse of sand and flatness stretched into the distance, the monotony of the view broken only by occasional walkers, like drawings of stick men, lingering among the pools of stranded water. The sea beyond was as still as a lake. The masts of sailing boats scarcely moved.

I was on Strand Road.

Not far now.

Fitzgerald lived in a cul-de-sac across the sea with a view of Howth Head from her bedroom. Cul-de-sac: they had to be the three most terrifying words in any language, next to *I love you* and *it's a boy*. The houses had been put up about five years ago, and they didn't look like they'd last much longer than the stuff I'd bought for lunch. They were the sort of houses that a child would make out of Lego. Front door, four windows, chimney, like a sketch of something that might one day be a house rather than the real thing. I hated it here.

So did Fitzgerald, but for her it was just a place to eat, a place to sleep, a place to take a shower. It was like a hotel without chambermaids to root around in your underwear drawer and use your toothbrush to clean the toilet. She kept irregular hours. It was all she needed.

We'd often talked about getting a house together. It made no sense to keep two places going when as often as we could we were both either at one or the other. Living in two places simply multiplied the time we spent travelling between them, and travelling was getting more difficult round the city with every month that passed. Fitzgerald said she could remember a time when you could get from one side of Dublin to the other in a half-hour. Now you'd have no chance of doing that unless you grew wings. Traffic choked the city more tightly than a noose. But still, somehow, we'd never gotten beyond talking about it. There was always something else that pushed house-hunting on to the back burner.

We wanted different things, that was the problem. She may have hated her house, but cross the road and there was the Strand and the wide sweep of Dublin Bay, Howth Head opposite and Bray Head in the distance. This is where she liked to walk. If she could have her way, she'd live out in the country, with roaring fires, and logs piled by the stone hearth, and seven dogs sleeping at her feet. She should've married a farmer, and they could've gotten themselves a smallholding out West, where they could tend pigs and grow parsnips and make wine out of nettles. My longing had always been for the city, for bustle and noise. Trying to find a compromise between the two extremes was like negotiating an end to the Cold War. Not that we were likely to come to blows about it, just that what we wanted was so far apart as to make any chance of finding a happy medium pretty much impossible.

It was complicated by the fact that houses in Dublin were so expensive.

I had enough money not to have to worry about it, and Fitzgerald had her house to sell. Pooled together, we had plenty. But it never ceased to shock me what people in Dublin paid for what in any other city would've been regarded as unremarkable properties.

That was why people were moving further and further out of the city and commuting in each morning, just so they could afford a place of their own, and houses in the centre of town that would once have been lived in were now offices for insurance brokers and lawyers – Dublin was full of lawyers, and I used to think the States was overrun with them – and were locked up and dark at night, giving an eerie, otherworldly quality to the streets. The gardens in the middle of the old squares were dark and deserted. Take a small turn off the main street and the city, which a moment ago had been thronged and noisy, had almost ceased to exist at all. A vista emptier than the post-nuclear winter landscape had taken its place.

Yet even that had to be preferable to this, I thought, as I walked up the path to Fitzgerald's house and a curtain twitched in response in the window next door.

It was that kind of place. The kind where they keep tabs on you to make sure you never have any privacy. Your privacy offends them. And the fact that Fitzgerald wasn't married to a chartered surveyor and spending her days rearing three kids probably offended them too. I resisted the childish temptation to stick out my tongue at the neighbours, and let myself in. There was no sign of her yet, but then I hadn't expected there to be.

A murder investigation doesn't watch the clock.

I stacked the food in the fridge to keep for later.

Whenever later turned out to be.

To pass the time, I lifted a Coke from the ice box and turned on the large fan which Fitzgerald had set up on the worktop in an effort to keep cool, and I sat with the news reports about Jenkins Howler that Burke had printed off for me fanned out on the kitchen table, held down with various pieces of silverware to stop them blowing away.

And there was his last statement. The page must've gotten stuck to the back of another sheet. That was how I'd missed it. It was only the breeze from the fan that made it work loose. I read it through slowly, ending at Howler's last words.

'*Warden, I'm ready.*'

Well, bully for him.

That's what many condemned men said when the time came, and it always made me angry. They had no right to be ready. Their victims hadn't been given the chance to prepare themselves for death, to find Jesus or to make their peace with the world.

They had simply been snatched away from life, violently.

The Texas Department of Criminal Justice was certainly thorough, I'll say that. For each execution, there was not only a record of the offender's last statement but a sheet detailing their previous criminal convictions, history of education, height, weight, eye colour, the country they came from, you name it, as well as an account of the crimes for which they were being punished. There was even a note of

83

the ethnic origins of their victims. Killers tended to stay within their own ethnic group. It was black on black, white on white, Hispanic on Hispanic. Burke would say that proved him right when he argued how every act had its origins in the social, economic and racial circumstances out of which it had been born.

My own view was that killers simply took their opportunities for fun where they could find them, and in a country as segregated as the United States they were inevitably going to find most of those opportunities in the particular sub-group they belonged to. There was nothing profound about it, it was merely a reflection of where they were at.

Or was that just an example of the two of us finding different ways to describe the same pnenomenon?

In addition to all this, there was a list of those who had been present at the execution of each prisoner, and there used to be a description of the prisoner's chosen last meal until the publication of that information was deemed insensitive and ordered to be kept secret. Though why the revelation of a psychopath's Big Mac and fries should be considered out of the bounds of decency, while the final degradation and suffering of victims at the hands of these same losers with a grudge against society was published for all to see, was beyond me.

Depressed, I read through Howler's final statement again – the expressions of regret, the best wishes for the future for his friends and fellow inmates and guards, the born-again claptrap – looking for something I couldn't be certain I would recognize even if I saw it. Whatever Howler had done to get Kaminski on his scent, I still didn't have enough information to determine. All this effort, and I was no closer to an answer.

I scraped back my chair in frustration and roughly yanked

open the door of the fridge to get another Coke. Or, better still, a beer. The fridge shook in protest at my delicate, lady-like touch, dislodging some further sheets of paper which had been pushed into the gap between the top of the fridge and the microwave that sat up there.

I caught them as they fell. I saw at once what they were. They were brochures for house sales. Detached Victorian villa in Rathgar and Ranelagh. Edwardian semi-detacheds in Dalkey and Sandycove. Period features, orginal fireplaces, en suite bathrooms, fitted kitchens. I guess house-hunting wasn't as on the back burner as I'd thought.

'You're going bald,' I said, when they finally arrived at the door an hour later.

'Bald is sexy,' growled Healy.

'Whoever told you that must've had one sick sense of humour.'

'Stop talking nonsense, woman, and bring me some food.'

It was after two and Healy's car had just pulled into the driveway with Fitzgerald in the passenger seat, and I'd gotten up from the kitchen table, where I was still reading, to open the door for them. The scent of the sea was in the breezeless air.

They both looked spent. Not sleeping tends to have that effect. But, as it happened, Healy was right. His hair may have been thinning and greying a little, but it made him look more attractive. These days he almost looked distinguished.

He was nearly fifty now, a veteran of many cases, and remained the person in the department that Fitzgerald probably felt most comfortable with, the one she related to and could talk to. He'd never had the same problem working for a female Chief Superintendent that some of the other members of the team did, and just as important he'd never had a problem with our relationship. Plenty of the others found it either threatening or a vehicle for trademark crude humour. Healy just regarded ours as a normal relationship like any other.

We often found ourselves eating together when they were working a case.

He headed through to the tiny kitchen and threw himself into a chair.

'What a day,' he said.

I saw Fitzgerald's eye move to the pile of real estate brochures which had fallen on me from the top of the fridge, and then look at me sharply, like I'd caught her out.

'It's fine,' I said in a low voice.

'What's fine?' said Healy, not noticing anything was wrong.

'Lunch,' I said.

'I should think so,' he said. 'A man comes in after working hard, he expects to find some decent chow waiting for him at the table.'

'I'll get your pipe and slippers later, good master of mine,' I said. 'Meanwhile, why don't you help yourself to a cold drink while I get the food ready?'

'Beer?' he said hopefully.

'You're driving,' said Fitzgerald.

'Drat.'

I took the various trays of pre-prepared food from the fridge and began to scoop them out on to plates – cold chicken, falafels, olives, houmous, pitta bread.

Red Ned was right. I was turning into a housewife.

'What's all this?' said Healy, lifting a sheet and peering at it.

'Just some research I've been doing,' I said.

'*Death Row Killer in Final Appeals to Texas Governor*,' he read aloud. 'You know, I sometimes think it wouldn't be such a bad idea if we had the electric chair here too.'

'They don't have the electric chair in Texas,' I said, taking it neatly from him.

'They don't?'

'Lethal injection,' I said. 'Sodium thiopental to sedate the prisoner, pancuronium bromide to relax the muscles and collapse the lungs, potassium chloride to stop the heart.'

'You really know how to make a girl look forward to her food,' said Fitzgerald.

'Oh, I don't know. It doesn't sound too bad,' said Healy. 'Not compared to what they've usually done.'

'All assuming you get the right man,' Fitzgerald pointed out.

'That's true,' he admitted. 'Do you remember that guy in Churchtown?'

'Parker?'

'No,' said Healy. 'Parker was Islandbridge. The Church-town one was supposed to have killed his wife. Maybe it was before your time. They all merge into one after a while. Anyway, everything checked out. He did five years before the real killer was finally picked up. Standish something, that was his name. He's remarried now. Owns a pub. Bought it with his compensation money. If we'd had capital punishment, he'd probably have been hanged.'

'Exactly,' said Fitzgerald. 'The graveyards in Texas must be filled with men like Standish something.'

'But you can't help wishing sometimes,' said Healy, 'that there was *some* punishment in place that even came close to matching the crime. You kill someone now, and what do you get? Ten years, if you're unlucky. And it's not exactly a Siberian gulag when they're in there. More like a holiday camp.'

'Don't let's go there again,' said Fitzgerald, raising an eyebrow across the table at me. 'He gets so bad sometimes he even starts to sound like you.'

'I'm serious,' said Healy. 'It makes you wonder what the point is of catching them when all they get is a slap on the wrist and a few years somewhere warm and cosy, with all their meals cooked and paid for. And what then? Freedom, so they can do it all again.'

'And as I've told you a hundred times before,' said Grace, 'it's not our business to worry about that. We can only do our job. If the courts and the government don't do theirs, that's not our fault. We've done all we can.'

'I know, I know,' said Healy. 'It just pisses me off.'

'Sounds like you've both had a rough twenty-four hours,' I said.

'The first twenty-four hours are always the worst,' said Fitzgerald. 'Then routine kicks in.'

'You manage to find out anything more about her?'

'Did we?' asked Fitzgerald, talking to herself. She frowned. 'I suppose we must have done. We're building up a picture, let's put it that way, but I still couldn't honestly say that I have the slightest idea what she was like. She was twenty-eight. Blonde. Single. Not much by way of family. Good-looking. Drove a Ferrari. Lived in a recently converted chapel. She worked for one of those small theatre companies down in Temple Bar, off Fishamble Street.'

'An actress?'

'She had ambitions to be an actress, she'd taken a few small parts in some plays, even got her name on to some of the posters, but her day job was in publicity, PR, fundraising. To be honest, I don't know what she did exactly. You know what these groups are like, everyone does a bit of everything, it's hard to pin them down.'

'There can't be that many small theatre companies in Temple Bar doing so well that their part-time actresses can afford to drive a Ferrari and live in a converted chapel,' I said.

'It's not in such a terrific area. It's in the Liberties. But I take your point. The money came from her father,' explained Fitzgerald. 'He's a widower, made his money in the building trade, she was an only child. I think he probably spoiled her a bit.'

'Was it the father who found her?'

'No. That pleasure went to a girl she worked with in the theatre company. Name of Kim Denning. She was the one who told us about the ring. She says she hadn't heard from Marsha for a couple of days, so she went round last night to see what was wrong. When there was no answer, she made her way round the side of the church, climbed up to look through a window, and saw what seemed to be a body lying across the bed. That's when she spoiled our plans for an evening at the theatre by calling 999.'

'A starring role at last,' I said sadly.

'My words exactly,' said Fitzgerald.

'Did she have a boyfriend?'

'Did she ever,' said Healy between mouthfuls of food.

'Busy lady?'

'Seems like Marsha Reed was something of a swinger,' Fitzgerald explained. 'And not just your average swinger. From what we've been able to learn, she was heavily into the whole S & M scene. She belonged to some private members' club in town that puts on parties for broad-minded citizens who like to get their kicks in the modern equivalent of a medieval torture chamber. I exaggerate slightly but only slightly. She was a regular visitor.'

'Plus there was a diary,' said Healy, 'with dates and details of a whole bunch of men she'd been with, some women too, and what she'd been doing with them.'

'Names?'

'Mainly initials,' said Fitzgerald.

'Meaning it'll be all but impossible to trace each one,' I said.

'I certainly doubt they'll be lining up at HQ to identify themselves to the police.'

'It's a lead, at any rate,' I said. 'You've had less to work on in the past. What's your feeling? You think she met her killer that way?'

'Hard to tell. It's certainly a dangerous world to be getting into. On the other hand, it could be simpler than that. You know what it's like.'

'Sado-masochistic sex, or murder?'

Fitzgerald smiled.

'Both. But, seriously, sometimes we make things more complicated than they have to be. It could be unrelated. We're going to try to track down her movements, who she was seen with last, that sort of thing. We have statements coming out of our ears already, but nothing much that leaps out of the chart as yet. If anything, the club complicates things.'

'How?'

'Because how do we know what was part of her consensual sex life and what was part of her murder? Butler couldn't even say for sure whether Marsha was sexually assaulted. There were certainly signs she'd had some very rough sex a few hours before she died, but there were also old vaginal and anal abrasions that had healed up, suggesting she wasn't exactly a stranger to rough sex. Then there're the cords around her ankles and wrists. Were they restraints used to keep her under control or just a part of her usual lovemaking routine?'

'I see what you mean.'

'Butler says the cords were tied quite lightly, considering. The bindings weren't excessive. They were sufficient to render her helpless, but not any more than was needed to restrain her from getting away. Tying her to the bed looks

91

like a means to an end rather than an aim in itself. As for the bag over the head, it's not exactly the stuff of romantic fiction, but it's not unheard of in the kind of circles the victim was moving in to use partial suffocation as an aid to orgasm. What if this was just a sex game that went horribly wrong?'

'Sex games don't generally involve one party cutting off the other one's finger,' I pointed out. 'If she died accidentally while having weird sex, and he panicked, that's one thing. But post-mortem mutilation's something else. So is theft. You didn't find the ring?'

'No,' said Healy. 'And that wasn't all that was missing.'

'It wasn't?'

'She also had a necklace that she'd started wearing the last three months or so,' explained Fitzgerald. 'Never took it off, apparently. The taxi driver confirms she was wearing it when he dropped her off. That wasn't at the scene either.'

'So your guy took a ring *and* a necklace?'

'Maybe we're looking for a psychopathic jeweller,' said Healy.

'That's not funny,' said Fitzgerald.

'Never said it was.'

'And that's not even mentioning the cash,' I said. 'You don't really think theft was a motive, do you?'

'Right now, I can't see a motive at all. We just have to concentrate on eliminating names. The reasons why can come later.'

'Unfortunately,' said Healy, 'the swabs came back clean for semen, so that's not going to help. Either whoever she had sex with that night wore a condom, or else they were using some other kind of object for penetration. And let's face it, from what we saw and learned today, that could be practically anything, animal, vegetable or mineral.'

'We're just going to have to put the frighteners on all those bondage-type groups around the city,' said Fitzgerald. 'Crank up the pressure on them to come up with names.'

'Surely there can't be that many of them around,' I said.

'Where have you been?' said Healy. 'The things people get up to are limitless. When I was in Vice, we raided this place that made the club Marsha belonged to look like a kids' playground. There were all these men there chained up like slaves.'

'You see everything in this job.'

'You're not lying,' said Healy. 'They were even wearing these tight loincloths that made them look like babies with nappies on, and they had pins and chains stuck in places you wouldn't believe. Or places you probably would believe, knowing you. And you want to know the worst thing about it? They'd all paid for the privilege of being there. There were businessmen, priests, teachers.'

'Men are nuts,' I said. 'You're only realizing this now?'

'What can I say?' said Healy. 'Everyone needs a hobby. You women have shopping, we have perversion.'

'Give me shopping any day,' said Fitzgerald with feeling.

'Marsha Reed obviously didn't think so,' I said darkly.

'No,' she acknowledged.

'Do you have a picture?' I asked.

'Of Marsha?' she said. 'I've got one somewhere.'

'Here,' said Healy, reaching into his pocket and taking out his wallet. He opened it up and slid out a small snapshot. 'Her friend Kim gave me this one.'

I took the picture from his fingers – and gasped. A blonde-haired woman smiled shyly out of the photograph at me, and I was struck again by incomprehension at how the dead could not know what was going to happen to them. How could they be so unsuspecting?

How could they smile?

But it wasn't that which had made me gasp.

'I do know her,' I said.

'You knew Marsha Reed?' said Healy.

'I told you she recognized her name,' Fitzgerald reminded him.

'So where'd you meet her?'

'She was in my class,' I said. Then, realizing Healy probably didn't know what the hell I was talking about, I explained: 'I took an evening class for aspiring writers last year at a college in York Street. I was meant to be showing them the disparity between real police and FBI procedure and what you read in the books and see in the movies. But I'm not much of a teacher. We spent most of the time just shooting the breeze and eating chocolate-chip cookies. One of the other students used to bring them in each week.'

'What about Marsha?' said Fitzgerald.

'It's like you were saying earlier,' I said. 'I never felt I really got to know her at all. She did plenty of talking, don't get me wrong, she was real fascinated by the whole subject, used to ask detailed questions, take notes. But she never talked about herself, except to say that she was writing a novel.' I looked again at her photograph and shook my head. 'I'd never in a million years have pegged her as the kinky swinger type.'

'Do you still have a list of the other students?' asked Fitzgerald.

'Somewhere.'

'Try to dig it out,' she said. 'The more people we can find who knew Marsha, the better the picture we can draw up of her.'

'I'll do it when I get home. And if I can't find anything, I'll ring the college. They should have contact addresses and telephone numbers. Ironic, isn't it? They wanted to know more about authentic police procedure, and now they're going to get a lot closer experience of it than they ever imagined.'

'Hence the old proverb about being careful what you wish for,' said Fitzgerald.

I hitched a ride back with Healy. He was taking Fitzgerald to Dublin Castle for her meeting about the new Assistant Commissioner and where I wanted to go was on the way. She looked the picture of efficiency in her best suit, though she said she felt uncomfortable, and didn't even understand why she had to make this effort at all. It wouldn't make her any less of a detective if she turned up in pair of torn Levis and a Grateful Dead T-shirt.

I got him to stop and let me out near the Showgrounds on Merrion Road. Fitzgerald didn't ask why I wanted to be dropped off in that particular spot; I guess she was a little distracted and didn't have space in her head for queries about my own plans for the rest of the day. Or maybe she didn't think it was any of her concern. Fitzgerald and I had always known how to give one another space. That was one of the reasons our relationship worked.

I certainly didn't offer the information unprompted. It wasn't a secret as such, just something I wanted to keep to myself for now. Or maybe that's what a secret is, I don't know.

We made arrangements to meet up later; I stood on the sidewalk as the car pulled back into the traffic, watching until it was through the next set of lights. Then I turned and made my way along the narrow path that led between the sparkling narrow water of the Dodder on one side and the green haven of Herbert Park on the other.

The Dodder looked almost appealing that afternoon.

Almost clean.

As for the weather, there was still no prospect of a break in the sun's campaign yet. Rare breaths of wind stirred the leaves on the trees, but mostly the afternoon was as motionless as an oil painting.

Cecelia Corrigan's house, or the house which had been Cecelia Corrigan's before her death, was in a leafy backstreet off Morehampton Road on the other side of the park, where all was in blessed shadow from overhanging trees and the houses sheltered under the branches like they were sun-shades. As I turned into the street, I could hear a dog barking in one of the gardens. A cat lay sleeping on a wall. It opened one eye with a blink as the dog barked and regarded me as if to share a bewilderment that anything could bother making such an effort on a hot day like this.

I checked along the gates.

Here it was.

Number 8.

The gate swung open with a protest of a squeak, and I walked up to the front door, which was surrounded with roses like some country cottage on a picture postcard.

The brass door knocker was in the shape of a cat and there was a grey stone cat sitting on the step too, with a spider's web constructed neatly in the gap between its ear and shoulder. The garden looked small but neat, and a little overgrown. I guessed it must have been Cecelia Corrigan's concern, and now she had gone the garden had been left to its own devices and was declining gently into a quiet chaos of tangled growth.

I knew the feeling.

I knocked.

Waited.

Traffic buzzed by distantly on the main road, and a closer

buzzing denoted a bee that was hovering round the roses at the door, moving from flower to flower.

Apart from that, there was no other sound.

I knocked again, and this time a shadow abruptly loomed into view behind the glass, startling me. A moment later, the door swung open, and there stood a young woman, tall and slim with close-cropped dark hair, dressed in flat shoes and a loose-fitting summer dress with no bra. She was girlish-looking, with a tiny pointed nose, and definitely seemed younger than her mid twenties. I knew she was in her mid twenties because I knew who she was.

I'd seen her picture in the newspaper.

It was Cecelia Corrigan's niece.

Becky stopped in surprise when she saw me. She clearly hadn't realized I was there at all. She was wearing a shoulder bag, through which she had been rummaging for what I could only presume were her car keys, because that's what she was lifting out when we met.

'Oh,' she said.

It was a start.

'Becky Corrigan?' I said. 'I scared you. Didn't you hear me knocking?'

She didn't answer. She just looked at me and said, half to herself: 'Another American.' That threw me. 'I suppose you're here about dear departed Aunt Cecelia?'

If I was expecting to find a woman in mourning, I'd clearly come to the wrong place. She certainly didn't talk about her aunt as if the memory of her death was a painful one.

'If I'm not in your way.'

'You'd better come in,' she said with a sigh. 'But I'm warning you, I haven't got much time, I'm late for an appointment already.'

Before she could change her mind, I stepped inside to a long narrow hall in which stacks of boxes and old furniture were arranged untidily, virtually hiding a grandfather clock in the corner. Through doorways I could see more boxes, more chairs upended, piles of books and half-emptied shelves along the walls.

'I'm selling up,' she declared. 'Aunt Cecelia was a bit of a collector, but there's not much point keeping the place like a mausoleum just because she's dead.'

'I guess not,' I said non-committally, though her attitude seemed a little heartless, even to me.

'Did you know Aunt Cecelia?' asked Becky.

'Not as such.'

'She was a harmless old bag, I suppose. But I wouldn't say I was very close to her. I just started living here while I was studying at UCD. Afterwards, I sort of stayed on.'

'Did she leave you the house in her will?'

'She left me everything in her will,' she said. 'Apart from a few thousand which she wanted the Cats' Protection League to have. She was mad about cats. She had seven of them. They used to drive me mad.' *Used to*? She must have seen the confusion in my face. 'I had them put down after she died. I can't look after seven cats. I don't have the time.'

'I see.'

'What else was I supposed to do?' she said defensively. 'I'm not going to sit in every night looking after a bunch of cats that I never asked to be left in charge of in the first place. If you ask me, that's where Aunt Cecelia went wrong. If she'd spent more time with real human beings instead of her cats, maybe she wouldn't have gone so batty in the end. I don't intend to make the same mistake. I'm going to enjoy myself while I'm young.'

She smiled a little too brightly, and then the smile was replaced by a frown.

I'd been waiting for this moment.

'What did you say you wanted again?' she asked.

'I didn't.'

'I suppose it's about her old friend Howler?' she went on.

I was thrown a second time.

'Do lots of people come round to ask about him?'

'No. But it's what the other American wanted to talk about too. And I told him the same thing I'm going to tell you. I don't know anything about Jenkins Howler, and I don't *want* to know anything. I knew my aunt wrote to him, and I knew about her campaign for him. She was always writing to the Minister for Justice demanding that he intervene and save lover boy from the electric chair, but of course he wasn't interested. Why should he be?'

'You didn't support her campaign?'

'No.' She shook her head firmly. 'As far as I was concerned, they could have torn him apart limb from limb and I wouldn't have given a flying fuck. After what he did to those women . . .' So she knew *something* about Howler at least. 'Of course, *she* never told me what he'd done,' Becky added. 'I had to look him up on the internet. We had quite a row about it.'

'What did your aunt say?'

'That every sinner deserves a second chance. That's the kind she was. Always off to mass. She said Howler had found Jesus.' She rolled her eyes. 'Whatever.'

'But you didn't fall out permanently over him?'

'No, no, nothing like that. She was lonely. This was her obsession. She was only in her forties, but you'd think she was sixty or something from the way she used to go on. I don't know what she expected. That he'd be out one day and they'd get married, probably.'

'Had they talked about marriage?'

'I only looked at a couple of his letters. Maybe he meant it. Who knows? Someone like that, you wouldn't know what was really going on in their heads, would you? I don't know why there's such a fuss about the whole thing, really. He's dead now. She's dead.'

She regarded me oddly. It was as if she kept getting distracted by the sound of her own voice and then having to remind herself that there was someone else there.

'He was a reporter too,' she said.

'Jenkins Howler?'

'No, not Howler. Not as far as I know anyway. I meant the other American who came here. He worked for the *New York Post*. Or was it the *New York Times*? I can't remember. He said he was doing a piece on my aunt for the newspaper.'

So Kaminski was posing as a reporter now, and she obviously thought I was one too.

I chose not to put her right.

'When was this?' I asked.

'About a week ago,' she said. 'To be honest, I couldn't understand what was so interesting about my aunt's death. It's not like she was murdered or anything. And it was months ago.' She said it like months ago was another century. Sometimes it is when you're young. I wondered if she expected me to enlighten her as to why Cecelia Corrigan's passing should excite such intrigue. I only wished I knew.

'Are you so sure,' was all I said instead, 'that there really *was* nothing more to your aunt's death than meets the eye?'

Once more, she regarded me oddly.

'He asked me that as well. And, as I told him, my aunt was knocked down. It was an accident, that's all. Unless you both know something you're not telling me?'

'Me?' I said. 'I don't know anything.'

She continued staring at me for a moment, trying to read my expression. Then she jumped as the half-hidden grandfather clock chimed a muffled hour.

'And now I really am late,' she mumbled crossly. She glanced at her watch to back up the clock's unwelcome news. 'Look, Ms . . . I'm sorry, I didn't catch your name.'

'Er, Kaminski.'

'Then I wish I could be more help, Ms Kaminski, but I really have to scoot.'

'There *was* one more thing before you go.'

'Yes?'

'I wanted to ask if I could read the letters Jenkins Howler wrote to your aunt.'

'You can't.'

'Don't get me wrong. I realize they're private,' I said. 'I won't make them public if you'd rather –'

'You misunderstand me,' she said. 'I haven't got them any more.'

'You haven't got the letters?'

'I sold them,' she confessed. 'The reporter I told you about, he offered to buy them and I couldn't see any reason to refuse. He mentioned something about a book he wanted to write on women who struck up friendships with convicted killers. He said Aunt Cecelia's letters would be invaluable to him. I didn't think any more of it. They meant nothing to *me*.'

But they clearly meant something to Kaminski.

What could be in those letters that he was so desperate to get his hands on?

'I know it must be frustrating if you wanted to look at them,' Cecelia's niece said, her voice becoming tetchy now as if sensing my disapproval, 'but they do belong to me.'

'*Did*, you mean,' I pointed out.

12

My American cellphone rang the moment I sat down on the tram heading back into town. There was only a handful of other passengers, so thankfully talking openly wasn't a problem.

'Good morning,' said a voice.

It was Lucas Piper, calling from New Jersey.

'Piper, I thought you'd forgotten me.'

'How could I forget you, Saxon? The thought of talking to you again has been the only thing keeping me going.'

'I was beginning to think you wouldn't call back.'

'You jump to conclusions too quickly. Things take time.'

'You have to admit, it's not like we were ever best buddies.'

'No,' he said, 'we weren't. That's true. But we *were* both friends of JJ. I thought if I managed to get you back in touch with him, you might be able to help him.'

'Help him?'

'He's in a dark place right now. He needs all the friends he can get.'

'Why don't you get in touch with him yourself?'

'It's too late for that now. Too much was said. I wish it hadn't been, but it was. You can't simply wave a magic wand and make everything right again.' He stopped. 'Where the hell are you? I can hardly hear you speak.'

'I'm on a tram,' I said.

'San Francisco?'

'That's right. How did you guess?'

'I never guess,' he said. 'I simply used a process of logical deduction.'

'Is that what they call it?'

'I guess you just want me to shut up and tell you what I found out about Kaminski?' said Piper.

'That's the general idea.'

'Then I'll get straight to the point. I'm afraid the news isn't good. I haven't been able to find out where JJ is. He hasn't been back to his apartment for five months, and he's not been getting his mail forwarded anywhere either.'

'Terrific,' I said sarcastically. 'You must be losing your touch.'

'Hold on there,' Piper replied. 'I said I didn't know where he *is*, I didn't say I didn't find out where he went after New York.' He paused, like he was waiting for applause.

'Are you going to tell me,' I said, 'or do we have to play twenty questions?'

'He went to Texas.'

'*Texas?*'

'Yeah, Texas, you know, twenty-eighth state of the Union, big place, lots of oil?'

'I've heard of it, thanks for the geography lesson. Why'd he go there?'

'Maybe he liked the climate. Maybe he inherited an oil well. Or it could just be because the guy he suspected of killing his wife lived in Huntsville.'

'What kind of person lives in Huntsville?'

'The kind who works as a guard on Death Row,' said Piper.

'You're joking?'

'Do you hear me laughing? He worked at the Terrell Unit. Ten years' dedicated service. You want my opinion, Kaminski went down there to try to track him down.'

'For what purpose?'

'I wouldn't like to speculate,' said Piper.

'OK, so you're telling me he's in Texas?'

'I'm telling you he *was* in Texas. He was renting a cheap room on the outskirts of Huntsville. One day he cleared out and he hasn't been seen there since.'

'How do you know all this?'

'I spoke to the landlord of the house where he was staying. He told me Kaminski was a little wired, a little nervous, drank a bit too much, but was harmless enough. He didn't know where he'd gone. Kaminski certainly didn't tell him where he was going, didn't even say he *was* going. One week, the landlord went round for the rent money and he wasn't there.'

'And he definitely didn't return to New York?'

'Not so far as his old neighbours know. I left word for them to contact me if he turns up again. If I hear anything, I'll let you know. But I wouldn't go getting my hopes up.'

'What about the guard on Death Row?'

'That's the thing,' said Piper carefully. 'He's gone AWOL too. I spoke to the local cops down there. They told me he didn't turn up for work one morning about three months ago. When they went to search his house, they found him gone.'

A chill took hold of me, like it was January in July.

'Kaminski caught up with him, then?' I whispered.

'Like I say, I wouldn't like to speculate. The cops say they'd spoken to Kaminski a couple of weeks before. The guard had made a complaint. Said Kaminski was harassing him. They'd tried to warn him off, and, as far as they were concerned, it had had the desired effect. No more complaints. Then the complainant vanishes into thin air.'

'They didn't bring in JJ again?'

'They brought him in, all right, but they didn't have anything on him. Plus there was some doubt about the other guy's disappearance. Seems like he packed a case before he vanished, which suggests he intended to leave town. He also had some serious money issues. So they had to let Kaminski go. Apparently, he promised to stay in town in case they needed to speak to him again. Next thing, he vanishes as well.'

'Christ, what a mess.'

'You said it,' agreed Piper. 'So now you see why Kaminski might have good reason to want to make himself hard to find. And whatever he did, I hope it stays that way.'

'Even if he's got blood on his hands?'

'Not innocent blood,' he pointed out.

'You've only got Kaminski's word for it that this man killed his wife.'

'That'll have to be good enough for me.'

'It wasn't good enough when he called you afterwards.'

'I didn't say I felt good about it, did I?'

'Wasn't good enough for the FBI either.'

'You and I both know,' said Piper, 'that the FBI make mistakes. Every day. I've made plenty of them myself. But look, if you're so interested in all this, why don't you fly down to Huntsville and pick up the trail yourself? It's not that far.'

'It's not?'

'Not from San Francisco,' said Piper. I'd forgotten that's where I was supposed to be. 'Three hours on the plane, couple hours on the road. You'd be there easily by tonight.'

'It's really not that important,' I said hurriedly. 'I doubt he'd be in much of a mood to discuss a few old cases for my book over a beer. And you said it yourself – if he doesn't want to be found, he won't be.'

'I just wish I could've been more help.'

'You were help enough. I appreciate it.'

'So do I get to buy *you* a drink sometime?' asked Piper.

'What are you going to do – send it by courier?'

'I meant next time we're in the same general time zone.'

'I know what you meant, I was being sarcastic. Bad habit.'

'One of many.'

'You said it.'

It was getting near my stop now. I was about to end the call and make my way down to the door, when a thought suddenly struck me.

'Hey, Piper, can I ask you one more thing?'

'Shoot.'

'What was the name of the guard Kaminski suspected of killing his wife?'

That empty laugh of his rattled in my ear. 'It was Buck Randall III, if you can believe that.'

Believe it?

I would've put good money on it.

I returned to my apartment, but working was impossible. Thinking was impossible. The only thing that was possible was baking – and not the cakes and cookies type of baking either.

What was baking was me.

The heat in my apartment was hostile, offensive. It was playing rough with me in my own living room. Pushing me around, refusing to let me settle. I tried sitting out on the balcony, looking down at the traffic, but the heat seemed to strike off the ground and upwards and hit me straight between the eyes. Its aim was as clinical and as precise as a laser's.

The city was heating up, and the people were trapped in

its embrace. I couldn't bear it and retreated inside, lay down on the couch with an electric fan turning, pointing at my face. I tried to close my eyes and sleep, but there were too many thoughts in my head.

Through the window drifted the sound of one of the summer concerts that were held most days in St Stephen's Green. Today it was loud and unwelcome but I could hardly close the windows, without any air conditioning to keep the interior bearable.

Instead I had to put up with it.

I was supposed to be reading a script which had been sent to me. A couple of years ago, they'd made a TV movie from one of the cases in my first book. The movie had made me look good, not least because the actress they got to play me was more attractive than I could ever hope to be. It's nice to be flattered. They also made me look good in the sense that I was now being credited with single-handedly solving every crime I'd ever come into contact with.

It had been far more complex than that, but what do complexities matter when it comes to the movies? I was the photogenic one – correction: the actress playing me was the photogenic one – and hence by the infallible logic of Hollywood she had to be the one who caught the bad guy. I wasn't complaining. They'd paid me more for the movie rights than I considered they were worth, and I'd sold a lot of copies of the tie-in edition after it was shown, mainly I suspect because they'd put a picture of the actress who played me on the front cover. I should get her to stand in for me all the time. I'd make a fortune.

Fitzgerald probably wouldn't complain either.

Now they were in the process of making a sequel, which, if this latest script was anything to go by, had left the realms of reality behind and departed for Fantasy Island.

Not that I was objecting to that. I'm with Katharine Hepburn on that score: *Never complain, never explain.* The fact that a second film had come with a second cheque didn't hurt. Plus I'd managed to negotiate a percentage of the profits of the movie. Assuming that there were any. It wasn't a large percentage, but it was large enough to make me not care whether they made a movie claiming I'd personally captured Jack the Ripper.

I was supposed to be reading the new script and making suggestions. That had been my job on the last movie too. My name was listed on the credits as an Expert Consultant. Or was it Special Adviser? One or the other. Special Agent to Special Adviser in a few short years. Did that count as progress or retreat? My mind changed day to day on that question.

Sometimes minute to minute.

In the end, I flung the script aside impatiently and lay back on my couch, eyes closed, trying and failing to imagine that the breeze from the fan was a breeze from the sea.

I was confused.

No surprise there. Confusion is my natural state of mind. But today I was confused like I'd never been confused before.

I don't know why I should've been feeling so defeated. The pieces were finally fitting into shape. Kaminski's wife – Jenkins Howler – the Death Row guard he suspected of killing his wife – the spinster in Dublin who'd fallen for the condemned man – Kaminski in Dublin. The components were all there, but they wouldn't form any kind of pattern that made sense.

In the end, I knew the only thing I could do was to go round to the hotel and ask him right out what he was doing in Dublin. That had been the plan all along, after all. It's just that breaking and entering had somehow gotten in the way. It generally does.

This time would be different. From what Piper had told me, Kaminski needed a friend. Maybe I could help him out. Maybe I could help him face down whatever demons had brought him to Dublin. At the least, I could have a drink with him and take a human interest in what was happening with his life. All this running around was pathetic. It wasn't for him or for the truth, I was just trying to cover up some emptiness in my own life.

And if he *was* on the run from whatever bad things he'd done?

I'd have to deal with that dilemma when it arose.

It didn't take long to get round to the hotel. Everything inside was exactly the same. The same shabby lobby. The same music playing on the intercom.

Most of all, the same sulky receptionist.

She must've remembered me from last time but kept up the act all the same.

'Good afternoon, madam, can I help you?'

Talk about having a stick up her ass.

'I'd like to speak to Mr Randall, please.'

'I'm afraid you're too late, madam.'

'Too late?'

'Mr Randall checked out this morning.'

She seemed aggrieved by that and glowered at me like it was my fault.

I guess it was.

'He's gone?' I repeated blankly.

'I'm afraid so. He meant to stay till the end of the week, but said something had come up and he had to return to the States. Is your name' – she turned to check something on a sheet of paper on the desk behind her – 'Mrs Kaminski?'

That sinking feeling in my stomach sank a little lower.

He had some nerve.

'That's me,' I said.

I swore her eye dropped to my hand to see if I was wearing a ring. What was she going to do – demand to see a picture of me in my wedding dress?

'He left something here for you to pick up,' she said tightly. 'I told him you came here looking for him. He said he was sorry to have missed you, but to give this to you if you turned up again.' And she slid open a drawer in the desk and lifted out an envelope.

Handed it to me.

For the attention of Mrs Kaminski.

I recognized his handwriting at once.

'Sorry you missed him,' said the blonde, smiling slyly.

I knew what she was thinking – if you could describe what went on in her head as thinking. She had me pegged as some flaky, lovesick female chasing the handsome but melancholy and reluctant Buck Randall III. If so, she clearly had me confused with herself.

I didn't bother answering her. I simply took the envelope and went through the revolving door to the steps outside. I stood in the sunshine and tore the envelope open.

I knew without looking what would be inside.

Sure enough, it was the same leaflet from the theatre that I'd left for JJ that morning. Or half of it, at any rate. He'd torn it in two, and along the plain edge of one half of the leaflet he'd written me a message: *Saxon. Looks like our paths are destined not to cross. Hope you found what you were looking for in my room. – Buck.*

13

'Hey, you! Lady!' he said.

I'd only that moment carried my drink over to my table in this, the latest of a string of bars I'd been reacquainting myself with that day, and now I was looking up to find the barman on the other side of the room pointing at me accusingly.

Me, a lady?

He'd obviously never met me before.

'You can't smoke in here,' he said.

I looked down at my hand. I was in the process of lighting a rather fine cigar which, according to the store owner in Smithfield who had them shipped in for me from the States, comprised 50 per cent Dominican and 50 per cent long filter Cuban tobacco exported before the 1962 embargo, though they could've been made from dried Patagonian llama dung and I'd still have smoked them, they tasted so good. Though perhaps only on special occasions. And now, after one solitary puff, I was being told to put it out.

'You want to get me fined?' he said when I began to protest.

I held up my hand in apology. 'OK, OK, I'm sorry,' I said, 'I forgot.'

I stubbed it out, feeling as I did so that I was committing an unforgiveable crime against perfection, like scribbling with a ballpoint on the *Mona Lisa*.

That was a sure sign I'd had too much to drink. Not only too drunk to argue, but too drunk to remember that you couldn't smoke in this city any more

Actually, that wasn't strictly true. You could smoke, just not in any of the bars or restaurants. The city had taken a lead from Manhattan and imposed a public ban on tobacco. If you wanted to smoke and drink at the same time these days in Dublin, you had to stand outside, on rooftop terraces or crowded into courtyards with the other social renegades. The rationale behind the ban was to protect employees in bars and restaurants from the effects of passive smoke. My opinion was that if employees didn't want to breathe in someone else's smoke, they shouldn't get a job in a bar, they should go work in a kindergarten or something. But who listened to me? Grace thought the new rule was great, waxing lyrical about how you could go into bars and restaurants and, for the first time in years, not find them wreathed in second-hand smoke. But then she was the kind of woman who wanted to eat organic fruit and knew the carbohydrate and fibre concentration of just about every meal she ever ate. Me, I thought they'd ruined the whole atmosphere of bars – an opinion intensified by drinking, after which nothing seems as good as it used to.

And I was feeling sorry enough for myself as it was.

I got to my feet, took my bottle of Budweiser and wandered out to the beer garden. It was a small place, not much more room than it took to raise an elbow to bring the cigar to my lips, but it was enough. I lit up for a second time. At least it was warm out here tonight.

Tonight?

Well, nearly. Shadows were creeping in. I could almost see stars.

Where *had* the day gone?

The only company in the garden was an old man sitting on the wall, smoking a pipe. We nodded at one another with the quiet, unspoken solidarity of a despised minority.

The two last smokers in a city of people determined to be the healthiest on the planet.

I wished now I'd gone somewhere else for a drink. There were a few places in Dublin where they knew how to treat a lady who wanted a quiet cigar. There was nowhere you could smoke inside, but there were establishments which put aside great spaces outside where you could destroy your lungs in comfort. It wasn't so great in winter, when the ice on the pipes had frozen or the terraces were ankle-deep in the city's trademark rain, but right now, with the temperature on the thermometer heading high, it could be fantastic.

You got a better quality of people out here too.

Leave the interior for the saints who wanted to feel pious in the worship of their own bodily purity, and come out here with the people who simply wanted to have a good time and be left alone long enough to enjoy life without interference or disapproval.

Though I had to admit that, just this minute, me and the old guy were going to be pushed to make a party of it. He looked like the last party he'd been at was in 1947.

I sat down on the edge of the wall and regarded the area round me, lit brightly by overhanging lamps. It seemed like a metaphor for all that had gone wrong in the last twenty-four hours or so. I'd always thought of Dublin as a city of shadows. Not the hard-edged shadows that the sun was casting on the summer streets each afternoon, their edges so sharp on the ground that you felt you should step over them to avoid cutting yourself. Rather I thought of Dublin as a city of the shadows of night, of secrets. Partly that was because I lived much of my life nocturnally. I'd happily sleep all day and spend the night wandering round. I was an owl. A hunter. That made me perfect for hunting out other hunters. They preferred the dark too. It was what I was made for. It was as though I could see the city more truly at night. See it in its own shape. Light distorted rather than revealed. If it got too bright, the city had to step back and give the light room. After nightfall the city shuffled off the burden of daylight and revealed itself to those who shared its passion for concealment.

Dublin, more than most other cities, was a place that came into its own after dark.

Fogged by dark, it was at its most alluring and beautiful.

A little like me.

I smiled.

That was the attraction of the city. It was a place a girl could hide out. You could disappear inside it like an ant inside an old hollowed-out tree, where no one could find you if you didn't want them to. You could be overlooked. And that was what I wanted. I wanted to be a ghost drifting, unnoticed, through the city, just watching, observing, listening.

Now it was like there was too much illumination. The city was overly determined to show itself to the world. To show that it had nothing and nowhere to hide. That it was respectable. It wanted to be liked. I call that a pity. The smoking ban was one part of it. They had attempted to wipe away something they saw as anomalous and in fact had wiped away something that added to the city's charm. At least that's what I thought when I'd started to have too much to drink and remembered I couldn't smoke a damn cigar. It's the way I am. I need to make everything more dramatic than it really is or I feel only half alive.

Right now, I was feeling sorry for myself because of JJ. I might not be able to find anywhere to hide in the city any more, but *he* had managed it. He had hidden from *me*.

And there really wasn't much I could do about it.

Sure, I could try calling a few hotels and hope I got lucky, but I didn't fancy my chances. He wouldn't be using any name I could guess at, so what was I going to do? Ring them all up and say: 'Excuse me, by chance have any Americans checked in lately?'

I could have kicked myself for allowing it to happen. Losing him was one thing. Losing him in such a foolish way only made me feel all the more powerless. Like I'd lost control of my life and everything that counted was being decided by other people.

I should've realized he'd figure the whole thing out. He sees me in Temple Bar, then an American woman turns up out of the blue at his hotel? There was no doubt he'd have guessed someone had been in his room also. Dammit. Being so clever, I had simply been outmanoeuvred, and I had a dreadful premonition as I sat here that I'd never find out what his presence in Dublin had all been about. And not knowing had always been my worst nightmare.

It was strange. I had the definite sense that he'd won some game we were playing, and yet I didn't even know what the game was or how the rules worked.

To hell with it, I said to myself. It didn't matter.

Didn't.

Matter.

And yet I knew that it did. The crust of my defiance was as thin as the ozone layer.

I guess I could've spent all night there, getting more pissed with myself, but at that moment my cellphone went off. The old boy looked at me reproachfully, like I'd broken some unwritten but sacred agreement, like I wasn't the woman he'd taken me for, regardless of the cigar and the bottle of Budweiser. I shrugged a mute apology. He was probably right.

I barked out a hello.

'No need to bite off my nose.'

'Fitzgerald?'

'Of course it's me,' she said. 'Who else were you expecting? A secret lover?' She laughed like the thought was absurd. Which it was. Wasn't it? 'Where are you?'

'Last time I looked, I was in the yard of an atmospheric little place off . . . let me think now . . . Baggot Street. I think.'

'You're in the pub?'

'I'm in a bar, that's right. Or outside it, I should say, me and my illicit cigar. I'm expecting the tobacco police to swoop any moment and drag me away for questioning.'

'Are you drunk?'

'Am I drunk? Of course I'm not drunk. I'm outraged you could ask me such a question. I've hardly touched a drip . . . I mean, I've hardly touched a drop . . .'

'I think that answers my question. Well, listen. Don't go anywhere, I'm coming over. Healy can drop me off on his way home. I'll expect to have a drink waiting for me.'

'Are we celebrating?'

'We might be.'

'You've not cracked the case yet, have you?'

'No such luck.'

'What's the big deal, then?'

'The new Assistant Commissioner, remember?'

'Screw it, I completely forgot. What am I thinking? How did it go? What's he like?'

'I think the new Assistant Commissioner's going to work out just fine,' Fitzgerald said with a conspiratorial laugh. 'I'll tell you all about it when I get there. Think you can manage to get me a drink without spilling it? I shouldn't be long.'

*

Soon my mood of self-pity and resentment at Kaminski was replaced by one of bemusement.

'She wants to what?'

'She wants to meet you.'

This was the last thing I'd expected. I'd only just got over the shock of learning from Fitzgerald that the next Assistant Commissioner in charge of the Murder Squad was going to be a woman, and now it turned out that she wanted to meet me as well.

It was the same bar, except we were inside now. Fitzgerald had arrived about ten minutes earlier, looking harassed but sensational as always. Didn't matter if she hadn't slept all night or had spent the day at a crime scene, she still always had that elusive glitz that had certainly eluded me most of my life, no matter how hard I tried to nurture it.

I think you must either be born with it or not.

She was sitting on the stool opposite me with her legs crossed, white wine to hand. Men in the bar were watching her purely for the pleasure of seeing her sit there.

I shrugged in incomprehension.

Not at the fact men were looking at her – I understood that part – but because of what she was saying. The words sounded straightforward enough, but they might as well have been in Sanskrit for all the sense they were making in my skull.

'What would anyone want to meet *me* for?'

'Beats me,' teased Fitzgerald. 'Unless you owed them money.'

I raised an eyebrow.

'Or maybe she wants your autograph.'

'You're being flippant again,' I warned her.

'Or maybe,' Grace continued, ignoring the warning, 'she wants to ask you out on a date.'

'I thought you said she was married.'

'Divorced. I said divorced. And you know what these divorced women are like. I've heard a girl can get some of her most successful pick-ups with recently divorced women. Sadly, I was never able to find out. You came along and spoiled things.'

'Then it'll be you she's after, not me. You're a better catch.'

'I never mix business with pleasure,' she said. 'Besides, we're both out of luck. She's not the type. If anything, I'd say she's more likely to want to ask you about the case.'

Now I really *was* baffled.

'Marsha Reed? How can I help there?'

'I don't know, I'm merely speculating. She's already suggested that I ask Fisher to team up on it.' She meant Dr Lawrence Fisher, a celebrated forensic psychologist who had worked on a small number of cases with Fitzgerald before and who'd recently moved to Dublin for tax purposes. He made most of his money now writing popular books on criminal psychology and appearing on TV, and writers pay no tax in Dublin. 'I spoke to him this afternoon. He's taking a look at Marsha's journal. There's a lot of nasty stuff in there, stuff she's written about other people. I thought he might be able to make something of it.'

'That'll be right up his street,' I nodded.

'What about you?' she said.

'Me?'

'Remember I asked you to draw up a list of the people who were in your class?'

I couldn't believe I'd forgotten about that.

Nor could Fitzgerald.

I considered telling her about Piper's call, which had driven Marsha Reed out of my mind. But it would take too long, and she had too much else on her plate to start worrying about potential fugitives from justice like Leon Kaminski. More than that, forgetting what she had asked me to do was unjustifiable, whatever my other distractions.

'I'll get it for you first thing in the morning,' I promised.

'You'd better. Or I'll tell Stella you're not to be trusted.'

'You didn't mention that the new Assistant Commissioner Carson and you were already on first-name terms.'

'It must have slipped my mind. Like making that list slipped yours.'

'Touché.'

'You'll be on first names with her yourself after you meet her tomorrow,' Fitzgerald said.

'Who said anything about tomorrow?'

'She did. And she's the boss, remember, so don't be late. Ten thirty, on the dot.'

I took a deep breath. I hate being backed into a corner.

I hate losing the initiative even more. I didn't even remember agreeing to this meeting, and suddenly I was being warned against being late for it.

'I guess you'd better tell me about her again, then,' I said resignedly.

'What can I tell you? She's from the North. Late forties. She comes from a pretty rough background. She has an uncle in jail for armed robbery. From the point of view of her family, joining the police must have been like a little Palestinian girl suddenly deciding that she wants to be a rabbi rather than a suicide bomber. You'll get along,' Fitzgerald went on confidently. 'She doesn't believe in tiptoeing carefully around for fear of whose nose might be put out of joint. In fact, I think she rather enjoys putting them out of joint.'

'I like the sound of her already.'

121

'She's definitely going to ruffle some feathers down here. Not only have they got a woman, but one from the North too. That won't go down well.'

'How'd she get the job?'

'Our masters obviously felt they needed to make a radical break to convince the public we're still capable of doing our job. You know what things are like in there.'

She didn't have to elucidate. The Dublin Metropolitan Police had been under inquiry for the best part of the last two years. There had been talk for decades of corruption, sharp practice, incompetence, occasional misdirected brutality. A retired judge had been appointed to investigate allegations of malpractice. His report had uncovered major institutional failings, widespread nepotism and a culture of hapless endemic ineptitude, not to mention evidence of racist and sexist bullying, at the very heart of the force.

Fitzgerald had found out that last part to her cost. Every step she'd taken along the path had been against the force of tradition weighing her down. She knew there were still powerful people in the DMP who didn't think a woman was capable of running a major department, especially one as vital as Murder. That she'd gotten as far as she had was a miracle.

'How do you know so much about her anyway?' I said.

'Policing is a small world. I'd seen her around,' said Fitzgerald. 'You know, at conferences and the like. We're always being sent on these courses where police from the North and from Dublin are supposed to meet up, share experience, build contacts, that sort of thing. I even worked with her once, but that was years ago, before I knew you and I was only an Inspector. A doorman was shot at a pub in the inner city. Turned out he was a member of the glorious Irish Republican Army and came from Belfast originally, so

I ended up liaising with Stella Carson. She was rooting out some suspects who'd fled after the murder.'

'You close the case?'

'Are you questioning my professional capabilities, Special Agent? Of course we closed the case. Not that there was very much to it. It turned out he was killed by one of his paramilitary colleagues in a row over drug money. So much for the revolution.'

'Did you like her?'

'She was fine. She's like they all are up in the North. She's hard to get to know. There's a reticence there, a barrier you never quite cross. And they have these voices.'

'Most people do.'

'Not like these voices,' she said. 'People from the North have the kind of voices where, even if they're only asking you to pass the salt, it sounds like they're really intending to haul you up an entryway and kneecap you.'

I felt immediate empathy.

'People think I'm aggressive because of my voice too,' I said.

'No, that's different. You *are* aggressive. *She* only seems like it.'

'Everyone's a critic.'

'Still,' she said, 'it'll be worth having her around just to see the looks on everyone's faces. You should've seen Dalton.' Seamus Dalton was one of the longest-serving detectives in the Murder Squad. A man with a chip on his shoulder so high that it could probably be seen from Boston Harbor on a clear day. He thought a woman's place was either in the kitchen or in the bedroom. Or just in the wrong. He'd see this as an assault on his entire world. 'I thought he'd lost all powers of intelligent speech when he heard the news.'

'You mean, he has some to lose?'

'All powers of speech, then. This is going to be a bigger culture shock to him than the day he was told to stop making homophobic jokes in the canteen. That was suffering enough for him, poor thing. This could finish him off. He was no fan of Draker, but Draker was from his world. He has about as much chance of understanding Stella Carson as he does of understanding nuclear physics. In the meantime, how about you get me another drink?'

'Why do I always have to go get them?'

'Because they take notice of you,' she answered. 'Barmen just ignore me.'

'Fair enough. I'll do it, as long as we can go sit outside so I can smoke.'

'You win.'

So I got us more drinks, fending off the attentions of the pinstriped man on the next stool who was taking the opportunity to talk to Fitzgerald by offering to pay for them, and we sat outside where it was still warm, and drank, and I smoked, and then we had a couple more drinks, until it got too crowded outside with people who'd realized at last that bars are no fun without the smokers, and we made our escape, strolling round to a place in Wicklow Street that sold great tapas, and walked further, eating them, as more people wandered past, enjoying the summer evening. The turquoise sky above the city was speckled with pale stars like glitter, and a busker somewhere was playing a distant protest song.

His angry voice was the only discordant note to the evening.

We talked a little about the investigation into Marsha Reed's death, but mostly we talked about nothing much at all, which is sometimes the best thing to talk about, or else let the city talk to us as we walked in silence, eavesdropping on a thousand other conversations. And then we walked back to my apartment, taking the long way so that the walk would last longer. There was something magical about the city that night. An older spirit suppressed in the relentless commerce of the day had come alive and walked among the living. Lights sparkled and shone all around. Or was it just the thought of possible new beginnings?

The morning would tell me.

For the moment, I tried to savour it for what it was. Tried to feel content. The feeling never lasted long. It was important to hold on to it as long as possible when it came.

14

He almost collided with me. He was coming down the steps of Dublin Castle as I was climbing up them, and he didn't see me till it was too late. It was nobody's fault, but he scowled at me in annoyance all the same, his high forehead bulging alarmingly.

I stepped aside to let him pass and then watched as he crossed the courtyard.

Fleetingly, I wondered if this was some bigwig in the DMP that I'd never met before, furious at Stella Carson's appointment and determined to take it out that day on any woman he encountered. But he didn't look like a policeman. There was something too casual about his appearance. His grey hair was slightly too long, certainly for a man who must have been in his fifties. He wore brown corduroys. The collar of his shirt was unbuttoned and tieless. He was walking with a kind of defiant sashay, as if he was struggling to contain an energy that was bubbling up inside him. And were those moccasins he had on his feet? They were. No one ever got anywhere in the Dublin Metropolitan Police wearing moccasins and corduroy trousers.

Or sashaying, for that matter.

The younger man accompanying him was having to hurry to keep up. He wore a dark suit – no moccasins here – and his arms overflowed with cardboard files.

At the gate, the older man turned round and threw a *what the hell are you looking at?* glare back in the general direction of the building. Then he turned and was gone.

'What did you make of him?' a familiar voice said behind me.

Fitzgerald was standing at the top of the steps, watching me watching him.

I hadn't seen her come out.

'Who is he?' I said, climbing up to stand by her.

'That's Victor Solomon.'

'Should the name mean something to me?'

'Do you remember the night Marsha Reed's body was found, we were supposed to be going to the theatre?' said Fitzgerald. 'He's the director of the play we were supposed to see.'

'*Hamlet?*'

'*Othello*, actually. But you were close.'

'Whatever. What's he doing here? Did he hear you had to miss the play and came round to offer you free tickets?'

'Not exactly. He was sleeping with Marsha Reed.'

'I don't know why I'm taken aback. You did say she was sleeping with everyone.'

'Not all of them, though, gave her an expensive necklace.'

'The missing necklace was from Solomon?'

'The very same,' she said, and held the door open for me as I stepped inside.

I knew this place well enough. Dublin Castle was where the Murder Squad of the Dublin Metropolitan Police had its headquarters, along with a number of other major departments, such as Vice, Anti-terrorism and Drugs. There were cells in other parts of the city, local police stations where less serious crimes were dealt with. There was even the main administration block out in the Phoenix Park, where the Commissioner and his cronies were to be found and where most of the important decisions were made. But Dublin Castle was where what really counted went on. Didn't matter how many robberies were solved or how many tax evaders convicted, or how many people the Dogs Division picked up for not having a dog licence, or even how many pick-pockets were rounded up for swiping wallets from tourists who seemed to think they were safe in Dublin – it was how a police department dealt with murder cases that made the difference to their reputation and standing.

Dublin didn't exactly have a shining record in this respect, though it was not for lack of trying on Fitzgerald's part. She was a fine detective, just frequently frustrated by the lack of proper structures and resources. Uniformed police in the city couldn't always be relied upon even to preserve a crime scene properly for forensic analysis. Sometimes it felt like the cops were lagging decades behind. Unless Fitzgerald was called in quickly, it was often too late.

As always when I came here, I had to suppress the vague feeling that I had strayed into unfriendly territory. It was easy to forget that the police and I were supposed to be on the same side. Too often in the past, I had been made to feel as welcome as an outbreak of bird flu, even when I was meant to be offering a helping hand with particular cases.

Make that *especially* when I was meant to be helping out.

'Here,' said Fitzgerald.

'What is it?'

'Your pass,' she said, pinning it to my collar. 'Now you're official.'

'Thanks. Are we going up?'

'Follow me.'

And follow her I did, up the main stairway to the upper floors where most of the Murder Squad's real work was done, and wishing we could've taken the elevator instead. Unfortunately, she told me that was broken too, like the one in my apartment building.

Did anything work any more?

I was out of shape. Long gone were the days of my FBI training, when I could do a hundred push-ups without giving it a second thought. Lately I found getting out of bed a struggle.

'So was that his lawyer with him?' I said between breaths as we climbed.

'His solicitor brought him in this morning, said his client wanted to make a statement,' Fitzgerald explained, taking the steps with ease. 'He knew we'd be digging into Marsha's background and obviously realized it was inevitable that his name would come up eventually. He decided to take the initiative and present himself for questioning. It wouldn't look good if we'd turned up at the theatre unannounced. Not good for business, I mean.'

'*Did* you know he was Marsha's boyfriend?'

'Her friend, who found the body, said Marsha had told her she was sleeping with someone important in theatre circles here in the city, but she wouldn't reveal who it was. Not initially. She badgered her until Marsha eventually admitted it was Solomon.'

'What's his story?'

'That he and Marsha had been sleeping together on and off for the last six months or so, but that it was no big affair as far as he was concerned. But then he *would* say that. He's engaged to be married to the actress who's starring in his latest play. They're quite a well-known couple. You can understand why he wouldn't want it getting into the papers that he was seeing Marsha Reed as well. He says he last slept with her about a month ago.'

'They'd split up?'

'He says it wasn't even the kind of relationship where you needed to split up,' said Fitzgerald. 'They just saw one another when they saw one another. I got the impression that if he bumped into her around town in the evening and he didn't have anything else lined up, he was happy enough to appoint her as his temporary bedwarmer, but that he wasn't going to be calling her up to make a date for dinner or drinks or anything like that.'

'He gave her the necklace, didn't he?'

'A meaningless trinket, if you listen to him.'

'Was he part of her little S & M set?'

'He says not,' said Fitzgerald. 'According to him, he knew nothing about that part of her life and, if he *had* known about it, he'd never have got involved with her in the first place.'

'The morally upright type, huh?'

'That's the general picture. Though more upright than moral, if you ask me. You know what these artistic types are like. See? Here we are now. Do try and stop panting. People will think we were up to something.'

And she ushered me through the door into the upstairs corridor off which the Murder Squad was housed. Her own office was at the end of the hall. The main incident rooms were down the left. The windows along the other side looked on to the street below.

Patrick Walsh was standing in the corridor, waiting.

What was there to say about Walsh? He was young, lean, ambitious, capable, sharply dressed, good-looking, and those were just a few of the reasons why so many of the other detectives loathed him. I liked him well enough, though I admit there was a cockiness to him that could be jarring on first contact. He considered himself to be God's gift to the women of Dublin, and felt that women should be grateful to the Lord for blessing them with such a gift.

He'd even asked Fitzgerald out once.

Whatever other faults he had, he certainly didn't lack chutzpah.

He did, though, have a bad habit of calling me –

'Babe! If I'd known you were coming in, I'd have put on my best aftershave.'

'Save it for someone who doesn't mind being called babe,' I said. 'Though to do that, I guess you'd have to find a time-machine to take you back to the 1970s.'

'I love it when you get angry,' Walsh said.

'Break it up, you two,' said Fitzgerald. 'If you want to flirt, do it on your time.'

Flirt? That woman sure knew how to get on my wrong side.

'I heard you wanted to talk to me, Chief,' Walsh went on before I could object.

'Yeah, there's something I want you to take a look at for me. Saxon,' she said, 'did you manage to finish that list?'

'I have it here in my pocket.'

I fished it out and passed it to her. She unfolded the sheet of paper and glanced quickly through the names.

'Is this the whole list of people who took your class?' she said.

'There were seven,' I confirmed. 'Eight, if you include Marsha Reed.'

'Popular course,' murmured Walsh sarcastically.

I ignored him.

'I put down a few impressions of each one, just as a pointer for you. Sarah O'Leary – that's her there at the top – was the one who seemed to know Marsha best. They sat together, sometimes they left together. I heard them making arrangements once to meet up for a drink.'

'Has her name come up in the investigation yet?' she asked Walsh.

'It doesn't ring any bells.'

'That guy there', I said, pointing to another name on the list, 'might be worth talking to as well. He arrived for one class with Marsha. I remember hearing them laughing on the stairs up to the lecture room. They may've only just seen each other as they arrived, but it's probably worth following up anyway to see how well he did know her.'

'What about the others?' asked Walsh.

'That's for you to find out,' said Fitzgerald.

'Chief?'

'Take this list round to the college and find addresses and phone numbers for all seven. Pay them a call, see if they have any further information about Marsha Reed.'

'Will do. And Solomon's alibi? Shall I check that out first?'

'Leave that to me,' Fitzgerald said. 'I'm just going back to my room to pick up some files, then I'm going over to speak to his fiancée with Healy.'

'Solomon claims he was at the theatre until eleven on the night of the killing,' Walsh explained to me. 'Then with his fiancée until ten the next morning.'

'You never know, he might be telling the truth,' Fitzgerald said. 'It happens.'

'Shall I make my own way up to the Assistant Commissioner's office, then?' I said.

'Walsh will take you. Won't you, Walsh?'

A grimace. 'Yes, Chief.'

'What's the matter with you?' I said after Fitzgerald had gone out of earshot. 'Don't you want to take me up there?'

'It's not that, babe. You know nothing gives me more pleasure than spending time with you. I just want to get these interviews over as soon as I can,' he explained, waving the list of names Fitzgerald had handed to him a moment earlier. 'I have a date tonight.'

'From what I hear, you have a date every night.'

'But *this* date is something special,' he said. 'This one I have high hopes for. Her name's Lucy and she works downstairs in Vice.'

'Is that part of the attraction?'

'If a woman chooses to works in Vice, she's got to be kind of kinky, right?'

'Walsh, you're a sick man. Logical but sick.'

'I'll take that as a compliment,' he said. 'I just wish I could've gone with the Chief instead of being stuck with the job of tracking down your ex-students. No offence.'

'None taken.'

'I bet Healy gets to meet Zak Kirby too. I worship that guy.'

'Healy or Kirby?'

'Very funny. You should be a stand-up comedian.'

'That's what my doorman tells me.'

I'd forgotten that Walsh had a thing about the theatre. He'd often admitted that acting was his first love, and police work only came second when it became clear that the acting was going nowhere. He still took part in amateur productions occasionally. Getting a foot in the door with Victor Solomon's crowd at the Liffey Theatre, even under these circumstances, would've been even more irresistible to him than an evening with Lucy from Vice.

Was Fitzgerald keeping him away from that part of the investigation because she feared he might not be able to keep his mind on the job, or that he might be too starstruck by the people he'd be seeing there to stay objective? If he had any sense, he wouldn't mention his hero worship of Zak Kirby. The American was surely already beginning to wonder what he'd got into, with the cops turning up to interrogate him about the movements of his own director on the night of a brutal murder.

If they started asking for his autograph as well . . .

I was being unfair. Walsh had always shown total integrity when it came to doing his job, even if he did leave his brain in his pants when it came to the rest of his life. He probably just wanted this one rare chance to soak up some of the atmosphere of the real theatre.

It wasn't a crime.

'Come on,' he said dolefully. 'I'd better get you to the Assistant Commissioner before the Chief comes back and gives me hell.'

15

Stella Carson came out from behind the desk and held out her hand to greet me.

'You must be Saxon.'

Now that I was hearing it for myself, the voice didn't sound so bad. It wasn't going to win any prizes for musicality, that's for sure, but I'd been on the receiving end of worse.

'I've heard a lot about you,' she added.

'That's what I was afraid of.'

She was smaller than I'd expected – smaller than Fitzgerald, that is, if not as small as me – with a sharp, clever face, an impression accentuated by the way she had her dark hair pinned back severely. The smile she offered was warm enough, however, and her eyes didn't have that deceitful look you often saw, where the eyes are sizing you up critically even as the mouth plays the part of smiling. She had a strong, athletic look to her, still looked trim. Most men her age in the force had already succumbed to middle-aged spread, the side-effect of consuming too many long liquid lunches with the other administrative overlords at whatever gentlemen's club they hunkered down in. There was none of that with her.

'Won't you sit down?'

I took my place in the chair she waved me into and watched as she made her way back round to the other side of the desk. There was an open cardboard box on her desk from which she'd been taking out various files and books and diaries – as well as a framed photograph showing a young woman in her mid twenties in a graduation gown and mortarboard hat, holding a rolled-up degree. The photograph had been given pride of place on the desk. Quite a contrast from the way the office had been when Assistant Commissioner Draker had occupied it, when any trace of his ordinary home life had been ruthlessly expunged, like it didn't matter. Either that or Draker had never *had* an ordinary home life of which to be reminded.

'My daughter,' Draker's successor explained when she saw me glancing at it. 'She recently finished her law degree. She's starting work soon with the Prosecutions Office.'

'That's a relief,' I said. 'For a second there, I thought you were going to say she was becoming a defence lawyer.'

'The enemy,' agreed Carson. 'What a dreadful thought.'

'Will she be following you down to Dublin?'

'She's already down here. She went to Trinity. So you could say I'm the one who's following her. I'm staying in her place right now while I look for a house and trying hard not to interfere too much with her life. It's a difficult habit to break.'

'At least you're *trying* to break it,' I said. 'Some mothers never learn to let go.'

'Are you speaking from experience?'

'Not me. I think my mother decided to let go approximately five minutes after she gave birth,' I said wryly. 'I'm not objecting. It suited me fine.'

She paused briefly before continuing. 'You're probably wondering why I asked to see you.'

'It had crossed my mind.'

'It wasn't to talk about my family troubles, if that's what you're thinking. I'm saving *that* up for my memoirs. Fitzgerald didn't tell you what I wanted?'

'She said she didn't know,' I said.

'I didn't say anything directly,' Carson said, 'but I think she guessed what I was thinking all the same.' Another pause. 'Do you want something to drink? Coffee? Tea?'

'I'm good.'

'Straight to the point. That's what I would've expected. I read your book. Your first book, that is. I don't get much time for reading, but I did read that. I like your point of view.'

'I appreciate it.'

'Fitzgerald tells me you knew this woman who died.'

Is that what this was about?

'I wouldn't say I knew her.'

'You'd met her, though?'

'Dublin's a small town in many ways,' I said. 'She sat a course I was teaching.'

'Do you think she admired you?'

'She gave no hint of it if she did,' I said. 'Why do you ask?'

'She had a lot of books about crime, murder, in her room. Serial killers, you know.'

'Novels?'

'Mostly non-fiction. Yours were among them.'

'You think that's important?'

'You know how it is, you have to examine every possible lead. If nothing else, it helps flesh out the kind of woman Marsha was. From what I've seen of the initial reports, there's not much else to go on.' She paused and picked up a cardboard file from her desk. 'Have you seen the crime-scene photographs?'

I shook my head.

That was her cue to slide the cardboard file across the desk toward me.

'Take a look,' she said.

The first picture I took out of the file was one of Marsha Reed lying dead where she was found, naked, tied to the bedposts with cords, a bag over her head. Her last desperate breaths had made the bag cling to her face like a second skin. The sheets underneath her body had become tangled with the violence of her struggle to capture air.

There were plenty more of the same. Close-ups, wide-angle shots, panoramas of the interior of the converted church where she'd lived, each photograph overlapping with the next, so that not one inch of the dead woman's final surroundings would be missed.

Most curious to me were a series of snapshots showing Marsha Reed's body lying on the bed covered with a sheet.

'Did one of the police officers at the scene cover her body?' I said.

'No,' the other woman said. 'She was found like that. Didn't you know?'

I hadn't known. Fitzgerald hadn't mentioned it.

I found myself considering what it meant. Did the killer feel ashamed of what he'd done? Killers sometimes covered the bodies of their victims if they couldn't accept what they'd done. Covering the body was a way of pretending that it hadn't happened. Sometimes too they didn't want the dead eyes of their victims staring back at them accusingly, though in Marsha's case she had died face down. Whatever the reason, covering the body certainly tied in with the investigation's assessment of a sexually motivated killer who knew his victim.

'He didn't cover the body straight away,' Carson said.

'He didn't?'

'The blood was dry when it touched the sheet. That meant some time must have elapsed between the killing and the covering.'

But why leave the body uncovered so long just to get suddenly squeamish? Had he come back, intending to wrap up the body for transport elsewhere, only to be interrupted?

'You see why we need your help,' I heard her say distantly as I leafed slowly and with grim fascination through the crime-scene pictures.

'Sorry?'

For a moment, the pictures were forgotten.

'I realize what I'm asking must come as a surprise. But you know what I'm saying makes sense. For years now things haven't been as they should have in this place. The Commissioner knows it. Draker knew it too, but he was too stubborn to do anything about it. Procedures have been lax. Standards have been allowed to slip. Fitzgerald has held the place together for a long while, but there's only so much she can do.'

'It's been a struggle, yes.'

'Exactly. Every new direction has been resisted. Every last penny of funding has had to be prised out of reluctant fingers. It's no way to run a department. Frankly, I wouldn't have stood for it in Belfast, and I'm not going to stand for it here. I intend to shake things up. We need to be ahead of the game for once and not forever running along behind trying to catch up. At times it feels here like they're still struggling to get to grips with the twentieth century, never mind the twenty-first. I've spoken to Dr Fisher already; he's agreed to get on board.'

'Fitzgerald mentioned he was looking at Marsha Reed's diary.'

'I hope that'll only be the start of it,' she said. 'Since he's here in the city permanently now, it makes sense to use his expertise as much as we can. You're smiling.'

'I'm imagining Fisher's reaction when he realizes how

you're reeling him in,' I said. 'He protests so much at his workload already, and yet he allows himself to be drawn every time into offering his services. I half wonder if that isn't the real reason he left London, so that Scotland Yard wouldn't be on the phone to him every week with another case.'

'Thankfully, we don't have the same crime rate as London yet,' the Assistant Commissioner said. 'But the key word there is "yet". Long gone are the days when Dublin could console itself that murder was something that happened elsewhere.'

'Sounds like Fisher picked the wrong city for a quiet life.'

'You too, perhaps.'

'The difference is that *I* don't have the same specialist skills to offer as Fisher,' I said. 'I don't even have a proper job any more. I'm just an inquisitive meddler.'

'I don't care what you call the talents you have. All I know is that your experience is something I can't afford to simply throw away. I've already talked this over with Grace. She's totally behind me. She knows the problems we have. Both of us need to know there's a collection of people out there that we can call upon when needs be. That's how it is in most police departments round the world. They understand the value of using the abilities of people with experience to make investigation easier. And you're an outsider here. Like me. Outsiders see things other people can't. They make connections and spot anomalies where others on the inside can't.' She raised an eyebrow sardonically. 'At least that's the theory.'

'And that's what you think I can do?'

'I don't know. What I do know is that Dublin's changing, and the DMP has to change with it. We're already in the middle of a recruitment drive to try to get more non-nationals into the force. Poles. Lithuanians. Nigerians. There are so many different nationalities and cultures out there now that have been thrown together, it creates new problems, but new opportunities as well. The DMP has to reflect the people who actually live here.'

She suddenly pulled a face.

'Listen to me,' she went on, 'I sound like a bloody recruitment ad. Think about it, that's all I ask. Like I say, you can see for yourself why your input could prove invaluable.'

And she nodded toward the crime-scene photographs I was still cradling in my hands. I saw what she'd done now. She'd let me see the photographs to soften me up for the approach, knowing I'd be horrified and angry at what I saw but intrigued too.

Intrigued enough not to want to walk away without getting close to the truth.

I took a long time answering, and when my answer came, it sounded weak even to my ears. 'I'm not sure I know what I can do,' I said.

'Me neither,' she said, 'but I'm willing to find out. Are you?'

16

'And what precisely are you asking me for?'

'I wanted the benefit of the esteemed Dr Lawrence Fisher's advice.'

'You know what to do,' said Fisher. 'You don't need me to tell you. You should accept. You've complained often enough about being out of the loop, about never having enough to do. This is the perfect opportunity to put that right. Plus you'd have the chance to work alongside Grace. With me too, for a while. What more could a girl want?'

'I guess you're right,' I said a little sulkily.

'Of course I'm right,' said Fisher. 'Just make sure you get paid handsomely for your efforts. You know what your problem is, Saxon?'

'You mean, there's only one?'

'Let me rephrase that. Do you know what *one* of your problems is? You don't know how to simply take what you want, even when it's being offered to you on a plate. You think because it seems too easy that there must be something wrong with it.'

'There usually is.'

'But plenty of times there isn't,' he retorted. 'Sometimes things really are what they seem. Sometimes there are no hidden catches. You agonize about things too much.'

'I don't trust simplicity,' I admitted.

'Well, it's about time you started,' he said briskly.

The way he said it reminded me so much of Fitzgerald. They were the two people in my life to whose advice I should always listen to stop myself making bad choices. Like he said, Stella Carson was holding out a possibility that I'd longed for, vaguely, hopelessly, for years: the chance to get back into the centre of things, no longer stranded on the sidelines.

The only problem was Kaminski.

If I hadn't seen him a couple of days ago, I would probably have said yes already. But there was something about his presence here in the city which demanded a response from me, and if I did accept the new Assistant Commissioner's invitation, then what would that mean for Kaminski? I couldn't go on sneaking around behind Fitzgerald's back, keeping her in the dark about what I'd learned about his presence here. And yet could I really tell her what I knew, or thought I knew, when the police would inevitably have to become involved? Could I betray him like that? Or should I just back off and forget I ever saw him?

But what then if he did something stupid?

Kaminski could certainly be impetuous. In the past, he could coil himself so tight you didn't know when he might snap. When he did, he himself was usually the one who suffered. His lost year in North Carolina proved that much. But there'd also been one or two rumours I'd heard down the years about him getting rough with suspects when he felt the situation called for it.

I'd never seen it happen myself, but then nor had I asked him about the rumours. That was the weird thing that happened when you worked so closely with someone. You turned a blind eye to things which, in normal circumstances, would make you distinctly uneasy.

So no, I didn't know if that part was true. But it rang true. When Kaminski got an idea into his head, there was no stopping him. Until I knew what idea he had in his head this time, I didn't feel in all conscience that I could wash my hands of him.

I almost began to wish as I sat there that I hadn't seen him at all.

It would've made the decision I had to make so much easier.

Not that Fisher was to know that.

As it was, right now we were supposed to be having lunch with Miranda Gray, Fisher's new Significant Other, as they say in certain circles. Idiot circles, that is. But then, what else could you call her? *Girlfriend* sounded faintly absurd for a middle-aged man. *Partner* always seemed like the whole thing should come with a business agreement attached. As for *lover*, I really didn't want to picture Fisher in the throes of ecstasy. At least not while I was eating. The two of them had recently dropped the pretence that they were simply good friends and set up home together in a large Victorian house in the mellow, leafy, bourgeois district round the Rathmines Road. He'd left his wife, Laura, and children, back in London, although he saw them as often as he could, and I know he missed them terribly.

Laura especially, though he'd never admit it.

Miranda's not being here had its advantages, however. It meant he could fill me in on what he'd found in Marsha Reed's journal. Though, as he spoke, I soon realized that it might have been quicker to tell me what *wasn't* in it. As Fitzgerald had said, she had had a busy life.

'I don't even know whether half of what I'm reading is true or not,' Fisher said. 'I've completed plenty of profiles before on sexual obsessives, people whose entire lives were dedicated to the pursuit of it, but I've never known a woman so fiercely driven by the same impulses as Marsha Reed.

Her every waking and sleeping thought seems to have been consumed by sex: its planning, execution and aftermath. Everything was written down in detail from her dreams to her regular encounters at the S & M club in town.'

'What makes you doubt the truth of what you've read?' I asked.

'Nothing I can put my finger on exactly, except that Victor Solomon doesn't appear in the pages of her book at all. Why leave him out? Was it because he was her real lover and the rest of them were nothing but figments of her own imagination?'

'They couldn't be. Fitzgerald has already spoken to people at the club. They remember Marsha well. She seems to have been game for anything.'

'Was she protecting him, then, by rendering him invisible in her journal?'

'Journals are private. Who would she be protecting him from?'

'Not all journals are private. It could be that she used her journal as part of her erotic life, maybe shared it together in bed with her conquests. She might not have wanted anyone stumbling on the secret of her relationship with Solomon, if secret it was. Also,' he noted with a frown, 'I have to say that the people I've known previously who shared the same sexual obsessions as Marsha increasingly found it hard to continue any normal sort of social or professional or family life whatsoever, whereas to all outward appearances *her* existence seemed unremarkable. Humdrum even. How she managed that is a mystery. Also there were other manuscripts found in her possession besides her journal which suggested she had a talent for fiction. Or for fictionalizing her actual experiences, perhaps I should say.'

'What were they like?'

'Erotic crime fiction, you'd have to call it. Short stories in which sex and murder become inextricably linked, often written in the first person so that it's only small details which make it clear it's not herself directly that she's writing about.'

'Did she cast herself as the victim in these stories?' I said.

'Victim or perpetrator, she seemed to have had an equal preference for either role.'

'You think she was acting out one of her fantasies the night she died?'

'It's certainly a possibility,' Fisher said, 'though there was nothing in her writings which corresponded precisely to the circumstances of her own death.'

'Maybe she preferred to try them out first before writing them down.'

'And this time she didn't get the opportunity? It's possible.'

It certainly put a new slant on her presence in my classes on criminal procedure. Something darker than mere curiosity had led her there. I only hoped nothing I'd said had unwittingly led her imagination down that one-way corridor where it was snuffed out for ever.

'You wouldn't be responsible for it even if it had,' said Fisher, when I confessed my fear to him. 'That's the uncomfortable thing about people. They have minds of their own, and no one else is ultimately responsible for what goes on inside them. Not that I should be talking to you about all this business,' he added unexpectedly, 'since you insist on still pretending to be undecided about accepting the Assistant Commissioner's offer.'

'What do you mean, pretending?'

But all he could say in reply was: 'What the –?'

And immediately I discovered what had distracted him.

Some drunk, folded in a filthy coat that seemed more fit for winter than the bright summer's day, had appeared in the street out of my sight through the window of the restaurant and now fell heavily against the glass before slumping in a heap to the ground.

As we watched, he hauled himself with difficulty to his feet, his hands gripping the glass, leaving greasy stains where he touched it, and turned on unsteady legs to face us through the window, looking in as though we were alien fish in an aquarium on which he couldn't quite focus. His hair was matted and bird-nested with unknown filth, and his face was hidden beneath a tangled beard that looked more like a growth of the same dirt than hair.

Silently he mouthed something to us, but whatever it was we would never know because the waiter had appeared belatedly from the direction of the kitchen and was hurrying toward the door, waving a towel in his hands like he was shooing away a fly.

The old hobo took awkwardly to his heels.

'Charming,' said Fisher as we watched him hobble away.

'I guess that's what you get for taking a table by the window.'

The waiter by this time was standing at the entrance, looking severe and disapproving, arms folded, the picture of a man who has escaped some fight but wants it to be known that he'd have been up for it if only he'd been around when it started.

My eye, though, was fixed on the road down which the drunk was clumsily making his getaway. As he reached the corner, he turned and looked back at the restaurant where we were sitting. I saw him reach into his pocket and take out a bank note. He held it in both hands and kissed it, then did a stiff little jig on the corner with delight.

Then he was gone.

'That's an odd thing,' said Fisher.

'What?'

'Look.'

He pointed to where the old man had climbed up against the glass.

A scrap of paper was stuck there now with chewing gum. I recognized it at once as the other half of the leaflet I'd left for Kaminski at his hotel and which he, in turn, had left for me. On the edge of this half was scribbled a cellphone number.

'He left you his contact details,' said Fisher. 'He must want a date. Your lucky day.'

'Ever think it might've been you he wanted, Fisher?'

And I laughed to cover my irritation that Kaminski had trumped me again.

I didn't know where *he* was to be found in the whole city, but seemingly he even knew where I was having lunch. Was there anything he didn't know about me?

I finished up with Fisher as quickly as I could, turning down his prompting to accompany him to Marsha Reed's house. As soon as he finished the rest of the wine, he would be heading over there to take a look at the place where she'd died. There were some curious details of her murder, he added, trying to reel me in mischievously, that he thought I might find interesting.

I told him I needed longer to decide whether I should get involved.

'Just make sure you make the right choice,' he left me with.

*

Once I was safely outside, I dialled the number that had been scribbled on the edge of the leaflet on the glass. It rang only once before it was answered.

'You've had your fun, JJ. Now are you going to tell me what you want?'

'I'm not JJ,' the voice on the other end answered. 'I'm Buck Randall, remember? You can't have forgotten me already. Or do you make a habit of breaking into everyone's room?'

'Oh, *that* Buck Randall? I knew the name sounded familiar. So how are you, Buck?'

'I'm doing terrifically. You?'

'Never been better. A bit tired from chasing old friends through Temple Bar, you know how it is.'

'What can I say? I suddenly remembered an urgent appointment I had to get to.'

'Was that what it was? And there was me thinking you were trying to avoid me.'

'You always *were* on the paranoid side.'

'Look who's talking. I'm not the one who's changed my name and dyed my hair.'

'Everything changes. Nothing lasts for ever.'

'Did you get that little pearl of wisdom from a fortune cookie, JJ?'

'Buck,' he corrected me.

'Don't start that again,' I sighed. 'Are you going to give me a break or not?'

'I'm considering it, what more can I do?'

'*Hey, watch where you're going!*'

'Excuse me?'

'I wasn't talking to you,' I said. 'It's tricky, walking along here and trying to listen to your lectures in philosophy at the same time. You should try it.'

'Who says I'm not doing it right now?'

That was true.

Listening hard, I could hear traffic, faint and discordant, on the other end of the line. I wondered if it was the same traffic I could hear in my other ear, the traffic on the street I was walking along. Then I wondered if he was watching me now, if he was near.

I spun round quickly.

There was a short laugh at the other end, but there was nothing of amusement in it.

I guessed I was right.

He *was* watching me.

But if I knew Kaminski, I wouldn't see him no matter how hard I looked. Like me, he knew how to make himself inconspicuous. Or at least like I *used* to.

'I have to admit,' I said, 'that was a neat trick with the hobo.'

'It's amazing what a few crisp new bills will get you,' said Kaminski. 'I told him you were friends of mine, and I wanted to play a prank on you for your birthday. He didn't even ask any questions, just took the money and did exactly what I asked him to do.'

'Maybe he has Americans asking him to fall into windows all the time.'

'Could be,' said Kaminski. 'Still, it got us talking again.'

'You wanted that, you could've just walked into the restaurant.'

'Now look who's talking. I didn't ask for any of this, in case you've forgotten. You started it. You knew where I was staying, why didn't *you* just come round and say hello?'

'That was the initial plan.'

'What went wrong?'

'You were out.'

'So you broke into my room?'

'Strictly speaking, I didn't break in,' I said. 'All I did was ask the maid to let me in.'

'She told me. Did you really say you were my wife?'

'It was the first thing I could think of.'

'I'd have thought being married to me was the *last* thing you'd have thought of.'

'I must've been feeling desperate,' I said.

'Desperate?'

'To know what you were doing in Dublin.'

Silence greeted that remark. I sensed he wanted to ask me if I'd found out what he *was* doing in Dublin, but he didn't want to just come right out with it. Instead he said: 'I didn't even know to begin with that you were in Dublin. Didn't know you were still here, that is. I knew you'd come here years ago. It's not like you to stay in one place so long.'

'You said it yourself,' I reminded him. 'Everything changes.'

'Not you,' he said. 'The Saxon I used to know wouldn't have hung around the same city for . . . what is it now? Ten years?'

Ten years. Suddenly I felt old.

'The Saxon I knew was always moving on.'

'Then we're even, because the JJ I knew wouldn't have picked a name like Buck Randall III to book into hotels under.'

'I have my reasons.'

'You want to share them with me?'

'Maybe,' he said, as if he was learning that fact about himself for the first time. 'I just need to be sure I can trust you first.'

'Trust me?'

151

'Yeah, trust. You know, the thing two people have between them that means one of them doesn't go breaking into the other one's bedroom uninvited.'

'There you go again. I told you. I didn't break in. I'm sorry it bugged you so much.'

And *I* realized as I spoke that I meant it. 'I'd no right,' I said.

'Not then you didn't,' said Kaminski, 'no. But now?'

He let the prospect hang like a spider on a thread.

'Now?'

'Like I said, I didn't know you were in Dublin at first. Then I saw you in Temple Bar. It spooked me out. I'd just been passing through and I saw your book lying on a table. I picked it up. The next thing I knew, there you were, standing on the other side of the square. It felt like . . . you'll say this is insane . . . it felt like a sign.'

'I don't think it's insane.'

'Later, I realized someone had broken into my room, and made it my business to find out who it was. The widow who owns the place told me someone had been asking for me at the desk. A short, dark American *female*. It didn't take long to figure it out.'

'I'm not that short,' I protested.

'I'm only telling you what she told me. Plus she said my mysterious caller had bad attitude coming out of her ears. I knew at once it was you.'

'She said *I* had a bad attitude?'

'She didn't put it exactly like that. She simply said you were a little . . . what was the word she used again? Argumentative, that was it. Not even you can deny that.'

'OK, you got me there.'

'So I began to ask myself,' said Kaminski, 'if that was a sign too. If you were being directed toward me. There was no way I'd expected you to track me down so quickly. I knew you'd do it eventually, I already had plans in place to move on. But that was fast work, Special Agent. I allowed myself to hope there was a reason for it.'

'You found me pretty fast yourself,' I pointed out.

'That wasn't so hard. *You're* not hiding out under a false name.'

'Fair point. But if you wanted my help, why not just come right up and ask me?'

'I could have done that,' he conceded. 'But then I wouldn't have had all the fun of seeing you put out for once. Of getting one over on you. That's a rare pleasure. Let me indulge it for a while. Besides, I wanted you to realize you weren't the only one who could play games. You can't expect to get your own way the whole time.'

If only he knew.

I don't think I'd gotten my own way in years.

How times change.

'So what now?' I said impatiently.

'We meet up, I guess. Talk.'

'And you'll tell me what your being here is all about?'

'If you're anything like the Saxon I once knew,' he said, 'you'll have figured some of it out by now.'

'I saw the newspaper clipping, if that's what you mean.'

'And?' He sounded apprehensive.

'And I know the woman who died was writing to someone on Death Row in Texas by the name of Jenkins Howler. I know too that Howler has passed over to the great beyond.'

'Anything else?'

I hesitated before continuing. 'I also know what happened to your wife.'

In the long pause before he responded, I became convinced that he'd broken the connection between us. Only the continuing traffic in that ear told me otherwise.

'Who told you?' came his voice finally.

How long did I consider telling him straight that it was Lucas Piper?

Not even one second.

If I asked myself why I held that part back, I couldn't have put it into words. There was something about not wanting him to know that Piper had been talking behind his back. They might have fallen out, but they'd been friends for so long it was bound to feel like betrayal. There was also a worry in me that telling him that part would lead to all sorts of other questions: what had Piper told me, how much did I know, what was I going to do with the information I had. It would take too long to explain to him where I was at in my understanding, and in the time it took to reach the end of the explanation he might've become unnerved enough to decide I was too high a risk to whatever plan of action he had in mind.

In addition, a part of me liked being able to keep this nugget back from him.

It gave me some reason to believe he wasn't holding all the aces.

'I read about it in the newspaper,' I told him in preference to the truth.

I'm not sure he believed me, but he accepted the lie with good grace.

'Then it's all the more important that we meet,' he said.

'What about right now?'

'Not so fast,' said Kaminski. 'I need to prepare the ground first.'

'When, then?'

'I'll be in touch,' he said.

'You're just going to hang up and disappear again? No. Come on, you can't do that.'

I was wrong.

He just had.

I couldn't believe it. He was doing it again, teasing me, taunting me, taking control of me, and I was letting him. *I was letting him.* I stood in the middle of that summer street, suppressing the urge to kick something, anything, feeling as if everything in existence had been created in that instant just to irritate me. The blaring horns of impatient, over-heated drivers as they took out their frustrations on one another. The courier cyclists weaving in and out of the traffic, sinister and silent, looking like aliens peering out through flylike shades. The office girls going by lost in their iPods, frowning slightly as if in concentration to hide the fact they didn't know how to work them. The men in suits walking by almost in slow motion, like they were auditioning for a part in *Reservoir Dogs*, over-compensating for the fact they were accountants. The world was going about its business without asking for permission or approval, but I was letting my every move be controlled by *him*.

I remembered suddenly the way I'd felt when I'd gone round to the hotel and found him gone. How I felt like I'd lost control of my life. That everything was being decided by other people. I was exhausted by being the tumbleweed that gets blown from place to place by someone else's will. I was tired of being other people's fool.

That's when I decided I would take back control of my own life. Whatever happened after that, I would deal with it when it happened. Kaminski had no right to expect anything more from me. I turned and made my way back to the restaurant.

*

Fisher was still at the table, finishing the last of the wine.

'Did you forget something?' he said.

'Yes,' I said. 'I forgot to tell you I'm coming with you.'

17

West of Aungier Street lay the Liberties. Originally known by the grand designation of the Liberties of the Monastery of St Thomas of Canterbury, this district got its name from the fact that it was self-governing and didn't come under central control until the nineteenth century, though whether it was under effective control even now is a matter for some debate.

At one time the area was outside the city walls. A place of poverty, deprivation and political rebellion, where tanners and weavers and linen-workers from Continental Europe were thrown together to sink or swim. However hairy the modern city could get at times, it had nothing on that Dublin of old, when you took your life into your hands just walking these same streets. In past decades there'd been occasional half-hearted attempts at gentrification, with the small, often one-roomed cottages that lined the narrow streets being knocked together and renovated. But the area still had a rough edge to it. It felt raw. Some of the city's more refined residents wouldn't venture this way if you paid them, let alone live here.

Marsha Reed hadn't been one of them.

This was where she had lived.

More to the point, this was where she had died, and where Fisher and I came after leaving the restaurant, picking up my Jeep on the way since it was quicker than heading over to Dublin Castle and begging a lift. The church stood out among the low houses as incongruously as a Mother

Superior in a strip joint, and when I first caught sight of the narrow lane running up between the other houses toward it, I feared my presence here would be more incongruous still. But to hell with my misgivings. It was too late for them.

I found a parking space as near as I could to her house, climbed out and left the car in Ossory Square – initially misreading the sign as Ossuary Square, which was grimly appropriate, considering why we were here – before doubling back to the right entrance.

The cop standing guard at the wooden gate that closed off the lane must have been briefed to expect me, because he didn't seem too troubled when I came along with Fisher. He didn't even ask to see my ID. He simply pushed open the gate and let us through.

Beyond the gate stretched a gravel driveway, wide enough for one car, at the end of which stood the church itself. It was only a small building, barely taller than the crouching terraced houses which surrounded it. The doorway on the facing gable took up most of the front wall, with room above for only one modest stained-glass window.

A small spire pointed crookedly at the sky.

Around the church, the land was laid out in a pretty garden, and the boundary was marked first with trees and then a wall, shielding the house from view. That may have partly explained why none of the neighbours saw or heard a thing the night she was murdered.

The garden, I noticed as we drew closer, was waiting to be filled by light, like a bowl by water, and right now, in high summer, I doubted there was a more peaceful spot in the whole city. I could scarcely even hear the traffic. I could well understand why Marsha Reed would have wanted to live here, whatever people said about the area's dangers.

Next to the door was a stone nameplate with ST GOBNAT'S

inscribed upon it, the *o* in the name represented by the shape of a bee. There were plenty more bees cut into the heavy oaken door as well, buzzing round chiselled wooden hives.

I ran my fingers over them, losing count.

'Apparently, she kept bees,' said Fisher as he stepped aside to let me in.

'Marsha Reed?'

'St Gobnat,' he said with a bewildered look. 'Does Marsha Reed strike you as the kind of woman to keep bees? Though maybe they'd have come in handy. There's a legend that says St Gobnat used her bees to see off a band of raiders who were trying to steal cattle.'

'You might say she told them to buzz off,' I answered.

'For that joke, I'm almost tempted to refuse to let you in,' said Fisher. 'But since I have no authority to stop you, I'll give you a second chance.'

I took a deep breath and crossed the threshold into Marsha Reed's house, pausing briefly before going in because there was always a moment before entering a place where someone has been killed when you find yourself wondering if you'll be able to tell something bad has happened there from the very air itself. Whether the poisonous aura which you suspect such places must possess as a result of what happened in them will be detectable, or whether it's only there in your own imagination. The truth, of course, was that the places where people die are generally indistinguishable from anywhere else at first glance and scent.

That was what Marsha Reed's house was like.

First impressions? That Marsha Reed had money, and plenty of it. Her father had obviously ensured that she wanted for nothing. Once you stepped out of the small stone hallway behind the door, there was essentially just one large open space, laid out with polished wooden floorboards, and with stained-glass windows all around and a lofty ceiling above ribbed like the inside of a whale. Medieval-style lights hung like descending spiders.

Expensive designer furniture had been arranged at the front of the room to make an improvised sitting area centred around a table strewn with movie and TV magazines bearing the grinning faces of identikit movie stars, the detritus of Marsha's aspirations, together with a huge plasma TV screen and a tottering pile of DVDs. Behind that a bookcase was stuffed with the novels and true-crime paperbacks that Stella Carson had already told me Marsha collected.

A little further on, steps led to a raised section in the centre of the room, surrounded by a wooden railing, like an altar, where the victim's iron-framed bed stood.

This was where Marsha had snatched her final breath before having the next one, and all the others that should have followed it, snatched from her. I recognized the scene from the photographs the Assistant Commissioner had shown me in her office.

The bed had been stripped of sheets since then, bagged up and taken away by forensics, and the bare mattress looked forlorn and exposed. Going up to see where she died, I could still identify traces of white powder on the bedposts where the technical team had dusted for prints, a reminder of how easy it was to turn an ordinary home into a crime scene.

All it took was one random, or not so random, act of violence.

As for the rest of the church, there wasn't much to say.

There were two doors on either side of the far wall. The first led into a small vestry that had been converted into a kitchen, though there was little sign that much in the way of cooking had ever gone on there. Marsha Reed's active social life had seen to that. The other door opened into a short corridor, off which were a number of equally small rooms where Marsha had hung her clothes and stored her shoes. Again, no expense had been spared. Each label carried the mark of some designer whose name was vaguely familiar to me.

The final room on this corridor contained the bathroom, white as heaven.

More bees buzzed in the stained glass above the bath.

I opened the door of the medicine cabinet, knowing it would be bare. Taking away a victim's pills was one of the first things police did following a murder. They had to check what was actually in the bloodstream of the dead against what was supposed to be there.

'What medication was she on?' I asked Fisher.

'Prozac for depression,' he said. 'Diazepam for stress. There was a small cocktail of other prescription drugs in there too, for which she didn't have a prescription. It seems she was self-medicating, basically taking whatever she could get her hands on.'

'Recreational drugs?'

'Some of the surfaces dusted positive for cocaine, and there were a couple of tabs of ecstasy wrapped up and stuffed down the side of a chair in the main room. The lab results aren't back yet, but her friends confirm she indulged chemically on a fairly regular basis.'

'Did Daddy know that's where his money went?'

Fisher shrugged. 'Who knows what anybody really knows or thinks?'

'That's a reassuring sentiment, coming from a criminal psychologist.'

'You know what I mean,' said Fisher. 'I can make educated guesses with the best of them, but people are always going to spring surprises on you. That's what they do best.'

'Did Marsha Reed spring any surprises on you?'

'Only insofar as there's not a trace here of her other more unconventional pursuits.'

'What did you expect to find – whips and chains hanging in the closet?'

'I expected to find *something*,' he said. 'Instead it's as if she worked hard to keep the two parts of her life separate and they're still not on speaking terms now she's gone.'

'That's not so unusual.'

'No,' he acknowledged. 'But it's *noteworthy*.'

'Maybe she didn't want her father finding out what was really going on in his baby daughter's head,' I suggested. 'Maybe she feared he wouldn't approve.'

'So she keeps things neat and anodyne to stop him cutting off her cash supply, saving it all for the privacy of her journal? It's a possibility.'

'Have you come to any other conclusions?' I asked.

'Tell me what you think first.'

'Me? I don't know what to think. Everything seems so' – I searched for the word – 'unremarkable. You'd never guess anything out of the ordinary had happened here.'

'You've hit the nail on the head. Unless I'm missing something blindingly obvious,' Fisher said.

'It wouldn't be the first time.'

'You keep your sarcastic put-downs to yourself, Special Agent. All I mean is that this looks like one of these rare cases when what you see really might be all there *is* to see.'

'That's significant in itself, surely?'

'It's the most significant aspect of the whole business. No one blundered in here unexpectedly and murdered this poor woman. You only have to look at the crime scene to know whoever did this felt *comfortable* here. At home even. He wasn't rushed or stressed.'

'So you're saying it wasn't one of her casual pick-ups?'

'I'm not saying it couldn't be, but I don't think she would've brought someone she met through the S & M scene back here for sex. The environment is just too sexless and anonymous to match their requirements. I'm assuming she went elsewhere for that. To clubs, or to the men's own houses. Besides, would a casual pick-up have felt so comfortable here?'

'More of a regular boyfriend, then?'

'A boyfriend? Yes, that might work. But the truth is we don't know *who* felt comfortable here. There could have been men in and out of Marsha's house all the time that we don't know about, men who could have become familiar with the layout of the place. They could fit the bill as easily. Till we know who they are, we can't rule anything out.'

'It definitely wasn't a random attack, though?'

'No way.' Fisher shook his head firmly.

'You mean this was an organized scene?'

'Organized is too simple a description. It's more complex than that.'

I knew what Fisher meant. Amateur profilers made much of the differences between organized and disorganized crime scenes and what they meant, but nothing was ever that straightforward. It was one of the things I'd explained in my lectures to my students: the difference between a fictional crime scene, where the evidence and the nature of the attack were signposted and clear, and an actual crime scene, where things were less absolute.

Not that the classifications were worthless.

Everyone had to start somewhere.

It was all a question of trying to determine how motive affected a crime scene. Basically an organized crime scene reflects the control which the killer brings to the place of killing. The scene shows planning, premeditation. There would be an effort to avoid detection. The killer is aware of what he's doing and does all he can to avoid leaving incriminating evidence behind. Disorganized crime scenes, by contrast, display clear signs of spontaneous action and frenzied assaults. Victims are selected at random. Weapons might be chosen the same way. The attack will be hurried, the crime scene disarrayed.

At least, that's what the textbooks say.

In that sense, Marsha Reed's house fitted the classic organized scene, especially when it came to the use of restraints. Organized killers need to *control* their victims. They need to minimize resistance. On the other hand, organized killers usually picked targeted strangers as their victims, and, if Fisher was right, Marsha was no stranger to her killer.

They also usually took the body away, or made some effort to conceal it. That accorded with the desire to escape detection. The most inexperienced killer would know that the longer a body is kept away from the police, the better his own chances of getting away with the crime. Here, no attempt was made to hide the body at all. In fact, it was openly displayed, making discovery inevitable. Covering it with a sheet certainly hadn't been a serious attempt at concealment. The significance of that act lay elsewhere.

The body hadn't even been moved after death, though that could simply have been a consequence of necessity. The killer would have found it difficult to shift a body from Marsha's house down the lane and into the street without being seen.

Alternatively, it could be a sign of his confidence again. He didn't *care* whether the body was found, because he didn't expect the police to be able to catch him whatever he did.

Another difference was that Marsha's killer must have lingered on the scene for some time after committing the murder, hence the dried blood on the sheet. Equally, that could point to the killer having returned subsequently to the scene of crime, which in itself was recognized as a reason why a crime scene showed signs of organized and disorganized behaviour simultaneously. But why would he have taken the risk or returning?

Because he'd left incriminating evidence behind?

Or because the need to take some trophy overrode any sense of caution?

Another commonly cited reason for finding conflicting evidence at a crime scene was because there were *two* killers. Could that have been the explanation in this case?

'Or it could be,' I said slowly, groping my way through the possibilities, 'that this whole scene has been staged to throw investigators off the scent.'

'Now you're getting somewhere,' Fisher said with a smile.

I realized that he'd been gently leading me to this point the whole time.

'You're saying you think the scene *was* staged?'

'I think there is no doubt that this scene was staged,' said Fisher. 'The place was arranged to make some point, to tell some story. The question is, what story?'

'To know that, you'd have to know first what it looked like before.'

'Now that forensics have finished up, Grace is planning to get some of Marsha's friends in here individually to take a look around. We certainly don't want them coming by in a crowd and confusing one another. If anything has been moved around and changed by the killer in an attempt to convey some message, they're the ones most likely to spot it.'

'Sounds like a good idea.'

'The only problem,' Fisher replied, 'is that her friends don't seem to have come round here much. She seemed to socialize with them mainly in town, or at their houses.'

'The solitary type.'

'In that respect, she was. In others, obviously she was a little less shy. But any friends from her secret life who *did* come here aren't exactly going to be rushing round to help the police make an inventory of the fixtures and fittings. Of course,' he added, 'I could be wrong about her knowing her killer at all. Maybe he's just the type who feels confident enough to move in spaces that are foreign to him as easily as he moves in his own house.'

'Then that makes him all the more dangerous,' I said.

'I don't think we need any further proof that the man we're looking for is a dangerous individual,' commented Fisher bleakly. 'We have his handiwork as evidence.'

18

Fitzgerald was standing on the gravel drive in front of the church, talking to Seamus Dalton, when we finally stepped outside. It was Dalton who noticed me first – and if I could've anticipated the look of mingled confusion and loathing on his face at the sight of me, it would have single-handedly dispelled any doubts I had about accepting Stella Carson's offer.

He couldn't have been more taken aback if Marsha Reed herself had come out of the church, and made a noise in response somewhere between a worldless moan and a profanity.

The noise alerted Fitzgerald to the fact something was wrong with Dalton, and she followed his gaze until her eyes met mine. She hid her own surprise well, but I could tell she was pleased. That was harder to hide. A smile was flickering on the edges of her mouth.

'There you are, Saxon,' she said. 'No need for any introductions in present company, at any rate. You both know each other. I did mention Saxon'd be joining us for a time, didn't I, Dalton? The new Assistant Commissioner has invited her to offer her expertise on the investigation.'

Dalton didn't answer.

Most likely, he didn't trust himself to answer civilly. I doubt I would've been able to either if the roles were reversed. I tried not to enjoy his discomfort too obviously.

'Detective Dalton's just brought round Marsha's phone records,' Fitzgerald went on, pretending not to notice the strained atmosphere which had descended on proceedings.

'I didn't realize you were here,' I said.

'Only arrived a moment ago. I spent the morning with Desdemona.'

'Desdemona?'

'Solomon's girlfriend. She's playing the main female lead in his latest production.'

'Desdemona's the name of the character,' Fisher whispered to me helpfully.

'Right. I did wonder. What's her real name?'

'Ellen Forwood. Seems Solomon was either telling the truth, or they're both lying. She says he was with her from after the play ended on Saturday night until the next morning.'

'So he couldn't have sneaked over here and killed Marsha?'

'Not unless he has a body double,' muttered Dalton.

No chance of Dalton ever getting a body double, that's for sure. Where would they ever find that much excess fat to replicate his waistline?

'Did his fiancée know about Solomon's relationship with Marsha?' asked Fisher.

'Not until this morning, when he confessed all – and not, I hasten to add, out of the goodness of his heart. The press got wind of his relationship with Marsha Reed.'

'And?'

'She says she's forgiven him. That everyone makes mistakes. According to her, they were planning on an autumn wedding before all this blew up, and nothing has changed.'

'If marriage was in the offing, that would've made it all the more inconvenient,' I said, 'if Marsha Reed decided to make life difficult for Victor Solomon. It would give him the perfect motive to want rid of her.'

'That still doesn't explain how he can be in two places at once,' said Fitzgerald.

'True.'

'Plus we've been through the records we can find of cars in the area at the time and there's not a sniff of Solomon's presence. Not that that's conclusive proof,' she added.

'Any joy with the phone records?' pressed Fisher.

'Sort of. That's why I came round to let you take a look at them.'

She handed a bundle of sheets to Fisher.

'The top sheet is a list of the calls she made on the night she died,' said Fitzgerald. 'Then they go back in reverse chronological order for six weeks.'

'The highlighted ones?'

'Those are the calls to Solomon,' she explained.

'Did she always call him this often?'

'Quite the contrary. Initially she hardly called him at all. It could be she didn't need to, because she was seeing enough of him. Or it could be she was more careful at the start to maintain his privacy. She must've known about his relationship with Ellen Forwood. Then, as her own relationship with Solomon started to cool off, the calls increased in frequency.'

'There must be over a dozen each day,' observed Fisher, lifting each sheet in turn.

'And on the last day, more than twenty.'

'Few of them lasting more than a few seconds,' I said, as Fisher handed me the record.

'Solomon says she kept calling and begging him to meet her again. He kept telling her it was over and to stop harassing her. Harassing was his word. By the end, he was just cutting Marsha off every time as soon as he realized it was her on the other end.'

'What about the other numbers?' I said.

'Some are probably men she met through the club she belonged to,' said Fitzgerald. 'A handful have already come forward to admit they knew her. The others –'

'Are probably married,' I finished for her.

'I shouldn't wonder. I've already put Dalton on to the job of tracing them.'

And boy, did he look delighted with it.

'And this one?'

'That,' Fitzgerald said, 'is the last number Marsha Reed ever called.'

The call had lasted only a couple of minutes, but the time recorded meant that it must have taken place less than an hour before the pathologist's estimate of the time Marsha died.

'Who is it?'

'His name is Todd Fleming. And', she said to me, 'there's one curious feature I thought might grab you. He used to work as a locksmith. Remember what Niall Boland said about the criminal propensities of errant locksmiths? Here's someone who wouldn't have had any trouble getting in and out of Marsha Reed's house if he wanted to.'

'You say he *used* to work as a locksmith?'

'That's right. Currently he's working the night shift at a 24-hour internet café down in Temple Bar.'

'Has his name come up in the investigation thus far or not?'

'Not. It's the first we've heard of him,' said Fitzgerald. 'We're going over there now to have a word with him. Healy's waiting in the car. You can come with us,' she added to me.

I didn't need to be asked twice.

I felt Dalton's eyes burning resentfully into the space

between my shoulderblades as Fitzgerald and I walked down the lane back to the road. He wasn't going to be pacified by being told my presence was the Assistant Commissioner's idea. That only gave him additional excuses to mistrust her and me together. Like he didn't have enough already.

'Damn,' I said.

'What is it?'

'I forgot about my car. I parked it round in Ossory Square earlier.'

'Give me the keys,' said Fitzgerald. 'I'll get one of the drivers to bring it round to Dublin Castle later. If it still has any tyres on it by then, that is. Some of the kids round here can strip a car back to its constituent elements quicker than a school of piranha can strip a shark's carcass back to the bone. What were you thinking of, leaving a car unattended down here? Not that your Jeep being burned out by joyriders would be any loss, you understand.'

'You leave my Jeep out of this. That car's like family to me.'

'In your case, that's not much of a compliment. The last time you saw your mother more than twice in the same calendar year was when you were in high school. And Saxon?' She checked over her shoulder quickly to make sure we were out of earshot. 'I'm glad you decided to accept Stella's invitation,' she said. 'Really I am. I think this is what you need.'

'I don't want to get in your way –'

'You're not in anyone's way.'

'Try telling that to Dalton,' I pointed out.

'Dalton's just going to have to learn to adjust,' Fitzgerald said firmly. 'It wouldn't be before time. Though coming on top of the new Assistant Commissioner being a woman as well, the shock of your arrival might just tip him over the edge.'

'We can only hope.'

'Here,' she said.

We were back in the street.

Healy was parked up on the sidewalk, and was sitting with his head back on the seat and his eyes closed. Fitzgerald rapped on the glass good-naturedly to wake him up.

'Look sharp,' she said. 'We've got company.'

'I see that,' said Healy, as Fitzgerald slid easily into the front seat and I clambered more awkwardly into the back. 'It's good to have you back on board, Special Agent.'

'Don't give me that Special Agent crap, or I might be tempted to change my mind.'

'You're the boss.'

'No, I'm the boss,' said Fitzgerald. 'She's not taken the whole place over yet.'

'Only a matter of time,' said Healy. 'Only a matter of time.'

It was way too early to find Todd Fleming at work in the café. Instead we headed north, up Francis Street, over the river on to Church Street and Phibsborough Road. At Cross Guns Bridge, we turned right into Whitworth Road and from there took another left into the network of streets that thronged darkly, despite the sunshine, underneath the railway line.

Healy and I waited in the car while Fitzgerald strode to the front door of the house.

She was back within moments.

'No luck,' she said. 'A neighbour in the flat below says he's usually out around this time picking up his son from nursery school. He should be back in ten minutes.'

But ten minutes turned into fifteen.

And fifteen into a half-hour.

Still there was no sign of him.

'Do you think the neighbour warned him we were here?' suggested Healy.

'So he decides not to come home?' said Fitzgerald. 'He might as well just tattoo the word GUILTY on to the front of his forehead. No one is that stupid.'

'Half our arrests happen because people are that stupid,' said Healy.

'Is this him now?' I said.

A man had turned the corner at the end of the road, walking hand in hand with a young child of five or six, a little blond-haired boy in blue shorts, awkwardly carrying a large box underneath his arm with the name of a famous toy store written on the edge.

The man whose hand the boy held was about thirty years old, and he looked, from the rumpled state of his long hair and unshaven cheeks, like he'd only recently gotten out of bed. Maybe he had. If this was the right man, he had the working hours of an owl. The day would be for sleeping. He was dressed casually in jeans and a T-shirt bearing the name of some local football team, and in his free hand he carried a half-empty shopping bag. He had piercing eyes, which he trained on us as he neared the place where we waited.

'Todd Fleming?' said Fitzgerald through the open window.

'Who wants to know?'

She got out and showed him her badge.

'Chief Superintendent Fitzgerald,' she said. 'I wonder if we could have a word?'

Fleming glanced from her to Healy and me in the car, then back to Fitzgerald.

'Wait here. I'll just get someone to look after Jake.'

The badge hadn't phased him at all.

I heard the little boy asking what was wrong as his father led him up the path to the front door, and Fleming making some excuse about having to talk to friends of the boy's mother, and then their voices faded as they went indoors.

A couple of minutes later Fleming reappeared.

'What do you want?' he said cagily.

'Don't play games,' said Fitzgerald. 'It's predictable, it's tedious, and it only wastes your time and ours. You know what we've come here to talk about.'

Fleming considered her words.

It didn't take long for him to see sense.

'I knew it was only a matter of time before I heard from you,' he said. He was about to say more when he changed his mind. 'Can we go somewhere quieter?'

'If that's what you want,' said Fitzgerald.

'I don't want to stand on the street like a lemon, that's for sure,' said Fleming. 'You've already made me the chief topic of conversation round here for the next month as it is. If Jake's mother gets to hear that the police have been knocking on the door, she'll let me see him even less of him than she does already.'

'In that case, climb in the back. Healy?'

'There's a park not far from here,' said Healy. 'We can go there.'

Fitzgerald walked round to the other side of the car and held the door open for Fleming. He manoeuvred in next to me, his piercing eyes holding mine dispassionately for a second before Fitzgerald made her way back round to her own door and got back in, forcing him to fumble quickly with his belt before Healy could pull out from the kerb again.

He was in a car with what he thought were three police officers.

He didn't want to make things worse by forgetting his seatbelt.

'How did you find out about me?' he said as we drove.

'Your mobile number was in Marsha Reed's phone records,' Fitzgerald told him, turning round in her seat so that she could look directly at him where he sat in the seat behind Healy. 'In fact, you were the last person she called before she died.'

That didn't throw him either.

'I thought I might be,' he said. 'I mean, I knew I had to be *one* of the last people she spoke to, because of the time. I heard on the news afterwards that she died around midnight.'

'Why didn't you come forward and tell the police you heard from her that night?'

'What would've been the point? I didn't know anything.'

'You weren't worried it might look suspicious if you kept quiet?'

'Suspicious in what way?'

'Someone killed Marsha,' said Fitzgerald. 'If I was in your shoes, I wouldn't want to give the police any more reason than necessary to suspect me of being the one who did.'

'I wasn't worried about *that*,' Fleming said dismissively.

'Why not?'

'She called me at work,' he said, as though the answer was obvious. 'I was there until after three o'clock in the morning. Scores of people must've seen me there. I knew no one could say *I* killed her.'

He had a point. It was certainly a better alibi than Victor Solomon's forgiving fiancée.

'What would I want to kill her for, anyway?' he added.

'Why would anyone?' said Fitzgerald.

'I thought that's what *you* were supposed to find out,' Fleming replied testily.

'All in good time,' said Fitzgerald. 'This'll do.'

She was talking to Healy, telling him to stop the car again.

Outside was a playground. Children played on slides and swings. We could hear them laughing through the open windows. Inside the car it was hot.

Fleming was wiping the palms of his hands on his jeans. 'I should've brought Jake,' he said sardonically, gazing out at the playground. 'Made a day of it.'

'How did you know Marsha Reed?'

'You mean, how did a badly paid shop worker get to know someone like Marsha with her own Ferrari and little black book filled with the numbers of important people?'

'That's not what I meant at all,' said Fitzgerald. 'What I meant is, were you one of her whip and leather crowd? Money doesn't come into it. Well? *Is* that how you met her?'

'Christ, no.' He actually sounded shocked by the suggestion. 'That's not my scene at all. I met her because she used to come into the café some nights. We got talking.'

'Were you lovers?'

'I wanted us to be,' said Fleming. 'I'm not going to deny it.'

'She wasn't interested?'

'She only wanted us to be friends,' he said, injecting all the sarcasm he could into the last word. 'Isn't that what women always say when they don't fancy you? I suppose she was getting her pleasure in other ways.'

'Did you know about that side of her life?'

'It wasn't a secret. She used to tell me stories of the men she met at the club she belonged to,' he recalled. 'The way she talked about it, it sounded like a meat market.'

'You didn't approve?'

'I didn't *understand*. There's a difference. I wasn't judging her. She was a nice girl. I cared about her. I didn't want anything bad to happen to her. I told her it was dangerous.'

'What did she say to that?'

'That she was a big girl, and she knew what she was doing. She told me it was just a bit of fun,' Fleming said, 'and that I should come along one night and see for myself. I never did, before you ask. The only time I ever saw Marsha was in the café. She came in two, three times a week, usually late at night, to use the computers. She said she didn't have one at home. We used to have a coffee together, talk for a while. I hoped one night it might turn into something else. But it never did. I was a shoulder to cry on, that's all.'

'What about the night she died?' said Grace. 'Why did she call?'

Fleming took a deep breath, as if this was the part he'd been dreading. 'She was upset,' he said. 'She'd been seeing Victor fucking Solomon.'

'She told you that?'

'It was no secret. He'd told Marsha he could help her make it as an actress. I told her it was the oldest story in the book, but she wouldn't listen. She'd started sleeping with him, and then, of course, when he got what he wanted he dumped her. Or rather, he stopped sleeping with her as often as he had before. He still used to call her up for sex when he felt horny and there was nothing better on offer, and she always used to oblige.'

'She still thought he could help out her career?'

'That's what she *said* it was,' Fleming said, avoiding Fitzgerald's eye. 'She even tried to say he might be able to help me.'

'How could he have helped you?'

'Even shop assistants can have ambitions, you know.

I write plays. I had one put on last year at the Dublin Fringe Festival. I'm working on a new one now. I just work at the café to pay the rent. Marsha reckoned if she could make the right connections, we could both get something out of it. We used to talk about the future all the time, about her starring in a play of mine. Then again,' he said thickly, 'maybe she just *wanted* to sleep with Solomon. She slept with plenty of others as well as him. It was only me she didn't want to go to bed with.'

He didn't try to hide the bitterness in his voice.

'You say she was upset about Solomon the night she died?'

'She said she'd met him earlier that evening, and that he'd demanded she give back some necklace he'd given her. Said now they weren't together any more, that she should return it. He wanted to give it to his fiancée as a wedding present. It was expensive, though what's money to a man like him? I also got the impression that she'd been asking him to get back together, begging him by the sound of it, and he'd turned violent. It was hard to get much sense out of her, she was crying so much.'

It certainly didn't sound like the taxi driver's description of Marsha that night.

He'd said she was giddy and excitable.

'What did she want *you* to do?' said Healy. 'Go to Solomon's house and rough him up on her behalf?'

'Nothing like that. And believe me, I offered. That only made her cry more. She just wanted me to come round to her place. She said she needed someone to talk to.'

'But you didn't go.'

'I was working, I told you, I couldn't get away.' Fleming sounded defensive now. 'It was going to be another three hours before I finished work, and I couldn't just drop everything and run round because she'd summoned me. I didn't want to lose my job. And I was tired of her thinking I could just be dangled like some puppet she could play with.'

'You sound angry,' said Fitzgerald.

'I *was* angry. I *am* angry. I'm angry with her because she had to die like that. Marsha could've been with me instead of all those creeps she threw herself at, instead of Solomon. She would've been safe with me, but no, she wasn't inter-ested. I didn't turn her on, because *I* wouldn't hurt her like those other sick bastards did. And don't bother looking at me like that, as if you think I killed her out of jealousy because she rejected me. You're not listening. I spent the whole night at the café. You can check up on me on the CCTV.'

'Then you have nothing to fear, do you?'

'Did I say I was afraid?' he shot back. 'Are you deaf? I don't give a damn what you think you know about me. I'm the one who has to live with the knowledge that if I'd gone round to Marsha's house when she called that night, she might still be alive. Do you have any idea what that's like? I was afraid that night all right. Afraid of losing my job. And because of that, Marsha was the one who ended up losing her life. It's all my fault.'

'Then why', said Fitzgerald coldly, 'didn't you come immediately and tell us all this when you heard what had happened to Marsha? If you cared for her so much, didn't you want to help put Solomon away for what he'd taken away from you?'

'Don't you worry about Victor Solomon,' said Fleming. 'I don't intend to let him get away with anything. I have *plenty* of plans for him.'

19

Outside Dublin Castle, reporters were massed like cavalry before a battle. Cameras flashed as Healy's car slowed to turn at the gates; there was shouting; a blur of faces through the glass; microphones were pushed forward in the vain hope that a window would be lowered and a few words offered by Fitzgerald. The throng surged forward and was barely held back by the clutch of uniformed officers sent out to keep them at bay. Fitzgerald ignored them all. She scarcely gave any impression of having noticed them. Maybe she was used to it.

Nothing sells newspapers more than a good murder, after all, and the murder of Marsha Reed was one of the more lurid cases to have come to attention in recent months.

Once the pack scented blood, they rarely let up.

Victor Solomon's name had given the case the added glamour of showbusiness too. The lovers of famous Shakespearean directors were not found murdered and mutilated every day. I wondered if his fiancée would be so forgiving when she had to face this barrage.

Nor had the severed finger remained secret for long. Fitzgerald hadn't seriously expected that it would. Reporters knew where to find Murder Squad detectives after hours. A few drinks, some flattery, maybe even a little money changing hands, and tongues were inevitably loosened, strict instructions to silence forgotten, discretion abandoned.

So would the killer strike again? That was what the reporters had gathered at the gates of Dublin Castle to find out, though they could have learned the answer to the question much more quickly by simply familiarizing themselves with the available literature on murder.

Of course Marsha Reed's killer would strike again. He would keep striking until he was caught. No sexually motivated murderer ever stopped of his own volition.

Why would he?

We climbed out of the car at the back of Dublin Castle and took the rear entrance into the building. It seemed strange to have to move about so surreptitiously, as if we were the ones who'd done something wrong, but I understood Fitzgerald's preference for keeping things low key. She wanted nothing to interfere with the investigation. She needed to stay focused.

Upstairs, she asked me to wait while she went to speak to someone on the desk about getting the uniformed presence outside increased. I stood at the window of her office, looking down at the now distant, silenced crowd gathered for scraps, like gulls on fishing day.

There were others watching the proceedings too. Lone figures at the edge of the larger group, semi-detached from what was happening but still lingering as if hoping some of the air of suppressed excitement might rub off on them. That was nothing new. The world was full of voyeurs attaching themselves to things that were none of their business, filling the empty spaces in their own existence with the detritus of other people's lives.

Other people's deaths.

Murder always had and always would act as a malignant magnet.

Looking down now, though, I couldn't help wondering who else might be out there, watching. The kind of controlled, organized killer who had taken Marsha Reed's life from her would undoubtedly be anxious to follow the course of the investigation, to know every detail of what was going on. He would listen to each news show, devour each newspaper. He would keep cuttings. He might even find a way to inveigle himself into the proceedings, itching to see the police at work closer to hand, to gain an insight into their thinking on the case.

Often men like that were frustrated would-be policemen themselves.

He might be out there right at this moment, in the street below, getting off on being so close to the heart of the Murder Squad inquiry, on knowing that just behind the grey walls of Dublin Castle the pictures of his handiwork were on display, and that scores of detectives were wrapped entirely in the world that he had created out of the darkness of his own mind. To the killer, it would be like they were paying homage to his work.

Being so close, he might also hope to catch any whisper of new developments. Of possible leads. Reporters talked. They couldn't help it. It wasn't in their nature to be discreet. Sadly, their ceaseless chatter was a highly effective advance-warning system for any killer.

I found myself scanning the loiterers and the watchers below, and even any passer-by who lingered a moment longer than necessary, for signs that they might be the one we were seeking. A young man in an Hawaiian shirt stood smoking in the doorway on the other side of the street, laughing to himself as if at a private joke. What was he doing there?

A businessman driving up Dame Street missed the traffic lights and had to be beeped into action by the cars behind, so preoccupied had he been by the scene at the gate.

What did he find so fascinating?

A streetsweeper leaned on his brush and stared through the gates.

Hadn't he seen reporters here before?

That was the worrying thing. You want the wicked and the damned to bear some kind of mark that distinguishes them from the rest of us. That sets them apart. But they don't. They look as normal as everyone else. Or, that is to say, as abnormal. Because once you started looking at people in a particular light, they almost all began to seem suspicious. To simply not feel right. You stopped believing in anything good or decent. All you saw in the eyes of strangers was some flicker or flash of inner wickedness struggling to remain under control.

To remain hidden.

'Scavengers,' said Fitzgerald behind me, and I turned, not realizing until then that she'd been there. She must've thought I was still watching the reporters.

'It keeps them out of trouble,' I remarked lightly.

'And how are we going to keep you out of trouble?'

'You could lock me up.'

'And have the American Embassy on my back for mistreating one of their most valued citizens?' said Fitzgerald. 'Not likely. I'll try this instead.'

She tossed a file down on to her desk.

A man's photograph was pinned to the front, one of those ordinary, unremarkable-looking people whose existence I'd been pondering when she came in.

'His name's Mulligan,' she said. 'John Arthur Mulligan. Thirty-two. He's got more convictions than you've got grudges. Yeah, that many. Rape. Sexual assault. You name it. One of the officers in Vice, Walsh's bit of stuff that he thinks we don't know about, came up with his name as a possible for Marsha Reed's killing. Apparently, he liked to tie up his ex-girlfriend naked and threaten her with a knife when he was feeling horny.'

'They don't teach you that in the Kama Sutra.'

'I wouldn't know. Your reading's obviously more varied than mine.'

'Have you brought him in for questioning?' I said, ignoring the jibe.

'No need. Turns out he was rearrested two weeks ago for breaching an exclusion order against the same ex-girlfriend and was locked up when Marsha Reed was killed.'

'Then I don't –'

'See what I'm getting at? You will,' said Fitzgerald. 'Mulligan was out of circulation at the time of the murder, but he's very far from being the only man in Dublin with a known penchant for a little light bondage and violence against women. I thought you could head down to Records and check the files, see if anyone else like Mulligan comes back.'

'Good idea,' I said.

'Nice of you to say so,' she answered with a smile. 'I was going to ask one of the detectives to do it, but since you're around . . . You do have a sharp eye for deviance.'

'That doesn't sound like a compliment,' I said.

'It wasn't.'

And so, dutifully, if without much enthusiasm, I headed downstairs to Records.

This had been Niall Boland's special domain before he'd fled the Murder Squad for the exciting world of locks and keys. He'd frequently squirrelled himself away here in the basement of Dublin Castle for as many hours as he could manage before his absence was noted, king of all he surveyed – that being mainly row upon row of cold metal shelves, lined with cardboard folders in boxes, all overseen by bare and unforgiving lightbulbs.

For the next couple of hours, I familiarized myself with the contents of the files, at least insofar as they related to the Marsha Reed case. That meant locating any offender or ex-prisoner whose habits or modus operandi touched in even the most incidental way upon the manner and circumstances of her death. Rapists who tricked their way into women's homes rather than breaking and entering; attackers who preferred to tie up their victims, for whatever practical or symbolic reasons; those who used or threatened to use knives – they were all here.

It was the same pattern I'd noticed earlier when watching passers-by from Fitzgerald's window. The more you looked, the less light there seemed to be in the world. Everybody became a suspect. The world scarcely seemed large enough to contain the evil that was done in one small city on the edge of Europe like Dublin, let alone in the rest of its swarming farthest reaches. The basement echoed with the voices of the nameless and forgotten victims.

I decided to confine myself to the last three years, otherwise I would have been down there all night and left at the end of it with more files than there was time to process efficiently. Then came the business of sorting the assembled names into more easily manageable categories – Impossibles, Unlikelys, Could Bes and Possibles – and then subdividing them still further the more information I had at my disposal.

A had carved his initials into his pregnant wife's belly, but he'd subsequently been killed in a gangland shooting in North Dublin. *B* had tied up and raped three women, but he was still in prison. *C* had posed as a policeman to gain access to the homes of numerous women down the years, but he had never done more than steal their underwear.

One by one, the list was whittled down to size.

Eventually I was left with perhaps half a dozen men

who could be regarded, without too much stretch of the imagination, as capable of the murder of Marsha Reed or significant aspects of it. And that was a depressing enough number in itself. It's comforting to believe that murder and mutilation are esoteric affairs, of practical interest only to the few. The terrible truth is that there are more people with the required diseased distortions of the brain to carry them through than it is altogether healthy to count, and it is often in administrative caves such as the Records Office that their scent can first be picked up and followed.

That day, it was Terence Dargan's scent that got into my nose.

And in more ways than one.

20

A fly was trapped in the gap between the window and the closed curtains of Terence Dargan's house, struggling to escape from its prison in that manic, slightly sinister way flies have.

Fitzgerald and I stood on the doorstep, waiting for the man himself to answer the door. He, however, showed no signs of urgency. Perhaps he was out.

But out where?

Dargan's file had been the one Fitzgerald had seized on when I brought my collection of Possibles back upstairs. She remembered Dargan. She'd worked on his case years ago at the start of her career when he was charged with murdering a woman who lived in the next street and the attempted murder of another woman not five minutes' walk from his home. He wasn't a man who believed in putting too much effort into finding victims. He wasn't fussy.

As long as they were near by, she said, they'd suffice.

That's probably why he was caught so quickly.

What she didn't know was that he'd been released from prison two months ago and was now living in the Liberties, near Marsha Reed's house. The small spire of St Gobnat's peeked above the house opposite. Dargan must've seen it every day when he opened his curtains.

If he ever *did* open them.

'God knows why they let the creep out,' Fitzgerald muttered, her eyes hidden behind dark glasses. 'He can't have done more than ten years. Some justice.'

'What happened to you telling Healy yesterday that it wasn't your business what happened to offenders after they got to court?'

'Screw that,' she said. 'And screw Dargan as well. Where *is* he?'

She rapped again impatiently on the front door.

'Maybe he's skipped town,' I suggested. 'Would *you* hang around waiting for the police to come and pick you up if you really *had* killed Marsha Reed?'

'Dargan wasn't too bright,' she pointed out, 'and I doubt he's become a brain surgeon in the intervening years. He's probably hiding behind the sofa, hoping we'll go away. For Christ's sake, Terence,' she raised her voice, knocking at the door again, 'we only want to ask you a few questions.' Then she stopped abruptly. 'You hear that?'

'No, what?'

'*That.*'

We both pressed our ears to the door and listened. Now that she'd pointed it out to me, I *could* hear it. A low humming, like machinery, coming from somewhere within.

'Maybe that's why he can't hear us,' I said.

'The noise isn't that loud,' said Fitzgerald.

She knelt down and lifted the flap of the letterbox to peer inside.

'Nothing,' she said. 'You take a look.'

I saw a narrow corridor, threadbare carpet, peeling wallpaper. The light inside was yellow, the filtered essence of the few fragments of sunlight that had managed to find their way inside and then been trapped, as surely as the fly in the window.

A small pile of letters lay behind the door, undisturbed.

'What do you think?' said Fitzgerald.

'I'd say he *has* run out on you.'

'*Bastard.*'

'He can't have gone far,' I reassured her. 'Like you said, he's not the sharpest tool in the box, and he's only recently out of prison. He'll not have much money on him.'

'Come on, then. No point hanging around.'

It only took one phone call from Fitzgerald's car to get the necessary warrant to enter Terence Dargan's property. In that time, a van had arrived with the equipment to break down the door and a couple of extra armed officers in case of trouble, and an ordinary summer's day in the city suddenly took on a new air of curiosity for nearby residents.

They hung on their gates, watching expectantly.

'Soon as you're ready,' Fitzgerald told the newly arrived officers.

The muffled bang as the front door of Terence Dargan's house was thrown off its hinges and back into the dingy hallway sounded like distant thunder, but almost as soon as it had faded it was replaced by that humming again, only it was louder now and less like machinery. Now it sounded more like some kind of demented chanting coming from deep underground, the kind of noise that could drive a being crazy if they listened to it too long, looking for meaning or sense in its relentless rhythm. *What could it be?*

The answer came as soon as Fitzgerald entered the house and opened the door of the front room, where the curtains had been closed against the light.

'Dargan, are you –?'

Through the first crack, flies swarmed out, the hum broken free at last and given shape and form, filling the air and turning it black, a spreading cloud that kept expanding like smoke until the air around us was almost used up greedily by them, and I had to cover my mouth to stop myself swallowing them. The two armed officers who had accompanied us were not so lucky. They bent over, coughing, as their mouths filled up, and they knelt, spitting out what looked like thick black blood but was only the bodies of the flies they hadn't been fast enough to avoid tasting. One ran back to the garden and vomited violently.

The flies caught in our hair, shivered their way inside our clothes.

I felt sick as I watched them, as I *felt* them, but what made me even more nauseous was the acrid stench that they carried out with them from the enclosed room.

The unmistakable sweet smell of the dead.

Slowly the cloud of flies was getting smaller. It had found the open door and headed for light and freedom, and if I was superstitious I could almost have imagined it as the physical manifestation of an evil soul let loose on the world, dispersing to continue its dark work in new homes now that the old one was of no further use as nourishment or shelter.

The old house was Terence Dargan.

At least I presume it had been Terence Dargan once. All it was now was a corpse in the advanced stages of decomposition, sitting by a rusty gas fire set with screws into the wall. By now he was little more than rotting rags hanging from a frame of bone and still looking moist, the corrupted flesh partly fused into the fibres of the chair on which he sat.

This was where the flies had come from.

Sarcophagidae.

More commonly known as flesh flies. They could smell a fresh corpse from several miles away. They were attracted to the bodies of the dead once the maggots and the blowflies had done their work. Not that there was often much left once the maggots had taken their fill. Maggots could devour half a corpse in a week. Up to 300 other insects could also be present, depending on where and when the body was left after death. Spiders. Beetles.

Analysis of the larvae of the flies would help pinpoint exactly when death had occurred in this room. It could take as little as ten minutes before the first blowflies arrived, colonizing open wounds and orifices, and from that moment the parasites appeared in a predictable sequence. All you needed to do was to calculate backwards to the time the victim died.

Studying the insect activity in the bodies of the dead could also determine whether wounds were inflicted pre- or post-mortem, whether the body had been moved, sometimes even the cause of death. Not that it would matter much in this case, I guessed.

I'm no forensic entomolgist, but even I could tell that Terence Dargan, if indeed this was him, must have been dead before Marsha Reed met her killer.

He couldn't be our man.

It was after midnight by the time I picked up my Jeep from Dublin Castle and returned, alone, to my building, turning off the street and down the short ramp into the underground car park that was shared among the residents of this building and the adjoining one.

I never liked coming down here. During the day was not so bad, but after dark it was a claustrophobic, dank, eerie place. Couple of times I'd even heard rats running around. Rats are creatures I just can't stomach. There must be something primeval in the fear, something that goes right back to the time when we squatted in mud huts and rats meant death.

There was also a stale smell that suggested the winos used it as a place to sleep.

And worse.

It was supposed to be patrolled. That was why we paid our service charge, right? But I'd never seen anyone else down here the times I came except fellow residents with whom to pass on the same complaints. And tonight there was no one there at all, and all the lights but one over by the door leading to the elevator looked like they were broken.

The headlights skittered across the walls as I turned into my usual space and switched off the engine. Then I saw – what?

Something had moved. I'd caught a glimpse of it shifting slightly in the rear-view mirror, but when I turned it was gone. Probably one of the bums, I told myself sternly. Get a grip. But I felt nervous as I climbed out. I paused a moment with the door open under my hand in case I needed to get back in again and lock the doors behind me.

Nothing happened.

I reassured myself there was nothing there, that I was just feeling jumpy after the events at Terence Dargan's house a few hours earlier, and locked the door with a high-pitched beep. The light in the car flashed brightly for a moment, then extinguished itself; and now there was only the pale orange light from the streetlights outside at the top of the ramp leaking in for illumination, and what seemed like the distant haven of the light above the door.

Between the pillars that held up the roof, shadows lurked. The windshields of the parked cars were like black mirrors reflecting blackness back, so that the more you stared at them the more they began to look like holes into which you might fall if you weren't careful.

The air was stifling and hot, even after midnight. It was like all the hot air of the city had fled here during the day to escape and had then become trapped. Now it was heating up this space like the blast from a restaurant kitchen. I could feel the heat pounding in my head, which in turn dulled my sense of hearing, and that made things seem worse.

Carefully, I began to make my way across the car park.

I could hear the murmur of traffic in the streets above head level, and even the sound of music drifting over from some bar. But in here my footsteps sounded unnaturally loud.

I found myself concentrating on the sound they made, like a monk contemplating the sound of running water as an aid to prayer. My heart was racing in my chest. I didn't know what was wrong with me. It wasn't like me to be so nervous. I didn't usually –

I spun round.

There.

There *was* something, I knew it. Something behind that car over there, the Mini which belonged to the neurotic woman who lived opposite me, who fed the pigeons from her balcony and even let them fly inside, according to Hugh.

Not that you could always believe what Hugh said.

Christ alone knew what he told people about *me*.

But something *was* moving there.

I could see it.

'Come out!' I said with more confidence than I felt. 'I know you're there!'

Something shifted slightly in the dark.

I took a step forward.

'Come out, I said.'

A couple more steps toward the Mini, quickening my pace to cover my trepidation, wishing that I had something more than keys in my hand to defend myself.

Though you could do worse than have keys for a weapon.

There were times in the past when I *had* done worse, and I was still around to tell the tale.

I paused a final moment, before jerking forward quickly to startle whoever was hiding there into revealing themselves – and then I jumped as something rushed out past my feet, and I let out a cry, remembering the rats. Only it wasn't a rat, but a black cat with luminous green eyes which must have wandered in here to get some shelter from the heat.

Or else someone in the building had taken in a cat against regulations.

The cat was now cowering under the next car, staring out at me with wide frightened eyes. Feeling guilty, I got down on my haunches and held out a hand and tried to make some cat-friendly noises, but they obviously didn't convince this cat because he didn't look like he intended coming anywhere near me. And I can't say I blame him.

I wouldn't have trusted me either.

'Go fuck yourself, then, you fleabitten little rag,' I muttered to myself irritably as I got to my feet again and turned round.

The cry was out of me before I could hold it in.

Kaminski was standing right behind me.

'What're you playing at?' I yelled at him. 'You near scared me to death.'

'What were you doing at Marsha Reed's house?' was all he said to that.

I couldn't speak. I saw him in the dimness and he looked half deranged. In fact, forget the bit about being only half deranged. His eyes were wide and staring, like he'd just stuck his finger into a live socket. His skin looked flushed and blotchy. He had the vague, slightly unfocused look of a man who'd been drinking. Though in truth, I only remembered what he looked like afterwards. At the time, all I could think of was what he'd just said.

'Marsha Reed?' I echoed, taking a step back as I did so, not liking anyone to get that close. It makes me uneasy. Especially when they're clearly in an emotionally unsteady mood.

'Yeah, Marsha Reed. The dead woman. You know who I'm talking about,' Kaminski said, his voice rising with irritation. 'What were you doing there earlier?'

'What were *you* doing there?' I answered.

He paused at that.

'I had my reasons,' he muttered.

'Then I had my reasons too. Two can play at that game.'

'What game?'

'I haven't a clue. Whatever game it is you're playing here right now, hiding out here, sneaking up on me . . .'

He suddenly looked apologetic.

'Look, I'm sorry about that, OK? I was pissed with you. I just wanted to –'

'Scare the crap out of me. Yeah, I noticed.'

'I was going to say I wanted to give you a taste of your own medicine,' he said quietly. 'It was a bad idea, I see that now. I've said I'm sorry.'

I took a deep breath. 'Look,' I said, 'we can't talk here. You'd better come up to my apartment. I've been in your hotel room, it's only fair I return the compliment, right?'

He caught my eye and smiled at the reminder. Suddenly he didn't look so unnerving. He was under pressure and I was jumpy, that's all it was.

'And then,' I added, 'you can tell me what the hell's going on.'

'I'm not sure I know the answer to that question myself,' Kaminski said.

A loud rattle alerted us to the fact that another car had crossed the grate at the top of the ramp, and in the next second a bright explosion of headlights cut the gloom around us, like an intruder bursting in. I recognized the Mercedes as it turned into a far corner.

'It's just a man who lives on the floor below me. Come on,' I said, 'why don't we go upstairs where it's quieter and I can fix you coffee or something?'

He didn't say anything on the way up the stairs, nor in the hall as I stood looking in my pocket for my new key. Only when I stepped inside and switched on the lights did he break his silence, whistling appreciatively as he looked around at my apartment.

'So this is where you're hiding out these days,' he said. 'Nice place.'

'You're the one who's hiding, JJ,' I said.

'Don't call me that,' he said.

'Don't call you what?'

'JJ,' he said. 'I hate it. I always hated it.'

'I'm sorry,' I shrugged. 'I didn't realize you felt so strongly about it.'

'You never bothered to ask,' he said, and then, as if to cover his embarrassment for having been so touchy about a mere name, he said: 'Nice apartment.'

'Make yourself at home,' I said. 'I'll get the coffee.'

From the kitchen, I watched him walk over and take a seat, leafing idly through a pile of academic periodicals on the low table in front of him.

'*The Journal of Research on Crime and Delinquency* ... *The Canadian Journal of Criminology and Corrections* ... *Advances in Criminological Research*,' he read out as he rifled through them. 'I can see your reading habits haven't changed much.'

'There's a copy of the *National Enquirer* in there somewhere, if the other stuff's a bit too highbrow for you,' I said, spooning coffee into the cafetière. 'Apparently, the latest issue says that Nixon was an alien. Like this is supposed to be a surprise. Or was it Jerry Springer? I can't remember. One or the other.'

'Are you ever serious about anything?'

'Not if I can avoid it. Here.'

I handed a cup to Kaminski, then sat down opposite him across the table, taking my chance to get a better look at him in a brighter light. The deranged look had almost entirely vanished now, replaced by something that looked more like weariness. The sort of weariness that makes your bones ache with the misery of the effort of staying awake and the greater misery of not knowing why it's even worth staying awake to begin with.

'So,' I said. 'You going to tell me what this is all about?'

21

Kaminski didn't answer directly. For a long time, he didn't answer at all. He just nursed his cup of coffee like it was winter out and he needed the warmth. Eventually he put it down on top of one of the magazines, reached into his pants, took out his wallet and opened it up.

He withdrew a photograph and held it out to me.

Taking it in my fingers, I saw a picture of a woman in her mid thirties, with her hair in dreadlocks and wearing shades. She had just turned round, perhaps someone had called her name, and the camera had caught her unguarded and unposed. She was laughing.

'Is this your wife?' I said.

'Heather,' said Kaminski. 'Her name was Heather. I met her through work. She was a secretary in one of the field offices. She wanted to be a Special Agent. She was going out with someone at the time, he was in the FBI too, he didn't want her to get involved, said it was too dangerous, but I tried to encourage her. Told her to go for it. You only live once.'

The words caught in his throat, and he looked away, to the window, staring out, then took another swig of coffee. By the time he spoke again, he'd managed to get it together.

'Nothing happened at first because, like I say, she was with this other guy. Then they split up and I took the chance to ask her out. We got married three months later. Had our honeymoon in Vegas.'

'I never had you down as the marrying type,' I said gently.

'I wasn't. You know me. Girl in every port. Marrying was never on my agenda. Then Heather came along. You said it yourself the other day. People change. We all do.'

'You want to tell me what happened?'

'We were living in New York, at my apartment. You remember my apartment?'

'I'll never forget it. Your office had more human touches than that place.'

'Heather gave it the human touch. She made it more homely. She bought curtains, new stuff for the bedroom, sheets in pastel colours, all that kind of shit. There were ornaments everywhere too. She filled the place with them. I don't know why women buy them.'

'I don't either,' I admitted.

'I didn't mind. I was glad she was making the place her own. She was still working as a secretary, but I was trying to see if I could get her on a training programme for the Bureau. I had these visions of our working together. Man and wife crime-fighting team.' He smiled at the memory. 'It was probably insane, but when you're in love you think insane thoughts. Maybe that's how you *know* you're in love.'

'What happened?'

'I was at home. A rare day off. I'd spent the morning pottering around the place aimlessly, enjoying being free. She was at work. On the way home, she called to ask if there was anything we needed. I said we needed milk. That was the last time I spoke to her. She never got home. A couple of days later, they found her. She'd been abducted, murdered. Her body was dumped down by the river. The rats had eaten away half her face. She still had the milk in her bag when the body was found. That and a Hershey's Cookies 'n' Crème candy bar. She knew I loved those. I found out later she'd stopped off at a 7/11 a couple of blocks from the apartment. Somewhere between there and home she disappeared.'

The flow of words was halted again. His hands gripped the cup tightly.

'I'm sorry,' I said quietly. I hate people who take refuge behind those trite catchphrases, but what else was there to say?

'The man who found the body and raised the alarm', Kaminski said, 'was called Buck Randall.' He said the name with distaste, like each syllable hurt. 'Buck Randall III, for Christ's sakes. He was a prison officer on Death Row down in Texas. The Terrell Unit. You know. He told the police he was up in New York seeing friends and sightseeing, and just saw her body on the mud down by the river when he was passing over the bridge.'

'You obviously didn't believe he found it merely by accident.'

'Nor did the cops initially. They said he was edgy, he kept changing little details of his story, nothing that amounted to anything in itself but taken together set your alarm bells ringing. You know how it is. When they examined the CCTV footage from the store where Heather had bought the milk on the way home, they discovered that he'd been in there around the same time. He left a couple of minutes after she did.'

'That's some coincidence.'

'Damn right it was. I checked his records and I also found he had priors for assaulting his ex-wife. An ex-wife, what's more, who'd later disappeared herself after moving, supposedly, to Arizona, only no one in Arizona had ever heard of her. He'd also been questioned about another murder in New Mexico five, six years ago. I knew it was him. He probably saw Heather in the store, maybe he'd been looking for the right woman to target and she came along, he decided she was the one. But in the end the cops let him go. They said they had nothing. Forensics didn't match up. He had a witness who said he met him in a bar down the street five minutes after he left the store. What could they do? They held him for a while, questioned him, next thing he's walking out of there, no charges, nothing.'

'It was risky,' I said, 'being the one to discover the body. He must've have known his face would show on the CCTV.'

'Some of these bastards get a kick out of taking risks like that. Who knows what goes through these assholes' heads? You were in the FBI. You studied the same stuff as me. They have impulses we can't even being to fathom. They take trophies, they want to be acknowledged, they play games with the cops.'

'But the cops didn't think so?'

'They told me to go home. They even made a complaint about me to the Bureau.'

'A complaint?'

'They said I was harassing them. Harassing them. What are they? Choir girls? More like they couldn't stand the fact I wasn't willing to simply let the whole thing go. Sure, what was my problem? It was only my wife.'

'How did the Bureau react?'

'I was hauled up and told to drop the whole thing. Take six months off. Go to Barbados. You know the kind of bullshit they pull. They said I'd feel better if I had a break, that maybe I'd be able to put it all in perspective. That's the word they used. Perspective.'

'I'm guessing you didn't make it to Barbados.'

'I told them to stick their job. I quit. Said I couldn't see the point any more. Upholding justice and going after the bad guys and all that crap when I couldn't even protect my own wife, when a woman's murder could just be put down on the It Can Wait shelf.'

'What was your plan?'

'I just wanted to do some digging. I'd been in the FBI. I knew how to find things out. I wanted to find out all I could about him. From what I'd seen of the crime scene in New York, I knew the whole thing had been planned more closely than they thought. There was a determination there. A direction. That kind of thing didn't come out of nowhere. The guy who did it had done it before. And, even if he hadn't, he'd do it again.'

'So you followed him back home?'

'To Huntsville,' he nodded. 'I got an apartment near the prison where he worked. I didn't need money. I had plenty of that saved. My folks were dead by then, they'd left me some stocks and a house that I could sell quickly if I needed extra cash. I found out where Randall lived. I found out where he went to the gym, where he hung out with his friends, the bars where he drank, the strip joints where he usually went after work. I used to sit a couple of tables away from him and he had no idea who I was. Probably thought I was another pathetic inadequate loser like him. It was hard, though. I had a hunch that maybe he was committing his crimes away from Texas, maybe he took a trip each vacation somewhere new and did what he had to do. I couldn't know if or when he made a booking. What was I to do? All I could do was follow him around and wait for him to make a mistake.'

'And did he?'

'He didn't put a foot wrong,' said Kaminski. 'He went to work, he came home, he visited his little elderly mother in Austin once a week. So that's when I had to start making some new moves. Taking some risks. I found the people he worked with inside the prison and asked a few questions.

I found out that Randall was pretty close to a guy inside named Jenkins Howler. Howler had killed several women about ten years back and had spent the whole time in prison since waiting to get what was coming to him. You know that much. You checked him out. He and Randall were apparently thick as thieves. Randall used to bring him in books, dirty magazines, give him extra rations, that sort of thing.'

'Very cosy,' I said.

'It'd make you sick,' said Kaminski. 'Howler was scheduled for execution in two months' time, they were going through the usual appeals and stuff, I used to see crowds protesting outside the prison sometimes, though it wasn't going to do any good. Howler was dead meat. But it didn't surprise me that Randall and Howler were friends. If Randall was the sort of man I thought he was, he was bound to find the company agreeable, right? Those people can smell their own. Could be it was getting so close to Howler that had given Randall the courage to act out his own fantasies, who knows? Maybe Howler had seen his weakness and worked on him, wanting someone to continue the good work after he'd gone. I didn't have it nailed yet, but I knew that I was getting close, that this was the key to where it all lay.'

'It sounds like there's a but coming up,' I said.

'There was a *big* but. One morning I got a knock on my door from the local police. Someone had tipped them off to where I was, what I was doing. It was my own fault. I took too many risks asking round about Randall. I got too close to him. The cops were there to warn me to stay away from him. He'd taken out a exclusion order on me. I wasn't allowed within half a mile of where he lived or worked. They said he was afraid I was going to do something. I reminded them it was a free country, and I could go where

I liked. They reminded me that there was an arrest warrant pending if I stepped one inch out of line.'

'So let me guess. You flew straight back to New York and forgot all about it.'

Kaminski smiled genuinely for the first time that night.

'You know me well,' he said. 'I kept my head down for a few days, realized I needed to go more carefully. Only it didn't turn out that way. Couple of weeks later, Randall did a bunk. He didn't come into work one day, or the next, contacted no one to tell them where he was. Next thing I know the police are back, accusing me of having murdered him.'

'You must admit you were the obvious suspect.'

'Thankfully, like I said, I'd been keeping my head down, hanging out, doing normal stuff, and there were plenty of people who could vouch for me. But it was tricky for a while. They even tried to suggest that I'd paid some hitman to finish him off.'

'You hadn't?' I said.

He looked at me across the table.

'If I wanted Randall dead, I'd have finished the job myself,' he said starkly, and I believed him. I remembered the similar threats Todd Fleming had made earlier that day about the man who killed Marsha Reed. Kaminski wasn't the only one who felt the need for revenge. 'But at least I thought now they'd listen, now they'd know that Randall was up to no good. He'd realized I was on to him and that was why he'd flitted. How obvious did he have to make it before they'd see? But they *still* wouldn't listen. Told me to forget it again. That I was obsessed. They said *I* was the one who needed locking up. They said it was being afraid of me that had made Randall run, and he'd turn up eventually when he felt safe again. They actually felt sorry for the guy. They said I was persecuting him. They couldn't see I was the victim, I was the one who was suffering. I felt like I was further away from my goal than ever. I wasn't ever going to find him now. He could be anywhere. I couldn't even be sure he was still in the States. For all I knew, he'd gone down to Mexico . . .' Behind Kaminski, the sound of the traffic was dulled, lessened. I realized how long we must have been talking.

I stole a glance at the clock and saw that it was 2 a.m.

'What did you do?'

'I didn't really have a plan,' he admitted. 'I thought maybe I'd go back to New York and see if I could persuade some of the guys in the Bureau to help me out, see if they could turn up Randall somewhere in the system. It's not so easy to vanish. There're social security numbers, people need to rent cars, take planes. He was bound to leave a trail some time. Slugs always do. Part of me also thought that if I could get them to provide me with lists of similar attacks on women, maybe women killed in convenience stores, 7/11s, that maybe I'd get a pattern in my head of what he'd done before and be able to predict where he might hit next.'

'Sounds like a long shot,' I said.

'It *was* a long shot. It was the longest shot I've ever attempted in my life. I was just grasping at straws, trying not to sink. As it happened, what I actually did was just hang around Texas for a few months to see if he came back. I'd reached the end of whatever ingenuity I had. I was spent. And then,' he paused for effect, 'I got something in the mail.'

'The newspaper clipping at the hotel,' I said.

'The very same. That clipping told me about the death in Dublin of a woman I'd never heard of; with it was a typewritten note saying *Are you really going to give up that easily?* It said that if I really wanted to meet up with him, I had to fly to

Dublin and book into the hotel where you tracked me down under the name Buck Randall and wait. He'd make contact.'

'What did you think?'

'What did I think? I didn't know what to think. I couldn't see how a woman being run over in Dublin connected to what Randall had done to Heather, and yet there it was in black and white. He'd sent it to me. It had to mean something.'

'You're sure it came from him?'

'By that time, I wasn't sure about anything. But I didn't have the luxury of sitting round waiting to see what would happen. I was out of ideas. It was all I had. I found an internet café and went online to see what I could find out about her, but I didn't find out much more than was contained in the news item I'd been sent. It wasn't exactly the kind of story CNN had covered in depth, put it that way. But I did learn that she'd been writing to Jenkins Howler. And then I was more confused than ever. She'd been writing to Howler, and now she was dead. Had Howler sent Randall over to kill her? You know what those relationships are like. They're sick enough to start with. They certainly don't want the woman they're writing to striking up another sick romance with the next guy along on Death Row after they've gone. What better way of putting a line under the relationship than to have her done away with?'

'But she hadn't *been* killed,' I reminded him. 'She died in an accident.'

'Exactly. And there was one other flaw to the theory.'

'She died while Randall was still in Texas.'

'So how could he have done it? Yeah, that was the problem. But there was still the same question. Why then had Randall sent me the note telling me about this woman? I had a few theories about that. That he wanted us to continue

206

whatever game we'd been playing elsewhere. That he hadn't liked the odds back home and preferred to take his chances elsewhere, in a new arena, and that this was the lure to get me to follow him. Equally, I wondered if there *was* more to the woman's death than met the eye, and I knew I wasn't going to learn the answer to that out in Texas. That's why I came to Dublin.'

'Why didn't you just give the note the police in Texas? Or the FBI?'

'They hadn't listened to me all along. Why should they suddenly listen now? They'd just think it was more evidence I was for the funny farm. Or they'd say I sent it to myself or something. I'd be wasting my time – and worse, they'd know what my next move would be. They'd know I was bound to follow Randall to Dublin. I'd have made it too easy for them.'

It sounded fair enough.

I lifted the empty mugs and carried them back into the kitchen.

'I checked out Cecelia Corrigan's death myself,' I told him as I rinsed out the mugs and put them into the dishwasher, 'and I absolutely don't think there *was* anything more to it than an accident. The local police know who did it, he was never under any suspicion, there were witnesses. There was nothing mysterious about it at all.'

'I know,' he said. 'That's the part that got me. I seemed to be back again where I started. And that's why I thought about contacting you, seeing if you could help. You were on the outside too, like me. The difference was that you know this city and I don't. If anyone could find Randall, I knew it was you. Especially after you found *me*.'

'And then what?'

'I just want justice,' said Kaminski.

I wondered what exactly he meant, but I was almost afraid to ask.

Did he want justice or revenge of a more immediate kind?

'Don't get me wrong,' I said. 'I don't have any objection to murderers getting what's coming to them. I'm the last person in the world to take the moral high ground where that's concerned. But making sure you get the right guy is kind of important too.'

'That's why I thought working together made sense.'

'If it was so important, why give me the brush-off this lunchtime?'

'Like I told you, I wanted to make you sweat it. I wanted to make you wait a while to put you in your place. I thought I had time.'

'You're saying you don't?'

'I don't have a single minute to waste any more. When I got back to my hotel after talking to you, there was *another* note from Buck Randall waiting for me.'

The room was white, anonymous, antiseptic, made almost unbearable by the heat – and even more unbearable by some of the people sitting round the table that morning.

At the head of the table sat Fitzgerald, with Sean Healy on one side of her and Patrick Walsh on the other. Those three, I didn't mind. Dr Fisher was supposed to be there too but hadn't been able to make it, so I felt like a captured cowboy in injun territory. I was sitting down near the other end of the desk, marvelling at how history repeats itself. At school I was always hiding out at the back of the class, hoping not to be noticed, hating the people up front with their hands in the air, desperate for approval. Now here I was lurking near the back again, though my chances of going unnoticed this morning were about as good as a goat's chances of making it to a long and happy retirement when placed in the lions' enclosure at the zoo.

Seamus Dalton, who was sitting at the other end of the table to me, near where the action was, kept shooting sly glances off in my direction, making it clear what he thought of seeing me back again. There were other detectives there too that I knew by sight – Stack, Kilbane, Ledger. They weren't openly hostile as such, just indifferent to whatever difficulties I might be experiencing or how isolated I felt. And I wasn't going to blame them for that.

No one likes an intruder.

I remembered the first time I'd been here to help on a case. I'd found myself sitting next to Niall Boland, who'd done his best to make me welcome. I'd valued his friendship. This morning I was appreciating him all the more, and simultaneously cursing him for ducking out in search of the quiet life and leaving me to face all this crap alone.

At least this wasn't the full team that had been assembled over the murder of Marsha Reed, only the lead detectives. I couldn't say I was sorry to have missed the whole team, since the scepticism which I could feel coming off this small group was bad enough.

'Let me get this straight,' Dalton was saying. 'Some screwball that you used to work with in the FBI has been playing hide-and-seek with the man he thinks murdered his wife, and now you want us to believe that the same man murdered Marsha Reed?'

'I'm not asking you to believe anything,' I said tightly, for what felt like the thousandth time since the meeting had begun. 'I'm just telling you what Kaminski told me. He got a delivery in his box at the hotel where he's staying yesterday morning. Inside was a newspaper clipping on the murder of Marsha Reed with a handwritten message saying: *How many more women have to die before you get your act together?* He took it as evidence that the man who killed his wife was taunting him about having killed Marsha Reed too.'

'And we're supposed to take the word of a guy who's been booking himself into hotels under the name of the man he thinks murdered his wife? Sounds fucked up to me.'

'He was only doing what he was told to do,' I said as patiently as I could. 'He was only following leads. That's why he went round to Marsha Reed's house to check things out.'

Which is where he saw me. It was no wonder he'd been confused. He thought I must've worked out myself the connection between what happened to his wife and Marsha Reed's death, but how could I have done that when he'd only been sent the note himself that morning? Had he missed something real obvious? He didn't know that I had no inkling there was any connection between the two strands before he himself pulled that rabbit out of the hat. I *still* didn't know if there was any connection. It all seemed so bizarre.

And now I felt like I was betraying him.

Felt it like a knot in my chest.

Last night he'd sworn me to secrecy. He didn't trust the police with the information, he said. If they got involved now, Randall would know it. He'd vanish again. Kaminski would lose him once more. '*You and me, we can get him, together,*' he'd said. '*We can bring him in. The cops have messed up too many times. They don't deserve another chance. I do.*'

I'd never seen him so desperate.

Instead, after he left, I'd watched him from on high through the window like his guardian angel as he crossed the road below, weaving through the minimal traffic on the road at that late hour. At the far kerb, he looked over his shoulder without breaking stride, glanced back toward the building and waved up at me. I waved back.

Soon as he was out of sight, I picked up the phone and called Grace.

I had no doubt I was doing the right thing. I'd seen the pictures of Marsha Reed's body. I couldn't conceal evidence that potentially might reel in her killer. Moreover, whatever he might think or say once he learned what I'd done, I knew this was the best way to help Kaminski. This was his best chance to catch Randall. No one had believed him before. Now the police were in the middle of an active murder investigation. They'd have to take his story on board. He just wasn't thinking straight right now.

Though if he saw Seamus Dalton that morning, Kaminski

would hardly be reassured that the police in Dublin would take him any more seriously than the police in Texas had.

'I'm just telling you what the man said,' I found myself telling Dalton and hating myself for even trying to mollify him. 'I didn't say Buck Randall actually killed Marsha.'

'Too right he didn't fucking kill her,' Dalton sneered right back.

'What makes you so sure?' said Walsh.

I was glad to see someone wasn't dismissing the idea out of hand.

'What makes me so sure?' echoed Dalton incredulously, looking at a couple of the other cops for confirmation, as if this was the dumbest thing he'd ever heard. 'What makes me so sure is a little thing called evidence. Namely, the lack of it.'

'There's not much evidence against Victor Solomon either,' Walsh said equably.

'What about what Todd Fleming said?' answered Dalton. 'We only have his word for it that Marsha told him Solomon had beaten her up. And she might have been lying herself. Even if it's true, it doesn't prove he killed her.'

'There's still more than there is against this Texan prison guard who might not even be in Dublin for all we know. You're forgetting the report from Dr Fisher.' Dalton hated psychological analysis, profiling, all that fancy bullshit, as he called it, but he didn't mind using it when it helped him make a point or put someone down. 'Most of what we got was the usual airy-fairy waffle about the killer having an emotionally stunted background and issues to do with self-esteem, like that has anything to do with anything. But one thing his report did say is that this was no stranger-on-stranger killing. You read it. It said the killer felt comfortable at the scene. How was the imaginary Buck Randall III supposed to get familiar with Marsha Reed's house when he didn't know her from a hole in the ground?'

'Imaginary?' I said. 'What's that supposed to mean?'

'It means we've got no reason to believe this Buck, Chuck, Fuck, whatever he's called, is even in the country. Since we all lost sleep overnight after being roused by your contribution to the investigation, Special Agent, everything's been checked, and what did we come up with? Zippo. Zilch. A big fat zero. Diddly squat, as you'd probably say.'

'He'd hardly come into the city under his own name,' I said testily.

'If you ask me, he didn't come into the country at all.'

'Then how did he send the messages to Kaminski?' said Walsh, jumping in again.

'Am I the only one who's noticed that there's no evidence anyone sent *anything* to Mr Leon Kaminski? Because strangely enough he didn't bring along the notes he claims he got from his wife's killer to show to Little Ms FBI, and the only evidence he got anything the first time is a scrap torn from a newspaper. I could've got that myself.'

'He left them back in his hotel,' I said.

'That's right, he conveniently left them in his hotel. But even if there were notes,' Dalton went on, his voice getting louder to stop Walsh interrupting again, 'even if there were a thousand notes on pieces of parchment, written in gold ink, for all we know they could be coming from himself. For all we know, losing his wife could've sent him loco' — he mimed a twirling motion with his fingers at the side of his ear — 'he could have a whole colony of bats up there in the belfry now. You ever stop to think maybe this whole story about some killer on the run is just a fantasy he dreamed up?'

'You'll be saying next his wife wasn't killed at all.'

'She was killed all right,' said Sean Healy. 'That much we do know. I called the NYPD last night. They confirmed that the body of a woman named Heather Kaminski had been recovered from the side of the river in New York on October 10th last. They told me the case was still ongoing, though I think we can all guess what that means.'

'Then maybe *you* sent the notes to him,' Dalton said to me, 'so that you could get your foot back inside the door here.'

'Dalton, you're so full of crap they could use your body for fertilizer.'

'I'm serious. How come everything has to be about you? No sooner have you *graced* us with your presence again than the whole fucking case starts to revolve around you. We couldn't have an ordinary murder in the city. Oh no, that'd be too simple. That'd be too boring for you. Instead it has to all centre on you and your fancy American friends again.'

'That's enough,' said Fitzgerald quietly. 'I said enough,' she added when I opened my mouth to reply to Dalton. 'This isn't getting us anywhere.'

She was good at that. Like any good referee, she didn't police passion or argument, but she knew when it had gone too far and needed to be checked back into coolness. Nothing could be gained from Dalton and I sniping at one another like children. There was something about the man, though, that just made me lose it. His entire existence was calculated to offend me, and it was pretty clear that he felt the same way about me.

We didn't understand each other.

We never would.

What's more, we didn't *want* to.

'Dalton's right,' Fitzgerald went on, taking control. 'Up to a point,' she continued when Dalton started to look smug.

'Everything we know about the crime scene, about Marsha Reed's life, about the psychological shape of this crime, makes it unlikely that this man, Buck Randall, is our killer. But that doesn't mean we can casually ignore what Leon Kaminski told Saxon. Every lead has to be checked. Every path has to be followed.'

'But this Heather woman was strangled,' said Dalton insolently, refusing to let it go. 'And she wasn't killed in her house either. The MO's completely different.'

'Not entirely,' answered Fitzgerald, unruffled. 'She was tied up, remember, just like Marsha. What's more, when her body was found, Heather's ring was missing too. That's one connection we can't ignore.'

'Kaminski never told me that,' I said.

'Why would he? The press might know about the severed finger, but they haven't found out about Marsha's missing ring yet. He had no way of knowing that possibly tied the two crimes together.'

Dalton looked unconvinced but settled this time for a resentful silence.

'So you want us to look for this man, Chief?' said Walsh.

'First things first,' said Fitzgerald. 'That means establishing whether anyone can identify him as having been in the vicinity of the killing. I called the Texas police department this morning. They confirmed that Randall was close to this Jenkins Howler inside, and they also confirmed that Randall was reported missing when he failed to appear for work for a few days running, and was investigated as a missing persons case. But they said that three months later Randall called and said he'd been visiting his brother in Oklahoma and that he was sorry, he hadn't realized people were searching for him, but he wasn't coming back. Seems he had some debts hanging over him he wanted to escape.'

'Big debts?' said Healy.

'All debts are big if you can't afford to pay them off. Now whether you believe that or not, he's not wanted for any crime, he's not broken any laws, he hasn't skipped bail, nothing, so as far as they're concerned if he's in Dublin that's his concern. He's free to go where he likes. But I explained the situation, and' – she opened the file in front of her – 'they did send through this photograph of him from the prison records to help us look for him.'

She handed the picture to Sean Healy, who passed it to Dalton, who passed it down the line till it reached me. I saw a man like any other. Small square face, tiny eyes, neat moustache, untidy scar over his left eyebrow. I glanced at it briefly and passed it on. It went all the way round to Walsh, who tried to hand it back to Fitzgerald to complete the circuit.

She shook her head.

'Give it to Kilbane,' she said. 'Kilbane, I want you to run up some copies and then pass them round discreetly in the area where Marsha Reed lived. Talk to neighbours, shopkeepers, taxi drivers. Ask them if they've ever seen this man hanging round at all. Might turn out to be a thankless task, but if they *do* recognize him, that changes everything.'

'Shall I take it down now, Chief?' said Kilbane.

'Do,' Fitzgerald nodded, and Kilbane scraped back his chair and rose to take the picture downstairs to get copies made. 'And you, Stack, I want you to take these.' Again she handed a loose sheet over. 'Those are Randall's fingerprints. You're going to have to check them against the prints we lifted from Marsha Reed's flat. No need to look so happy about it. It's a tedious job but someone has to do it. Besides, if you get a match the effort will have been more than worth while and you can take all the credit for it. Walsh?'

'Yes, Chief?'

'I want you to run over to speak to Mark Hudson.'

'Mark Hudson?'

'The man who knocked down Cecelia Corrigan,' I said.

'The very same,' said Fitzgerald. 'If Leon Kaminski is right, and there's a killer on the loose in the city, then this is where it all began. Or didn't. The point is we just don't know. The evidence is even more tenuous in relation to this incident than it is with Marsha Reed's death, but we can't afford to blithely ignore it. It will all have to be checked out.'

'It really was an accident,' said Healy. 'I read the file.'

'That's true. But maybe Hudson saw something that could prove crucial. Maybe she stepped in front of the car deliberately. Maybe she was pushed. Maybe she was talking to someone immediately before she died who hasn't been positively IDed.'

'Hudson said nothing about it at the time.'

'It's a long shot,' she confessed, 'but people often remember things a long time after they happen. Especially when there's been a traumatic event. They get flashbacks. Memories. Sometimes they see what happened more clearly weeks after the event than they did when it was happening in front of their eyes. The mind makes an imprint of the event and stores it away for future use. Can we take the risk of ignoring the possibility?'

'No problem, Chief.'

'What about me?' said Dalton.

He had the correct proportion of insolence he could get away with in his voice worked out perfectly each time. He was a master of the nuances of contempt.

'What have you *been* doing?' said Fitzgerald.

'Checking out Marsha's movements the last few days before she died.'

'Then carry on doing that. I said I wanted to check out every lead, I didn't say I wanted to close down old roads every time a new road branches off the main one. This is an augmentation of what we've been doing so far, not a replacement for it. That goes for the rest of you. Just follow the same lines of inquiry as before. There, we're done for this morning. Meet again here at four to see what you've got. Now go to it. And Sean,' she said, as chairs were scraped back and the detectives began to head for the door, 'I want you to take over from me here for the next couple of hours and hold the fort. You know what needs done.'

'Consider it done. What's the story?' asked Healy.

'I want to speak to this Leon Kaminski myself. And you're coming with me, Saxon. I think you should be there when I introduce myself. He knows you. You know him. I want to hear from him myself what he knows about this whole affair.'

'I don't know where he's staying,' I admitted ruefully. 'Last night he left without –'

'That's OK,' said Fitzgerald. 'Dalton found him.'

'Dalton?'

'It was easy,' said Dalton. I hadn't realized he was still there, eavesdropping. He was standing by the door, watching me. 'A few phone calls, that's all it took.'

He made no effort to conceal his glee at having bested me.

'Don't let him bother you,' Healy said to me after Dalton's wide smug ass had made its exit. 'He got one of the sergeants to do it this morning. It makes a difference when you tell hotels you're calling from the DMP for information. They take you much more seriously.'

'The main thing is we know where he is now,' said Fitzgerald. 'He's not the one who's in control like he has been hitherto. Let's go see how he likes that.'

'Right now that doesn't feel like much of an advantage.'

'Every little helps,' she replied, unperturbed. 'Besides, it's all we've got.'

23

It took him so long to answer the door that I began to suspect he wasn't there.

'You think he's moved on again?' I whispered.

'No,' said Fitzgerald. 'Someone's coming.'

A number of emotions crossed Kaminski's face when he opened the door and saw me standing there. First came the shock that I was there at all, then a resigned smile crept into his features, and he murmured: 'So you tracked me down. Does this mean you've decided to –'

And then the door swung open wider and he saw who was standing behind me.

The smile vanished.

'Don't tell me,' he said. 'You're the tooth fairy.'

Fitzgerald held out her badge for him.

Kaminski looked at it, rubbing his face as he did so, rubbing away sleep.

He looked ashen. He needed to shave. I wondered again what his former self would think if he could see himself now. Whether he would even recognize himself.

It was as if the outer form remained roughly similiar, but the person inside had been transplanted and couldn't help exposing itself periodically. Some metaphorical Invasion of the Body Snatchers had taken place in Kaminski. He was like a building whose interior had been ripped out and refashioned. The two halves of himself didn't fit together any more.

'Detective Chief Superintendent Grace Fitzgerald,' he

read aloud. 'I'm honoured.' He handed the ID back without looking at Grace after the initial realization that she was there. Instead his eyes were fixed firmly on me. 'So you sold me out,' was all he said.

'I didn't sell anybody out,' I said thickly.

He didn't answer that. Instead he stepped back and waved a hand. 'I guess you'd better come in,' he said to the both of us. 'Unless you're here to put me under arrest?'

This time he did look at her.

'Why would we be putting you under arrest, Mr Kaminski?' asked Fitzgerald.

He shrugged. 'For withholding vital information from the police, for being in the country under false papers, for sounding my horn in a built-up area after 11 p.m., that sort of thing. I'm sure you can think of something.'

'You didn't tell me you were here on a false passport,' I said.

'You didn't ask,' Kaminski pointed out. 'But you didn't seriously think I'd have come here under my own name, did you? I'm a little tired of everyone knowing where I am.'

'Right now,' said Fitzgerald, stepping into the room briskly, 'I don't much care what name you're travelling under. Our priorities are a little different.'

Kaminski shut the door behind us.

It was a small room, little more than enough space for a bed and a few sticks of furniture. Grey net curtains were drawn over. The light was so sickly it reminded me of Terence Dargan's house and that was something I didn't care to be reminded about. Those flies had haunted my dreams last night. I'd woken more than once imagining I could hear them humming again. In the corner, a TV was switched on. Kaminski had been watching golf. There were the remains of a meagre room-service lunch on a tray. His bag was on a chair, still only half unpacked, as if it hadn't made up its mind whether it was staying.

The bed was crumpled, like he'd been sleeping when we knocked. A half-empty bottle of Jack Daniel's stood on the bedside table next to a tumbler.

Kaminski made no move to remove it. He clearly didn't care what we saw.

Or what we thought about what we saw.

All he did was pick up the TV remote and snap the sound off. He kept the set on, though, so the sight of long acres of green, interrupted occasionally by flashes of blue sky as the camera followed the trajectory of the ball, remained in the background as we talked, and I found I couldn't help my eye straying unconsciously to the set as we spoke.

Kaminski wasn't distracted by it. He didn't glance at it once. He was still staring blankly at us. I sensed we could've been standing there stark naked, and he would scarcely have noticed. Something was dead inside him. Perhaps it was his own capacity to feel alive.

'You must be leading the investigation into that girl's death,' he said finally to Fitzgerald. 'Did Saxon tell you what I told her?'

'She did.'

'Then what are you doing here?' he asked bluntly 'Shouldn't you be out there looking for Buck Randall?'

'We're actively pursuing a number of lines of inquiry, including that one,' Fitzgerald said. 'I hope it turns out to be fruitful. But these things take time. In the meantime, I thought it might help if I spoke to you myself, heard your side of the story.'

'I'm not in the mood to talk right now,' Kaminski said with a show of feigned regret. 'Besides, I'm sure Saxon here has told you all you need to know. I'm confident she's repeated everything I said last night faithfully. What more needs to be said?'

'I realize this is a difficult time for you, Mr Kaminski –'

'Please,' said Kaminski. 'Call me JJ.'

'I thought you hated being called JJ?' I said.

'It doesn't look like it matters any more what I want or don't want,' he said. 'Just tell me this,' he added, turning to me again. 'Did you even give this any thought at all, like I asked you to, or did you just pick up the phone and dial 999 and tell her everything I said?'

'Of course I gave it some thought,' I said wearily. 'That's why I told her. I was the one who *was* thinking.'

'Well, I guess I should've known better than to trust you anyway,' he said to that. 'You always were an insubordinate little shit. You were always questioning everything, always dissatsifed with whatever we were doing, always wanting to take over and do things your own way. You always knew better. Though you've obviously changed some now, huh?'

'What does that mean?'

'It means, look at you, running round doing the police's work for them, running to do their bidding, like a dog fetching a stick. You put it down, you get a pat on the head, they throw you another one.'

'That's not fair,' I said.

'Saxon,' said Kaminski, 'I am way past caring about fair. No offence,' he went on, turning to Fitzgerald, 'but you know we used to have contempt for people like you when we were in the Bureau.'

'Is that so?' said Grace.

'It was always the same. We'd drop in on some little out of the way place, a town, somewhere, anywhere, Nowheresville most of the time, and then instantly you'd just hit this wall. The local police didn't want you treading on their patch, on this little patch of territory that they'd lovingly cultivated, where they were lords of everything, and suddenly here we were, the FBI, dropping in. It was warfare. Sure, the professional rivalry and creative tension could have its uses, keep us on our toes, but we still knew it was warfare.'

'Times change,' I said.

'You're telling me,' he said wryly.

'This is getting us nowhere,' said Fitzgerald. 'Whatever problems you have with involving the police in this matter, the fact is that it's too late now. It's out of your hands. Your best bet is to cooperate as fully as you can with the police in Dublin, whatever you think of our abilities, and see if between us we can't track down this man.'

Kaminski didn't answer. It was like the fight had gone out of him with his last defiant speech. He simply nodded mutely, then sat down on the edge of the bed and regarded us as if to say: *OK, then, what have you got?* Grace answered the unspoken challenge by taking out the original photograph of Buck Randall which she had retrieved from Dublin Castle after copies had been made. She dropped it on to the bed next to Kaminski.

'Is this the man you suspect of killing your wife?'

Kaminski looked at the picture for an eternity, almost like he was trying to decide whether this *was* the same man, but I could see how his fingers tightened on it.

'That's him,' he said grimly in the end.

'Is it a good likeness?' asked Fitzgerald.

'Randall's lost the moustache,' he said. 'This must've been taken when he first joined the prison guard. That must be about, let me think, seven years now? Maybe a little longer? He looks a little older now.' He took out his wallet and prised out a picture. It was a little battered from being in his pocket so long. In this one, Randall was out of uniform and walking in the sun. It looked more natural than the one we had. 'This is the best one I have,' he said. 'It's the one I show people when I want to know if they've seen him. I took this one of him when he came off duty one night,' Kaminski said. 'But it's been three months since I saw him, so I guess he could've changed his appearance again.'

'Can I keep this?' said Fitzgerald.

'No. Like I say, it's the best one I have.'

'You have more of them, then?'

Kaminski smiled grimly. 'You could say that . . .'

Kaminski got to his feet and walked over to the wardrobe. He opened the door and reached inside. He came back carrying a small black holdall. I wondered where he'd been keeping it. It certainly hadn't been in his last hotel room or I'd have found it. He unzipped it and tipped it upside down. A small shower of photographs fell out on to the bed.

There were dozens, all of them of Buck Randall. Kaminski had obviously been watching Randall for a long time. There were shots of him in his car, shots of him outside what I presumed was his front door, shots of him standing at a window, looking out, shots of him pushing a shopping cart piled high with groceries through a parking lot.

'It's lucky the cops never found your collection when they pulled you in,' I said. 'They'd have had you down as a stalker. Where have you been keeping all these?'

'I usually put them in the hotel safe, if that's what you're wondering,' he said. 'You never know who might be breaking into your room next.'

There was a short uncomfortable silence.

I could feel Fitzgerald looking at me.

'You broke into his room?' she said eventually.

'Didn't she tell you that part?' said Kaminski, and he smiled with genuine pleasure for the first time that morning.

I had to admit it was good to see it, even if it was at my expense. It suggested there was some of the old Kaminski still left in there.

'I wouldn't exactly call it breaking in,' I began carefully.

'What would you call it?'

'She bribed a chambermaid to let her in, isn't that right, Saxon?' said Kaminski.

'Shut up, Leon. Who said I bribed her? I spun her a line, is all. I wanted to have a look round, see what he was up to. I didn't know how else to do it. I should've told you,' I admitted to Fitzgerald. 'It didn't seem like the right time. I'm sorry.'

She didn't say anything, just shook her head in disbelief and turned back to the pictures, asking Kaminski: 'Do you mind if I take a couple of these?'

'Will you bring them back?'

'Soon as I've made copies,' she promised.

'Then be my guest.'

Fitzgerald carefully picked out three pictures which showed Randall at his best and slid them into her pocket. Kaminski pushed the other pictures to the side and sat down again on the bed. He made no move to put them away.

'When was the last time you saw this man?' Grace asked him.

'I told you. About three months ago. You're not trying to catch me out, are you, Detective Chief Superintendent? You'll have to try a bit harder than that.'

'You definitely haven't seen him since you arrived in Dublin?'

'No.'

'Then how do you know he's here?'

'Because he's communicated with me. I thought Saxon told you everything?'

'Don't get me wrong,' said Fitzgerald. 'I just need to get the facts straight. How do you *know* it was Buck Randall who was making contact with you?'

'Why would anyone else be trying to make me think they were Buck Randall?' said Kaminski, looking confused and still answering a different question. 'It doesn't make any sense. It was Randall I had the quarrel with. No one else hates me that much.'

'You think he hates you?'

'I'd take a wild guess that a man who takes the trouble to taunt the husband of the woman he murdered probably isn't filled with feelings of great affection.'

'Why does he hate you?'

'Because I'm the only one knows who knows who he is . . . what he is . . . I know his true nature. Everyone else fell for the act, they didn't recognize him. I did.'

'Why not just kill you too?'

'You'd have to ask him.'

'Take a guess.'

'Because this is more fun?'

'It's dangerous, though,' I said. 'You said yourself that no one else suspects him of being anything other than what he appears to be. That way he gets to carry on doing what he does. By playing games with you, he runs the risk of being discovered. Of being *stopped*. I still think it would be better to just get you out of the way.'

'I've wondered about that,' said Kaminski reluctantly. 'I can only think he's getting a kick out of this, that this has become part of the pleasure for him. Killing is a risk-taking business. It's the risk that people like Randall get off on.'

'And that's the same reason you think he killed Marsha Reed?'

'He didn't need a reason to do that. Killing women is

227

what he does. But he wanted me to know, yes, he wants to torment me, he wants to show me what he can do. To show me what he's going to carry on doing unless I stop him. Because no one else will. I don't think he's planned this whole thing through. I think he's improvising. He just wanted to kill Heather, but when I began to pursue him then that became woven into it too.'

'And now you're connected to him.'

'Through Heather, yes. She's what it's all about.'

'You're sure that he'll contact you again? That he won't just run now?'

'Why would he run? The only way he runs is if you make a mess of this and let him know the police are on to him. He has to think it's me and me alone. It has to be him and me, no one else. If he gets any hint the police have gotten involved, he'll be gone.'

'And you won't get your revenge,' I said.

'It's more than that. If he just vanishes now, it's not only me who loses. It's the other women he'll kill, because he will. He vanishes now more people are in danger. I hope you understand how serious this situation is, Chief Superintendent?'

'I have a long experience of these kinds of investigations,' Fitzgerald answered icily. 'I know what's at stake. I know how to be discreet. You should also know that the more information I have, the easier it becomes. If I could see the notes Randall sent you –'

'I lost them,' he interrupted bluntly.

'You told me you had them last night.'

'I'm a careless person, what can I say?'

'You're just keeping them to yourself now to spite me,' I said. 'Because I squealed on you, as you see it, you're throwing your toys out of the carriage, not cooperating.'

'It could make all the difference,' said Fitzgerald, more conciliatory.

He didn't waver. 'If they turn up, you'll be the first on my list.'

'I could have them analysed.'

'I'll keep it in mind.'

'We're only trying to help,' I said quietly.

'Is that what they call it now? Trying to help? It feels more like betrayal.'

'I haven't betrayed anyone.'

'Of all the people I thought I could trust, it was you. I was the one who gave you your first break. If it wasn't for me, you wouldn't have gotten near a big case for years. With your bad attitude, maybe never. Now the one time I need you, the one time I ask anything of you, you dump on me. I thought we meant more to each other than that.'

'I did what I thought was right. Whatever you say, however bad I feel about it, I still think it was the right thing to do. You can't find Buck Randall on your own.'

'He found me,' said Kaminski simply. 'I can find him.'

24

'I forgot to tell you,' said Fitzgerald as we made our way downstairs. 'Alastair Butler called this morning. He finished the autopsy on Dargan. Nothing official, but he's 80 per cent sure he died from breathing in the fumes of that gas fire we saw screwed to the wall of his room.'

'An accident, then?'

'Maybe not. The fire had been tampered with. Whoever did it must have known that, once it was switched on, the effects of inhalation could be fatal.'

'Someone wanted him dead?'

'The families of his victims are still out there, remember. Could be they thought Dargan got off too lightly and decided to take justice into their own hands.'

'Or feared', I said, 'that he might do it again to some other woman now he was free.'

'Alternatively,' she suggested, 'Dargan could've nobbled the fire himself.'

'Why would he want to commit suicide?'

'Apparently, he was facing new charges. The Prosecutions Office wanted to pursue him on further allegations made against him at the time of his original arrest. They weren't happy that he'd been released early. Maybe he just couldn't face going back inside.' She paused a moment as a man in a boiler suit passed us on the stairs, heading up. 'We'll probably never know for sure,' she said. 'The world is full of secrets, after all.'

Something about the way she spoke caught my attention.

'What do you mean?' I said.

'You and the hotel room,' she reminded me. 'You haven't forgotten already?'

'Oh . . . *that*.'

I was about to try to justify my actions, though Christ alone knows how I was going to, when Fitzgerald interrupted me with a question so out of left field that it took me a moment or two to recover.

'Do you think he knows about us?' she said.

'How *could* he?' I answered eventually.

'That's not what I asked.'

'True. Then I'd say not.'

'You didn't tell him?'

'If I did, I didn't mean to,' I said. I considered what she'd said for a moment, as we reached the ground floor and crossed the lobby to the entrance. 'JJ was always pretty perceptive,' I admitted. 'He picked up on things that weren't obvious to the rest of us.'

'Some people are like that,' she agreed. 'Maybe it was my reaction when he mentioned your breaking into his hotel room that gave it away.'

'I didn't break in.'

'Let's not split hairs. It was the not telling me which was the important part.'

We went out to the car in silence. I leaned on the roof on one side, resting my chin on my folded hands, as she searched her bag for the keys on the other side.

'I really am sorry,' I said.

'Are you?'

'Yes! At least, I don't know.' The car beeped open, and I climbed in. 'I didn't want to worry you. I still don't. It was nothing. Just me being me.'

'You being you will get you arrested one day.'

'Do you always do everything by the book?' I said.

'Not always,' she admitted.

'Do you always tell *me* when you've crossed the line?'

'Not always.'

'There you are, then.'

'What we don't know can't hurt us, is that what you're saying?'

'Something like that.'

'Does that include not telling me about you and Kaminski?'

Shit, that was the last thing I needed.

'I'm pretty perceptive myself when I need to be,' Fitzgerald said.

'There's not much to tell, really,' I said resignedly. 'One time we were working on a case together. We'd flown down to Denver, Colorado, had a frustrating day. We ended up going to some awful bar and drinking too much. One thing led to another.'

'You slept with him.'

'If you could call it that. It was nothing. Not something I cared to remember, at any rate. I just wanted to forget about it as quickly as possible. Next day I never mentioned it, he never mentioned it, and neither of us ever said a word about it again. Not once. It was . . . embarrassing. I felt I'd lost some contest. JJ was the kind of man that other agents wouldn't have trusted their wives around. He made Walsh look like a monk in comparison. I didn't want him to see what happened as a victory. The melting of the ice maiden, you know. They were always talking, all of them, in the field office, about how frigid I was. I just felt I'd let myself down, and all because I got drunk. I didn't know afterwards if they were talking about it among themselves, but I don't think so. I think I'd have known. There would've been looks, smiles, you know what it's like, sudden silences. They wouldn't have been able to hide it. Since there was nothing like that, I guessed Kaminski hadn't said a word about it.'

'You must've been relieved.'

'In a way, yeah, I was,' I said. 'But in another way, it made things worse.'

'Why worse?'

'Because by not saying, it made it seem as if it was somehow . . . what's the word? A guilty secret. Something illicit. So the more he didn't say anything, and I didn't say anything, the more it seemed to grow and take on a significance it didn't deserve. I always felt it was back there in reserve, and he could use it against me somehow. You're not mad, are you?'

'Why would I be mad?' she said. 'It was a long time before I met you.'

'I'd hate you to be jealous, is all. There's no need. My relationship with Kaminski, such as it was, isn't so much dead as never alive. It wasn't relevant.'

'At the risk of sounding picky, sleeping with someone is always relevant.' She offered a smile of reassurance. 'But, even so, I don't want you to feel bad. It was something I sensed up there, that's all. I needed to know. It makes things easier next time we all meet. But I don't deny it's weird. That's the first person I've ever met that you've slept with. The first person I know about, anyway. Unless you've been seeing Dalton behind my back.'

'I think we both know that's the least of your worries.'

'I'm just wondering,' she said.

'Wondering what?'

'Wondering if what you two had was more significant to Kaminski than to you.'

'In what way?'

233

'In this way,' she said. 'What if he really came to Dublin to see *you* again? What if this whole thing was planned from the start to get him into a position where he could see you? That you were *meant* to see him that day, it wasn't accidental at all.'

'That's not possible. Is it? His wife *was* killed. He *did* quit the FBI. He *did* follow Randall back down to Texas.'

'But still the only connection between the two events – the one in America and the one here – is him. And *you* are his only connection to Dublin.'

'What are you going to do?'

'I'm going to put him under surveillance and see what happens,' she said. 'Either way, it makes sense. If all this really does have something to do with Marsha Reed's death, I need to know where he goes. I don't think he'll cooperate. If Buck Randall gets in touch again, I think he'll keep it to himself. And if it *doesn't* have anything to do with her death, I have to know that too. The last thing I need on this case at this point, at any point, is distractions. Whichever it is, I want to know what he's doing.'

She was picking up her cellphone to give the instruction when it rang.

'Walsh, is that you? Speak up, I can hardly hear you. What is it?' Long pause. 'I've got you. I'll be there right away. What's the address?'

She wrote it down, then dropped the phone back in her pocket.

'Mark Hudson's gone,' she said.

'The guy who knocked down Cecelia Corrigan?' I said. 'What do you mean, gone?'

'Gone. Vanished. He hasn't been seen for over a week. He was reported missing by his cleaning woman to the local police station. Since then, nothing.'

'That doesn't make any sense. Her death really was an accident, wasn't it?'

'Maybe that's only what we were supposed to think,' she said.

It was only when we turned into the street that I realized where we were.

'Is this the street where Hudson lived?' I said.

'Yes,' she said. 'Number 11.'

'But this is where *she* lived too.'

'Where who lived?'

'The woman Hudson knocked down and killed. Howler's penfriend.'

'Cecelia Corrigan lived in this street too?'

'The very same.'

As we climbed out, I recognized the low white stone wall, the creaking gates, the sleepy summer trees dappling shadows on the ground.

The only difference was that now there was no sign of the black cat.

It was obviously getting too crowded for the poor creature.

I looked up at Cecelia Corrigan's house and thought I saw someone standing at an upstairs window, but, when I raised a hand to shield my eyes from the sun and get a better look, the someone vanished, and there was only the trembling of a curtain.

'Chief,' said a familiar voice.

'Walsh,' said Fitzgerald, 'what have you got?'

The young detective looked glum as he came down the path to meet us.

'Nothing, Chief. The place is empty. One of the neighbours had a key,' he said, 'so we were able to take a look inside. Everything seems in order, no signs of struggle or a hurried departure. There's someone in there you might want to talk to, though.'

He led the way up the path and through the door into Mark Hudson's house. I felt that peculiar sensation of nervousness you always get on walking into someone else's house when they aren't there. It's like an intrusion. It *is* an intrusion. That it's a necessary one doesn't make it feel any less like a violation of privacy. I felt like a peeping tom.

And yet who was here to feel offended? Something about this house smelled empty, like it had already adjusted itself to the business of being abandoned.

And at least I didn't have to worry about flies this time . . .

In the small rear kitchen stood a young man in a police officer's uniform, looking nervous. It wasn't every day a local cop got to meet the Chief Superintendent of the Murder Squad. This cop's face was slightly flushed. He was fidgeting on his feet.

Walsh introduced him as Sergeant Chase.

'He was on duty when Hudson was reported missing.'

'Is that Hudson?' said Fitzgerald. She was pointing to a framed photograph on the shelf above the fireplace, which showed a man of thirty, possibly, wearing dirt-spattered sports gear and holding up a trophy.

'He played rugby for his local club,' acknowledged Walsh. 'His teammates were the last ones to see him. He'd arranged to meet them mid week for training. When he didn't show and couldn't be contacted and they realized he hadn't been in work, they reported him missing. By which time someone else had reported him missing too. His cleaning lady.'

'That's Mrs Emily Nolan,' said Sergeant Chase. 'She came in at 9 a.m. on Tuesday to begin work. Mr Hudson normally left her wages in an envelope on the mantelpiece, but there was nothing. She thought it was a bit unusual, but did her work as usual. Next day, the money still wasn't there and he hadn't been home, so she called the local station.'

'Seems a bit drastic, calling in the police that quickly,' said Fitzgerald. 'Didn't she know any friends or family of his she could call?'

'She says she couldn't think of anyone else to ring,' said Sergeant Chase. 'He'd never mentioned any family, and the only neighbour Hudson really had any contact with lived across the way. She was the one who told Mrs Nolan to go the police.'

'Number 8,' I said quietly.

'How'd you know that?' said Walsh.

'That's where Becky Corrigan lives,' I said.

'Corrigan?' said Walsh with a frown. 'The old woman Hudson knocked down?'

'She wasn't that old,' I corrected him, though it was curious because that was the way I thought about her too. 'But yeah, that's Jenkins Howler's late penfriend. Becky was her niece. She still lives in the house. It's over there, see?'

I showed him where, through the window, the house opposite was clearly visible. Mark Hudson probably saw it every day, just as Ceclia Corrigan saw his. It could never have occurred to either of them that one day he would be the unwitting cause of her death.

If it *had* been unwitting.

Fitzgerald must have been nursing the same thought, for I heard her say next: 'Tell me what happened that day, the day Cecelia Corrigan was killed.'

'There's not much to tell really, er, sir,' Sergeant Chase answered her awkwardly. 'I'd only come on duty, it was about seven in the evening. There was a call-in saying there'd been an accident down on Herbert Park. A woman badly injured, it said. I was sent out to take a look at it. By the time I got there, the woman was already dead. She'd been crossing the road at the traffic lights when she'd been hit by a car turning into the street.'

'Was the driver . . . was Mark Hudson . . . still there?'

'Oh, yes, he was still there. He was in a pretty bad way, to be honest. He couldn't stop shaking. He was sitting on the kerb with his head in his hands, crying, shaking. Quite a crowd had built up by then, and they were gathered round asking him what had happened, but he couldn't talk. It was only when we eventually got him back here to the station and got him a cup of tea, that he calmed down enough to tell us what had happened.'

'Was he arrested?'

Sergeant Chase looked startled by the question, as if arresting people was the last thing he could imagine himself doing.

'No! He was breathalysed at the scene of the accident, of course, but he didn't have a drop of drink on him, and there was no evidence he'd been driving carelessly or too fast. Plenty of eyewitnesses saw it all happen. The dead woman didn't stand a chance. She'd just stepped out in front of the car. He couldn't stop. Miss Corrigan said so herself.'

'I thought you said she was dead by the time you got there?' I said.

The young cop turned reluctantly toward me, wondering perhaps if he'd said the wrong thing. 'I meant the young Miss Corrigan,' he said.

'Becky Corrigan was there when her aunt died?' said Fitzgerald in astonishment.

'Not only was she there,' said Sergeant Chase, 'she was in the passenger seat of the car. Mark Hudson was giving her a lift home when he hit her aunt.'

I whistled softly. Funny how she hadn't mentioned that when I spoke to her.

'And you're sure,' said Fitzgerald tentatively, 'that there was nothing more to what happened? Nothing suspicious? Something that didn't fit?'

'Nothing.' He shook his head bemusedly. 'It was an accident.'

How many times had I heard those words in the past days?

Fitzgerald and Walsh tried more questions, different angles, but they might as well have been speaking Mandarin Chinese for all the impact they were making on Sergeant Chase. As far as he was concerned, he had attended the scene of a routine road-traffic accident and nothing was going to shake him from that conviction. And maybe he was right.

Finally, Fitzgerald told him that would be all, and she went off to check out the rest of the house with Walsh. I retreated to the garden, found a bench to sit on and lit a cigar.

I had other things to think about. I was feeling guilty about Kaminski. I didn't want to say anything to Fitzgerald about it because she might get the wrong idea. Might think that somehow I still had feelings for him. I didn't. At least I didn't *think* I did. My only feeling for him right now was pity. I was struggling with the awful feeling that I'd taken away the one thing that kept him going, which had sustained him in the days since his wife was murdered, and that was the possibility of reeling in Buck Randall III.

There was something else too. What Kaminski had said hit home. As far as he was concerned, I was the cops' lapdog now. I was the thing we'd always fought against. I was the thing I'd always despised. Somewhere along the way I had become respectable.

Safe.

I still couldn't work out how I felt about that. Part of me needed to be on the outside. It was part of what defined me. Take that away, and what was left? And I was no nearer getting an answer to that when Fitzgerald and Walsh came out to join me.

'Any luck?' I asked.

They didn't need to speak to give me my answer.

Their faces said it all.

Or at least they did until Walsh's face suddenly brightened. 'Would you look at that?' he said appreciatively.

I followed the direction of his gaze. On the other side of the street, a slender woman in a revealing summer dress had emerged from the gate and was glancing over at us with a curious frown. She caught my eye, and there was a vague flicker of recognition on her face before she turned and began to make her way toward the main road.

'That's Becky,' I explained to him.

'The girl who was in the car?'

'And the one who inherited the money, don't forget that part.'

'Rich and hot with with it,' he said. 'It doesn't get any better than this. Leave her to me.' And he trotted to the gate to follow her. 'Excuse me, miss,' he called after her.

I saw her turn and wait until Walsh caught her up. He showed her his badge before reaching out an arm and shepherding her back toward her house.

'Say *she* did it,' I found myself saying.

'What?' said Fitzgerald, astonished.

'I'm serious. Say she was having an affair with Hudson. She gets him into her clutches, has him knock down the aunt so that she can inherit the money and the house, and then, when Hudson's outlived his usefulness, she bumps him off too.'

'What an imagination you have,' said Fitzgerald. 'Do you have any reason for thinking so or is this just one of your legendary intuitions?'

'Neither. Thinking aloud, is all.'

'You have the dimmest view of women of anyone I've ever known,' said Fitzgerald.

'That's because I am one,' I said. 'I don't have any illusions.'

I didn't really think that. A memory of her coldness on first meeting, the way she'd talked about Cecelia Corrigan, had merely hit me as I looked across at her.

Coldness was no crime, but it provoked mistrust.

'You know,' said Fitzgerald indulgently, 'you can't send everyone you don't like to the electric chair. The drain on the power supply would be too great.'

'Since when did you become so understanding?'

'Oh, I couldn't be compassionate all the time,' she smiled. 'Just now and again as a special treat. Now what say we get back to looking for the elusive Mr Hudson?'

25

The search for Mark Hudson was complicated by the small and inconvenient fact that we didn't know exactly what we were looking for. A straightforward missing person?

A fugitive?

A killer?

Or the victim of a killer, who had disappeared from his own life as effectively as he had disappeared from everyone else's? Or was his absence a complete non-mystery which would be solved by his suddenly turning up, unaware of the stir he had created?

The procedure for finding the lost was different in each case. Which one was followed could make all the difference to how successful the search turned out to be. I almost found myself wishing I could call up Lucas Piper and ask him for help. His famous skill in uncovering those who had seemingly been erased from the universe would be invaluable.

Or would it? This was a different city, a different country, a different world, than he was used to. He might be totally at sea here. Then again, he couldn't be any more at sea than I felt. And surely the principles were the same whether you were looking for someone in this Dublin or Dublin, Ohio? I should send him a postcard. *Wish you were here.*

Where to begin? Mark Hudson didn't have many friends, and the ones he did have knew of no earthly reason why he should have gone off the radar screen. Of a family there was no sign. There was no sign either of a girlfriend or boyfriend.

On that score, Hudson's sexuality remained stubbornly indeterminate. His few friends knew of no sexual partners, and there was no pornography in the house to indicate which way his inclinations lay. A study of his computer also found no clue in the websites he'd visited, or the emails that he sent. Most of those were related to his work as a salesman. Most of those sent *to* him were commercial pitches, offering the usual range of bizarre and generally unsavoury services.

Hudson's bank account had also remained untouched since he vanished. The last withdrawal from his account came from an ATM in Talbot Street, near where he worked. The CCTV at the bank had recorded him taking out money the day before he disappeared. Grey and grainy, it represented the last sighting of the missing man. If he had been planning on going away for any length of time, there was no hint of it in this transaction.

Nor were there any unusual patterns in his financial dealings in the months leading up to his disappearance. It wasn't like he was stockpiling money ready for a midnight flit.

His car hadn't turned up either. He'd switched cars after knocking down and killing Cecelia Corrigan. Popular psychology would suggest that he did so because the car reminded him of that painful memory. Well, maybe. He'd bought a used Honda, metallic blue, 2002 registration. A search of car parks and side-streets in the city had failed to uncover it abandoned. Police patrols remained on the lookout for it but without much hope.

Of course, if his disappearance *was* the result of foul play, whoever was responsible would make every effort to get rid of the incriminating evidence, including the car.

But how to dispose of a car? Bodies can be dumped down abandoned wells, buried under a new patio, put inside existing graves, fed to animals. Generally the best way to get cars out of sight effectively was either to send them to the auto crusher, or to have them resprayed and fitted with fresh number plates. Inquiries were pursued on both fronts.

It all came back to the same question: *why* was Mark Hudson missing? Dublin wasn't like London or New York. Unlike those places, it wasn't a place where the world's detritus came to burrow down, unseen, in the city's cracks, where those who have spent a lifetime cultivating anonymity for usually malicious ends congregate.

But until we answered that question, the rest might remain for ever hidden.

Becky Corrigan hadn't been much help. She recalled seeing Hudson around the weekend he vanished, but they hadn't spoken and she didn't know him well enough, she claimed, to detect any weirdness in his behaviour that might suggest something was up.

She also flat denied that he could have intended in any way to kill her aunt. She'd been in the car. She *knew* how it had happened. She'd *seen* it – 'with my own eyes', as she put it. (Why do people always say that? Like there was a way they could've seen it with someone else's eyes instead.) On this, she was certain. Maybe Hudson had been distracted by talking to her, maybe he'd taken his eyes off the road for a second, but do it deliberately? No way.

I didn't think much of her story, but Fitzgerald had an irritating habit of asking me to prove my hunches with evidence and that wasn't possible, mainly because there wasn't any.

All I knew is that it all seemed a bit too neat that Hudson would've given her a lift that night, but then Becky said he often picked her up on his way home, in fact she suspected he had a thing for her, that he deliberately arranged the times of his journeys in the hope that he'd get the chance to offer her a lift, though she insisted their relationship went no further than casual friendship. He wasn't her type, she said.

And, in truth, I had no good reason to suspect her of lying about it. Becky benefited from her aunt's death, but that didn't mean she'd colluded in it.

I'd benefit from my mother dying too, since I'd get a half share, along with my brother, in the family mansion – OK, so it's a decaying town house in downtown Boston, but I keep up to date with the real-estate prices in New England and it was still worth getting hold of – but that didn't mean I should be hauled in as a suspect when she finally croaks.

Not that I hadn't seriously considered the attractions of bumping the old girl off in my time. Sure, everyone's had the same thoughts, no? Or is that just me?

The more we delved, the less there seemed to go on. Hudson's mental state remained unfathomable. Was he depressed? Did he feel bad about killing Cecelia? Might he have taken his own life in despair? Guilt could do that to a person, but in Hudson's case such lines of inquiry couldn't be any more than guesswork and speculation. Whoever said no man is an island should have tried meeting Hudson. He wouldn't have been so sure then.

Normally in missing persons' cases, there's a long list of people whose testimony can be sifted for hints of the elusive one's likely whereabouts. Wives, ex-wives, cuckolded husbands, children, business associates, relatives, folks they owned money to, folks who owed *them* money, even the police if they'd ever found themselves on the wrong side of the law.

Hudson's only contact with the police had been following Cecelia Corrigan's death, and, like the dead woman's niece, Sergeant Chase continued to insist that there was no more to that than had been immediately apparent. There was no reason to doubt either of them.

But that still didn't explain where Hudson was right now.

Pictures of Buck Randall were circulated discreetly around the area, to Hudson's few friends, work colleagues, Becky herself, but they failed to elicit any positive response.

No one had seen Buck Randall here, just as no one had seen him in the vicinity where Marsha Reed died, and none of her friends, either those at the theatre or at the sex club where she'd gone to get her fun, could place his face. His fingerprints were also conspicious by their absence in the converted church where she died. The whole thing looked like one huge red herring, and Seamus Dalton didn't hesitate to remind me of this when I returned to Dublin Castle.

I sat at a borrowed desk, wondering again what the hell I was really doing here. It was early days, but I was painfully conscious of my failure to bring any of those skills to the table that Assistant Commissioner Stella Carson had hoped I would. At least with Kaminski, I would've known what I was doing. At least I would've been doing something useful, especially if, as I was increasingly starting to suspect, there turned out to be no connection whatsoever between Buck Randall's presence in the city and the death of Jenkins Howler's lonely penfriend.

And yet how could there *not* be a connection? The only other explanation was that the two things were a coincidence, and how likely was that? Though maybe I should revise my scepticism in the light of experience. Sometimes chance takes a hand. Like the time I saw Kaminski in Temple Bar. Likewise, if Dermot Bryce hadn't quarrelled with his wife on a particular night, or he hadn't left the house to go walking and calm down, or he'd taken a different path, or gone to a late-night café instead, or didn't watch the news, or didn't believe in helping the police, we might have floundered a lot longer.

But that was all still to come. At that precise moment, I'd never even heard of Dermot Bryce, and I had no idea how important his recollections would turn out to be.

'You look like you need rescuing,' said Healy eventually. 'Want to come with me?'

The trip was worth it alone for the look on Todd Fleming's face when we saw us walking into the café. I'd say we were both the last people he'd expected to see – and also the last ones he *wanted* to see, with the one exception of Fitzgerald herself. He'd been spared that at least.

'This is early for the night shift,' remarked Sean Healy affably.

'I'm covering for someone,' Fleming said.

'Sounds like a confession,' said Healy.

Fleming looked momentarily alarmed before recovering his composure.

'If I ever feel the need to confess, I'll go find a priest,' he said. 'In the meantime, what can I get you? Coffee?'

'Coffee would be good. Black. No sugar,' said Healy. 'Saxon?'

'Nothing for me.'

'You arrest Solomon yet?' Fleming asked as he reached for a cup and poured Healy his coffee. 'Or have you just come here to ask me some more pointless questions?'

'We're still in the middle of our investigation,' Healy answered. 'But, as it happens, we're not here to see you at all. Your boss left something for us. I'd say that's it up there.'

Fleming followed the line of Healy's gaze until it rested on a brown envelope tucked behind a jar on a shelf above his head. The words *FAO Sergeant Healy* were scrawled across the front. Looked like Healy had been secretly demoted somewhere along the line.

Fleming reluctantly lifted down the envelope and slid it across the counter. His curiosity was obviously pricked as to what was inside, but he wasn't going to admit it by asking. All he said was: 'Will that be everything?'

'No,' said Healy. 'We'll need the use of one of the computers. Is that a problem?'

'It's quiet,' said Fleming by way of an answer.

'Then lead the way.'

Fleming took us to one of the booths in the café. He was right about it being quiet. Apart from us, there was only one other customer, a young woman over by the door checking out cheap flights online. The lure of a foreign sun. Even so, Healy asked for the booth furthest from the counter, in a dim corner where we wouldn't be overlooked.

'This was where Marsha always sat,' said Fleming as he switched on the screen and typed in the password, before adding sharply: 'But then you probably knew that already.'

As it happened, we hadn't known, but it soon made sense that she would have chosen this spot. What Healy had in the envelope was a printout of the websites which Marsha Reed had looked at during her visits to the internet café. Fitzgerald had asked the owner for a list and, once he'd spluttered a little about civil liberties and the Big Brother state, he'd agreed to see what he could do. The internet was a felons' paradise. Terrorists, pornographers, people traffickers, drug smugglers: they all operated under its sheltering wing. And where they went, the law was bound to follow. First Amendment devotees might not like it, but the police couldn't afford to allow any public space to remain out of surveillance. And the internet, as many of its habitual users frequently failed to realize, was the most public space of all. Nothing that happened there was ever truly private. Hence, all it took to locate a record of Marsha Reed's internet use was the computer she had used and the times she had accessed it.

And, like I say, it then didn't take a genius to figure out why she preferred this dim haven in the corner. The kind of websites she'd visited in the café were not the kinds you'd want to share with any casual observer looking over your shoulder as you surfed.

First there were websites set up as anonymous forums where other like-minded souls who shared Marsha's sexual proclivities could make contact, swap stories and tips, arrange to meet up. There were sites listing clubs in other cities – maybe she'd visited them on her own travels, or maybe she was just curious to know what was out there – and weblogs by people who wanted to record every aspect of their sex lives, in considerable detail, for the benefit of strangers online. Mostly, though, Marsha's interests on the internet had revolved around her private studies into murder, which had also been evinced by her book collection.

From my own reading, I was anecdotally familiar with the content of many of the websites Marsha had regularly visited, but it still made me feel uncomfortable seeing them for myself. These were not forums which had been set up to collate academic research into serial murder, but more like fan sites on which users were invited and encouraged to trade their own enthusiasms for their 'favourite' killers or to rank crimes, as in a popularity poll, according to various sick criteria. There were plenty of photographs too, many of which must have come from the original police investigation teams from across the world: the United States, the Far East, Europe. Murder was the ultimate loss of privacy. The bodies of the dead were inevitably reduced to the raw stuff of police work. This, though, added a new and unnecessary dimension to the unavoidable indignity. At the click of a button, the intimacies of the crime scene were now translated into instant entertainment for voyeurs.

There was nothing in the photographs I hadn't seen a thousand times before, and not just through the impersonal gaze of the camera but up close, drawn inexorably into the dark aura that the dead weave around them, near enough to touch, near enough to smell. But it wasn't the content of the pictures which shocked, but the heartless context in which they were being so casually and thoughtlessly presented. It made me angry, wondering what Marsha Reed had seen in these places, what primitive pleasure she had taken from them, if it was indeed pleasure that she'd been looking for when she visited them. Would the pictures of *her* crime scene end up online too? I wondered what she would've thought of that. Would that have made her understand the violation involved? Or would it have turned her on more?

I didn't know her well enough to answer that.

I didn't know her at all.

Angry or not, I kept my feelings in check. My feelings had no place. This was what investigation was all about. It was about detaching yourself from the passions that surrounded murder so that you could see them more clearly. Getting too involved was fatal.

I should know.

I made that mistake all the time.

Sean Healy barely spoke a word as we worked. His eyes were fixed to the screen, silently taking in what he saw, missing nothing; he only made occasional notes.

His coffee grew cold.

Across the café, I sensed Todd Fleming watching intently whenever he got the chance. The radio had been playing when we walked in. It was now switched off, as if he needed to concentrate and the noise of it had been distracting him.

Did he know what we were looking at?

Did he fear we might find something we weren't supposed to know about?

Once, accidentally, I caught his gaze from across the café.

He didn't look away and I felt like I'd been caught out doing something shameful, without being able to say precisely what the shame was meant to be for.

Before I could say a word to Healy about it, though, he whistled softly.

'Would you take a look at this?' he said.

I found Fisher in the canteen at Dublin Castle, picking half-heartedly through a limp salad. Miranda must've put him on a diet. Poor chump.

'Have you got a moment?' I said.

'For you,' he said, pushing away the plate with gratitude, 'always. Besides, I have nothing much to do until the reception tonight.'

'The reception?'

I'd forgotten. There was going to be some party that night for Stella Carson to let her meet and greet the press and local bigwigs. I was supposed to be going there myself. I guess there wasn't much chance of getting out of it.

'You're not running home to Miranda, then?'

'Miranda won't be home till later,' he said, 'and I don't fancy being out there by myself. It's not like there's anything there for me when I'm on my own.'

He was probably thinking of Laura and the children again.

'You don't like the neighbours?'

'I hardly *see* the neighbours. Not during the day, anyway. It's a ghost town. They're all at work.'

'Not everyone is as fortunate as us. They have to work for a living.'

'I know. It's such a bore. But it's not that. It's the kind of people they are. They're all investment bankers, insurance brokers, MDs of their own companies. I have nothing in common with these people. Even when I do bump into them, I have nothing to say to them.'

'I'm sure you manage,' I observed wryly.

Fisher had never been lost for words for long.

'I manage,' he acknowledged, 'but with no conviction. Who are these people? Where did they come from? What language do they speak? They're an alien species to me. Still, I suppose that's what work's for, isn't it? To fill the emptiness.'

'Speaking of which . . .'

I opened the flap of the folder I was carrying and took out a sheaf of printouts to show Fisher what Healy and I had found on the computer at the internet café.

I soon had his attention.

'She was soliciting strangers online to murder her?' he said.

The merest raise of an eyebrow was the only surprise Fisher allowed himself to show. I guess when you've seen and heard everything, there's not much that can shock you any more. And Fisher had seen just about all there was to see in his time.

'Consensual homicide,' he said. 'Interesting. There was a similar case in the United States about ten years ago. I don't remember the precise details. A woman from Maryland – a happily married businesswoman, by all accounts – used the internet to arrange for a stranger to sexually torture and then kill her. Police found that her computer contained

252

hundreds of pages of email in which she'd been trying to convince people to kill her too.'

'Sharon Lopatka,' I said. 'I remember. She was tortured for days before being killed. Christ knows what was going on in her head. There was also a German man who agreed to torture and kill his companion and then eat his remains. He was only arrested when he posted a request for more victims. I'm sure Marsha Reed must've come across the cases.'

'And got the idea from that?'

'It's a possibility,' I said.

'If she was a willing participant, that would certainly explain why the cords weren't tightened so fast. The ethics of it are fascinating,' Fisher added. 'If the victim wants it to happen, does that make it murder? If death is what Marsha sought, was she victim or perpetrator?'

'Murder is murder,' I said with certainty. 'Just because the victim might want what happens to them doesn't mean you have the right to do it. And we can't say for certain that this was what Marsha really wanted. She might've been using the exchanges as an outlet for some private fantasy of hers. We don't know she ever really intended to go through with it. And she never once in all those emails reveals her real name. She only gives a phone number. That hasn't been traced either. There's no evidence it even belonged to her.'

'The Mardi Gras phenomenon, they call it,' said Fisher. 'You assume disguises, masks, to take on various personalities and act them out without consequences. The internet's the perfect place to do that. It explains, at any rate, why she didn't have a computer in her own house. I did wonder about that. Her father seems to have bought her everything else. This was another part of her life that she wanted to keep secret, separate, neatly fenced off.'

'Pretty risky, using a public computer in an internet café.'

'Not when you have someone who works there eating out of the palm of your hand. Besides, why should she worry that anyone would be interested in her internet activities? She was just another customer in just another café. Ms Anonymous.' He paused. 'Did anyone express an interest in taking her up on the offer, by the way?'

'She'd corresponded for weeks with a couple of dodgy characters,' I said, 'batting scenarios back and forth. There, all the details are on the next page. See? But it seemed to come to nothing. They expressed an initial interest, then backed off.'

'Maybe they got scared off when they began to suspect she was serious. Well, it shouldn't be too difficult to trace them and get their version of events. But even if they have a perfectly innocent explanation for what they were doing, that doesn't mean she didn't excite someone else's interest, someone who then managed to track her down independently.'

'So it could be anyone in the whole of cyberspace?'

'Practically,' said Fisher.

'That doesn't exactly narrow down the suspects, does it?'

'Don't forget the money too,' he added.

'The money?'

'In her purse the night she died. The taxi driver saw it when she was looking for her key. According to her bank records, Marsha had taken out five thousand in cash that afternoon. What if that money was to pay someone to kill her?'

'The subject of money's never mentioned in any of her emails.'

'But she didn't find anyone to do what she asked of them that way, did she? What if she realized she had to make other arrangements? Find a professional?'

'But what –? Why –?'

I gave up.

'Marsha's lost me,' I said. 'What was she *doing*?'

'You'll never understand other people's desires, other people's deepest needs,' Fisher said. 'It's futile to try. That's one thing I have learned. What goes on in people's heads will always be a mystery. That what makes them so dangerous.'

'Victims aren't supposed to be as dangerous as their killers,' I said stubbornly.

'When are you ever going to understand that there are no rules when it comes to murder? Everything is chaos and surprise. That's what makes this job so interesting.'

'You're saying I should see it as a good thing that nothing makes sense any more?'

'There are worse things than being baffled,' he observed placidly.

'There are also worse things than walking stark naked round St Stephen's Green,' I said, 'but that doesn't mean you have to recommend it as a lifestyle choice. And what if our bafflement leads to some other woman being butchered? Have you thought about that?'

'Saxon, my dear, right now I am thinking about precious little else.'

26

'This isn't my idea of a party,' said Walsh.

'This isn't anybody's idea of a party,' I answered. 'And if it *is* somebody's idea of a party, I don't want to have the misfortune of ever meeting them.'

We were standing in a large room in the Parliament Hotel, at the top of Dame Street, almost directly opposite Dublin Castle. A wall of windows looked out on to buses passing below. Traffic was heading home. Waiters circulated inside with trays bearing drinks, and there was a free bar until nine. That was something at least. I was clutching a bottle of warm beer and wondering what I was doing here. I knew what Kaminski would say I was doing here. Kissing ass, that's what he'd say. And maybe he was right.

The room was crowded with people I didn't know and didn't particularly want to get to know. Patrick Walsh, who'd grabbed hold of me almost as soon as I'd arrived and saved me from splendid isolation, was taking time to point out a few of them to me.

'See that guy over there with the bad hairpiece? He's in charge of the DMP press office. That short guy who looks a bit like Hitler, only not quite so pleasant? That's the Assistant Commissioner for Traffic.' And on he went, telling me who had screwed who to get what positions and the gossip about the various people in various departments. Some of the guests needed no introduction. I recognized their faces, in particular the huddles of reporters, getting snippets for the weekly social diaries charting who was hot and who was not in Dublin public life. It was certainly good for public relations to have a woman taking over the Murder Squad. They wanted to make sure they got as much capital out of it as they could.

'Here, pass me another one of those beers. I seem to be empty. Thanks. You know, you don't have to stand here with me. You can circulate if you want. I'll be fine.'

'No problem. Besides, I'm trying to avoid someone.'

'Anyone I know?'

'See the woman over there with the tits?'

'Don't they all have them?'

'Not like those,' said Walsh with an appreciative leer, then the smile vanished when he saw the look I returned. 'Sorry,' he said. 'Sometimes I forget you're a woman.'

'Thanks, I needed that.'

'No, I mean it in a good way,' he said quickly. 'Usually with a woman these days, you have to watch everything you say or they start looking at you like you've broken some golden rule of the sisterhood. With you, I don't feel like you're judging me. I don't have to be so careful what I say. I can say what I'm really thinking. That's a good thing, isn't it?'

'I guess so.' I was still trying to work out whether I'd just been on the receiving end of a compliment or an insult and whether it mattered whether someone actually insulted you when what they'd been trying to do was say something nice. In the end I gave up.

'You were telling me about the woman with the tits,' I reminded him. 'I presume you're seeing her?'

'And trust me, there's plenty worth seeing,' he said.

'So why are you trying to avoid her?'

'She's been moving a little too fast for my liking,' he said. 'She always wants us to be spending time together, she wants to know where I'm going, what I'm doing, she even asked me a couple of nights ago for my home phone number.'

'Women today,' I said sardonically. 'What are they like? Just because they've let you have ramblers' rights over their bodies, they think they ought to be able to call you.'

'She has my mobile phone number, what else does she want? I need my space,' said Walsh. 'I know the score. They start by asking for your number and then they want to know where you are all the time and then they tell you that you're drinking too much and before you know it they're saying they love you and want to have your baby.'

'And you deduced all this from the fact she asked for your home phone number?'

'I can read the signs,' he said confidently. 'And I figured that if she saw me with another woman, she'd make a scene. She can be ... fiery. Women can be very vengeful, you know.' And that was true enough. 'The truth is I don't believe in monogamy. It's not natural for men and women to stay together for ever, don't you agree?'

'I've never had a problem with monogamy,' I said. 'When I'm with someone, I'm with them. I don't usually look around for a replacement.'

'I couldn't be like that. It's only natural to try out what else is available.'

'Maybe it's a male thing,' I said with a shrug.

'Most of the women I know are like that too. Maybe there's just something wrong with your sex drive.' And he said it so pleasantly that I was again stumped as to how to respond to what sounded like an insult. But I never got the chance, because he suddenly interrupted his own thoughts with a low appreciative murmur: 'Hello.'

Another woman had caught his eye on the other side of the room. She was tall, dark-haired, with mischievous eyes and prominent cheekbones and a great figure. She was smiling politely at something her companion, a small dumpy man that Walsh had already identified to me as an inspector with the Immigration Office, had said to her.

The smile verged on a grimace.

'Now that's more like it,' he said. 'Who is she?'

'That's Stella Carson's daughter,' I said. 'I saw a picture of her in the Assistant Commissioner's office. She's a lawyer.'

'What's her name?'

'Sally, I think. You're not going to make a move, are you?'

'Why not?' he said. 'It could be good for my career, going out with the boss's daughter. I'd be like one of the family. I'd make Inspector two years tops.'

'Unless you cheated on her and broke her heart and the outraged mother decides you're being transferred to the Dogs Division. Mothers can be very protective.'

'I never thought of that.' Walsh looked disappointed, until another thought struck him: 'But it couldn't hurt to just talk, could it? Wait here. I'll not be long. I'm a fast worker.'

Walsh checked his appearance quickly in a nearby mirror before starting a nifty sideways dance to where Sally Carson was beginning to look a little less than delighted by the anecdotes of Mr Immigration. I couldn't help smiling at Walsh's talent for getting himself into emotional tangles, until I became aware that someone was staring at me.

I looked over and saw the infamous woman with the tits and the bad habit of asking men for their home phone numbers glaring at me with obvious dislike. I was clearly being put down as the big bad wolf who'd stolen boy wonder away from her.

'It's OK,' I wanted to tell her, 'I never date anyone who needs to shave their back.'

But I doubted she would've believed me.

Suddenly weary, I wondered how long it would be before I could sneak away without my absence being noted. Assuming, that is, that my presence had been noted anyway.

I began to walk slowly round the room because, when you're on the move, you can always pretend that you have something to do and somewhere to go. I estimated I could spend an hour making my way round and round the room, like a goldfish in a bowl, avoiding conversation, before I got so dizzy I fell over.

I hadn't gone far when I spotted Fitzgerald. She was standing with Stella Carson and Sean Healy and the mighty Commissioner himself at the far end of the room. I hadn't spoken to her since arriving. It was one of those occasions when we both decided it was judicious to stay discreetly apart – so as not to frighten the horses, as it were. The Commissioner knew about our relationship, sure he did, but I sensed it was something he preferred to know about in the abstract, like a mathematical equation, rather than have the evidence in front of him.

They were all laughing at something one of them had said. Probably one of the Commissioner's bad jokes. Fitzgerald had a very expressive mouth. I often found myself watching her talk, not necessarily hearing what she said, but just liking the way it moved.

She'd also loosened her hair so that it hung down her neck. She told me once that she'd had hair down to her waist as a child and having to cut it was the saddest thing she'd ever had to do. It was, she said, like the end of childhood. Me, I couldn't get out of my childhood fast enough, but I could see how the symbolism might've meant more to her.

When she wore her hair loose, it was like she was free in some indefinable way.

It was then that the Assistant Commissioner reached out and touched Fitzgerald's arm. It was nothing, a gesture to command attention, and yet for a moment it made me angry, and I was surprised at myself. I'd never been the jealous type before. It shocked me.

I turned away in irritation, hating the irrationality of thoughts. The way you had no power over them. The way they just came unbidden and unwanted, and drove out all self-possession. I took a deep breath and told myself not to be so stupid.

It didn't help.

At that moment, I wanted to get out of there.

Be alone.

On the way out, I met Walsh coming back from the men's room. He looked sheepish, but it was too dim at first for me to see what was wrong with him.

'You had enough?' he said.

'I need some air,' I told him.

It was a plausible enough lie.

'I'll come with you. I could do with getting some air myself.'

'Honestly, I just want some time to myself. What's up with you, anyway? I thought you were moving in on the younger Miss Carson?'

'Let's just say I don't think that's going to work out.'

He stepped forward a little into the light and I saw that he had the beginnings of an impressive black eye. So *that's* why he'd looked so sheepish.

'She hit you?' I said, amazed.

'Not Sally. Lucy.'

'Lucy being the girl from Vice?'

'She saw me chatting up Sally. I told you she'd make a scene. She just came right over and kapow. The woman's fucking nuts. What did I tell you about them being spiteful?'

'What did Sally Carson say?'

'When she stops laughing, I'll let you know.'

'Don't let it bother you. Women can be vengeful, surely you've realized that by now? And I'm sure your male ego will survive. There are plenty more women upstairs for you.'

'True,' he said, brightening. 'You're sure you don't want me to come with you?'

'Walsh, you're a sweet guy, and I appreciate the offer, I do. But I couldn't forgive myself if I came between you and your raging libido. I don't want to cramp your style.'

'If you put it like that,' he said, 'it does seem a shame to deny the women of Dublin the incomparable pleasure of my body on such a warm summer's evening. Wish me luck.'

'You don't seem to need it,' I pointed out. 'Except with Lucy.'

'Ouch,' he said. 'What'd you have to go reminding me about her for?'

27

I didn't feel like returning home straight away. I was restless, antsy, disgruntled with myself and the world. Nothing new there, then. I needed to walk. But I scarcely noticed where I was going because I was still thinking about Stella Carson's reception. Had Fitzgerald been trying to make me jealous back there, to punish me in some way for not telling her about Kaminski and me? Was she trying to send me a message not to take her for granted? Telling me that if I didn't appreciate her, there were plenty of other people who would?

No, I was being paranoid. She hadn't even known I was there. She had her back turned to me the whole time. I was making myself unhappy for no reason.

Perhaps I was simply feeling vulnerable. Fitzgerald had always spent more time in work than out of it, it came with the territory, but there'd never been anyone that she worked with before that I could have imagined her having anything other than a professional relationship with. Now there was someone who, given different circumstances, it didn't take a huge leap of imagination to suppose could spark a mutual attraction. Stella Carson was a good-looking woman. After her recent divorce, she was available. Nothing was unthinkable.

The city that night was hot. Suffocatingly hot. The weather still showed no signs of breaking. The streets were crowded and noisy, like they'd been a couple of nights ago when Fitzgerald and I had walked back to my apartment from the

263

bar. I even thought I recognized some of the same faces, taking advantage of the warm while it lasted – which in Dublin, it rarely did. It was exactly the same scene, except that tonight the city had become infested with a kind of malignancy. Everything which had seemed healthy and vital now seemed rank, rotten, like meat left out in the sun too long. It even felt like it was getting hotter rather than cooler as the night got later, as if everything were conspiring to just feel wrong.

I didn't know how the other people in the streets couldn't feel it too. How it didn't ruin everything for them. Could they not smell the city going bad?

It was the kind of heat that makes people angry. And maybe I'd been touched a little by that myself. It was almost as if something was about to explode or catch fire. The streets needed a dousing of rain to slake their thirst and cool their fever, but there was no chance of that. The sky was drier than an African plain, cloudless and cracked like a dirt track.

Everywhere I walked, I saw signs of the festering mood which had gripped the city. In the crimson sweating faces of the people that I passed. Their exposed roasted flesh. The scent of food in the air, usually so inviting, now sickened me. A man stood on the corner of Molesworth Street cramming a burger into his mouth like a python greedily swallowing its prey whole, and the juices ran down his chin like blood. Another stood near by, urinating through the bars of a metal grille covering the doorway of an office. A man and a woman stood arguing loudly on the junction of Ely Place and Merrion Row. There was a dead dog decaying on the banks of the Grand Canal. Garbage floated by on the water's oily surface. The smell was bad here, and getting worse. The weeds looked like strips of raw flesh.

Gradually I realized that I wasn't walking without purpose or direction. Without knowing it, I had been making my way to Kaminski's hotel. I found myself standing across the road from its weathered old stone façade, looking up to where I imagined his window to be.

Was he in?

Fitzgerald hadn't mentioned whether she'd put the tail on Kaminski that she'd talked about that morning, but I guessed so. If she said she'd do something, she did it. Even so, I knew any tail on Kaminski would prove fruitless. He'd know he was being followed and adjust his patterns accordingly. He knew how to make his daily existence as anonymous and lacking in trace evidence as Mark Hudson's was looking right now. He'd proved that in North Carolina. I checked out the street in front of the hotel quickly to see if I could detect where the watching officers might be positioned. A stationary silver car a hundred yards away with blacked-out windows looked the most promising. Unless, I thought, it was Buck Randall himself, keeping an eye on the object he was tormenting. Now wouldn't that be something?

I wandered over and knocked on the car window.

Nothing.

So I knocked again. Louder. This time, the window descended slowly with a whirr. In the driver's seat sat a man who couldn't have been more obviously a police officer had he walked about with the words *Police Officer* tattooed on his forehead in flourescent ink.

'What's he doing?' I said.

'Sorry?' he replied with a show of incomprehension. But he had the look of a schoolboy caught out looking at another kid's test.

'Kaminski,' I said. 'The guy you're watching. What's he been at?'

There was a long pause.

'Do I know you?' he said eventually.

I explained who I was.

Showed him my nice new shiny ID to prove it.

'I heard about you,' he conceded reluctantly.

'Then can I get in?' I said. 'Don't worry, I'm not going to ask to play with your truncheon. I just don't want JJ to see me if he's up there.'

He looked bemused again.

'JJ?'

'JJ . . . Kaminski . . . look, can we continue this conversation behind blacked-out glass?'

By now anyone walking by would've thought I was a hooker fishing for a client.

With a grunt, the surveillance guy finally unlocked the door and let me in, and I slid into the passenger seat, grateful at least for the air conditioning inside.

Cool air played with my hair, and I let it.

'So you know the target?' the driver said to me.

'We used to work together,' I said, 'back in the States. We were in the same FBI field unit. That's why I thought I'd come along tonight and see what's happening.'

Another expressive grunt.

'Nothing is what's happening,' he said. 'Far as we know, he hasn't left his room all afternoon. He had his dinner brought up, some drinks from the bar, and that's about it.'

'Who else is watching?'

'We've got one more keeping an eye on the rear of the building. That's the only exit apart from the firedoors, and they'll set off the alarm anyway if they're opened. He can't get out without our knowing.'

'Isn't that what they said about Clint Eastwood in *Escape from Alcatraz*?'

As if on cue, a voice crackled on to the police radio.

'*He's moving.*'

And a moment later, we were gazing out of the windshield at the steps of the hotel, where Kaminski could now be seen, still looking dishevelled, ruffling his hair. He barely looked up from the ground as he descended the steps and set off along the sidewalk in the direction of town. He certainly didn't look across at the car in which we sat. Maybe he really hadn't noticed it. He was distracted right now, after all. Or maybe he was only making it seem as if he hadn't. I couldn't help wondering if he'd seen me climbing inside and this was his way of yanking my chain. Making me think he was going somewhere.

Making me think he was on his way to meet someone.

Someone like Buck Randall.

Chances were he was just going to pick up another bottle of Jack Daniel's, but I still felt as if something was about to happen. Maybe that's what the strange atmosphere in the city that night had been preparing me for.

I reached for the door handle.

'What are you doing?'.

'I want to follow on foot.'

'You can't follow him, you don't have – Hey, come back!'

I stayed on the other side of the street, keeping Kaminski in view, ready to dodge out of sight if he became suspicious of being followed. But he didn't turn round once. He just walked straight on. A man with a purpose. Or was I simply reading in his actions what I wanted to see? Soon he had crossed the Grand Canal and continued on to Lower Baggot Street. Doubt grew. If Randall had managed to make contact with Kaminski to arrange a meeting, why not somewhere quieter? Or did he want the safety of the crowd around him?

The city began to fill up again, with the same sweating, shouting, laughing, partying summer souls as before, only now they made less impression on me than the breath of a butterfly. My entire attention was focused on Kaminski and his mission.

Wait.

What was this? Kaminski had approached a man standing in a doorway and was talking to him. Could this be . . . Then the man raised his arm and pointed further down the street, and I realized Kaminski had only been asking for directions.

A mute wave of thanks and he was on the move again.

I tried to suppress an ache of disappointment when I saw where Kaminski had apparently been going – an all-night chemist just past Roger's Lane.

Kaminski pushed open the door and disappeared inside.

I edged closer to the glass and looked inside.

Kaminski had stopped in an aisle less than six feet away from me, looking at boxes of painkillers. So much for the big mystery. He was probably just trying to shift a headache from all that Tennessee whiskey earlier. He lifted a packet down and headed to the counter to pay.

I turned and saw the surveillance guy from the car standing across the street at the bus stop, trying his best to look inconspicuous and failing miserably.

He made a gesture as if to say: *What's he doing?*

I shrugged.

I managed to get out of sight before Kaminski emerged from the chemist with his box of pills, and I smiled to myself as his eyes glanced across the street briefly at his pursuer. It would take more than pretending to check out a bus timetable to fool Kaminski.

Had he seen me too?

I wouldn't be surprised.

He set off again in the direction of his hotel, and I couldn't decide whether to bother following him back there. The whole evening seemed to have been a waste of effort on my part, like I'd been trying to prove something to myself without knowing what it was I was trying to prove. I should just head home. My apartment was close. At that moment, bed seemed like the best idea I'd had in a long while. But soon I was glad I stayed out.

There was some kind of disturbance up ahead on the corner of James Street East. A small huddle of people had gathered round in a ring, like they were getting ready for some impromptu teamtalk. Kaminski's steps slowed as he neared them.

In the gaps between the legs of the people watching, I could see a young woman kneeling on the ground, barefoot, grasping the front of her loose nightdress and pulling it tightly to her frame, in an effort to cover herself. The nightdress was torn. She was crying. As I got closer, unconcerned now whether Kaminski saw me, I heard her voice.

Choking.

Pleading.

The breath catching in her throat.

'Don't let him come back,' she was telling them. 'Please, keep him away from me.'

'What is it?' someone asked her.

Between sobs that racked her body like electric shocks, she finally managed to force out the words.

'He tried to kill me,' she said.

He tried to kill me.

And then she started screaming.

28

'What happened to *you* last night?' said Fitzgerald when she called next morning.

For a second, I didn't know what she was talking about.

'I was with Rose Downey, remember?' I said, naming the woman that I'd found crouched and frightened on the ground on the road to Kaminski's hotel the previous night.

'That's my point. You'd gone by the time I got there,' said Fitzgerald. 'I was looking for you. Healy told me you were on the scene when he arrived. Next thing, you were gone.'

'I didn't feel so hot.'

'A headache?'

'I just wanted to get home.'

I guess I didn't sound too convincing.

'You OK?' pressed Fitzgerald. 'You sound strange.'

'It's nothing. Forget it. Like I said, I don't feel so hot.'

'Last time you used that line it was in the past tense,' Fitzgerald said. 'You've deteriorated quickly. Would you rather stay home today?'

'I was thinking of dropping by the hospital to see Rose again.'

'There's not much point. The doctors still have her sedated. They won't let us question her yet. They say she's not strong enough. She had a pretty traumatic ordeal.'

'You didn't manage to get anything out of her about what happened, then?'

'All she said last night was that she came back to her

apartment in James's Place East after a night out with friends, got undressed and ready for bed, and as soon as she turned out the light he jumped on her. He must've been hiding in her bedroom the whole time. Christ knows how she managed to get out, but somehow she managed to open the door and escape.'

'No description?'

'Says she didn't see his face, nor did he say a word. And of course, by the time we got her address out of her, he was long gone.'

'You think it's the same guy?'

'Who knows? We'll have a better idea over the next couple of hours, once her apartment's been properly analysed. The lock on the door was already broken, apparently, so there's no sign of any break-in, there was no need for it, and no restraints were used, but then he didn't have time to finish the job, so who knows what way things may have turned out? I'll be able to give you more details over lunch, if you're interested. There's a price, though. I want you to do something for me first. You know Kim Denning?'

'Marsha Reed's friend. The one who found her body.'

'That's her. She's going round to Marsha's house today to pick up some stuff. We've finished with it now. The keys are being handed back to the father later this afternoon. Apparently he didn't want to deal with clearing out his daughter's personal stuff, so Kim said she'd do it for him. I said I'd go round this morning to open up for her, but after the attack on Rose Downey and what you found out yesterday about Marsha's trips to the internet café, I've got too much to follow up. So what about it? Would you do it for me? I can pick you up at Marsha's place about one and we can go get something to eat together . . .'

Which is how I found myself walking round to Dublin

Castle to pick up and sign for the key to Marsha Reed's house from the desk sergeant, and then continuing on down Patrick Street past the cathedral and over the junction toward Lower Clanbrassil Street.

At least an early night had cleared my head. I was feeling stupid again for allowing myself to be made to feel low by my suspicions. It's just that sometimes when you've lapsed into foolishness, it can be tempting to nurse the foolishness longer than is healthy. In all these years Fitzgerald had never given me a moment's cause to doubt her.

She deserved better than my paranoia.

My moods.

I turned off into Fumbally Lane, relishing, as I always did when I came here, the almost Dickensian quality of the old street names in this area of the city: Ebenezer Terrace, Marrowbone Lane, Black Pitts. When so much else in the city had been prettified and sanitized, it was good to be reminded of the ancient dark heart still beating here.

Marsha Reed's father, Healy had told me, was blaming himself for his daughter's death for buying her a house in this district. He hadn't wanted her to live here. He could have afforded to fix her up with a place of her own in any part of the city. But St Gobnat's was what she wanted, so St Gobnat's was what she got. I got the impression she was the kind of girl who was used to getting what she wanted. The father had been left a widower when Marsha was still young. She'd been spoiled. I wondered if that was what made her seek out such extremes in her sexual life. Was she punishing herself because life had been too easy?

Then I admonished myself for indulging in this pop psychology.

I should leave that to Fisher's new girlfriend.

It was strange, though, how people had an instinct to

blame themselves for things that weren't their fault. It wasn't living in this district which had killed Marsha. Most likely, it was her own bad choices which had done that, and there's nothing parents can do to stop their kids making those once they've flown the coop. Just ask my mother. It wouldn't have mattered where Marsha had lived in the city if her own desires were leading her into danger.

I guessed it would be sold now, I thought as I passed through the front gates and continued up the lane toward the church. Marsha's father would hardly want to keep the place after what had happened to his only child within its walls. For a moment, the thought crossed my mind that we should buy it, Grace and I. That's what she wanted, wasn't it? A place together. And two weeks ago, maybe, it would've been perfect for us. Close to the city for me, peaceful enough for Grace. Did it make a difference that Marsha had died here? *Someone* would live here again. Why not us? And yet I knew, even as I framed the notion in my brain, that this was a non-starter. The house would be tainted for ever now.

'Oh.'

The exclamation came from a red-haired young woman wearing flat shoes and what seemed like jodhpurs, siting on the steps of the church and clutching a purple shoulder bag on her lap. She had a startled look on her face. I guess she hadn't heard me coming.

'I wasn't really sure what time I was supposed to be here,' she explained, scrambling to her feet, once I'd introduced myself.

'You been waiting long?'

'About an hour,' she said, considering. 'I didn't mind. It's so beautiful in here, isn't it? I can't believe this is the last time I'll ever come here. I can't believe someone else is going to be moving in. Everything about it just reminds me so much of Marsha . . .'

She bit her lip gently. Whether it was simply an involuntary habit, or she was trying to stop herself from crying, I couldn't tell. I fitted the key into the lock to let us in.

'I know it sounds strange,' she said, 'but I'd buy it myself if I could. I wouldn't live here. I couldn't. I'd just hate someone to come and pull it down. Marsha loved it so much. After what happened, I wouldn't be surprised if her father had the whole place flattened.'

'Why *don't* you buy it?'

She laughed hollowly. 'I couldn't afford it. I'm an out-of-work actress. The last job I had was the voiceover for a radio ad for toothpaste. My work doesn't even pay my own rent, never mind the mortgage on a place like this.'

'You met Marsha through the theatre, right?'

She nodded as she stepped into the hallway 'We were appearing together in *A Midsummer Night's Dream* . . .' She stopped. 'Listen,' she said. 'It's so quiet.'

It was. The last time I'd been inside the church, Fisher had been talking, detectives had been coming and going, trailing a perpetual echo of footsteps and murmured voices.

Now I knew what the phrase 'silent as the grave' really meant.

This must have been what it was like for Marsha when she was on her own. This must have been what attracted her to the place. Once the door was shut, the world ceased to exist. All was still, undisturbed, uncomplicated. What a contrast to her own messy life.

'I should get started,' Kim said, but she made no move to do so.

'Do you want me to come with you?' I said.

'Would you?'

274

We went through, crossing the main floor to the doors at the other end of the church and walking down the narrow corridor toward Marsha's closet. Kim took out a roll of black garbage bags from her shoulder bag and began to tear them off one by one. She started to fill them methodically with the clothes in Marsha's drawers and her shoes.

'I don't know what I'll do with all this stuff. Give it to the charity shop, I suppose. It doesn't seem right somehow,' she said. 'I know it's not like she has any use for them any more, but she was so passionate about her clothes. She was passionate about *everything*.'

'Does that include Victor Solomon?' I said.

She shot me a look of flame.

'Don't talk to me about that bastard,' she said. 'He's the reason she's dead.'

'You think Solomon killed Marsha?'

'He has an alibi, doesn't he? That's what I heard,' said Kim. 'I didn't mean he physically killed her. Just that if it hadn't been for him, she might still be alive now. All she wanted was to be with him. She was crazy about him. When he rejected her –'

'She put herself at risk trying to forget him?' I finished for her.

'I warned her,' said Kim. 'I knew she'd been going to that club downtown. She used to tell me about it. It was a giggle, that's all.' I recalled that's what Todd Fleming said too. Marsha must have told that to everybody, trying to make the darkness of her desires seem routine and uncomplicated. 'It was mostly role-playing, she said, dressing up, pretending to be someone else for a few hours. Putting on a mask. It's like acting, yeah? I mean, I knew she had these *fantasies*,' she went on reluctantly, 'about being tied up, about being dominated, but if you knew her, you'd understand there was no harm in it. There's nothing wrong with a bit of kinkiness now and then, is there? It's not against the law. Everyone does it these days. They even sell those furry handcuffs on the high street now, don't they?'

From what we now knew of Marsha Reed's sex life, it had gone way beyond a bit of innocent kinky fun with furry handcuffs and silken binds, and I suspected that Kim Denning knew it too, which was why she was subconsciously turning all her statements about her friend into questions, like she was looking to me to back up her need to see all that Marsha did in the best light. I didn't puncture her illusions. I wanted to hear her talk.

'She told me she stopped going to the club after she met Victor,' Kim said. 'She wanted a different life. She wanted to be with him, but she said he wasn't interested in taking things further than a casual thing. Wham bam, thank you, ma'am. That was his style. He gets his kicks pushing the little people like me around on stage. But he wouldn't leave his adoring wife-to-be, and Marsha drifted back into her old world again. If she'd been with him, maybe she'd have been safe. Though whether he would've been is another matter.'

'What do you mean?'

'Marsha was very possessive. I've never met anyone who could get so jealous. She'd just lose it completely when she was mad. If anyone was going to kill anyone, I'd have said it was Marsha who'd kill him, never mind the other way round. She was furious when he said he didn't want her any more. She actually said she'd kill him. She said she'd kill him and then kill herself. I told her not to talk like that. It's ironic, really. If only she'd been more patient.'

'More patient in what way?'

'Didn't you know?' she said, eyes widening in surprise as she paused momentarily from what she was doing.

276

'Solomon's fiancée's dumped him. Everyone was talking about it last night. I met some friends for drinks last night. They're appearing in *Othello* at the moment. They said he was in a foul mood yesterday, and he had a blazing row with her and she ended up throwing his engagement ring back at him.'

'So much for her forgiving him for his relationship with Marsha.'

'I don't blame her,' said Kim. 'Marsha was no angel, I told her she shouldn't get involved with a man who was practically married. But Solomon's the one who was cheating, not Marsha. And it wasn't the first time either. He must've screwed most of the young actresses in Dublin. They think he's going to make them famous, but once he's taken what he wants he can't get rid of them fast enough. And yes, before you ask, he did it to me too. That's why I warned Marsha. I told her what he was like. But she wouldn't listen. She was convinced he really cared about her. I'm just glad he's finally got what was coming to him. Now he knows what it feels like. I'm sorry it didn't come out sooner, that's all.'

'What difference would it have made?' I asked.

'Maybe she'd have seen him for the scumbag that he really is,' she said. 'Maybe she'd have stopped torturing herself over him and found herself a nice guy for a change.'

A guy like Todd Fleming, I thought.

Though sadly, as he found out, she didn't seem to want *nice*.

She didn't even seem to have wanted normal.

29

'So where's lunch?' I said, when Fitzgerald finally pulled up in her Rover at the front gate of St Gobnat's. Kim Denning had left ten minutes earlier. She'd ordered a cab so that she could take all the black bags away with her. Now the church was empty of everything except furniture, and that would be taken away and sold soon enough, I guessed. All traces of Marsha would be gone.

'Bull Island,' Fitzgerald said.

'Is that some fancy new restaurant I haven't heard of?' I said, already knowing the answer by the frowning look of concentration on her face.

'I'm afraid lunch will have to wait,' she said.

'Something happened, huh? Is it Rose?'

'She's still not in a fit state to be interviewed formally. We've got a trauma counsellor on hand in case she feels like talking, but I'm not expecting a breakthrough any time soon. No, it's Mark Hudson. We found out this morning he spent some time in the States before taking up his job here in Dublin. He was living out in New Mexico.'

New Mexico.

'Kaminski claimed Randall killed a woman in New Mexico.'

'Hudson was staying in the same rooming house as the woman who died. He was questioned by the police and the FBI at the time, but he was never in the frame as a suspect.'

'So Randall allegedly kills a woman in the same house Hudson's staying in, then allegedly turns up in Dublin, if Kaminski's to be believed, and now Hudson's gone missing?'

'And there's no allegedly about that part,' Fitzgerald pointed out.

'There's something else too, isn't there?' I said.

'I think we may have found Hudson's car.'

And that was compensation enough for missing lunch.

My stomach could wait.

As we drove back through the city centre and over the river, up Parnell Street and Summerhill, past Fairview Park and on to the road that snaked round by Clontarf Promenade, she explained to me what had happened that morning.

A man by the name of Dermot Bryce had called Dublin Castle. He'd heard a report on the morning news that police were looking for a metallic-blue Honda with a 2002 registration and remembered seeing one a couple of weeks earlier out along the Bull Wall.

The wall had been constructed, I'd read once, about two hundred years ago on the north side of Dublin Bay to provide shelter for the city port and make the passage in and out easier for ships. Behind the wall, huge deposits of sand and silt had gradually been left by the tide and merged to form the so-called Bull Island, three miles long and still growing steadily.

The whole area was now a protected nature reserve, home to thousands of migrating birds such as geese and oystercatchers, as well as housing two golf courses (sometimes I think the whole world is being turned into a golf course). Dubliners often went out to walk or swim, crossing the wooden road-bridge that connected the island to the mainland.

It was the way Bryce had gone that night after quarrelling with his wife.

'I wanted to be by myself for a while,' he explained when we finally found him waiting for us near the coastguard station, as arranged. He worked as a porter at Central Station and was still wearing his uniform, peaked cap and all. He only had another twenty minutes of his lunch break to go, he informed Fitzgerald grumpily. She told him not to be concerned. If he was needed for longer, she'd make sure the station was kept informed.

He didn't look convinced. He looked, in fact, like he was thinking that a call from the Murder Squad was the last thing to make his boss feel happier about a missing employee.

'The sooner you tell us what you saw,' Fitzgerald urged, 'the sooner you can go.'

'I was over there,' Bryce said, pointing further along the road that ran along the Bull Wall and which looked from this angle as if it dropped eventually and disappeared into the sea. And maybe it did, for all I knew. 'Right where that red car is now. You see it? I was just standing there, having a cigarette, looking out, thinking.'

It was certainly one hell of a view, if you could ignore the huge container terminals that dominated the foreshore in the middle distance. Blank those out and the great sweep of Dublin Bay stretched before us, sparkling fiercely in the sunlight, with mountains huddled protectively in the distance, heads wreathed in white clouds so perfect they were like drawings, stone guardians watching over the city that crowded untidily at their feet.

'There was hardly anyone about,' Bryce said. 'It wasn't hot like it is now, it was raining, and it must've been after eleven o'clock. You don't see too many people out here when it's like that. That's probably why he thought I was this Peters fella.'

'Why *who* thought you were?' I said, bemused.

'This man who came along. He was an American, like you. Wearing one of those baseball caps. I'd seen him

280

coming over the bridge in this car, just as I told your people earlier, and he parked right next to me down there and got out and asked me if I was Peters.'

'What did he say when you told him you weren't?' asked Fitzgerald.

'He laughed, that was all, then he told me they had to meet a man here by the name of Peters, who was supposed to be buying the car off them.'

'Them?' I said.

'There was another man in the front seat. I didn't see his face.'

Mark Hudson?

'What did you think of his story?' asked Fitzgerald.

'Seemed like a funny place to be selling a car,' admitted Bryce, 'but it was none of my business. Even if he was up to no good, what was *I* supposed to do about it?'

'So what happened then?'

'To be honest with you, I was worried to start off that the pair of them might be queer, you know? That they might've thought I was that way inclined myself. But he wasn't interested once he knew I wasn't this Peters. He just got back in the car again.'

'Did the two men drive off?'

'No,' he said, shaking his head, 'all they did was sit there, looking out of the windscreen. They were still there when I left to go home about ten minutes later.'

'And you didn't think any more about it until you heard on the radio this morning that the police were looking for a blue Honda?'

'Why would I?' he answered, reasonably enough.

'I wonder if anyone else saw them,' I said to Fitzgerald.

'I told you,' answered Bryce on her behalf, 'there was hardly a sinner about.'

'You didn't see anyone who might've been this Peters, then?' said Fitzerald.

'Not unless he was disguised as a seagull,' he scoffed.

I found myself wondering if this Peters even existed, and noticing as I did so that Bryce was glancing down in an obvious way at his watch.

'Can I go now?' he said.

'In a moment,' said Fitzgerald. 'First I want you to take a look at this.'

'Yeah, that's him,' said Bryce as he took the picture from Fitzgerald's fingers. 'That's the fella I saw that night. So what's he supposed to have done, anyway?'

What had Buck Randall done? Finally proved he really was in the city, that's what.

At least Kaminski wasn't entirely off the wall.

'That'll be all, Mr Bryce,' was the only reply Fitzgerald gave him, returning the picture to her inside pocket. 'We'll be in touch if we need you again. Thanks for your help.'

It was what is officially known as getting the brush-off, and Bryce knew it. He went off muttering about wishing he hadn't bothered. What did he want? A medal?

'Come on,' said Fitzgerald when he was out of earshot.

We walked from the coastguard station along to where the red car that Bryce had pointed out was parked, keeping close to the edge to avoid the other cars that crawled regularly on this road toward the golf club.

I tried to imagine the road empty of people and getting dark. It had to be eerie. Somewhere out among the sand dunes, I could hear birds calling, screeching. At night they must sound like something from another world. I wouldn't like to come here after nightfall, even if I had walked out on a quarrel with my beloved and wanted to clear my head.

It could be cleared just as easily within range of a streetlight.

Immediately to the right of where the cars were parked, the ground dipped unevenly under grass and rocks down toward the sea. Seagulls hopped awkwardly among the stones. They flapped away, crying in protest, as Fitzgerald stepped off the road to join them.

'Let's hope Bryce remembered the right place,' she murmured as I followed her.

Together we crouched down to examine the rocks. She didn't need to tell me what she was looking for. Somewhere here might be the end of the search.

The seagulls returned and settled and watched with interest, heads to one side. Had we managed to find some source of food that they'd missed?

It only took a couple of minutes before Fitzgerald gave a low exclamation.

'Saxon, look.'

A scratch of metallic-blue paint on the edge of a rock.

'I think we'd better call in the divers,' she said softly.

It took them less than an hour to locate Hudson's blue Honda. That is, they found a Honda, though its colour was difficult to determine, the water was so murky down there.

Then came the problem of getting it out.

Getting the lifting crane across the wooden road-bridge was a logistical nightmare in itself. The bridge hadn't been built for that kind of punishment and creaked alarmingly under the strain. The engineers brought in by the DMP Water Unit to oversee the operation insisted it would hold, and hold it did, but I wouldn't have been surprised to see the crane go down to join Hudson's Honda under the water and be swallowed inexorably by the same sand and silt.

There wasn't much for me to do but stand around and watch as the crane manoeuvred bulkily into place on the road, and divers descended anew to attach a hook to the car's rear axle. The grinding of gears filled the air as the crane struggled with the bay for possession of the car. The afternoon was tense with the rasp and scrape of machinery. The seagulls had fled.

And slowly, slowly, fighting its fate, the car emerged, dripping and black with filth.

The fenders were buckled and the grill was pulled into a lopsided grin.

'What can it tell us?' said Fitzgerald.

'Not knowing the answer to that question,' I said, 'is why you have to ask it.'

'How very Zen you are today,' she replied.

She looked apprehensive, though.

Waiting was always worse than disappointment.

The Honda, which could now be seen to have been metallic blue, even if its colour had now become the subject of negotiation with the sea, was dragged over the rocks like a dog at the end of a leash, reluctant to do as it was bidden, until it sat, defeated, on the road.

Even now no one approached it.

'It won't bite, boys,' said Fitzgerald lightly as she stepped up and peered into the windshield and the windshield stared back blackly, guarding its secrets.

The driver's side door was more forthcoming. All the windows had been wound down, presumably to make the car sink more effectively once it entered the water.

Fitzgerald bent down and put her head inside.

There was still water inside and a stench like an open sewer. Christ alone knows what was trapped in the mud that coated the seats. Essence of Dublin Bay: I couldn't see it catching on as a new fragrance. Fitzgerald pulled on a pair of Latex gloves and tried the handle.

It didn't budge.

It was probably just as well, or what was inside the car would've ended up on her shoes.

The other doors wouldn't open either.

Before taking off the handbrake and pushing the car into the water, had Buck Randall crippled the locks to make them harder to open? Why would he have bothered?

Twenty feet down in Dublin Bay was surely barrier enough to the curious?

Fitzgerald shifted round to the back of the Honda and tried the button on the trunk.

Click.

'We're in,' she murmured as she lifted it open.

Then she staggered back violently, as the sweet, decadent, obscene smell of death escaped from the trunk where it had been trapped and took ownership of the shore.

I clasped my hand over my face in a futile attempt to stop the smell assaulting me.

Fitzgerald had the presence of mind not to do the same. She wouldn't want to lift the gloves to her mouth now. Instead she protected her face in the crook of her elbow and turned away. 'After all this time down there, what will be left?' she'd asked.

Not much, was my guess.

Fitzgerald was soon taking charge. She ordered everyone back while the City Pathologist was summoned. What we had now was a crime scene. Nothing was to be disturbed. The engineers and crane crew were told to return to the city. Uniforms were directed into place to keep unwanted onlookers away from the area. Blue tape appeared from nowhere. A shapeless white canopy was shouldered into place around the car, for the police's privacy rather than the victim's, though for that too. It wouldn't take long for the reporters to appear. We sat, waiting for the pathologist to arrive, in a room at the coastguard station which she had immediately requisitioned for use by the Murder Squad.

A young sergeant was dispatched for coffee.

The coffee he found wasn't going to win any awards for taste, but it sufficed. The smell of it at least offered some relief from the smell of decay. Once it gets into your nostrils, it's hard to shift. You keep imagining you can still smell it even when you're far away.

It clings to you.

You wonder why other people haven't noticed it on your hair and clothes.

She didn't need to tell me what she'd seen. Bodies decay much more slowly when immersed in water than in the air, but the process still ain't pretty. After only a few hours in water, the skin becomes wrinkled and white, especially on the soles of the feet and the palms of the hands. It's as if the dead one has been walking on icing sugar.

Within a few weeks, the skin slips off like clothing. Hair becomes loose and as easily lifted off as a badly fitted wig. The body becomes bloated and filled with gas. It easily breaks apart if not handled correctly. The pathologist would want to make as close an examination as he could out here. By the time the body reached the mortuary, many vital indications could have been corrupted or destroyed. Murderers had relied on this fact for centuries, disposing of bodies in water because it eradicated so much of the evidence against them.

'It was definitely a man?' I asked her as we sipped the coffee.

'I'm pretty sure,' she said. 'It looked like a man's clothes.'

'I wonder if he was dead already when he went into the water?'

Whoever it was, I hoped that he *had* been dead already. The alternative, that the victim drowned while trapped in the trunk of the car, was too grisly to contemplate.

Though would we ever know? Determining absolutely the cause of death in these circumstances could prove impossible. Even determining the identity of the victim might be beyond the reach of the science, unless there was adequate DNA or dental records to match against the corpse. In many instances, the body fat itself could be transformed into a greasy, pale, soft substance akin to butter or soap. There would be no face to speak of.

The City Pathologist reminded us of each and every one of these provisos when he arrived with Sean Healy about an hour after the car had been dredged out of the bay.

Alastair Butler was a careful man. He lived carefully, he dressed carefully, he spoke carefully, he worked carefully. It could make him frustrating to deal with, but it did mean that when he made a pronouncement it represented his most exact thinking on the matter.

He did not deal in speculation.

He dealt in facts.

Right now he was staring over the top of his half-moon spectacles, having declined coffee, listening while Fitzgerald outlined the circumstances in which the body had been found.

'Whether he was dead when he went into the water, I don't know,' she told him, 'but I'm assuming the body went into the water the night Bryce met Buck Randall.'

'Assuming, Chief Superintendent?' said Butler quizzically.

'Call it an educated guess, then. Why would he drive all the way out here with Hudson's car, only to come back a second time and double his chances of being seen?'

'Trial run?' I offered.

'Too risky,' she said.

'Murderers do strange things,' Healy said.

'Remember we don't know that he *is* a murderer,' pointed out Fitzgerald. 'We only have Leon Kaminski's word for that. The police in New York didn't think he'd killed anyone.'

'He acts like a murderer,' I said. 'Sneaking around, nameless, invisible.'

'Does that make Kaminski a murderer too?'

'Kaminski?'

'He's been sneaking around as well. Again, we only have his word for it that he's looking for his wife's killer. I don't like it when so much hangs on one man's testimony.' She sighed. 'For that matter, how do we know it isn't *Randall's* body in the boot? This is totally different from the MO Randall himself's used so far.'

'You mean he met . . . what did you say his name was again?' said Healy.

'Peters, according to the witness.'

'He's arranged to meet this Peters, then – Peters, whoever he is, murders him – stuffs him in the boot – pushes the car into the water.'

'That's what I was considering,' said Fitzgerald.

'What about the other man who was seen by Bryce in the front seat?'

'You got me on that one.'

'Randall certainly didn't seem to act like a man with something to hide,' I admitted grudgingly. 'Driving up to a complete stranger out of the blue and starting a conversation with him isn't the best plan of action if you're trying to dispose secretly of a body in the trunk of the car you've let witnesses see you driving.'

But no, Randall couldn't be dead, I told myself firmly,

refusing to follow my imagination down that avenue, because he'd subsequently contacted Kaminski to claim Marsha Reed's murder for himself. He mustn't have expected to meet anyone out here, I decided. The line about Peters must've been the first thing that came into his head to cover his back. Though wouldn't killing Bryce have covered it better?

For once, I could see the benefit of Alastair Butler's way of doing things. Speculation wasn't getting us anywhere. First we needed to know who was dead in the trunk.

Everything else would flow from that.

'I'd say it's over to you, Doc,' I told Butler.

'Don't expect any miracles,' he murmured disapprovingly. 'I only perform those on Sundays.' And with that, he and Fitzgerald went off to get themselves suitably boiler-suited for the gruesome task ahead. Fitzgerald did not look like she was relishing the prospect.

'I still don't see what any of this has to do with Marsha Reed,' said Healy, when we were left alone with the cold coffee and he was standing at the window watching them go.

I couldn't see any obvious connection either but didn't want to admit it.

'One thing at a time,' I said carelessly instead.

'You're not wrong there,' he said. 'In this job, one at a time is more than enough.'

30

'Is it so absurd?' I asked Fisher later as we sat in Fitzgerald's office in Dublin Castle.

'That Buck Randall would come to Dublin to kill Hudson?' said Fisher. 'Not absurd, no. Personally I've never come across it before, but I've certainly read of similar cases.'

Late afternoon was mingling into early evening. For the first time in weeks, low clouds had rolled in and were sagging heavily on the tops of buildings. There might even be rain later. I couldn't remember the last time it rained. The city needed it. Already there was relief in the streets below that the incessant jabbing of the sun's rays had eased temporarily.

A moment earlier Fitzgerald had gotten off the phone to Alastair Butler to confirm that the body in the trunk really was that of the missing Mark Hudson. Unsurprisingly, there was no possibility of a visual identification – the water had seen to that – but Hudson's driver's licence had been found in an inside pocket of the victim's jacket, as well as his house keys, and a wallet containing a couple of credit and store cards in his name.

More to the point, since those could have been planted on the body, Fitzgerald had already had the foresight to pull in Hudson's dental records before the body was returned to the mortuary for the autopsy. It was a relatively simple matter once the victim was X-rayed to establish that it was indeed Cecelia Corrigan's unfortunate neighbour dead in his own car.

What Butler also found was a non-fatal wound to the

back of the head, probably caused by some ordinary metal household tool such as a poker, as well as high levels of a particular brand of insecticide in the victim's bloodstream. It suggested that Hudson had been poisoned, though whether it would ever be possible to prove completely that this was how he met his death, considering the deteriorated state of the remains, was another matter. He may have been dead already when the wound was inflicted to his head. Butler still couldn't determine whether the wound was post-mortem or ante-mortem. More tests would be needed to prove that. All we knew for certain was that Mark Hudson's killer had exhibited an entirely different MO from the man who had killed Marsha Reed. Unless that was the point. Unless the change of tactic was nothing but a ruse designed, *staged*, again, to throw Buck Randall's pursuers off the scent. Presuming, that is, that Buck Randall was the killer.

Right now, he was the only angle we had to go on.

Randall's presence in the city had not been adequately explained.

He was seen with a car belonging to Mark Hudson at the water's edge.

The car was recovered with Hudson's murdered body inside.

Randall's fingerprints were, we had since learned, all over the interior.

Concluding that Buck Randall had serious questions to answer was not jumping to conclusions. It was simply following the evidence to its logical end.

But there was still the small question of why a prison guard from Huntsville, Texas, would come all this way to murder a man who had, apparently accidentally, killed a woman who had been writing to a prisoner the guard had known on Death Row.

Did it have anything to do with the death of the woman in New Mexico? If not, then the whole thing was a coincidence, and I believed in those even less than I believed in fairies.

'Maybe Jenkins Howler just *asked* him to do it,' said Fitzgerald.

'Why?' said Healy.

'Why did he agree to do it, do you mean, or why did Howler want him to?'

'Both.'

'Starting with the second, Howler might've believed that Hudson deliberately killed Cecelia Corrigan,' she said. 'We still can't say for definite that he didn't. We've no reason to suppose that he did, but that only means we have no evidence, not that it didn't happen.'

'OK,' said Healy, 'I'll accept that, but why then would this Buck Randall agree to do it? Cecelia wasn't *his* penfriend. She meant nothing to him.'

'But Howler meant something to him,' I said. 'You heard how close the two of them were. They were thick as thieves.'

'Thick as murderers even,' murmured Walsh, who was sitting with his feet up on the windowsill, drinking a cup of coffee and absently sending text messages on his cellphone as we all talked. From the frequency with which they were coming I suspected it must be one of his latest conquests. I hadn't even thought he was listening properly. Obviously I was wrong.

'Exactly,' I said. 'If Howler asked him, he might've felt it was his duty to do it.'

'A doomed friend's last wish, you mean?' said Fisher.

'That's not so unimaginable, is it?' I said.

'I already told you,' said Fisher. 'It's not unimaginable at all. Many perpetrators have committed murder in the past in order to please another person, a person who meant a lot to them. That's why we have laws against committing murder by proxy. If it didn't and couldn't happen, there'd be no point having a law against it.'

'I thought murder by proxy usually meant contract killings,' said Walsh.

'Those are the most common kind of proxy killings, where you simply pay someone to commit the murder that you are either unable or unwilling to commit yourself.'

'But you don't think that's what happened in this case?'

'I suppose Jenkins Howler *may* have found some convoluted way of financially reimbursing Buck Randall for committing this murder on his behalf, but it all looks rather implausible,' confessed Fisher. 'More likely, if he did come all this way to do this last favour for Howler, then it was because of a convergence of interests at that particular moment. They were each getting something out of it. Or he might not even have told Howler that he was going to do it. It might've been a posthumous tribute to a friend who'd died on Death Row.'

'You don't think he was under Howler's influence when he acted, then?' I said.

'He might've been,' said Fisher, though he was so cool about the idea I guessed it wasn't one he'd entertained for long. 'If there is one thing habitual killers are good at, apart from not getting caught, it's finding other human beings' weak spots and exploiting them for their own ends. They use charm, cunning, fear, pity, whatever it takes to get what they want. Making it seem, for example, that they're that person's only friend, or that something bad will happen if they don't do the thing which is being asked of them. They work at people insidiously until they do exactly what they're being directed to do. They act out their will using other people as the weapons. What can I say? It happens. Many are weak, and the few are strong. The few are bound to prey on the many. It's crime as Darwinism. The innocent often fall under the spell of psychopaths until they're completely in their power.'

'If Kaminski's right about Randall killing his wife and the other woman in New Mexico,' I pointed out, 'he's not so innocent.'

'I didn't say it was only the innocent,' said Fisher. 'In fact, if Randall did come to Dublin to kill Mark Hudson, it strongly suggests that he *was* the one who killed those two unfortunate women in the States, as your friend so vehemently suspects. Not least because the hold a killer has over a person who comes into his orbit inevitably diminishes the further away that person gets in time and place from the source of the influence, and Buck Randall's been away from Howler's influence for months now. He'll hardly still be acting under Howler's control.'

'In other words, Randall killed Hudson because he wanted to, not because he was being compelled to in some way by Howler's evil eye?'

'Undoubtedly. If he *did* kill Hudson, at any rate – which, I need hardly remind you, remains only a working hypothesis, however superficially attractive. I know, I know,' Fisher exclaimed, holding up his hand to repel our objections, 'the fingerprints, the witness statements. But it's still circumstantial evidence. It only means he was *there*.'

'I wonder if Howler knew Randall was a killer already,' I said, half to myself, ignoring his caveats.

'I seriously doubt that Randall would have taken the risk of letting him find out the precise details of his previous adventures,' said Fisher pointedly again. 'It would have given Howler too much power, and Randall can't be that stupid.

In fact, that's another discrepancy in this whole situation. Usually in these proxy relationships, there's a dominant, clever, manipulative one, and a weaker, more submissive partner. Here it's not so easy to disentangle which was which. It could be that Randall was the dominant one in the relationship all along. He may have been the one who latched on to Howler, feeding off his energy in some malignant way, not the other way round. Or maybe it was simply a meeting of minds, like souls with the same appetites and desires being drawn together.'

'Like falling in love,' I said.

'Now you mention it, that's another discrepancy,' Fisher said. 'These kinds of interdependent murderous relationships I'm talking about generally have some sexual basis. The wife or girlfriend of the killer does what he asks of them, even becoming a murderer in their own right, because they want to keep the connection they have with this man going, or to maintain an erotic intensity that needs blood to feed on. There's nothing to suggest there was anything like this between Buck Randall and Jenkins Howler.'

'They could've been doing one another through the bars,' remarked Walsh appreciatively. He offered the room a wide grin and got stony faces in reply.

'You know, Walsh,' said Fitzgerald, 'sometimes I worry about you.'

'I'm serious, Chief,' said Walsh. 'I had a drink once with this prison officer who worked up in the women's wing at Mountjoy. There was one girl in for shoplifting who used to offer him all sorts of off-the-cuff services in her cell. It happens all the time.'

'I'm surprised you don't quit and put in an application up there yourself,' I said.

He looked offended.

'*I* don't need to. This guy was one ugly fucker. He needed all the help he could get.' Suddenly he stopped himself. 'Oh, sorry for swearing, Chief.'

Fitzgerald simply shook her head in bewilderment.

'Can we get back to the subject?' she said wearily.

'To be fair,' said Fisher, suppressing a smile, 'it's not such an outlandish suggestion. Prisoners and prison officers do often find themselves in inappropriate sexual relationships. You don't stop being a sexual being just because you've been incarcerated. Prison officers have been known to abuse that need for intimacy to satisfy their own desires. It's a power thing. But in this instance? I don't know enough about them to rule it out or in.'

'That's why I've asked the police in Texas and the prison authorities there to send us all they have on Buck Randall,' explained Fitzgerald. 'The more we know about him, the easier it will be to predict his next move. Predict it and, let's hope, prevent it.'

'I only hope there's enough in what they send to get some handle on this man,' said Fisher. 'Right now, I feel like I'm blundering about in a room where all the windows have been blacked out. It's like making a psychiatric assessment of a patient that you've never even met and whose actions and motivations you only ever hear about third and fourth hand.'

'Anything that helps find him is an improvement on where we are now,' said Fitzgerald. 'Though I have to tell you that, from what I've heard so far, Randall had an exemplary record as an employee. There wasn't a single official complaint against him.'

'He did drink, didn't he, according to one report?' I said. She acknowledged it with a nod.

'There's a possible angle. Drink's a classic disinhibitor,' Fisher pointed out.

'Finding an American in the city has to be easier than finding a local, at any rate,' I added. 'We know from the witness on Bull Island that Randall's making no effort to conceal his accent. How many Americans can there be here? At the very least, he has to be living somewhere, eating somewhere, getting money somewhere. He'll have left a trace.'

'Unless he's being sheltered by someone,' Healy suggested.

'No object moves through space without causing some disturbance,' I said. 'And Randall doesn't seem to want to move through it without causing some ripples at least.'

'You mean Kaminski?' said Fitzgerald.

'I do. It's no fun for him playing his games alone. He wants others to join in too.'

'Two may be company,' said Healy, 'but he might consider *us* joining in as well to constitute a crowd.'

'Then we'd better do all we can', said Walsh, 'to make sure he doesn't know we have joined the game.'

'Isn't that going to be a bit difficult,' I pointed out, 'when he notices on the news that we've dredged up the evidence of his latest handiwork from Dublin Bay?'

'There's a message for you,' said the doorman, Hugh, when I finally made it through the front door of my building at eight o'clock that evening, looking forward to a shower and a drink.

I recognized Kaminski's handwriting at once when I took the envelope from him.

I tore it open and read the message inside.

I'll pick you up outside at 8.30.

The letters RSVP had been added in, then crossed out.

'When did this come?' I asked Hugh.

Hugh looked uncomfortable. 'I've been busy,' he said. 'Mrs Williams upstairs had a busted cistern again, I had to put out the bins —'

'What time did it come, Hugh?'

'About nine this morning,' he said sheepishly.

'In other words, it was already sitting in my mailbox about an hour before I stood here talking to you about your bunions, and you didn't even give it to me?'

'It was my ingrowing toenail actually,' said Hugh.

'That's not really the point, is it?'

'I'm sorry, my mind was on other things . . .'

'Forget it,' I sighed. 'It's done.'

I checked my watch.

It was now five after eight. I still had time to get ready if I got moving. There was no question but that I was going to accept the invitation. If Kaminski had decided to end his sulk, I wasn't about to screw it up because my doorman was a certifiable idiot.

I ran upstairs and into my apartment. Quickly checked that there were no messages waiting for me on the phone. There weren't. Another five minutes to shower and pull on a clean pair of jeans and a shirt, and as long as it took to send a hurried and badly spelled text message to Fitzgerald explaining what I was doing, and I was back down in the lobby again before the clock had reached the half hour.

Hugh was sitting with his feet up in his small office, watching soccer on TV.

'Any more messages for me,' I asked him, 'or are you planning to save them all up and give them to me tied up with a silk ribbon for Christmas?'

'Christmas isn't for months yet,' he said blankly.

'That's the point, Hugh, it was a . . . oh, never mind. Go back to sleep.'

I pushed open the door and stepped out into the evening air just as Kaminski appeared at the foot of the steps. He'd put on a jacket, shaved, combed his hair. It was an improvement.

'I expected you to be late,' he said when he saw me.

'Why?'

'I figured you'd want to make me wait in punishment for having gone cold on you.'

'It's true I thought you were pissed with me,' I said, 'but it never crossed my mind to take it out on you. I'm tired of playing games. I want to know what's going on, that's all.'

'It wasn't that you couldn't wait a moment longer than necessary to see me, then?'

'Don't flatter yourself, Kaminski.'

'I'm way past flattering myself,' Kaminski said. 'I was just jagging you. Must be the excitement of hitting the social scene again. You know, this is my first night out since my wife died. Most nights I just sit alone in front of the TV flicking channels.'

'You sound like my doorman,' I said.

'Is that a bad thing?'

'If you'd met him, you wouldn't have to ask. So tell me, where are we going?'

'That's a surprise.'

'I hate surprises,' I said. 'But I'm glad you're talking to me again. I never wanted to make you mad. I only wanted to help find the man who killed your wife, and I thought my way was the best way. I thought you weren't thinking right at the time.'

'It's water under the bridge,' Kaminski said. 'Things have moved on.'

'What is it? I can tell from your voice that something's up.'

'You could say that.'

'What happened?'

'What's happened is I'm making progress at last,' he said.

'Tell me, come on, don't make a meal of it.'

'Patience,' he said infuriatingly.

And he stopped any further questions by hailing a cab, and we climbed in the back while he gave an address written down on a scrap of paper to the driver up front.

The driver took one look at it and then made his way to the lights at the corner. He continued straight on past University College on our right before turning left on to Camden Street and away from town until we were over the canal and on to the Rathmines Road.

As we drove, a light rain began to brush the windshield, the fulfilment of the vague promise in the clouds I'd seen above the bay earlier in the day.

I wondered if the tail was keeping up.

'Here,' said Kaminski as we drove along.

He handed me a scrap of newspaper from of his pocket.

At first I thought it was the same story I'd found near his bed in his first hotel, until I noticed the typeface was different.

'What is it?' I said.

'Take a look.'

I took a look. It was an ad from the personal columns of a local newspaper. The *In Memoriam* column. It read: *Cecelia, fondly remembered, a friend of a friend from Texas.*

'It was in yesterday's edition,' he said.

'Who put it in?' I said.

'A friend of a friend from Texas,' said Kaminski. 'Can't you read?'

'Why would Buck Randall want to put a message like this in the local rag?'

'Because he knows I'll be looking for traces of him everywhere. He wanted me to see it. To show me that he's still in town. Still in the game.'

The message would certainly confirm what Fisher had been tentatively suggesting earlier that evening: that Randall might have killed Mark Hudson as a tribute to his late friend Howler. But had Kaminski gotten it confirmed that Randall paid for the message to go in?

'The newspaper wouldn't tell me who placed the message. Customer confidentiality. But I had a hunch. I went along to the cemetery where she's buried, and I was right. There were fresh flowers on the grave. The gardener who tends the place told me that fresh flowers had come for Cecelia Corrigan every morning for the past three weeks.'

'Becky might've sent them,' I said, though it didn't sound like something she'd do.

'The niece? I thought of that,' said Kaminski, 'so I went there this morning and talked to the guy who delivered the flowers. He said an American came in three weeks ago, put down a bundle of cash and instructed them to send flowers every day for the next month.'

I remembered the rough bouquet of flowers which had been stopped at customs a couple of weeks after Cecelia's funeral, purporting to come from Death Row.

'Randall?' I said.

'None other. The delivery boy IDed the picture.'

That man was everywhere.

Where the road forked beyond the Town Hall, we now continued left and soon disappeared into the maze of well-behaved residential streets and squares that dwelt in the en-folding arms of Rathmines Road on one side and Ranelagh Road on the other. A mellow mid-evening mood had settled on the district. Inside the houses, I imagined the city's tribe of urbane, well-dressed, well-paid couples sharing a glass of wine over spaghetti.

But where were *we* going?

I got my answer as we pulled up outside a small wooden door set into a wall and covered with graffiti. The back entrance to the cemetery.

Kaminski sure knew how to show a woman a good time.

The rain was getting harder as we climbed out. It was nothing much by Dublin's standards, but I still wished I'd brought a jacket with me as Kaminski handed money through the window to the driver and the cab pulled away from the kerb, leaving us alone.

'So this is your idea of a night out?' I said to him.

'I thought you'd want to see it for yourself.'

'The morning would've been just fine.'

'Waiting is for fools,' said Kaminski. 'Besides, I got a call about an hour ago from someone who works here saying he'd seen someone hanging around the grave. I thought it might be worth checking out and figured you wouldn't mind missing dinner to help me.'

'I guess it'd be a silly question to ask how we're going to get in?' I went on, trying the handle and finding it locked.

'Since when did you let a little door get in the way?'

I hoped he wasn't going to suggest we climb over the wall. I'd hate to fall off and have to explain to the docs in the emergency room that I'd been breaking into a cemetery.

People can be funny about things like that.

'Then aren't you glad I have a key?' said Kaminski, and he produced it with a flourish from his pocket like some street-corner card-sharp pulling out an ace from his sleeve. 'You're not the only one who knows how to bribe the staff to get inside where they're not supposed to be,' he said, and laughed to himself too loudly. I was beginning, I must confess, to find his manner disconcerting. There was something giddy about him.

Excitable.

'Let's get it over with,' I said.

Right now, I wanted to be off the street and out of sight, even if the graveyard was the only alternative. The company of the dead had never bothered me. They couldn't hurt anyone. Besides, there were old bones everywhere. Just because you couldn't see them didn't mean they weren't there. Cemeteries were just places to gather the bones up tidily.

Kaminski unlocked the door and we stepped inside. Thankfully, it was still light enough to see by, though the rain was quickly dimming the light as it got heavier. Puddles had started to form on the footpaths between the neatly tended graves.

Kaminski didn't hesitate but headed straight into the heart

of the cemetery, ignoring the paths and weaving instead among the headstones to where he needed to go.

That was a grave in a far corner, by the wall, overhung with the thin rain-dripping branches of a weeping-willow tree. By the time I caught up with him, he was standing mutely in front of it, staring down at the brown mound of earth topped with a large bouquet of flowers that marked the spot where Cecelia Corrigan was buried.

To be honest, I couldn't see why he'd needed to bring me here at all.

There was nothing to see beyond what he'd already told me about in the cab, and I was about to say so scornfully when I became aware that he hadn't moved a muscle since I'd caught up with him at the graveside. After his earlier restlessness, there was something unnerving about that too, and I looked across at him to check that he was all right.

'Kaminski?'

His eyes were wide.

'Someone's disturbed the earth,' he said.

'What?'

'Someone's been digging,' he said, and suddenly he knelt in front of the mound of soil and began to claw at it with his hands, oblivious to the wet dirt that soon caked his hands.

'Kaminski, stop it, you can't do that.'

He only dug all the more furiously.

'What are you —'

My voice failed as he stopped digging and held up something between his fingers.

Something shiny.

It was a ring.

'Marsha,' I breathed.

But there were tears in his eyes as he held it up, and I

realized it couldn't be Marsha Reed's missing ring. Why would he cry over that? It was Heather's. He didn't need to tell me.

'I have to call Fitzgerald,' I said.

I sensed him bristle with alarm.

'What has this got to do with her?' he snarled, and his fingers gripped the ring more tightly as if afraid I was about to take it off him. 'This is between Randall and me.'

I'd given away too much, but it was too late to back out.

'They found the body of the man who knocked down Cecelia Corrigan today,' I said.

'What?'

'His car was lifted out of Dublin Bay,' I said. 'Hudson was in the trunk.'

He clambered to his feet, his knees brown with wet earth, and something of the fight seemed to have gone out of him.

'This changes everything,' he said bleakly.

'In what way?'

'Everyone in this damn city is going to know about Buck Randall soon,' he said. 'How long do you think the press will take before they find out who he is? And how long do you think Randall's going to hang around in Dublin once his cover's blown? I've lost him.'

'No.'

'Yes! I know what he's like. I've been following his trail long enough. If he sees that Hudson's body's been found, he's going to be out of here faster than a fucking jet plane. It'll ruin everything. He'll not be there, I know he won't.'

There was something else going on here that he wasn't telling me about.

'He'll not be *where*, Kaminski?'

Kaminski turned his head away and wouldn't listen.

'He made contact again, didn't he?' I said. 'That's what

you were hinting about earlier outside my apartment when you told me to be patient? Shit, Kaminski, if you have any idea where Randall is, you have to tell the police, can't you see that?'

'I don't have to tell anyone anything,' he said bitterly. 'I thought I'd give you a second chance tonight to help me, but there's no way I'm going to let him slip through my fingers a second time.' And I knew from the cold way that he spoke that he'd made up his mind. I also knew there was only one way I could get him to change it.

32

'I can't believe you did this to me,' said Kaminski.

'I told you once before,' I said. 'If you're not thinking straight, I'm going to have to do your thinking for you.'

It was 2 a.m.

The trip to the cemetery had ended abruptly when police called to arrest Kaminski on suspicion of having entered the country using a false passport. It had been my idea. While he knelt at the graveside, I'd silently texted Fitzgerald and told her I thought Kaminski had information on Buck Randall that he had no intention of sharing willingly.

And if he wouldn't share it willingly, then unwillingly was the only other way.

Right now, Kaminski was on the wrong side of an interview desk in Dublin Castle, while Fitzgerald and I sat on the other side, a sergeant at the door on guard, waiting for the realization of his situation to hit him, at which point he might become more cooperative.

There was no sign of it happening yet.

The room was taut with Kaminski's rage.

I couldn't say I blamed him.

'I can't believe you did this to me,' he said again. Then he corrected himself. 'No, now I think of it, what I really can't believe is that I *let* you do this to me again. It was stupid, stupid, stupid. I should've learned my lesson the first time you betrayed me.'

'You use that word too easily,' I told him.

'It's the right word.'

'It's the wrong word, and you know it,' I said. 'Come on, Kaminski, stop playing the wounded innocent and start looking at things the right way up. Buck Randall's in the city someplace, *you* don't know where he is, *we* don't know where he is, and even if you do find out where he is he's going to be waiting for you to come to get him. You don't stand a chance.'

'And you think your friends in this dump do?'

'They stand a better chance than a guy who's acting like he's lost his mind and suddenly thinks he's Superman or something. Is it a bird? Is it a plane? No, it's Leon Kaminski, flying through the air in search of the man who killed his wife.'

'That's a cheap shot,' said Kaminski, looking at me with disgust.

'I'm just trying to make you see that you need help,' I said. 'You can't do this alone.'

'I managed to get this far on my own.'

'The only reason you managed to get this far was because he *told* you where he was,' I reminded him. 'If Buck Randall hadn't made contact with you and given you the come-on, you'd still be bumming around Texas trying to pick up his scent.'

'I'd have found him,' he said thickly.

'Maybe you would've, maybe you wouldn't, we'll never know,' I said. 'What we do know is that he's here someplace in the city right this minute, while we sit here swapping pleasantries, and if you seriously want to bring him down you're going to have to to start understanding that we can't let you run around Dublin like a grenade with the pin taken out, ready to blow. If you really want Randall brought in, you're going to have to get over this chip on your shoulder about the police and start cooperating – beginning by telling us what message he's given you this time. And don't bother pretending you don't know what I mean.'

'I've told you already, I'm not saying a goddam thing.'

Fitzgerald, who'd been sitting quietly the whole time, leafing through a sheaf of papers on her knee, tutted softly at that and shook her head, and she went on tutting softly and shaking her head without raising her eye once from the page, like everything she was reading there was shocking her profoundly, like she'd never known such a miscreant in all her days.

In the end, she sighed melodramatically and threw the papers face up on to the desk, before leaning back in her chair and fixing Kaminski with a faintly amused look.

'Do you know what the penalty is if you're found guilty of entering the country on a false passport?' she asked him.

'No. Should I?'

'If you're going to be travelling round the world on false passports, it's the sort of thing you should probably bone up on. To be honest, I'm not quite sure myself what the penalty is. Immigration law isn't my specialty, and that department'll be closed till nine this morning. Pity. But it couldn't be that severe, could it? It's not like this is North Korea.'

'I'm glad to hear it,' Kaminski said sarcastically.

'Then again,' she added, 'yours *is* a particularly provocative case. I just got a preliminary list of what my officers found when they searched your hotel room.' She nodded at the thin sheaf of papers. 'It makes fascinating reading. One false passport I can understand, two even, but how many was it you had again? I've forgotten.' She picked up the papers and flicked through to the relevant page. 'Five, that was it. That's a lot of false passports. Any judge worth his salt is going to think you were up to no good, Mr Kaminski.'

'We both know that, once I get an attorney, this case has no more chance of reaching the courtroom than Saxon here has of winning this year's Miss Charm contest.'

'True,' agreed Fitzgerald. 'She probably would struggle, though she's been working hard at her manners lately, haven't you, Saxon? Some of her handlers think they might even be able to start introducing her to polite society in the next few months.'

'Is there a point to this pantomime?' groaned Kaminski.

'Just killing time,' said Fitzgerald cheerfully. 'We've got another two or three days of each other's company to get through, so we might as well enjoy it.'

'Two or three days?'

The truth was slowly dawning on the poor klutz.

'That's how long we get to hold you before we either have to charge you or release you,' said Fitzgerald. 'So even if you're right and there's no chance of your being convicted of travelling on a false passport, or you *are* convicted and given a token fine in sympathy for your situation, the point remains that you'll still be spending the next seventy-two hours here with us.'

'You wouldn't do it,' said Kaminski but he didn't sound too confident.

'Wouldn't I?'

'You can't,' he said, and I thought I detected the first note of panic in his voice. 'I can't spend the next three days here. It'll fuck up everything.'

'Have somewhere to go, do you?' asked Fitzgerald disingenuously.

'You know I have somewhere to go,' Kaminski spat back. 'It's what this whole thing has been about. It's what it's all been leading up to. If I don't get out . . . Saxon, help me.'

The attempt at persuasion had turned into a plea now. His desperation was a pitiable sight.

'I'm sorry,' I said. 'There's nothing I can do for you now.'

'It's not Saxon you should be worried about, Mr Kaminski,' said Fitzgerald. 'It's me. Look at me. I'm a Detective Chief Superintendent with the Murder Squad of the Dublin Metropolitan Police. Do you honestly think I can just let you walk out of here, knowing that you may have information I need to locate a man that I urgently need to talk to? This isn't just about you and Buck Randall any more and what happened in New York, it's about what's happening right here, right now, outside that door, and what might happen in the future.'

'But if you don't let me go,' said Kaminski, 'you'll never find him.'

'And maybe nor will you. That's a risk we'll both be taking – unless you come to your senses and realize that you have to share with us what you know. I know you're afraid he'll slip out between your fingers if we get involved, but that's the last thing I can afford to let happen as well. You must see that. We have to give each other a break.'

'How do I know I can trust you?'

'Trust doesn't come into it. This is simply a mutually beneficial arrangement. And the sooner you're straight with us, the sooner you can start taking advantage of it.'

In response, Kaminski closed his eyes, considering, silent, still. I caught Fitzgerald's eye as we waited for an answer. She raised her eyebrows in a kind of shrug. She didn't know which way this was going to go either. Kaminski had always been unpredictable.

'OK,' he said eventually.

His eyes opened and met hers piercingly.

'You'll tell us what you know?' she said.

'I'll tell you. And in return, you let me go.'

'That's the deal,' she said.

Kaminski took a deep breath. 'Buck Randall sent me another message,' he said. 'It was slipped under my door when I came back to the hotel two nights ago. He was setting up a meeting.'

'There was no note in your room,' said Fitzgerald, tapping a finger on the inventory of stuff from Kaminski's hotel room that she'd been consulting earlier.

'I had it with me when you arrested me at the cemetery.'

Fitzgerald frowned. 'Bring in the box of Mr Kaminski's possessions that were taken from him when he arrived here tonight,' she said to the sergeant at the door. 'I'm warning you,' she added to Kaminski when the other policeman had gone, 'if you try anything clever, if you even think about double-crossing us or try to keep us in the dark in some way about what's going on here, I'm going to have you put back immediately under arrest. And this time it won't be for entering the country on a false passport, it'll be as an accessory to murder. I'm just going to have to assume that you *want* this bastard to get away.'

'I understand,' said Kaminski.

The sergeant returned presently with the box and passed it to Fitzgerald's outstretched hands. She began to sift through the contents. Not that there was much to sort. When he was brought in, Kaminski had been carrying a wallet with the usual assortment of credit cards and cash, some loose change, a cellphone, a book of matches from, of all places, the Mountain House Lodge in Aspen, Colorado, a flyer advertising some funfair that was opening later tonight down on Merrion Square West, a clipping from the newspaper about Marsha Reed's murder, a packet of mints, a ballpoint pen and a receipt for the headache pills I'd watched him buy when he was being followed the night before.

'I'm not seeing any message here,' said Fitzgerald menacingly.

Kaminski reached over and lifted out the flyer for the funfair.

'*This* is the message,' he said. 'Randall left it under my door. He means this is where I have to meet him.'

Fitzgerald took the flyer, unfolded it and read through it quickly, turning it over a couple of times to make sure that she hadn't missed anything.

'There's no writing on it,' she said. 'How do you know it's a message from him?'

'I put two and two together is how.'

'What makes you so sure you haven't come up with five?' I said.

'Or a hundred and one,' said Fitzgerald.

'Maybe everyone on your floor got one of these pushed under their door,' I added.

'I asked,' said Kaminski. 'They didn't.'

'Still seems a bit weak to me,' said Fitzgerald.

'Listen,' said Kaminski. 'I know this bastard. I've lived with him inside my head for months now. Trying to think like him. Trying to see the world as he sees it. That's what we were taught, right, Saxon? You become one with the killer. That's how you catch him. So when I say I know this came from Randall, you're just going to have to take my word for it.'

'Very well,' said Fitzgerald. 'I've got no choice. You're doing no good to me taking up space here. You can go. You can make your date at the funfair. And we'll be there too.'

'Just make sure you don't mess up,' he warned her.

'It's stopping you from messing up that this is all about,' she replied. 'You don't have to worry about us. Buck Randall won't know we're there.'

He didn't answer that.

I guess trusting the local police was still a step too far for the former FBI man.

'You're not bullshitting us, are you, Kaminski?' I said quietly.

He fixed me with a look of such bitterness that it almost made me gasp.

'You're the expert on everything,' he snapped. 'You're the one who always knows best. So you tell me, Special Agent. Can I be trusted? Is my word my bond?'

'I honestly don't know any more,' I answered.

'Honestly?' he echoed with a harsh laugh. 'There's an ironic word from a woman who's just had someone she calls her friend arrested.'

'At least I know now that I don't have to worry about you two still harbouring feelings for one another,' said Fitzgerald, as, from an upstairs window, we watched, Kaminski crossing the yard of Dublin Castle on his way back to freedom. 'If looks could kill . . .'

It had taken a while to get rid of Kaminski. As Fitzgerald had explained to him when he complained about how long it was taking, Dublin wasn't some Third World dictatorship. You couldn't just arrest and then unarrest someone without finishing the paperwork.

'Do you think he was telling the truth?' I asked her now, as Kaminski turned down Dame Street and disappeared from view.

'You tell me. You know him better than I do. But I'm

going to send someone round to personally babysit him until it's time to go to the funfair. There's not much more I can do than that. Letting him go is a risk I have to take. If it gives us Buck Randall, I'll be a hero. If Kaminski's leading us up the garden path, I'll look like a fool. That's life.'

We remained at the window, looking out as the rooftops began to lighten. Summer mornings came early, and by now it was well after five. The traffic had begun. At times it felt like it never stopped, not really. The streets still retained a film of wet from the overnight rain, but it would be gone by the time the sun had risen fully. A few hours of rain couldn't stop the summer in its tracks. Already I thought I could detect its intensity rising steadily once more.

'You should try to get some sleep,' she said to me eventually.

'What's the point?' I said.

'You'll need to save your strength for tonight, if you intend to be there.'

'At the fair?' I said. 'Try keeping me away. I love carnivals. That's where I first learned to drive, on the dodgem cars.'

'So that's why your insurance premiums are so high.'

'What about you?' I asked her. 'Don't you need sleep any more?'

'I can't. Not for a while yet,' she admitted. 'I had a call last night after you left. It was from Victor Solomon's fiancée. Ex-fiancée, I should say. They've split up.'

'Marsha's friend told me,' I said. 'What did she want?'

'She didn't want to talk over the phone,' said Fitzgerald. 'She asked if I could go round to her place this morning at eight. So you see, there's not much point in my trying to sleep.'

'Oh, well, sleep is overrated. We already waste enough of our lives in its grip as it is. One minute out of every three we ever live, we're unconscious. Think of all the things we could be doing with that time instead. It'll do us good to skip it for a night.'

'You think so?' said Fitzgerald. 'I've always thought it was the other two thirds we spend awake which were really wasted. I'd happily spend the rest of my life in bed.'

'Mmm, me too, now you mention it.'

'That's not what I meant.'

'Spoilsport.'

'But since you're so keen to defy the sandman,' she said, 'why don't you come along with me later to interview the woman who narrowly escaped becoming Victor Solomon's third wife? I'm sure if we get enough coffee inside us between now and eight o'clock, we might even be able to manage to look vaguely human by then.'

'I wouldn't bank on that,' I said, 'but sure. Sounds fun.'

'I'm not sure fun's the first word I'd choose, but each to their own.' She paused. 'You know, I'm really glad you accepted Stella's offer,' she went on. 'It makes a difference knowing there's another person here I can rely on. I just hope you're not feeling too guilty about abandoning Kaminski. I don't want you to think you've settled for second best.'

'I don't,' I said. 'I know I made the right choice.'

I trusted my voice to sound convincing. The truth was that I still wasn't sure I'd made the right choice. Doing everything by the book didn't come easily for me. I always wanted to cross that line and find out what life was like on the other side. Something about Kaminski's intensity appealed to me, thrilled me. I recognized it as the echo of my own heart.

And if it hadn't been for Fitzgerald, I'd be out there with him right now.

Stalking the prey.

Something in me still sensed too that it would be better for us all if I was. Without me, there was nothing to hold Kaminski back and rein him in. No one to tell him when he was going too far. Alone, the ferocity of his hatred for Buck Randall was unchecked and untamed. I dreaded to think what would happen if he finally caught up with him, and there was no one around to stay his hand. How would I feel then about the decisions I'd made?

33

It was Seamus Dalton, of all people, who woke me, knocking thunderously on the door and barging his way into Fitzgerald's office. I must have fallen into my own private nothingness sometime during those early hours, my head on her desk.

So much for that jazz about time spent asleep being time wasted.

I felt hot and disoriented for a moment, not knowing where I was or how I'd gotten there. It's a common sensation. Often on first waking I can't even remember whether I'm back home in Boston, and always feel a sort of longing that it might be true, until the familiar contours of a room melt into shape. Hence Dalton found me at a disadvantage, bemused by sleep, and he looked at me with disgust as though he'd caught me doing something disreputable. He must've known I was there alone. He wouldn't have forced his way so belligerently into Fitzgerald's office if he'd expected her to be there too.

He wouldn't have dared.

'What time is it?' I said, unfurling myself stiffly from the position in which I'd managed to arrange my limbs and rubbing my face in an attempt to bring back some feeling to my cheekbones. My face must have looked at that moment like a rumpled bedsheet with an imprint of my sleeve pressed into the mould of my skin. Not a good look.

I was glad there was no mirror to confirm my worst fears.

'After eight,' Dalton barked. 'Here.'

If a plastic cup could be slammed on to a desk, Dalton came as close as anyone could to slamming it. A little coffee spilled out over the rim, and he cursed as the hot liquid burned his skin.

He wiped his hand on the seat of his pants.

'You're bringing me coffee?' I looked at him suspiciously. 'What is this – your belated contribution to International Women's Day?'

'It's just a cup of coffee, don't make a big issue out of it. Walsh bought it for you from the vending machine downstairs to help you wake up, then the Chief called him away. I was coming this way so he asked me to bring it up to you. He must think I'm your fucking housemaid or something. Feel free not to drink it.'

'No, coffee's good, er, thanks.'

'You've got five minutes.'

He was gone before the fact that I'd just thanked him for something really sank in.

I wondered if this was some kind of peace offering.

Peace offerings weren't what I associated with Dalton.

Five minutes? It must be time to go talk to Victor Solomon's ex-fiancée. I lifted the coffee gingerly and sniffed at it. It smelled harmless enough, but I decided not to take my chances. I slid back the window and poured it out, making sure there was no one below first. Anything Dalton had been that close to should probably be filed under Best Avoided.

The man himself wasn't so easily avoided, however, because he was waiting in the lobby when I got downstairs. Looked like he was going too. Terrific.

He grunted his second greeting of the morning, but we were mercifully spared the ordeal of trying to make conversation by the arrival of Patrick Walsh, shouldering his way through the front door and coming to a halt when he saw us standing there.

'The Chief's waiting,' he said.

'Whose car are we taking?' I asked.

'The Chief said to take one out of the car pool, so I did.'

'I'll drive, then,' said Dalton.

'But I was going to –'

'I said I'll drive, son. I'd rather not put my life in the hands of someone who probably spent half the night banging some blonde bimbo he picked up in a nightclub.'

'She was a redhead actually.' Walsh grinned at me as Dalton snatched the keys and pushed his way out of the lobby. 'I met her in the bar after work. I don't know what I've got, but whatever it is they all seem to want it. I need a stick to keep them away.'

The door swung open again.

'Are you two coming or not?' snapped Dalton.

'There's someone who really *could* do with getting laid,' said Walsh when the other detective had disappeared again. 'Don't suppose you want to volunteer, do you?'

'You first,' I said. 'I haven't had my shots.'

The car Walsh had picked out of the car pool was a silver Audi. Even when he was working, Walsh was obviously still looking to impress any passing female. Not that he expected to be on the back seat with me while Fitzgerald and Dalton sat up front.

'Saxon,' said Fitzgerald brightly as I clicked my seatbelt into place. 'Are we working you too hard? Dalton tells me you were sleeping when he went up to fetch you.'

'That's just what it looked like to the untrained eye,' I answered slickly.

'Is that so?'

Ellen Forwood lived in North Great George's Street, a

steep incline of Georgian terraces whose doorways alone made it a Mecca for architectural groupies. They were certainly impressive, each one flanked by pilasters and crowned with some elaborate shining fanlights above the door. This area of the city, together with Mountjoy Square to the east, had once been the hub of polite Dublin society until the money moved south of the river. Now these houses, where wealthy landed families had dwelt not so long ago, were mainly occupied by language schools, solicitors' offices, art galleries, even a museum dedicated to James Joyce, a writer so beloved of the locals that they drove him into exile during his lifetime and only decided they adored him after he died. The usual story.

Previous years had seen heroic attempts at restoring the street and its surroundings to their former glory, and many of the houses remained in private hands. But there was something rather melancholy about their efforts when the general area around them was as dispiriting and rundown as ever, with a definite, dark criminal undertow to everyday life that meant most people still preferred to keep their distance. In that respect, it reminded me of the district where Marsha Reed had lived too. It took a certain nerve to live here.

What did Ellen Forwood see in it? There were plenty of theatres in the surrounding streets, that might have been one thing, not to mention the undoubted cultural cachet of living in a street immortalized by a great writer. North Great George's Street was still a name to conjure with in the kind of circles that Victor Solomon and company moved in.

We pulled to a stop outside Ellen's front door and Fitzgerald clambered out.

Walsh and I followed.

Dalton turned off the engine but stayed behind.

I'd been right about the weather. The day was growing

warm again, like the rain had been nothing but an implausible memory. There was a morning clatter in the air. A hum of traffic from the city's main thoroughfare of O'Connell Street a couple of hundred yards away beyond the high brown buildings, buses and cars on those endless journey to nowhere.

When Fitzgerald lifted the doorknocker, carved into the shape of an animal's golden head, and rapped the door with it, the sound rang out loudly in the enclosed street, the echo ricocheting from wall to wall.

'Hello,' she said curiously to herself in the aftermath of silence.

Hammering the knocker had made the door shiver and open inward slightly, like it had been left open accidentally by someone entering or leaving.

'Ms Forwood?' she called into the gap that had appeared.

There was no answer.

'Ms Forwood, this is Detective Chief Superintendent Fitzgerald.'

She knocked again, and the door opened wider, but this time the sound was on the inside of the house, almost like it was going from room to room, looking for an answer.

No answer came.

Fitzgerald stepped into the gap – and stopped.

A woman lay curled on the floor at the end of the hallway.

Fitzgerald rushed forward and knelt down by the woman's side. Careful not to touch anything, she bent a head to the woman's mouth and listened.

'She's breathing,' she said to Walsh. 'Call for an ambulance.'

'Is it Solomon's fiancée?' I said as Walsh hurried out into the street.

Taking a step forward, I could see a knot of blood on the

back of the woman's hair, and a further smear of blood on the floorboard near to a rear window and more on the pane itself. She must have turned herself over after falling there. But what had made her fall?

'It's her all right,' said Fitzgerald.

'I think she's trying to speak,' I said.

Trying to open her eyes too.

'Lie still, Ellen. Help's on the way.'

Another low murmur.

Fitzgerald hooked her hair behind her ear and bent her head once more to the woman's lips. But even I could hear what she whispered when the word finally came out.

'*Victor.*'

'Solomon,' I said.

'Did he do this?'

The woman tried to nod her head but winced in pain.

'No more talking,' Fitzgerald said.

Ellen Forwood closed her eyes once more. Fitzgerald got back to her feet and hurriedly examined the scene immediately around the prone figure while we waited anxiously for the ambulance. The moments seemed to drag longer than hours.

'What's taking it so long?' said Fitzgerald. 'The hospital can't be more than three streets away.' But, even as she spoke, the faint howl of a siren could be heard through the open door, approaching, getting louder as it turned the corner at the top of the street.

Doors slammed, footsteps hammered on the sidewalk, paramedics appeared.

Fitzgerald identified herself, then stepped back to let them do their job.

'Come on,' she said to me.

'Shall I stay here?' said Walsh.

'Has Dalton called Dublin Castle yet?'

'They're sending another car.'

'Then I'm leaving you in charge,' she said. 'Make sure Ellen Forwood's accompanied to the hospital, we mustn't let her out of our sight. Secure the scene. Search the rest of the house. Find witnesses if there are any. Don't try to talk to Ms Forwood herself until I get back. Leave her to the paramedics.'

'Are you going to find Solomon?' I said.

'Who else?'

Dalton already had the car running. I'd barely shut the door behind me when he was away and picking up speed. At the top of the street, he turned left and headed toward Parnell Square. Fitzgerald took out the siren and, winding down the window, attached it to the roof.

'Where does Solomon live?' I shouted above the sudden din.

'Prussia Street,' Fitzgerald said.

'Prussia Street?' I said. 'I didn't have him down as the Prussia Street sort.'

'Solomon hasn't a cent to his name,' Fitzgerald said. 'We've been checking him out ever since we knew he was involved with Marsha Reed. He's lost hundreds of thousands through gambling in the last few years. He did have a big house out by Killiney Bay, but he had to sell it to pay off his debts. He's been living out this way for the last six months or so. I think his circumstances being made public was the thing he feared the most. He said that if the press ever got wind of how he was living now, he'd sue us for everything we've got. He's obviously never seen my budget. I'm presuming that's one of the reasons he fixed on Ellen Forwood to marry. He was looking to go up in the world.'

'Well,' I said, 'I'd say a reconciliation's out of the question now.'

'Fuck it,' cursed Dalton.

The traffic was snarled at the top of Capel Street, and many drivers seemed to consider it a point of honour to wait until the very last moment to pull over and let the police through. By the time we were running down King Street toward Stoneybatter, more precious moments had been wasted. Fitzgerald was on the radio, ordering a second car to meet us at Solomon's place and another unit to head to the theatre in case the director had gone there.

'That must be it,' she said, as Prussia Street opened up before us.

A blue-and-white squad car was parked by the side of the road near the 24-hour supermarket, and an officer in uniform was holding up a hand like a traffic cop trying to stop oncoming traffic. Dalton pulled sharply into the left and tugged on the handbrake.

'Is he in?' Fitzgerald asked the uniform as she jumped out.

'There's no answer from inside.'

A narrow doorway between two low-rent stores, one with its window boarded up, led to a flight of uncarpeted stairs. Fitzgerald, closely followed by Dalton, ran up to the second floor, where another uniform was standing guard at the open door. He looked faintly alarmed to see us.

'Any sign of Solomon?' Fitzgerald asked him.

The cop shook his head.

'OK, you can go back downstairs now, we'll take over.'

'And remember,' Fitzgerald said to us, 'careful not to touch anything.'

She stepped through the doorway.

A mean little apartment opened up before her.

I couldn't believe a man like Victor Solomon could live in a place like this. He must have fallen on hard times indeed. I wondered if Ellen Forwood knew how desperately the man she had intended to marry must have felt the need to make her his own, regardless of all other considerations. This was the apartment of a man who had sold virtually everything that wasn't nailed down, and would have sold his soul too if only he could have found the right bidder. I'd known plenty of people like it at the poker table, men whose eyes blazed with the violence of the desire not so much to win as to just stop losing.

It certainly wasn't the apartment of a man who could afford to give away necklaces as meaningless trinkets to casual sexual partners that he claimed meant nothing to him.

'He's gone,' said Fitzgerald.

The diagnosis was hard to refute. Drawers had been pulled out, doors hung open, dirty dishes were piled high in the sink, all was emptiness and abandonment. A handful of suits lay in crumpled heaps on the floor of the wardrobe. Shirts had been flung over the backs of chairs. A pair of shoes sat awkwardly on the windowsill. Someone had been packing.

And hurriedly.

'I want theories,' said Fitzgerald. 'Where is he?'

'He's doing a bunk,' said Dalton. 'and there are only two places to go.'

'The airport.'

'Or the boat.'

There was no point in trying to escape by road. The country beyond Dublin was too small to hide out in for long.

'The airport,' I said firmly. 'He needs to get as far away as possible. The boat doesn't go far enough. And it's way too slow. You could have police waiting for him by the time he reaches the other side of the water. He couldn't take the chance. He's banking on being far outside your jurisdiction before you even realize he's gone.'

'And the next boat's not till lunchtime,' said Dalton.

That settled the argument.

'The airport it is, then,' said Fitzgerald.

'Are we on the move again?'

We were.

Getting north to the airport was easier once we hit the main road out. The streets became wider, and the drivers took it less personally when commanded by the siren to pull over and let us through. I heard Fitzgerald back again on the police radio, sending more officers out to the harbour just in case we were wrong about Solomon's preferred escape route.

She also requested back-up, preferably armed, at the airport.

The police would be getting stretched soon if Solomon was not found.

And when we finally reached the airport, not finding Solomon began to look like a distinct possibility. It was summer, after all. The airport's busiest time. There didn't seem to be a square inch of the airport terminal that was not already occupied by someone who was either on their way somewhere else or waiting to greet someone returning from elsewhere. Call it organized chaos, except there were times when it didn't seem very organized at all.

On the board above our heads, destinations fluttered by faster than birds.

Paris.

Chicago.

Rome.
Bangkok.
Toronto.

There was a world to hide out in. Solomon could have been here an hour ago, two hours, we didn't know when he'd attacked his fiancée. He could have paid cash for the first plane out – he didn't even care where. By the time we had been through the passenger lists and established where he'd gone, he could be a continent away, in a place where it might be impossible to find him or to get him back even if we did find him.

And in the back of my mind constantly now there was another thought.

If Solomon had run, it was because he was most likely guilty of Marsha Reed's murder. *And if he was guilty of that, then what about Buck Randall?*

Was that nothing to do with this at all?

Slow down, girl.

One problem at a time.

Fitzgerald had already taken charge of airport security and got them looking for Victor Solomon, though, since it took more than ten minutes to get the theatre director's picture forwarded electronically from Dublin Castle to the airport office, their contribution to the search was more symbolic than practical. She sat in front of a bank of TV screens, scanning faces in the crowds as the cameras picked them out, shouting frequently for the camera to be pulled in closer or further back when she thought she recognized someone.

Dalton couldn't bear to sit watching TV, so he went off to make a circuit of the coffee bars and gift stores in the terminal, restless with an energy that had no release.

Occasionally he appeared on the TV screens in front of us, each time almost prompting a cry of recognition, his face becoming confused in our heads with Solomon's, so desperate were we to find a face we recognized, until we remembered it was only Dalton.

'This is some haystack,' murmured Fitzgerald as she scanned another sea of faces.

And the needle in it wasn't giving out so much as a gleam.

I felt the same impatience that had sent Dalton out into the terminal starting to eat at me too. If I sat there much longer, holding myself in. I'd grow a tumour.

'I'm going to see if Dalton needs a hand,' I said eventually.

Fitzgerald was so engrossed in the screens that she didn't even acknowledge the unlikelihood of what I'd said. Or maybe she knew it was nothing but words, the first excuse my head could dream up to get me out of that suffocating office.

Whatever it was, I was out.

Everything had slowed right down. The crowds seemed to move and sway in syrup. Sound was a background hum throbbing in my ears. Announcements of flights crackled distantly but might as well have been in a foreign language for all the sense they were making to me. I was trying to tune them all out in order to concentrate on the one thing that mattered – seeing Victor Solomon's face. Or could he be far from here already?

'Dalton,' I said.

The detective spun round at the sound of his name.

'The fucker's not here,' he said. 'I've been round this place a million bleeding times. I'd have seen him. He's gone. What's the Chief doing?'

'She's on the phone to the Assistant Commissioner.'

He snorted. 'What are they doing?' he said scornfully. 'Swapping beauty tips?'

'You know that's not fair, Dalton.'

'Don't tell me what's fair and what's not. I'm the one who's trying to search this whole building on my own while she sits in there on her arse talking on the telephone.'

I was tempted to inquire what else he expected her to sit on. Her elbow, perhaps? But it was a fair presumption that he wasn't in the mood for jokes. He rarely was. Dalton was one of those people in whose soul humour has never found a welcoming home.

'Chill out,' I said instead.

'Chill out?' He pulled his face into an exaggerated grimace of disbelief. 'Tell you what, why don't you chill out while I go take a piss?'

The guy had a way with words that made a lady feel real special around him.

'Where're the jacks round here, anyway?'

'If you mean the men's room, it's over there,' I said, pointing. 'You can't miss it, it's the one with the picture on the door of the stick figure that's *not* wearing a skirt.'

He'd only taken one step toward the far door when he stopped.

'Fuck me,' he said.

Not an invitation I could ever imagine taking him up on.

The outburst was forgivable this time, because at that precise moment Victor Solomon had emerged from the men's room, clutching a holdall, and was inching his way nervously toward one of the departure gates, his eyes restlessly scanning the airport lounge as if he expected to be challenged at any moment. His face looked flushed, and the bag kept slipping through his fingers like his hands were damp with sweat.

I guess he didn't have much practice in fleeing the country.

'Get the Chief!' Dalton demanded over his shoulder, as

he hastened his step and made to intercept Solomon, who still seemed unaware that his cover was blown.

Fitzgerald, however, was already coming toward us. She must have seen her fugitive on the security cameras. By the time she caught up with Dalton, we were only a hundred yards or so from Solomon and he was almost at the check-in desk for Air Italia.

'*This is the last call for the 9.25 flight to Rome.*'

So that's where he was going.

Solomon reached into the pocket of his pants and pulled out his passport, sliding it across the counter at the blandly smiling girl behind it.

Then the smile vanished as she looked up and saw us approaching.

Fitzgerald held out her hand and took the passport as Solomon turned, the nervous half-smile he'd rustled up for the check-in girl crumbling as he realized what was happening.

'Victor Solomon,' she said, 'I am arresting you on suspicion of the murder of Marsha Reed and for the attempted murder of Ellen For –.'

'I want my lawyer,' said Solomon, interrupting. 'I know my rights.'

He was still griping when Dalton put the cuffs on him and led him out to the car.

34

'He swears he didn't mean to hurt her,' I told Fisher as we sat together on the steps of City Hall in the sunshine, watching the people go by and sharing some grapes out of a bag, like we didn't have a care in the world, like we were tourists. Which, in a way, we both were.

'That's what they all say,' said Fisher. 'How does he explain the fact she had a plastic bag over her head if he didn't mean to hurt her?'

'Not Marsha,' I said. 'Ellen, the fiancée. Or ex-fiancée, I should say. He still totally denies having anything to do with Marsha's murder.'

'But I thought they found the necklace in his room at the theatre?'

'Says he has no idea where it came from.'

'That's what they all say too.'

'Don't they just?'

The discovery of the necklace had certainly been unexpected. A search warrant had been obtained for the theatre following Solomon's apprehension, and, within the hour, it had been been uncovered in a plastic supermarket bag stuffed behind a cupboard in Solomon's office. Why he hadn't gotten rid of such incriminating evidence was anyone's guess, but even his lawyer had looked taken aback when presented with news of it.

That's where Fitzgerald was now with Sean Healy, talking to the director's colleagues and supervising forensics as they made a fingertip search of his office, vacuuming up fibres, dusting for prints, looking for fragments of leaf or soil that could be matched to those taken from the grounds surrounding Marsha's house. Getting a match would undermine Solomon's contention that he'd never been there, which is why the Murder Squad was treating the place where her necklace had been uncovered as respectfully as a crime scene.

They were looking for the missing ring too.

So far, it had failed to show.

That night's performance of *Othello* had been cancelled. With the director in custody on a murder charge, the leading lady in hospital and the theatre itself occupied by scores of grim-faced technical staff in white overalls and face masks, that wasn't so astonishing. A sign outside informed the public that the play would open again tomorrow.

Solomon had refused to speak any further after hearing that the necklace had been found, except to say that he was being stitched up for a murder he hadn't committed and would sue everyone in the building. It was a pity, really, because up until then he'd been doing plenty of talking. This was a man with no intention of exercising his right to remain silent. The police had given him a spade, and he'd kept on digging, digging, digging, ranting angrily at Marsha for having, as he now claimed, stolen from him the necklace he'd bought with the last of his savings for Ellen Forwood and then refused to return it, taunting him with his desperate financial circumstances, offering one moment to use her father's fortune to help him out if he carried on seeing her, the next moment refusing him a cent.

He didn't seem to appreciate that his palpable anger against Marsha might not exactly be helping his assertion of being innocent of her killing.

Mainly, though, he talked about what had happened that morning at Ellen's house.

How he'd heard she'd contacted the police the night before and was intending to withdraw her alibi following their break-up. He hadn't really been with her the night Marsha Reed died; he'd simply asked her to say that he was in order to take the heat off him.

Ellen hadn't suspected for a moment that he was guilty of the young actress's murder, but she knew that any adverse publicity would be damaging for both of them. There certainly wouldn't be many celebrity magazines interested in the photos of their wedding if the truth had become known. Only after Ellen learned that her husband-to-be had been involved in a sexual relationship with Marsha at the same time as they were planning their own wedding had she decided to call the whole thing off and stopped taking Solomon's calls. The show of forgiveness for the police when they first spoke to her had simply been a front.

She wasn't an actress for nothing.

Soon after, she further decided, whether from a desire for revenge or guilt at having lied in the first instance, to come clean to the police. And not just about his alibi.

Now she was also claiming that Solomon enjoyed tying her up during sex. It wasn't her thing, she said, but she went along with it to please him. Sometimes he hurt her. He claimed to be sorry, but she'd seen the bright look in his eyes when he was doing it.

So much for his offended claim not to share Marsha Reed's appetites.

Somehow, Solomon had found out that Ellen Forwood had been about to come clean about both things to the police. He'd gone round that morning to beg her not to reveal his secret. He told her she was the only woman he'd ever loved. He threw himself on her mercy.

When that didn't work, he threatened to finish off her

career as an actress. A ludicrous claim, considering that she was most likely about to bring his own career to a close by blowing his alibi for murder. There was a quarrel, the quarrel had turned into a struggle, she slapped him, he pushed her, Ellen fell and cracked her head against the windowpane, hence the blood smears. She ended up in a heap in the hall. He panicked and ran.

That was his version of events, at any rate.

Fitzgerald was waiting for a chance to talk to Ellen to hear her version.

'Is she going to be all right?' asked Fisher.

'The hospital says she'll be in for a while yet,' I told him, 'but there should be no permanent damage. She'll have one hell of a headache for a while, though.'

'I can imagine,' he said. 'What I don't understand is why he didn't just call for an ambulance if he really was sorry that he'd hurt her.'

'He says he thought she was dead. He thought he'd killed her. And, to be fair, he did look relieved when he learned that she was alive. Then again, he's a former actor too. How much you can take what either of them says and does at face value is anyone's guess.'

'You're such a cynic.'

'I'm only going by the evidence,' I said. 'The urge for self-preservation is definitely what kicked in when he thought he'd killed Ellen Forwood. First thing he did was race round to his rooms, pack a bag and head to the airport to get the first flight out of the city. That's what he was doing when we found him. He was hiding in the men's room, waiting for the last call for his flight before coming out. It was pure chance that he came out just at the same moment Dalton was headed to the door. Solomon's just a stage name, apparently. His passport was in his real name of Mahoney. That's why he wasn't coming up on computer records of flight bookings. If he'd gotten on to the plane, we might never have seen him again.'

'What was he intending to do once he reached Rome?'

'He grew up in Italy,' I said. 'Speaks fluent Italian without an accent. He says the plan was to hide out until he had the chance to clear his name.'

'Clear him of what? He admits attacking Ellen Forwood.'

'It was clearing his name of the murder of Marsha Reed he was interested in. He knew once his alibi fell apart that the police would blame him again for her death. He thought that if he could stay out of sight for long enough, then the real murderer would be found.'

'He'd still have to answer for the attack on his fiancée.'

'He thought people would understand once they knew what had happened, and the pressure he was under. I know, it's mad, he wasn't thinking straight.'

'I know the feeling,' said Fisher intently.

'What do you mean?'

'Just that I've obviously had this whole thing the wrong way up from the start. Solomon's behaviour – fighting with his fiancée – making a metaphorical break for the border like that this morning. It doesn't really fit the profile I had in mind of Marsha Reed's killer.'

'The careful, methodical, make-no-mistakes kind of guy, you mean?'

'That was the general idea.'

'Even methodical types can panic,' I pointed out.

'And everyone makes mistakes, I know.' He leaned back, extended his arms, folded his hands, and cracked his knuckles softly. The noise always makes me shudder. 'You know how it works. You try to insinuate your way into the killer's head, working back step by step until your thought

336

patterns correspond to theirs. When I did that, it was never Solomon's eyes I was looking out of. Why would such a careful man take the risk of keeping the proof of his guilt badly hidden where police were bound to find it if they searched? And what about Marsha's online requests for someone to kill her? Where do they fit in?'

I said nothing, because Fisher had given a voice to a doubt which I had so far left unspoken and which I wasn't sure I was ready to admit even to myself.

The DMP had everything they needed on Victor Solomon.

He had motive – the need to protect his secret affair from his future wife.

He had opportunity – no alibi for the night of the murder.

He had the necklace back in his possession.

He certainly had a reason for wanting it back. Maybe two reasons. One, because it was proof of his relationship with Marsha. Two, because he needed the money he could get for it.

What's more, he had incriminated himself by running.

So why did catching him not feel better than it did? I'd kept the doubt silent in my mind because I couldn't be sure that I wasn't simply refusing to see the evidence for what it was out of a misguided sense of loyalty to Leon Kaminski, that I wasn't being misled by his aching need to blame Buck Randall for this murder as well as that of his wife. And yet what of the clipping that Randall had sent Kaminski, boasting of Marsha Reed's murder?

Did that now mean nothing?

Or had it meant nothing all along?

I tried mentioning the doubts tentatively to Fitzgerald as we walked back to my apartment later, the sun cutting deep shadows into the ground at our backs as we walked into its path, but she had a plausible answer to every one of my questions.

'You know what Dalton would say, don't you?' she said.

'That Kaminski sent the clipping to himself,' I said. 'But you don't believe that.'

'No, I don't. But we haven't found a single scrap of evidence to connect Buck Randall to the murder of Marsha Reed,' Fitzgerald said. She paused as we waited for a chance to cross St Andrews's Street. 'All we have is Kaminski's conviction that there *must* be a connection somewhere. And how do we know that Buck Randall, even if he did send that clipping to Kaminski, didn't simply *want* him to think he'd killed this woman? If he's playing tricks with Kaminski's mind, it makes sense.'

'So you're saying these two strands are entirely separate?' I said.

'Why not? We thought there was some connection between Marsha's secret sado-masochistic life online and what happened to her, between her online fantasy life and her murder, but now we're faced with the likelihood that there wasn't. Why shouldn't these strands be separate too? They make no sense if we try to make them intersect. If we see them as separate strands which merely happened to run together for a while at a given point, then everything falls into place. Solomon killed Marsha. Buck Randall is involved somehow in the disappearance and death of Mark Hudson. Randall simply used Marsha as a weapon in the psychological battle he's waging on Kaminski. *And,*' she added hastily before I could object, 'even if there is some further connection between the two strands that we are failing to see clearly, the next course of action remains entirely the same. It's about reeling in Buck Randall. Once we have him in custody, we can take it from there.'

'OK, I'll buy that,' I said reluctantly.

'Then let's get on with it,' said Fitzgerald. 'We're already searching the city for him. Did you know Randall was a heavy drinker? Practically an alcoholic, according to the reports I got from Texas. That means he has to surface somewhere: bars, off-licences, supermarkets. Most of all, there's tonight. That's still our best chance to apprehend him.'

I couldn't argue with that.

Our steps were leading us away from Dublin Castle where, for the last couple of hours, the final briefing before tonight's huge surveillance operation had been taking place. I hadn't got a chance to talk to Fitzgerald during the meeting, the room was so crowded. That had its advantages too. It had been crowded enough that I'd become blessedly invisible again.

A small clutch of officers had tagged along undercover earlier that day as part of a final routine police inspection to check that safety regulations were in order. It had given them a good working knowledge of the layout of the site, which they then proceeded to pass on to the team which would be carrying out that evening's surveillance. There'd been a tense mood in the air that always came when something major was in the offing.

The presence alone of Finbar Donnelly from the armed-response unit was sufficient to ensure no one took what was happening lightly, though as always on such occasions it seemed like half the room was engaged in a testosterone contest with him. Seamus Dalton in particular had spent the meeting leaning back in his chair, chewing gum, feet up on the table, doing everything bar unzipping himself and slapping it on the table to prove that he was man enough to match any fellow officer with a gun. Dalton's mood was high too because he'd captured Solomon that morning and was currently feeling like a cross between Eliot Ness and Philip Marlowe.

Sometimes you wonder how far man really has evolved from the Stone Age – and when I say man, I don't mean it in the all-inclusive sense of mankind. I mean those members of society who seem to keep half their IQ hidden in their pants. And as to where the other half's hidden, no one knows because they've never managed to locate it.

Donnelly had used a map of the area around Merrion Square that was pinned to the wall, and a smaller rough sketch of the layout of the fair itself, to explain precisely where the armed response officers would be located in case of trouble, stressing all the while that his men were there only as a last resort and the best outcome would be if they went unneeded.

Dalton had snorted scornfully at that.

'That's right,' he was heard to mutter. 'Leave the hard work to us as usual.'

It was, to say the least, a blessing when the meeting was called to an end, and we could head back to my apartment to snatch a shower and something to eat. We didn't have much time. Fitzgerald wanted to see Kaminski one last time before waving him off to the fair.

For me, the night couldn't come quickly enough. I was impatient to begin. An end of sorts seemed tantalizingly close, like we only had to reach out and take it. But the minutes between now and then stretched out like the vastness separating stars, and the light itself seemed to be trying to frustrate us. The day never wants to step aside and hand the world to darkness in summer, but there was no chance of Buck Randall turning up at the fair until it had. Everything until then was just a question of waiting. I'd never been good at that.

I let Fitzgerald climb into the shower first while I found a few fragments of salad hiding out in the corners of the fridge, threw them together with a dressing, cut some bread that didn't feel too stale and tried to make an omelette to go with it all. Unfortunately, there's something about an omelette that always defeats me, and this one was no exception.

'That looks good,' Fitzgerald said appreciatively all the same when she appeared ten minute later from the bedroom with wet hair and clean clothes.

The hot water had knocked some of the exhaustion out of her face, but she still wasn't going to fool anyone that she'd been giving Sleeping Beauty a run for her money in recent days. Her mouth yawned involuntarily at regular intervals. Her eyes were too wide with the effort of keeping them open.

She groaned as her cellphone made a pleading noise at the exact moment we sat down to eat, and she reached down for the jacket which she'd dropped on the floor next to the couch on her way to the bathroom, rummaging around in the inside pocket until she found it.

She checked her messages cursorily.

'I need to recharge,' she said. 'The phone and me likewise.'

'Any messages?'

'Nothing,' she said. 'Unless you count the press. No matter how often I change my private number, they always get it. I don't know why they bother going to all the trouble. It's not like I ever tell them anything.'

'Have you heard any more about Ellen Forwood?' I asked.

'I dropped in on her at the hospital again before going to Dublin Castle,' Fitzgerald explained. 'She's in the same hospital as Rose Downey, so I was able to kill two birds with one stone, pardon the expression. Ellen's been in and out of consciousness, so I only managed to spend a few minutes with her, but I've never seen anyone more eager to make a statement.'

'She did withdraw her alibi, then?'

'She did. Unfortunately she also *confirmed* his story about what happened between them at her house in North Great George's Street. He came round to confront her, they argued, grappled briefly, she fell and hit her head. Pure accident, she says.'

'So the attempted murder charge will need to be quietly dropped?'

'That was always the icing on the cake anyway,' she said. 'More important is making the murder charge stick. That, and what happens tonight.' She suddenly looked apologetic. 'Actually, Saxon, do you mind if I don't finish this omelette?'

'I wasn't aware', I said, 'that you'd even started it.'

35

It took me a while to notice later that we were walking down
Kildare Street past the front gate of Parliament Buildings
and on toward the huge grounds of Trinity College where,
behind the railings on College Green, a group of men in
shorts were playing cricket for fun in the last of the light, the
thwack of the ball hitting the bat hanging dully in the air.

'This isn't the way to Kaminski's hotel,' I said.

'How observant you are today,' teased Fitzgerald. 'I didn't
want to take the risk of just turning up at Kaminski's door.
For all we know, Buck Randall may be watching the hotel. He
always seems to know where Kaminski is. I asked Malachy
Stack – you remember him from the crime team meeting? –
to bring Kaminski along somewhere quiet near by.'

Fitzgerald's definition of quiet was evidently different
from mine. A couple of minutes later we were turning into
Lincoln Place, and I found myself being led up the steps of
the Dublin Dental School and Hospital, into a reception
area on the first floor lined with plastic chairs. Luckily, there
was no sign of any patients. Either the place was closed or
they'd all been put off the idea of coming in for treatment
by the gruesome posters lining the walls.

They made the inside of your mouth look like Vietnam
circa 1975.

In the middle of one row, Kaminski was sitting on a chair
next to Detective Stack.

He didn't look happy.

Kaminski, that is, not Stack. Though on second thoughts,

Stack didn't exactly look the picture of joy either. The conversation had obviously been a little strained.

'Stack,' said Fitzgerald, 'take the door, will you, check no one comes in after us?'

The detective rose gratefully and did as he was told.

'What's with the babysitter?' asked Kaminski when the other man had gone.

'I had to make sure you were behaving yourself,' Fitzgerald said, taking the seat next to him while I sat on the row in front, turning round in my seat to face him.

'I'm a big boy,' said Kaminski. 'I don't need Mary Poppins holding my hand. And what's with this place? A dental hospital? Do you offer all the people you're holding against their will a free dental check-up, or is this a special offer for me alone?'

'No one's holding you prisoner,' said Fitzgerald. 'How melodramatic you are sometimes. You remind me of Saxon. You're free to walk away at any time.'

'Free to get subsequently arrested for being an accessory to murder, you mean.'

'All choices have consequences,' she said smugly. 'That doesn't mean we're not free to make them. It's one of the perplexities of the human condition.'

Kaminski must have decided there wasn't much mileage in that complaint, because he didn't bother answering her. Instead he turned his attention to me.

'What's with the dark rings round the eyes?' he asked. 'Didn't you get any sleep last night? Or did you two hit the town to celebrate screwing up all my plans?'

'We were otherwise engaged,' I said.

'Actually,' said Fitzgerald, 'we arrested someone for the murder of Marsha Reed.'

Kaminski looked stunned. 'You've got Buck Randall?'

344

'I said we arrested someone for Marsha Reed's murder. I didn't say it was Randall.'

'Then who was it?'

'Victor Solomon,' I told him.

He wore a bemused expression that said my answer didn't make logical sense.

'So Randall gets away scot-free?' he said.

'He's still wanted in connection with Mark Hudson's murder,' said Fitzgerald defensively. 'I'd hardly call that getting away with anything.'

'Randall won't have been so stupid as to let you pin that one on him.'

'He was stupid enough to be seen at the spot where Hudson's body was found.'

'Yeah, that was convenient for you, wasn't it?' said Kaminski. He shook his head roughly. 'No, there was a reason for that. There was a reason for everything. He has it all worked out. He's been ahead of you every step of the way.'

'His fingerprints were all over Hudson's car,' Fitzgerald insisted. 'Inside and out.'

That silenced him for a moment.

Then he shrugged that off too.

'He'll have an answer,' said Kaminski. 'He always does. He's going to wriggle off the hook for this the same way he wriggled off it when he murdered my wife. Even if you do pick him up, you'll end up holding him for a couple of days and then wave him off at the airport with a slap on the wrist for breaching immigration rules.'

'You don't have much faith in the police here in Dublin, do you, Mr Kaminski?'

'Do you blame me?' he said. 'Look at that chump you sent to watch over me.' He gestured toward Stack, who was standing by the door looking about as inconspicuous as an elephant at a geisha party. 'He has cop written all over him. Did you ever stop to wonder,' he continued, 'what would've happened if Randall had seen *that* trailing around after me like a devoted puppy all day? He'd know you were going to be waiting for him at the fair tonight. He wouldn't show. Maybe it's already too late. Maybe he already has seen him.'

'And I told you, that's a risk we're both going to have to take,' said Fitzgerald, though I could tell she understood what Kaminski meant. 'I couldn't let you wander about on your own. I don't trust you. I still don't know that you're even telling the truth about the fair.'

'Just make sure you keep well away from me tonight,' he warned. 'I'm not having you messing up my chance to get Randall after all the work I've put into hunting him down.'

'I know how to do my job,' Fitzgerald said coldly.

'Make sure you do.'

To avoid any further conflict, she showed him the map of the funfair and the surrounding streets, pointing out the relevant details of the surveillance operation to him, but he scarcely glanced at it.

'You've been wired up?' she asked him eventually, giving up on the briefing.

Kaminski nodded.

'Then if you see Randall, simply say the word and we'll take over.'

'Yippee,' he said sarcastically. 'Can I go now?'

Fitzgerald checked her watch.

'It's almost nine,' she said. 'You can go. But be warned. No games. There are more than enough of my officers around out there to stop you doing something stupid, so don't even bother trying. You'll only embarrass yourself.'

I thought he was going to say something in response to that, but whatever it was he decided to keep it to himself.

Maybe he felt contemptuous silence was all that we, his tormentors, deserved. Instead he turned and walked away, weaving through the lines of plastic chairs to the door where Detective Stack was waiting.

'Good luck,' my voice rose after him, trying to sound encouraging.

He flinched slightly, but that was all.

'Should I follow him?' asked Stack once Kaminski had gone.

'He's on his own now,' Fitzgerald replied. 'Did you search him before we arrived?'

'Yes, Chief. He wasn't too pleased about that either.'

'He wouldn't be. He was clean?'

'He didn't have anything on him.'

'Good. There's no way I wanted him taking any kind of weapon along with him tonight. The temptation would be too great. Unless he's received some special Marines training in unarmed combat, I doubt there's much danger of Buck Randall coming to harm.'

'Let's hope you're right,' I said, but even as I said it I wasn't sure if I believed it. Part of me feared that Kaminski was right. That Buck Randall, even if he was placed in custody, would somehow contrive to ensure that no dirt stuck to him. What was better – for a guilty man to escape justice, or for Kaminski to finish this once and for all?

I didn't trust myself to give the right answer.

By now the shadows were lengthening at last, the sky was fading. Night wouldn't be long.

There was also no sign of Kaminski as we left the building soon after.

'You don't think –'

'That he's run out on us? No, I don't think he's run out on us.'

347

Still, it was a relief when Fitzgerald managed to get through to Walsh and he told her he could see Kaminski approaching Merrion Square from the other direction.

'Why's he going that way?' I wondered aloud as we made our own way to the square. 'He must've walked straight past the road leading to Merrion Square, gone the complete wrong way and then turned back on himself further on.'

'Probably trying to piss us off,' she suggested.

He was succeeding.

'Come on, let's go join the party.'

The light was noticeably more strained than it had been before we went into the dental hospital. Night took a long time coming in summer, but once it started it came on fast. I felt a sense of growing expectation gathering inside my chest.

This was it.

Within the hour, we might be face to face with the elusive Buck Randall.

We took a more immediate route than Kaminski, for all the world like two women out for a summer evening's walk to the fair. At least, that's how I hoped we looked. Kaminski's words about Detective Stack practically having the word cop written all over him. Fitzgerald blended in to my eyes, but then I might be too familiar with her to be able to judge her dispassionately. *Did* she look like a cop?

What, for that matter, did *I* look like?

Certainly no one gave us a second glance as we joined the increasing mass of people making their way down toward Merrion Square where, above the rooftops, the top of a Ferris wheel could be seen now turning slowly, lights flashing in the shape of the metal, standing out more sharply against the thickening dark sky. Dark – yes it really was now.

I could hear music thudding, bass and drum, into the

warm night, mingled with snatches of laughter, the squeals of the nervous on the fairground rides.

There was a sign above the gate: *Opening Night*.

'You know,' Fitzgerald said as we walked through the gate into the square, and looked around all the stalls and rides laid out before us, 'it's a shame we have to waste a night like this. I love funfairs. I remember the one we always used to go to out in the West every summer when I was a child. It sat right at the edge of the sea. It probably only had a couple of dodgems and a few arcade games, but to me in those days it was like Las Vegas.'

'You mean, hookers and Mafia hitmen everywhere you look, and little old ladies from Idaho feeding their life savings into the slot machines?'

'Something like that,' she said. 'Only without the hookers and the hitmen.'

'And the little old ladies didn't come from Idaho.'

'I doubt it,' agreed Fitzgerald.

I didn't say anything about what I felt. I'd always hated carnivals, whatever I'd said to Fitzgerald last night. Always seen something seedy and untrustworthy in them. If the carnival was a man, he'd be the kind of man who could as easily knock you around as show you a good time. There's an air of jollity about them, but underlying that simmers a barely concealed mood of anger and menace and resentment. The people who attach themselves to the wandering carnivals are those who have nothing else left. They've been driven out of the world of light and on to the road in broken-down trucks, the modern-day equivalent of outlaws and renegades. There's always the feeling at the carnival that someone is going to get hurt, and you just hope it isn't you. And, caught up with that, there is the promise, or maybe that should be the threat, of bad sex and sudden intimacies

349

that could feel more like violence. Strange enemies lurk in the shadows, and you're never quite sure if they belong there or not.

People did, admittedly, seem to be having a good time at the fair tonight – stumbling dizzily out of the funhouse and showing off at the test-your-strength machines – so maybe it was just me who got grouchy under their influence. There were plenty of small children running round too, eating candy apples and cotton candy, clinging on to oversized teddy bears that their fathers had won by tossing wonky rings on to hooks on a wall or firing corks out of mounted shotguns at moving yellow plastic ducks. Couples walked arm in arm. Bursts of tinny music competed raucously with each other from every ride that we passed.

I tried to look as if I was there to enjoy myself like everyone else, and to stay alert for any sign of Buck Randall. That wasn't proving so easy. I knew what his picture was like, but the man himself might've come here tonight in disguise. That was most likely how he *had* come. He wanted to keep the advantage over Kaminski.

The crowds didn't help. I hadn't expected the fair to be so busy, but then why wouldn't it be? It was a mild night, not a chance of rain. The lights and music beckoned.

I began to think half the city had turned out for the fair's first night.

A couple of times I caught a glimpse of someone who might be Randall ... or was I only projecting Randall's features on to some other stranger because I wanted to see him so badly? And I couldn't stare too long, because if it *was* Randall then I couldn't alert him to the fact that other people besides Kaminski might be expecting him to turn up.

Once I caught myself staring and realized it was Kaminski I was staring at. He was staring back at me like he'd been trapped by the same trick of the mind, his eye latching unconsciously on to something known.

So I had to content myself with sideways glances and stolen looks, and couldn't decide whether they were better or worse than nothing. In fact, I soon realized, I'd have been better placed to see Randall if I was watching the fair from one of the windows in the surrounding buildings. And who knows, that might've been exactly what Randall was doing.

Say he was holed up in one of those apartments. Say he'd rented an office for the week or the month. It was the easiest thing in the world to camp up there tonight and observe the scene below, god-like, through binoculars. I saw Kaminski, standing by a hot-dog stand, squeezing mustard on to his food and trying to look nonchalant. What if Randall was watching him that very second? What if every move he'd taken had been observed from the moment he'd passed through the gate?

And what if Kaminski wasn't the only one who was being watched?

Everywhere I looked now, I seemed to see one of the surveillance team lingering, lurking, idling self-consciously – a figure here by the coconut shy, another there by the dodgems. Or was it only the fair's own security guards, talking to one another over walkie-talkies, watching out for possible trouble? They were all looking alike to me now, and a kind of panic gripped me temporarily, a sense that the situation was not as much under control as we'd imagined. I turned to speak to Fitzgerald – and found that I'd lost her somewhere along the way. A moment before, I was sure, she'd been there. I'd felt her hand touch my elbow, guiding me in the right direction as the crowd threatened to carry me on the wrong path.

Now there was no sign of her.

And there was no sign of Kaminski at the hot-dog stand. Where was he?

I pushed my way back into the pressing throng of bodies and on through toward the place where I'd last seen him. The sizzle of meat cooking turned the air rancid again, as it had the night Rose Downey was attacked. The stench of burning fat was as offensive as stale sweat. The paper in which the food came wrapped, now scrunched into stained, greasy balls, littered the ground around the food stall like flowers at a funeral.

And then I thought I saw not Kaminski but Fitzgerald, a couple of hundred yards away from where I was standing now, her back turned to me, walking toward the helter-skelter.

I resisted the urge to call her name and instead plunged back into the tide.

Waded through the crowd as if through heavy water.

But she wasn't at the helter-skelter. Nor at the carousel beyond. I was walking now without direction, simply going round, searching for some anchor to fasten my fractured impressions of the scene that evening back into place. Light was throbbing in my temples, and with it the screech and whine of machinery. The music was getting louder. The carousel spun crazily, horses hurtling round after one another's tails, mouths pulled back in demonic grins. Indistinct figures stepped expertly among the waltzers as the cars turned in a blur of faces.

And then I heard a voice.

Shouting.

'*Stop!*'

It was Kaminski. And soon other voices had joined his.

A murmur was spreading through the crowd, like Chinese whispers. I couldn't catch what it said, but I could see where it was coming from. The hot-dog stand. The direction I'd come from minutes before.

'It's the police,' I heard a woman ahead of me in the crowd say to her companion.

'What the fuck are they doing here?' he answered testily.

The idea that the police might actually have a good reason to be somewhere was one which many citizens of Dublin still considered too implausible to be entertained for a second.

As I got closer, I heard someone else say that the police had some guy on the ground – could it be Buck Randall? – and there was a crackle of police radios. The music continued from the rides but seemed to have fallen back until it was hardly audible any more.

All I could hear was the commotion up ahead.

'Stand back!'

'Let her through,' said Fitzgerald, because there she was, standing with a cellphone pressed to her ear and reaching out with her other hand for my arm to drag me into the circle. And the plain clothes cop who'd been trying to keep a boundary between the police who'd grouped together at this point and the restless crowd threw up his hands theatrically in exasperation, as if the futility of the task had just become apparent to him.

'Have you got him?' I mouthed to her, but she was talking so fast and so loud that nothing I said could get through. She simply pointed at Patrick Walsh, who, I now saw, was standing looking somewhat redundant and ineffectual a couple of yards away.

'Walsh,' I said, 'what's going on? Have you got Randall?'

Before he could answer, Kaminski's voice cut in angrily.

'Don't you tell me to calm down, you fucking incompetent fuckheads!'

He was standing in the middle of a group of police officers who were trying to hold him back. His nose was bleeding. His shirt was torn. Another man I didn't recognize, an unpleasant-looking character with a ring of studs through his lower lip, sat on the grass near by in handcuffs, trying to kick out at Kaminski's legs whenever he got the chance.

'What is it, JJ?'

'They lost him!' he spat when he saw me. 'They fucking lost him! How in God's fucking name did you people let him get away? What the fuck were you thinking?'

At which point I considered it safe to assume that no, we hadn't gotten Buck Randall.

36

'I got a call,' said Fitzgerald as she lay back on Kaminski's bed next morning, pillow at her back, arms folded behind her head, legs outstretched to the end of her boots. 'One of the surveillance team said Kaminski had seen someone who might be Buck Randall. I tried to get your attention, but the place was too noisy and you were distracted, you weren't hearing me.'

I'd been surveying the windows round Merrion Square, imagining our every move being watched and missing entirely what was happening right there on the ground.

I guess I must be more out of practice than I knew.

'By the time I reached the place where Randall had apparently been spotted,' explained Fitzgerald, 'it was too late. Kaminski said he'd lost visual contact. No one else had seen him, so I wasn't sure what to think – or, more to the point, what to do next. Melt back into the crowd again and wait for another sighting? Try to move in and close him down, shutting off the exits and searching the crowd one by one? Well, I knew I couldn't do that. It would've been chaos, there were too many people milling around.'

'So what did you decide?' I asked.

'I didn't have the chance to decide *anything*,' she said with feeling. 'Suddenly there was another shout. I heard someone calling out Buck Randall's name. It was Kaminski again. Next thing a scuffle had broken out. I ran over. It looked like some guy had punched Kaminski and they were grappling together like the worst pro wrestlers you ever saw. It was almost comic. The one thing I *could* see was that it wasn't Randall he was fighting with.'

'Who was it?'

'I can't even remember his name. He was just some scanger who'd gone along to the fairground with his girl-friend.'

'Scanger?'

'Yeah, a scanger, you must know what a scanger is. Let me think. What would you say? White trash maybe. It's an old Dublin word. Think young person of limited intelligence and even more limited vocabulary, who has an inordinate fondness for shaving his head, dressing in cheap sportsgear and piercing his body with too many pieces of metal.'

'I'm following you. It's a new word on me, but I'm following you.'

'This particular representative of the species, anyway, was at the fairground last night. Kaminski claimed he saw Buck Randall through the crowd; he tried to push his way towards him, ended up upsetting some popcorn belonging to this delightful individual's girlfriend. Next thing you know he's landed one on Kaminski's nose, and they're rolling around in the dirt trying to knock one another's lights out – the young scanger to defend his fair maiden's honour for the grievous hurt of losing her popcorn, and Kaminski just so he could get away and pursue what he said was Randall. The surveillance team came running, thinking Kaminski had their man, and instead found the world's most pathetic fight in progress at their feet. By the time it had been broken up, the evening's work was comprehensively ruined.'

'And Kaminski?'

'Came right back here, packed his things and made a bolt for it. In all the confusion, I forgot to keep a tail on him.' She slid her legs off the bed and walked to the wardrobe, opening the door to show me the empty hangers where Kaminski's shirts had hung, the absence in the corner where his holdall had sat. 'I screwed up. I was too tired. And now I can't help asking myself whether the whole thing was a set-up from the start.'

'You mean he created the confusion so that he *could* slip away?'

'He was the one who cried out Buck Randall's name. I don't think he saw a damn thing,' said Fitzgerald. 'I don't think Randall was ever there. There was no meeting arranged at the funfair. Kaminski just made it up to give him a chance to get out of our line of sight.'

'We had him backed into a corner.'

'He had to think fast.'

'And he did.'

I remembered that night at Dublin Castle following our visit to the graveyard, when he was brought in for questioning. He had somewhere he needed to be. Buck Randall had made contact. He was being threatened with a cell for the next three days, he was going to miss whatever appointment he'd made with the man who'd killed his wife. The only way he could get out was to offer us a false meeting instead.

I recalled how he'd closed his eyes in his chair while he considered what Fitzgerald was telling him. He was searching for something inside his mind.

'And then it must've come back to him that he had the leaflet,' she said. 'Someone probably handed it to him in the street as he walked by; he'd stuffed it in his pocket without thinking, and it gave him the perfect bluff. He could say the leaflet was the message from Randall, go along with the charade, start a fight in the funfair and sneak away under the cover of the ensuing pandemonium, leaving himself free to get to the *real* meeting alone.'

'It was my fault,' I insisted. 'You said it yourself. I knew him better than anyone else in this town. I should've known he was spinning a line.'

'He was another good actor. The city seems to be full of them these days. And you know what? I don't blame him for splitting,' she said, shutting the wardrobe door and dropping heavily on to the edge of the bed again. 'Look how we screwed up last night. Why *should* he trust us to help him find Randall when we fell for a blatant ruse like that?'

'You mustn't blame yourself.'

'You're right. There'll be plenty of other people willing to do that on my behalf. *This* certainly isn't what the Assistant Commissioner was hoping for in her first week in charge.'

She stabbed a finger at the newspaper lying thrown on to the bed at her side.

Mystery over Dublin Police Operation in City Fairground read the headline.

'I read it,' I said. 'The story's thinner than an anorexic ghost.'

'It's thin now, but it won't take them too long to flesh out what the surveillance team was really doing in Merrion Square,' Fitzgerald said. 'They can't be fobbed off for ever.'

'The press have the attention span of a cranefly,' I said fiercely. 'Couple of days and they'll have moved on to the next story. There was some trouble at the fairground, so what? Happens all the time. Just feed them a line about how it was an operation to round up illegal immigrants or crack down on drug trafficking. Reporters love that crap.'

'Even the press aren't stupid enough to fall for that one,' said Fitzgerald. 'Since when did the Murder Squad spearhead trawling expeditions against illegal immigrants? No, they know already there was more to it than that. All they have to do is put the jigsaw together.'

'Then be straight with them. Call a press conference. Tell them you're looking for a man called Buck Randall. Give them his picture. Let them put it on the front page. There's no point taking the softly-softly approach any more,' I said. 'What use is secrecy? Randall will probably guess last night was about him. The best chance of finding him now is to flush him out of wherever he's been hiding. Make him a celebrity. Deprive him of his anonymity.'

'We might drive him underground instead,' said Fitzgerald.

'There's always that chance. But it will also make him nervous, and nervous people make mistakes. He'll feel watched wherever he goes. He'll be a wanted man. And even if he doesn't break cover, Kaminski might. He'll know his window of opportunity's running out.'

'Do you really think it could work?' asked Fitzgerald expectantly.

'It couldn't hurt,' I said.

Fitzgerald got to her feet again.

She was restless, like she wanted to pace to think, but there was scarcely the space in that tiny room for breathing, let alone pacing. She was working out the permutations. Totting up what could go wrong and matching that against the possible benefits.

'Saxon,' she said eventually, 'you're either a genius or a fool. What say we find out which it is?'

That my genius would be confirmed so fast came as a surprise even to me. Not that I'd ever doubted it, you understand, it just made a pleasing change to have the hard evidence.

There were sightings of Buck Randall at an amusement arcade in Westmoreland Street, a cinema in Poolbeg Street, a bar in Camden Row, and the outpatients clinic at St James's Hospital. Either he was a very busy guy or there were a lot of cases of mistaken identity out there. Most promising of all was the landlord in Kilmainham, not that far from where Marsha Reed had died, who called to say he'd rented a room to a man with an American accent who resembled the photograph of Randall which had been issued.

'Yeah, that's him,' he said lazily, lifting the front of his T-shirt to scratch at his overhanging belly – but he wasn't really looking at the photograph Fitzgerald had laid down flat on the desk in front of him. Instead he was staring at a young woman in the road outside, skimpily dressed for the heat, bending down to pick up something she'd dropped.

He was old enough to be her grandfather. For all I know, he *was* her grandfather. He didn't look like he'd let a little thing like that get in the way.

His wife – bloated and sweating and squeezed painfully into a dress that looked like it was begging for mercy – sat next to him, watching him non-judgementally.

She hadn't spoken a word since Fitzgerald, Patrick Walsh and I had arrived.

'Please look closely at the picture,' said Fitzgerald, her voice rising to get his attention. 'It's very important that you're sure this really is the man who stayed here.'

The man sighed and reluctantly forced his gaze away to look at the picture.

'It's him. I already told you it was,' he said. 'How many more times? He wasn't using the name the police gave on the TV, mind. He called himself ... what was it now? O'Brien. Said he was an Irish-American over looking into his roots. Soon as I saw his picture on the news at one, I knew it was him. Said to you it was him, didn't I?'

That last remark was addressed to the wife, who suddenly

seemed to be jerked out of her lethargy by the words of her loving husband. Roused at last, she managed a nod of agreement and then returned to the semi-catatonic state she'd been in since we got here.

He, meanwhile, narrowed his eyes and peered at Fitzgerald.

'It was you, wasn't it? At that press conference?'

Fitzgerald confirmed stiffly that it was.

'Thought it was. I never forget a face.'

'That's a useful habit to have.'

'You look a lot younger on TV.'

'Is that so?'

'Yeah. Must be all those lights. Still, don't suppose you'd be so high up in the police if you were still nineteen, eh?'

And he chuckled to himself like he'd just told the world's funniest joke.

Seemed like women to him were there to be put in their place, leered at or ground into passive, defeated submission like the one slumped next to him in her chair.

With the patience not so much of a saint as half a dozen saints combined, Grace managed to guide his attention back to the picture. 'When did you first meet him?' she asked, stressing each syllable coldly.

'Three weeks ago. I know, because the rent was due Friday.'

'How did he pay?'

'Cash. Two weeks' deposit, rent one week in advance.'

'Did you ask for any ID?'

'I haven't got time to be asking people for their passports and driving licences,' he said scornfully. 'As long as they have the money and I've got a room for them to stay in, they're welcome to it. I'm not their bleeding nanny.'

'Can you remember *anything* about him?' Fitzgerald asked.

'Not much,' he admitted. 'I hardly saw him, and when

I did he didn't speak. Used to pass him on the stairs occasionally. He didn't keep regular hours.'

'Did he say what he did for a living?'

'Didn't ask.'

'He didn't let anything slip?'

'Not that I noticed.'

'What about visitors?'

'None that I saw.'

'Phone calls in or out?'

'There's a payphone out there on the wall.' He gestured to the door leading out into the hall. 'Couple of times I saw him sitting out there, waiting for a call.'

'You ever listen in?' I said.

'I've got better things to do.'

Like lust after every young girl who passed the window.

'So you noticed nothing unusual about him, you didn't know who he talked to or about what the whole time he was here, and then he was just gone?' said Fitzgerald.

'He must've left this morning,' the landlord said. 'He was definitely here last night. I heard him moving about, didn't I? Then, when I saw your press conference on TV on the news, I went up to check he was still there and found he'd cleared out without a word.'

Randall must've seen the press conference when it was televised live that morning. Either that or someone else had alerted him to it. He knew his cover was blown, so he ran.

If only the landlord and his wife had seen the press conference live instead of the highlights on the lunchtime news, he mightn't have had such a head start.

'I suppose all this will get into the papers now, won't it?' the man continued gloomily, starting off on his scratching again. And, to be fair, he had a lot of flesh to scratch. 'I almost wish I hadn't picked up the phone. I don't want people getting the wrong impression. I run a respectable business here. Still' – and he brightened visibly as an idea struck him – 'at least I can say I've had someone famous staying here.'

'Famous?'

I could see that Fitzgerald was getting near to the point where homicide was looking like a good alternative strategy for dealing with this witness.

'This man you're looking for,' he said. 'He must be famous if you're after him, mustn't he? Stands to reason. So go on, tell me. What'd he do? Did he murder someone?'

He said the word with such relish, it was like he was tasting it on his tongue.

'I'm afraid I'm not at liberty to discuss that,' said Fitzgerald.

The man's eyes opened wide with affront.

'Excuse me for breathing, I'm sure.'

He was still muttering under his breath about who did the police think they were, and whose taxes did they think paid their wages, when we finally escaped upstairs to check out the room where the elusive Buck Randall had been staying for the past few weeks.

It made Kaminski's original hotel room look like the Hilton. I was struck by the resemblances between the two men, both hiding out in a strange city in down-at-heel surroundings, their contact with the world around them reduced to furtive, obscure excursions on missions only they fully understood. And now, within the space of twenty-four hours, the two of them had both cut loose and vanished into the city. Where were they now?

Randall had left little behind him, save for a couple of odd socks, a shirt still hanging in the wardrobe and a shaving brush next to the sink in the bathroom.

Not exactly much to go on.

There was a stale smell in the room of sweat and un-washed flesh.

Fitzgerald right now was standing by the TV. There was a tape left in the VCR. She pressed the switch and ejected it.

'*Muff City*,' she read when it came out. 'Charming.'

'I think I've got that one on DVD,' Walsh whispered to me. 'It's very good.'

'Tragic how the Academy Awards always overlook the best films,' I replied.

'Ironic, isn't it?' said Fitzgerald. 'He needs to hide out, not make himself too conspicuous, but he still takes the risk of popping along to the local perverts' pleasure palace to pick up a copy of this crap.'

'Actually,' said the unexpected voice of the landlord from the doorway at our backs, 'that's one of mine.' He must have followed us upstairs to eavesdrop on the conversation. 'Mr O'Brien must've taken it from my library downstairs. Can I have it back?'

In the middle of everything, it was reassuring to see some people still had their priorities in the right order.

37

Walsh stayed behind at the rooming house to continue the search while Fitzgerald and I returned to Dublin Castle. She had to brief the Assistant Commissioner later, both on the case against Solomon and also on what had happened last night, and now she had today's events to add to the mix. She needed to make sure she was up to speed on the investigation.

That meant getting through the reports which had been gradually mounting in the last couple of days on her desk. The reports so far covering the attack on Rose Downey were scant. That was still being handled as a simple assault, whatever hunch we might have had about it being connected in some way with Marsha's murder. In that respect, Rose was fortunate it hadn't gone far enough for any possible similarities to emerge.

It was the reports on Marsha Reed which were going to take time to get through.

First up there were statements from confidential informants at the S & M club to which Marsha Reed belonged, and the transcript of an interview with one of the men Marsha had contacted through an internet chatroom to share her fantasies of being murdered. He turned out to be the happily married owner of a health-food shop in the city centre who had no idea that the woman he'd been corresponding with online was the same one who'd been found murdered less than a week ago. His story was that the whole exchange between the two of them was nothing more than a fantasy, and that he'd stopped once she suggested meeting up and maybe trying out a few scenarios. Lucky for him, the police didn't intend to tell his wife about the matter.

I would have.

Added to that were the profiles on Marsha's fellow students in the class I'd taken, though again it all seemed somewhat redundant in the light of subsequent events, and page after page of messages left on the email hotline which had been set up following her murder.

An accompanying detailed fingerprint analysis of the necklace found in Solomon's office showed, frustratingly, that it had been wiped clean and had no fingerprints of any kind upon it. Forensics did, however, confirm that microscopic traces of mud and grass matching those samples taken from Marsha's house had been picked up in the same office, though the finding of the Shoe Identification and Retrieval team was that there were no footprints matching his at the scene itself. A number as yet remained unidentified.

There was also the psychological report on Solomon from Fisher, who'd interviewed him briefly since his arrest. Solomon had not been forthcoming, to say the least, and indeed found the very idea of being psychologically profiled offensive and absurd.

Fisher could come to few conclusions, save that Solomon was a domineering personality, controlling and narcissistic, which struck me as something which could be said about most of the people in the theatre. As to whether he considered Solomon capable of such extreme violence, he didn't say, but I could read between the lines. Solomon was capable of extreme violence, as we all were, but Fisher did not think him particularly high risk.

There was also a rundown of everything that was known about Solomon's movements in the days before and after the killing of Marsha Reed, and especially his whereabouts on the night itself. There was undoubtedly a black hole in the record now that his alibi had collapsed. He'd left the Liffey Theatre when the night's performance ended shortly after 11 p.m., not staying for his usual drink, and no one could place him anywhere until the following morning when he had a late breakfast at Bewley's coffee shop in town with a postgraduate student who was writing a profile of him for a journal called *Dublin Theatre Studies*. The student revealed that Solomon had been hungover that morning and in bad form, and also that he'd attempted unsuccessfully to lure her into bed, promising that he could help her get her play produced in London. It seemed to be something of a pattern with him.

Like all police reports, getting through them was a thankless task, giving, as they did, the distinct impression of having been written by people with only a passing acquaintance with the English language and rules of grammar. Paragraphs came at random, or not at all. Spelling was atrocious. Malapropisms abounded. Many simple pieces of information, from dates and times to further contact numbers, were omitted entirely.

It's no wonder so many criminal cases fall down when they come to court because the police reports are so badly written. Often contradictory, and speckled with information which cannot be properly verified, they're a goldmine for unscrupulous defence attorneys.

The most crucial sheet among the multitude on Fitzgerald's desk would have been all too easy to overlook. It was stapled to the end of the report on his movements, almost like an afterthought, and came from the pen of a patrol cop on the night Marsha Reed died. This was about 2.45 a.m. and revealed that Solomon had been seen in the area round Fitzwilliam Place East in a dishevelled and drunken state, not seeming to know where he was. A patrol car had stopped him to make sure he was OK and then let him proceed on his way.

What was interesting about this was not only that it was the only confirmed sighting between his leaving the theatre and the following morning, but that he'd said he was on his way at the time to see the actor Zak Kirby at his apartment block in the same area of the city.

'Kirby isn't staying at a hotel?' said Fitzgerald.

'He doesn't like hotels,' said Walsh, and then he flushed slightly as we turned to look at him curiously. 'I read an interview with him in one of the American film magazines,' he explained sheepishly. 'It said he found them artificial, unreal, and that when he's in a city he likes to get an authentic feel for the place rather than the front they put on for visitors.'

Fitzgerald rolled her eyes.

'So where *is* he staying?' I asked.

She checked the notes on the desk in front of her.

'Mullingar Studios, apparently,' she said. 'You know it?'

I shook my head.

'It's a big fancy building off Leeson Street,' she said. 'All shiny glass and chrome.'

'Very authentic,' I said sarcastically. 'He'll really get a feel for the rough side of the city there.'

'Don't be so dismissive,' said Fitzgerald. 'A woman pushed her husband off the thirteenth floor last year, don't you remember? It doesn't get much more authentic than that.'

'What does Kirby say about all this?'

'That's the thing. He gave a statement to the police when Solomon's name first came up. He said he didn't see

Solomon from the time the play ended Saturday night until the following evening.'

'You think Kirby was lying?'

'No idea. But you heard what Fisher said about the mixed scene, the different knots, the possibility of two killers. By Kirby's own testimony, he wasn't back at his apartment until after one. That gives him plenty of time to have taken part in the killing.'

'You're not saying Zak Kirby is a killer?' I said.

'Why not?'

'Because too many people would recognize him if he suddenly started wandering round the city, slaughtering women,' I said. 'That's one of the perils of being famous. OJ apart, it severely limits your chances of committing murder.'

'I think you'll find that OJ Simpson was found not guilty,' said Fitzgerald.

'Whatever. My point is that every step he takes is ten times more likely to be seen and remembered than if it had been someone anonymous like you or me taking it.' I paused. 'Still, I wonder if he ever came into contact with Buck Randall —'

'Let's not even go there,' said Fitzgerald firmly. 'I told you, we've got to treat these stories like they're completely self-contained. I can't start trying to make them link up. That way lies madness. It couldn't hurt, though, to pull up the CCTV from the building where our American movie star is staying and see if Solomon ever did arrive there that night.'

And it certainly didn't.

'I have absolutely no idea,' said Zak Kirby, and if he really was innocent as charged then it was a perfectly reasonable answer to the question Fitzgerald had asked him a moment earlier.

Having said that, Kirby was, like most of the people we seemed to have encountered during this case, an actor, so if he *did* know why Victor Solomon had turned up at the door of his apartment building at 3 a.m. on the night Marsha Reed died, as the CCTV footage had revealed he had, then it wouldn't be so difficult to pretend ignorance as it might be for the rest of us mere mortals. Though if he *was* lying, it was a damned good act.

We'd found him sitting in his dressing room at the Liffey Theatre, preparing for that night's performance of *Othello*. The show must go on, isn't that what they say? This one had closed for only one night following the near-death of the leading lady and the arrest of the director on a murder charge. The company was clearly taking the old adage literally.

Kirby had an enviable reputation among young American actors. He'd made the transition from obscure off-Broadway shows and small-budget independent, slightly left-field movies to big-screen Hollywood fame without once being dogged by the usual accusations of selling out. He managed to keep his street cred intact while simultaneously beaming out from the cover of every celebrity magazine. He'd mastered the trick of being good-looking enough for teenage girls to want his poster on their walls, but cool enough for teenage boys not to think he was trying too hard, lending his face and name along the way to all the best progressive causes, and hacking his hair into a faux-punky style that fooled enough people into thinking he didn't care what it looked like. Every couple of years, he also stepped off the celebrity carousel to ostentatiously rediscover his artistic roots by treading the boards, giving the showbiz magazines another opportunity to write at length about what an intriguing, unconventional character he was. Hence the summer's sojourn here in Dublin.

Oh, and did I mention that he'd written a novel too? A slim, sensitive, coming-of-age tale set among young actors dreaming of better things in a rooming house in Brooklyn.

It would be.

Right now, he was lighting a cigarette and trying to remember that night.

'Let me think,' he said, mussing up his hair self-consciously and creasing his forehead into a photogenic frown. 'You have to appreciate that I get a lot of people ringing my buzzer. Lot of people calling my line. Calls all the time. Night. Day. Day. Night. You know how it is,' he added to me. He'd recognized my name as soon as Fitzgerald introduced me. Turned out too that he knew some of the people who'd worked on the TV movie of my first book. Now he was drawing me into his story for back-up. 'Their names all blur into one after a while. Just this morning, I took what must've been thirty calls from various TV stations and newspapers wanting to hear about this new script I've been working on about the war in Iraq. I'm calling it *American Dream, Arab Nightmare*. I think it's going to totally expose the hypocrisy of what we're doing out there in the Mid-East. It's the new colonialism, it genuinely is. What we're doing now is no better than what the Europeans did in Africa for centuries, carving up the land, stealing the natural resources, keeping down its true owners.'

I was beginning to appreciate why Dublin had taken Zak Kirby to their hearts.

He talked their language.

'I've no idea how they found out about it,' he continued smartly about his host of morning callers. 'I was trying to keep the project under wraps. I loathe publicity.'

You could've fooled me.

Having more manners than me, however, Fitzgerald waited till he'd finished his little speech on global geopolitics before pressing on.

'This wasn't some reporter on the hunt for a scoop,' she said. 'It was your own director. You're saying you don't remember him coming round that night at all?'

'I know I didn't let him in.'

'We know you didn't let him in as well,' said Fitzgerald. 'The CCTV shows he stood there for five or six minutes, ringing the buzzer, before he went away. Were you out?'

'No. I gave a statement about that already. I was asleep. The CCTV shows me coming in, right?'

'It does. It was a little after one.'

'Then how could I have left again without being seen?'

'The CCTV on the back entrance is broken,' Fitzgerald said. 'Anyone could get in and out without being seen.'

He looked shocked. 'They could? I'll have to get my people on to that. I can't have fans getting into the place where I'm staying that easily. I've had similar problems before in LA.'

'You had a stalker?'

'A teenage girl broke in while I was away filming,' said Kirby. 'Lived in my house for a week before she was discovered. She'd been sleeping in my bed. Wearing my clothes.'

'So you don't remember Solomon buzzing?'

'I don't. That's the gospel truth.'

'You're a heavy sleeper.'

'Acting takes its toll. More so when it's a part like Iago. Come to think of it,' he said, 'I shouldn't wonder if that wasn't what Vic wanted to talk to me about that night.'

'Did he make a habit of calling round after midnight to discuss your part?'

'As a matter of fact, he did. He must've been round six, seven times since we started rehearsals. He's a very learned man. I could listen to him talk all night. And believe me, sometimes it feels like I have.' He laughed indulgently at his own joke. 'Solomon must've read virtually every word that's been written about the play. He loved to talk about the part, and the range of different actors down the years who've portrayed Iago. Most of the other great actors through the years have tried their hand at it.' I loved that sly use of the word *other* there. 'Olivier, Spacey, Branagh, McKellen, we've all had a shot.'

'And this is what you used to spend all night talking about?' I asked.

'You could talk about this material for ever and still not get to the bottom of it. The role of Iago is one of the most important parts in the whole of Shakespeare's canon. I'm not boasting when I say the play should really be called *Iago*, not *Othello*. The whole structure of it is about how manipulation and deceit work together to precipitate tragedy. About how Iago works his will through Othello. I guess Victor and I often got a bit carried away with it.'

'But not that night?'

'Like I say, that night I don't have any memory of him coming round. I certainly didn't talk to him. It's always a rough period, coming up to the end of the first week of a show. I generally pop a pill, put on my earmuffs and say goodnight to the world. Particularly when it's a part this demanding. I've never stretched myself so much. Do you know *Othello*?'

'I had a part in it once at drama school,' answered Walsh unexpectedly.

I'd forgotten he was there. He'd been so quiet, standing by the dressing-room door the whole time we were talking, not contributing a word, taking in the backstage ambience, if the sound of hammering from the floor above and a radio blaring counted as ambience.

I guess he was a little starstruck. He'd mentioned a couple of days ago how much he admired Zak Kirby. His smile could have lit up the dark side of the moon when Fitzgerald told him earlier that he could tag along to the theatre this time while she interviewed him.

'You were at drama school?' Kirby said to Walsh, and to give him credit he sounded genuinely interested. Walsh flushed ever so slightly.

'Three years,' he said, 'but it didn't work out.'

'Please tell me you haven't given up acting completely.'

'I'm in a small amateur company. We put on a couple of plays a year. We did *Othello* a couple of springs ago,' Walsh said.

'Who were you?'

'Cassio,' said Walsh. 'I know it's not a huge part or anything.'

'Hey,' said Kirby, 'Cassio's a good role. You should keep going. Never give up. I'm serious. Once you give up wanting to make a difference, that's the day you start to die inside. You never know what's around the corner. I was twenty-six before I got my first lead role.'

The pleasure Walsh clearly took from this exchange almost made me ashamed that I'd been giving Kirby such a tough time in my estimation. Maybe he wasn't such a schmuck, after all, even if he was a walking mouthpiece for all those liberal clichés I so despised.

'You should come along to tonight's performance,' Kirby was telling Walsh. 'I'll get you three tickets, one for each of you, and leave them at the desk. This is a big night.'

'You're not missing Victor Solomon too much, then?' said Fitzgerald.

'Don't you folks have a little rule about being innocent until proven guilty?' the actor said in all seriousness. 'I know he's been through the wringer lately, but Vic's not such a loser. He lost his way a little, is all. I don't think he murdered anyone.'

'Shame for him you're not eligible to serve on his jury,' I said.

'I'd rather play the murderer,' he flashed me his big-screen grin good-naturedly. 'All those weeks centre stage on the stand, all eyes fixed on you and you alone. It's the ideal role for any actor. It's always more fun to play the villain.'

'I doubt Solomon's looking forward to the prospect quite so eagerly,' said Fitzgerald.

38

'Well, I think you should go,' said Burke, refilling my glass. 'Zak Kirby's one of the good guys. I saw him on TV talking about a film he's making about the US occupation of Iraq.'

'You couldn't have seen him on TV. He hates publicity. You must've imagined it.'

'I wouldn't expect *you* to like him,' he went on decisively. 'Unless someone's a fully paid-up member of the National Rifle Association, you practically write them off as a pinko.'

'You're a pinko. I haven't written you off.'

'True,' he conceded. 'You're a mass of contradictions.'

'Don't knock them. My inconsistency is my best feature. That and my ass. Only difference is it's my ass that talks most sense some days.'

Burke laughed so loud that he made his cat Hare dart in alarm from the chair where he'd been curled up making preparations for sleep and the last of the day's customers in his own store turn round in the aisles of books to see what he was laughing at.

They looked blank on realizing it was me.

'I still think you should go,' he said. 'I know it's a regular poker night, but Shakespeare's more important than poker . . .'

'Blasphemer.'

'. . . and *Othello* is one great play.'

'So everyone keeps telling me,' I answered grouchily.

'You know what your problem is, Saxon?'

'Yes,' I said, 'I do. Fisher asked me that exact same

question. In all honesty, I can't remember precisely which of my many faults it was that he proceeded to elevate into the number one position, but I'm sure it was a good one.'

'Your problem,' said Burke, refusing to be sidetracked from what he intended to say, 'is you think because everyone's telling you something that it must, by definition, be wrong.'

'How's that a problem?'

'It's a problem because you miss out on too much that way. Like *Othello*.'

'If the play's all you're worried about, then have no fear. I'm going,' I declared. 'Fitzgerald missed it the first time we had tickets because that was the night they found Marsha Reed's body. I'm not lucky enough to get out of it a second time. Unless you know someone who can arrange another murder for me at short notice?'

'Sorry, I sold my last copy of the *Psychopaths' Phone Directory*.'

'Pity. Shakespeare it is, then. If she ever turns up, that is.'

I checked my watch.

There was more than an hour to go before the play started, but in a town where time is notoriously relative and an arrangement to meet someone is regarded by most of the people living here as more of a well-meaning aspiration than a definite commitment, Fitzgerald was one of the few who could be relied upon to be where and when she said she'd be.

But tonight she still hadn't arrived.

There had to be a reason for it.

I wasn't worried about her as such. Fitzgerald was one of the few people I did let myself worry about but not on this occasion. I knew where she was. She'd returned to Dublin Castle to give her briefing to Assistant Commissioner

Carson. But that had been more than two hours ago and there'd been no word since. Should I call and make sure she was OK?

'Maybe she just got fed up with your bad moods and decided to dump you for another former Special Agent with a better temperament,' suggested Burke helpfully.

'Kaminski's the only other former Special Agent in town, far as I know, and he's not her type. Besides, he's playing hide-and-seek again. She wouldn't know where to find him.'

'Then drink your whiskey and relax. She'll be here.' And he retrieved the fleeing cat from the store room and made it sit on his lap, using his big hands to stroke the affronted creature into forgiving him for the earlier fright. 'You know,' he added more softly now so as not to disturb it, 'you might even find the evening interesting.'

'Want to make a bet on that?'

'I'd sure bet Buck Randall III would find it interesting.'

'Buck Randall probably couldn't even spell Shakespeare, let alone understand it,' I said. 'What's he got to do with Othello?'

'He's got everything to do with Othello,' said Burke. 'Or maybe not Othello so much as Iago. Don't you see?' I had to admit that I didn't. 'You know the story, right?'

'Vaguely,' I said. 'I caught the Orson Welles version on TV one night years ago, but I was pretty drunk at the time. I don't remember much about it.'

'That was in the bad old days when actors used to black up to play Othello,' said Burke. 'In some of those old productions, Othello couldn't even touch the fellow actors in case the boot polish came off and stained their nice new costumes.'

'Al Jolson, eat your heart out.'

'They did everything but give Othello a banjo and get

him to sing "Old Man River" in between eating courses of fried chicken and gumbo,' Burke growled disapprovingly.

I resisted the urge to confess that such an alternative sounded like it'd be a lot more fun than the version I'd seen all those years ago after coming home late from the bar.

'All you have to know,' he continued, conveniently saving me from my lifelong tendency to put my foot in it, 'is that Iago, a soldier, has been passed over for promotion by Othello, his captain, in favour of another man called Cassio.'

'That's the part Walsh played.'

'Don't interrupt. In revenge, Iago then plots to make Othello suspect his wife, Desdemona, of having an affair with Cassio so that he'll kill her and ruin his reputation.'

'Seems a bit of an overreaction to missing out on promotion,' I said. 'Just as well it never caught on. It'd be a bloodbath out there every time a position was filled.'

He ignored me.

It was usually the best way.

'Iago calls it his cunning pattern,' Burke explained. 'He works on Othello's decent, trusting nature, tormenting him with words, placing one layer of deception on top of another, so that no single character apart from Iago ever knows the truth, they only know their own part in it, until Othello is driven into a kind of temporary insanity by jealousy and murders the one thing he loves best. That's why the play's named after Othello, not Iago. It's his tragedy.'

'Sounds to me,' I said, 'like it was his wife's tragedy for marrying a man who'd kill his supposed beloved just because he thinks she's getting a bit of action elsewhere. Didn't they have divorce in those days? And that's another thing. How come we're supposed to feel sorry for this man when he was the one who murdered his wife? That was his decision.'

'It's symbolic,' he said. 'Think of it as a dark fable of how jealousy and suspicion can corrupt the most honest and noble souls.'

'You're starting to sound like one of those cultural programmes I always try to miss on cable,' I said confusedly. 'So where does the pound of flesh come into it?'

'It doesn't,' said Burke patiently. 'That's *The Merchant of Venice*.'

'Right,' I said slowly, running over what he'd said once more in my mind. 'So Iago twists Othello's mind and sends him mad and then Othello murders his wife and we're all supposed to feel sorry for him. I can follow that. Apart from the feeling sorry for him part. What I don't see is how that ties in to Kaminski and Randall. Randall isn't trying to get Kaminski to murder his wife. According to Kaminski, it's Randall who did that already.'

'You're taking it too literally.'

'I am?'

'It's not the details that matter so much as the way Iago sits at the centre of his web, spinning lies and plots. He even compares himself to a spider right at the start of the play. Iago manipulates Othello's weaknesses until he has no control any more over his own mind. He's like the Pied Piper of Hamelin, leading the children on a merry dance into the darkness. Think about it. Isn't that what Buck Randall's been doing to your friend Kaminski the whole time? He's been jerking his strings from the moment their paths crossed. Even Kaminski's weak spot is the same as Othello's: his love for his wife. That's what makes him vulnerable.'

'But to what end?' I said. 'Why would he want Kaminski to fall for this line about him being the city's very own killing machine? What does he want him to *do*?'

'Finding the answer to that is your job,' said Burke, 'not mine.'

I considered what he'd told me.

'Maybe', I said, venturing tentatively toward a possible answer, 'Randall wanted Kaminski to come after him all along. He wasn't trying to escape. He was the hunted leading the hunter into a trap so that the roles could be reversed. He knew Kaminski would never give up, so why not just face the inevitable confrontation and get it over and done with?'

'Only it's better to do it on your own terms than your enemy's?'

'And in the arena of your choosing. Exactly,' I said. 'Which means Buck Randall won't simply vanish, whatever else Kaminski feared. He'll stay and finish what he started.'

'He's running out of time if that's the plan,' Burke reminded me.

'All the more important, then, that we find Kaminski fast. He's our only lead to Buck Randall.' I checked my watch again, suppressing irasciability. Though not for long, probably. It wasn't only Randall that time was running out on. 'Where *is* that damn woman?'

I was standing on the kerb at Crampton Quay, waiting for a gap in the hurtling traffic to cross over to the Ha'penny Bridge, when I finally got my answer to that question.

'Saxon,' she said. 'Can you hear me? This signal isn't good.'

'You're cracking up,' I told her.

'You wouldn't be the first to tell me that.'

'Where are you?'

'I'm with Walsh. We're on our way to the theatre as we speak.'

'Weren't we supposed to be meeting up at Burke's place?'

'Change of plan,' she crackled in my ear.

The rest of the sentence was lost in static.

'Fitzgerald?'

I had my finger in one ear and my cellphone pressed tightly to the other, straining to differentiate her voice from the other noises around me, but I quickly learned that a warm summer's evening on the riverside in Dublin is not the best place to try to conduct a conversation with a woman in a car any number of streets away.

'Hello? Hello?'

In the end, I gave up.

It didn't matter. She'd said she was on her way to the theatre. I could talk to her there. Getting back to the theatre had been the plan anyway when I decided to leave Burke and Hare's five minutes earlier. In the meantime, all I had to do was get across this road.

Preferably without being run over.

Before long, I was striding across the bridge, looking down at the strollers idling down the boardwalk that now ran along this stretch of the river as it slapped and wound through the heart of the city. The evening sunshine cut low shadows over the wooden slats at the walkers' feet and glanced like fire off the steel railings.

Even the water seemed in a better mood than usual that evening, sparkling and blue-green and innocent where usually it was grey-brown and hungry and resentful of the walls that held it back and told it where to go. The city was gazing languorously down at its reflection in the river and liking what it was. The low quayside buildings glowed contentedly.

The fetid, feverish atmosphere of two nights ago seemed to have evaporated again.

Outside the Liffey Theatre, the same easy mood was in evidence. People stood chatting, enjoying the last of the evening sunshine before plunging inside to Othello's tormented world, others merely escaping the smoking ban by having a final deliciously wicked cigarette. Zak Kirby stared out menacingly from the posters.

He was right. *This* version of the play at least should've been named after him. The guy playing Othello peeped out on the posters from behind the great actor's back, almost apologetic for muscling in on his moment of glory.

Kirby's billing was even bigger than Shakespeare's.

Fitzgerald arrived a few moments after me, climbing out of the front seat of a marked police car as it pulled into the kerb. Then Walsh got out the back door too, and they both walked over to me. That certainly got the attention of the waiting theatre-goers.

'Shall we go inside and get a quick drink?' she said.

'You think we have time?'

'There's always time for a drink.'

The people around us seemed faintly disappointed. Maybe they'd hoped they were going to see an arrest, namely mine. Instead the three of us now climbed the steps into the theatre, and the police car drove off in the direction of O'Connell Street.

The bar was crowded when we got inside, so we took up a position by the door and sent Walsh to buy the drinks. I didn't waste any time.

'Something happened, didn't it?' I said.

'Am I that transparent?' answered Fitzgerald. 'Yes, something happened. Though what it means, I still haven't quite managed to figure out.'

'Well, are you going to tell me what it is, or do I have to beat it out of you?'

'You'll have to get a pair of stepladders first,' she teased me gently. Then her face became grave, and she lowered her voice so as not to be overheard by the people pressing in around us. 'We found something,' she said. 'Well, I say we found it. What I mean is that her friend Kim found it. You remember you met her at Marsha's house the other day?'

'She was picking up Marsha's stuff,' I recalled.

'And inadvertently picking up a mobile phone too,' Fitzgerald said.

'I'm guessing the phone was for the number she left on the online chat rooms for people to call?' Fitzgerald confirmed it. 'Where was it?'

'It was in the pocket of one of Marsha's dresses. Kim found it entirely by accident. God knows how we missed it. She just happened to notice something hard when she was packing the clothes away into boxes. She looked to see what it was and then brought it round today to Dublin Castle. That's what kept me. That's why I wasn't at Burke's.'

'What was on it?'

'There were calls to only one other number. We don't know who that belonged to, and she hardly ever spoke to him directly, only sent a whole series of text messages covering a period of two weeks. Basically, she was telling him exactly what she wanted him to do when he came to her house that night and making arrangements to pay him.'

'The missing money from her purse –'

'Exactly.'

'So she *did* set up her own murder?'

'That's the thing,' said Fitzgerald. 'It seems that Marsha didn't really want to go the whole way. She saw it simply as a kind of play-acting. They were going to carry out a simulation of her murder, so that she could feel what it was like, test the boundaries of her desire, as she put it, but within a controlled environment. The man was to go through with the act exactly as if it was real, right up until the last moment, when he would stop.'

'Except he didn't.'

'Except he didn't,' agreed Fitzgerald. 'Either because it all went horribly wrong –'

'Or because he never intended to stop in the first place,' I finished for her, 'and she walked right into the trap.' I sighed. 'There was no name? No clues as to his identity?'

'Nothing whatsoever,' Fitzgerald said. 'She told him she didn't want to know anything about him. I think the mystery of the whole thing turned her on. She talked to him about her pretend murder like they were planning on making love.'

'When did he last make contact with her?'

'She called him two nights before she died.'

'She was making the final arrangements?'

'That's what it looks like.'

I was about to say something else when Walsh returned with our drinks.

Our faces must have said it all.

'No need to ask what you've been talking about,' he remarked as he passed cold bottles of beer into our warm and grateful hands. I noticed he also had a programme with him. He must've picked it up at the bar. There was a telephone number scribbled along the edge.

The programme clearly wasn't the only thing he'd picked up.

That boy never stopped.

It's a wonder it didn't drop off.

'Either way,' I said, 'I don't see how Victor Solomon fits into it.'

'Don't say that.'

'Someone has to. You can't claim Solomon was trying to silence a woman who was threatening to destroy him and was so desperate for cash he stole her necklace and cut off her finger to get a ring that no one can find anyway, and then admit she'd been sending texts to another man begging him to kill her only days before she was actually killed. His lawyers will tear your case to shreds.'

'Who says Solomon wasn't her mysterious phone caller himself?'

'It didn't sound like it,' said Walsh gently. 'In one of the texts she wrote to him: *I can't wait to meet you*. She wouldn't use that phrase if she was talking to Solomon.'

Fitzgerald groaned. 'Don't do this to me. Not tonight,' she said. 'I'm just bushed, I can't think straight. Tomorrow. We'll talk about it tomorrow. Tonight was meant to be an escape.'

'I'm sorry,' I said. 'Forget I said anything. You know what I'm like. I'm the land that diplomacy forgot. Though you know, I'm not sure *Othello* will be much of an escape.'

'What do you mean?'

'Jealousy, murder, sex, lies, revenge – it sounds more like a normal day's work for you than like an escape,' I commented.

'I'm impressed,' she said. 'Since when did you get to be such an expert on Shakespeare?'

'Burke was cribbing me in your absence,' I said. 'The way he talked about it, he almost made me look forward to seeing the damn thing.'

'Only almost?'

'Only almost,' I conceded gruffly. 'But you know what they say. Every oak tree started out once as a little acorn.'

'I see you more as a little nut,' said Fitzgerald. 'What do *they* grow into?'

'I'll take a look in the mirror when I get home and let you know.'

'I think we're going in,' said Walsh, and, looking round, I saw that the crowd in the bar had gotten much thinner since we arrived. Either the play was about to start, or they were definitely trying to tell us something. Hastily, I finished my beer and followed him up the steps into the dim theatre, where a half-musical murmur, like an orchestra tuning up, was moving through the massed ranks of disembodied heads, the last remnants of conversation before the evening play began. We took our seats in the centre of one row toward the front, and waited, and I wished I'd gone to the bathroom before sitting down here because there was no way I could ask all these people to move again, especially not now the lights were dimming further, and the voices with it, as though the same switch which turned down the lights was able to turn down conversation at the same time. Neat trick if you could do it.

Oh, well, it served me right for never being able to resist a cold beer.

Gradual as dawn, a pale blue light appeared behind the curtain up on stage, moving, shivering, and, as the curtain drew back, I saw that it was a light like water rippling, which cast restless shadows over the flat façades of frowning buildings.

Venice, wasn't that where the play began?

Moments later there came approaching footsteps, echoes at first, then louder, and Zak Kirby appeared, followed by another man.

'*Tush! never tell me . . .*'

And so we began.

I settled down in my seat and tried to concentrate.

Kirby was good, I had to give him that. The brash young actor had gone. He was Iago now, the slighted soldier, world-weary and cynical and burning with the need for revenge, angry at seeing others less capable promoted ahead of him.

And I could understand that part at least. I'd seen it often enough in the FBI, as those who came garlanded with qualifications and meaningless academic recommendations strode ahead of the rest, overtaking agents who'd given years of their lives to the Bureau and had worked more cases than the newcomers had even read about. Promotion too often was for the golden circle. If you weren't in it to begin with, you stayed where you were.

Always the outsider.

His face was snarled with resentment at his ill-treatment, then would switch in an instant so that anyone seeing it would think at once they were in the company of a friend.

Someone who only had their best interests at heart.

And then it came to me.

Unexpectedly.

Unclearly as yet.

But undeniably too. At least it was to me. Whether Fitzgerald would be convinced that here lay the lock and key of all the villainous secrets which had occupied us for these past days remained to be seen.

'We have to go,' I whispered to her.

'What are you talking about? We can't go. We only just got here.'

'I can't explain,' I said. 'I know who he is. I know who Iago is. At least I think I do. I don't have a name for him yet, but I know where to get one.'

Someone shushed me loudly from the row behind.

'You're not making sense,' Fitzgerald hissed.

'You have to trust me,' I said.

'Shit, why do I hate hearing those words?'

39

'This had better be good,' said Fitzgerald as soon as we were outside the door of the theatre and had a chance to talk, 'and not just another one of your feeble excuses to wriggle out of improving your mind with a bit of culture.'

'Blame Burke,' I said. 'He's the one who got me thinking.'

'Burke?'

'He pointed out the parallels between the play and what was happening with Kaminski and Buck Randall. It all made sense. *Someone* was leading Kaminski on, setting a trap to entangle him, but think about it. Whoever was jerking his chain had to be subtle, clever, manipulative. Like Iago. Does that really fit what we know about Buck Randall III?'

'He never struck me as a candidate for *Mastermind*,' she conceded.

'It's like I said to Burke earlier. What does Randall want? In the play, everything's simple. Iago wants Othello to murder his own wife, so he keeps planting suspicions and winding him tighter till he blows, right? But if Buck Randall's the Iago in all this, then he's only planting suspicion against himself. Why would he do that?'

'I take it that's a rhetorical question?'

'If you mean, do I have the answer already, I think so,' I said. 'It just came to me in there, out of nowhere. Randall's not Iago in all this. He's Desdemona. He's the one against whom suspicion's being planted. And maybe, like her, he's been innocent all along.'

That would certainly explain a lot. Why Randall would let

himself be seen so openly out at Bull Island. Why should he hide his face if he'd done nothing wrong? It explained too why he didn't care if his fingerprints were found all over the car that was pulled from the water. He had no reason to believe anyone would even be interested in his fingerprints. He probably didn't even know that Mark Hudson's body was in the trunk. Maybe he just drove the car out there because that's what he'd been instructed to do, to meet this mythical Peters perhaps, and someone else came later to dispose of it. Each step along the way, he could've been planting suspicion against himself without even realizing he was doing it.

'The point is,' I said, 'that he's the one that someone wants to die.'

'And they're using Kaminski to do it?'

'Remember how Fisher described the same phenomenon when he spoke of how it was possible for a killer to act out his will using other people as the weapons?'

'But who could hate Buck Randall that much to want him dead?' asked Fitzgerald. 'The only person we know who hates Randall sufficiently is Kaminski.'

'But it isn't necessary for anyone to *hate* Randall to want him dead. Iago didn't hate Desdemona either. He simply wanted to use her death to bring about the downfall of Othello. It was Othello that he despised. So surely it's Kaminski that our own Iago hates too?'

'Then let me change the question round slightly. Who hates *Kaminski* enough to want to turn him into a killer?'

'There was a part in the play early on,' I said, trying to recall exactly how it went, 'when Iago was explaining his reasons for wanting revenge. How did it go? Something about Othello getting it on between the sheets with his woman.'

'*It is thought abroad that 'twixt my sheets he's done my office,*' she quoted effortlessly.

'That was it. It reminded me of something Kaminski told me that night in my apartment when he showed up. He said Heather was going out with someone else when they first met.'

'You mean, Kaminski had been doing someone else's office between the sheets too?'

'That's what I'm thinking.'

And now I could tell that she was interested.

'You have a plan,' she said.

'Follow me.'

I couldn't hang about waiting for Fitzgerald to call a car to bring us back to Dublin Castle and walking would take too long. Nor did I have enough power in my American cellphone for what I had to do. That left only one option.

Round the corner on O'Connell Street stood one of the international call centres that had sprung up across the city in recent years to let the thousands of people who'd arrived here from Eastern Europe and elsewhere call home cheaply. Small booths lined the wall like confessionals, and the light shone from the glass out front like a warm welcome.

I was out of breath by the time I'd run round there, then I had to search through my cellphone for the number I needed. I felt I was wasting time. Time I didn't have.

Time Kaminski didn't have.

Certainly time that Buck Randall didn't have.

Then I punched in the number wrongly.

Cursed.

Tried again.

At last it rang.

'Piper,' he said when he answered.

'Piper, it's me, Saxon. Listen, I need your help again.'

That familiar empty laugh. 'Who're you trying to get in touch with now?'

'It's nothing like that,' I said. 'I've got something to tell you. I found Kaminski.'

'You found him?'

He sounded hesitant, like he didn't believe me.

'I found Buck Randall too,' I went on. 'Leastways, I know he's here, and I know *why* he's here. I *think* I know at last what's been going on.'

'Right,' he said slowly.

He still didn't sound sure.

'So where are they now?'

'I don't know,' I admitted.

'But I thought you said –'

'I know what I said. I had Kaminski, but he's split on me again. Piper, are you listening to me? Buck Randall didn't kill Kaminski's wife.'

'He didn't?'

'He couldn't have. Nothing he does makes any sense if he really did kill her. Someone just wants Kaminski to believe that he did.'

'I'm not following you,' Piper said.

'It's complicated,' I said. 'You have to trust me. Someone's trying to set up Kaminski. That's what it's been about all along.'

'Who?' he said.

'That's the problem. I don't know. I thought you might be able to help me. I know who it is, I just don't know who it is, if you understand what I mean.'

'Saxon, there's probably not another soul on the planet right now who understands what you mean.'

'I think Heather was seeing someone in the Bureau before she met Kaminski. I think Kaminski was having an affair with her while she was seeing this other guy, and *that's* why he killed her. And now he's making Kaminski pay too.'

'Saxon, listen to me, you have to stop this,' said Piper. 'What you're doing here, it's too dangerous. I don't know what Kaminski's up to, but he's got you involved in it too now. He's been out of his head ever since his wife died, he's just been waiting to blow, and you don't want to be near him when he does. You have to walk away.'

'You were the one who told me Kaminski needed a friend.'

'It was wrong of me. I shouldn't have let you get involved. I didn't think you'd go this far. Listen to yourself. You sound half crazy. You've got to forget about Kaminski before he drags you down with him.'

'It's too late for that,' I said. 'The only thing I can do now is get to him before he destroys everything. I just need to know, was Heather seeing someone else in the Bureau when she met Kaminski? I need a name, nothing else.'

'You're serious,' he said.

'I've never been more serious in my whole life.'

'Then this is what I'm going to do,' said Piper. 'I don't want you to do anything until I get to Dublin. I'll get a plane first thing tomorrow morning. We can discuss it then. Together we'll figure out a way to help Kaminski. I shouldn't have left you to do this on your own . . .'

Finally, he noticed my silence.

'Saxon?'

He's like the Pied Piper, Burke had said.

Piper.

I almost laughed. It was so simple. You call a cellphone in New Jersey, you have no idea where it really rings.

'Saxon, are you there?'

'*How do you know I'm in Dublin?*' I said.

Traffic roared softly down O'Connell Street, the sound dulled by the glass.

It was like a wind rushing in my head.

'I never said I was in Dublin,' I said, more loudly.

'What are you talking about?'

'I never said *Kaminski* was in Dublin.'

Now it was Piper's turn to go silent.

'It was you, wasn't it?'

'For Christ's sake, what was me?'

'It was you that Heather was going out with when she met Kaminski. It was you she left to be with him. That's why you and Kaminski had fallen out. I am such a fool.'

'You're raving.'

'You're lying,' I said.

'I'm lying? You were the one who said you were in San Francisco.'

'Why, Piper? Why did you kill her?'

I counted ten cars passing, and a truck whose brakes squealed like an animal in pain as it came to a belated stop at a red light, before he answered.

Before he stopped pretending.

'They betrayed me,' he said simply. 'I don't know if you understand what that's like, if you can comprehend what it's like to have your insides torn out by the one person you thought you could trust, but I don't recommend the feeling.'

'All she did was fall in love,' I said.

'I'm not talking about Heather,' he said scornfully. 'I'm talking about Kaminski. How could he do that to me? And don't talk to me about love. She made me puke the way she tried to tell me she couldn't help herself, she had to be with him. Well, she paid the price.'

'And Kaminski?'

'I thought killing her would be enough. I thought that would punish Kaminski enough. But it wasn't. It wasn't nearly enough. He had to suffer more. Then he called me and asked for my help in bringing down Randall – after what he'd done to me, he wanted my help! And I knew how easy it would be to lead him by the nose. I remembered Randall from the case down in New Mexico. He was the perfect fall guy. I could've sent Kaminski a leaflet saying Randall was the second gunman in Dallas in '63 and he'd have believed it. All I had to do was make him think, right until the last moment, that he was getting revenge for Heather's death, and then finally let him see the truth: that the one he really should have gone after had gotten clean away, and he'd never have the chance to finish what he'd started. He'd simply sit rotting in a prison cell somewhere, torturing himself with what ifs and guilt at killing Randall. All I had to do was provide the bait and he'd fall right into the trap.'

'So that's why you killed Marsha Reed?'

'Don't expect me to feel guilty about that. It's what she wanted. She was the one who made all the arrangements. I simply played my part.'

'She thought it was all a pretence,' I said thickly.

'Be careful what you wish for,' said Piper, 'it might just come true.' And I remembered that Fitzgerald had used similar words once about Marsha too.

Desires can be dangerous things.

Who knows where they might lead?

'I'd come across people like Marsha Reed before, when I was in the FBI. She wasn't too hard to find. All I had to do was persuade her she'd be safe, and she was up for it. She thought it was a huge joke. Right until the very end . . . It meant coming to Dublin, but that was OK. I knew Randall would be easier to control here anyway. After that, it was easy to get Kaminski to follow us. And once he was here, I just had to convince him that the man who killed his wife had struck again and I knew he'd respond accordingly.'

'You took the ring from Marsha.'

'I'd taken the ring from Heather's body because I wanted it back. I'd bought it for her. She had no right to have it any more. Therefore I had to take the ring from Marsha too. It proved a little harder to get at than last time, but it had to be done. After that, it was simply a matter of giving Kaminski repeated reminders that Randall had to be stopped.'

'The ring in the grave . . . Rose Downey . . .'

'That one didn't work out so well, but, hey, you can't win 'em all.'

'And Mark Hudson?'

'He recognized me from New Mexico when I went round to Becky Corrigan's house to buy those ridiculous letters Jenkins Howler had sent her,' said Piper bluntly. 'I bumped into him as I was leaving. He said hello. What else could I do? I couldn't risk being IDed.'

'You didn't strangle *him*.'

'I figured I'd make the MO different in his case. Keep you all on your toes. Besides, I didn't want too much heat from the police in Dublin. My purpose was to play out the rest of the game with Kaminski. I only wanted those letters to make him suspicious, to make him wonder what was in them that someone wanted to hide.'

Some game.

It wasn't hard to imagine how things might have gone

with Hudson. How maybe he saw Piper and got talking, invited him in for a drink, how Piper slipped something into his glass when he wasn't looking . . . Then, when he started feeling groggy, he simply struck him on the back of the head to knock him out, put Hudson's body in the trunk of his Honda and got Randall to come with him out to Bull Island to dump it, making up some story about how they were going to meet some guy called Peters, that way making sure Randall was seen.

'You still haven't won yet,' I said.

'How do you figure that?'

'All I have to do is find Kaminski. Once he knows the truth –'

'But I have Kaminski here with me right now. He's sleeping in the next room. He has a busy night ahead of him. Why do you think he was so keen to get out from under your watching eye at the fair? I'd arranged the real rendezvous with Randall for him. You can't imagine how grateful he was when I turned up to make amends and offer my help. Buck's looking forward to it too. I told him I knew someone who could help him. He seems to have got the idea from your press conference this morning that he's in some kind of trouble.'

And he laughed.

I felt the panic rising inside me.

'Piper, don't do it. Randall doesn't deserve this. Kaminski doesn't deserve it.'

'Goodbye, Saxon. No hard feelings,' he said. 'I never intended for you to get involved. I tried to warn you off, but once you got involved I knew you'd be useful. You're even crazier than Kaminski. Once he got you involved, you were bound to reinforce his sense of what he had to do. He just needed a little push. But you know, Saxon, despite everything I always liked you. Maybe that's why we were always at each other's throats. We were too alike. And maybe we *can* still have that drink someday, huh? I'd enjoy that.'

Those were the last words I ever heard him speak. I never heard his voice again. Never saw his face. In fact, I realized as I sat there in the booth and watched Fitzgerald, unaware of the truth, gesturing me outside to ask what I'd learned, I hadn't seen his face this whole time except in a picture. The last time I'd seen him face to face was ten years ago, and yet he'd been directing my whole life in these last days. Now he'd vanished more completely than ever, like Kaminski had vanished into the trees in New England. Only Piper knew how to do it properly. He wouldn't be found again. The only other contact I had with him at all was one night, couple of days later, when I came home to find Marsha Reed's missing ring dangling from a frayed piece of string and slung around my door handle . . .

I took it as a warning from Piper to stay well away from him.

And the world would keep on turning in his absence, the sun would keep on shining, the rain keep on falling. That was the thing about murder. It didn't disturb normality, it scarcely even scratched the surface of it. The dead went into the ground, and the living forgot them. Thousands every day, killed a hundred different ways. Lucas Piper had gone, but there were always Lucas Pipers, just as there were always innocent fools like Leon Kaminski and Buck Randall III. None of us amounted to much in the end. A hundred years from now, we'd all be forgotten. There was a strange kind of comfort in it.

In the meantime, as Kaminski had known and had tried to make real in his wrong-headed way, there was always justice and there was always vengeance. In one way or another, one place or another, I hoped Piper would get what was coming to him.

The rest of that evening passed largely in a haze. There were phone calls and questions. I was distantly aware of voices. But something in me had become detached. I couldn't make sense of what had happened. It was like everything I'd thought was true was now lined up against the wall, laughing at me. Fitzgerald said I shouldn't blame myself. She said you never really know what these people are thinking, and I thought: is that what he was now? One of those people? And I realized I didn't even know any more what kind of person Lucas Piper was. Everything I thought I'd known about him turned out to be as insubstantial as cigar smoke.

If only, I found myself wishing futilely, I'd been straight with Kaminski from the start. I hadn't wanted to say too much because Lucas Piper told me that first night I called him how he and Kaminski were no longer friends and I didn't want to complicate things by admitting to Kaminski how I knew about his wife's death. *Who* had told me.

I didn't want to make him mad.

Hence I said nothing. Maybe together we would have seen through Piper's lies. I'd never know.

All I can say is that it seemed like a good idea at the time.

That's the story of my life. Things look like a good idea at the time, and they rarely are. In fact, I would go so far as to advise running like a cat out of a rabid dogs' home from anything which seems like a good idea at the time. Most of the greatest disasters in history have started out that way. But then that was part of what I was too. What I'd done, what I'd become, where I was now – none of it had been part of any plan. There hadn't been a plan. Maybe that was the problem. Everything in my life had been accidental.

Even seeing Kaminski in Temple Bar a week ago.

None of it had been planned.

But I was still finding it difficult to accept that it was the FBI man who'd been leading Kaminski by the nose, ass-like, into the darkness. But Becky Corrigan had confirmed that it was Lucas Piper who'd tried to buy Jenkins Howler's letters to her aunt.

One photograph.

That's all it had taken in the end to confirm his identity.

She also told us that it was Hudson's talking about the time he was questioned by the FBI in New Mexico for the murder of a woman that had got her aunt interested in the whole subject in the first place. Hudson had talked up how easy it would be to end up on Death Row for something that you'd never done. Something in his words tugged at her bleeding heart.

Soon after, she'd started writing to Jenkins Howler.

Strange how everything turned out to be connected in some way.

By this time Piper's fingerprints, which had been sent over from the personnel division at the FBI, had also been matched up to those found all over the inside of the trunk of the car in which Mark Hudson's rotting body had been found.

As for Buck Randall, it soon became clear that he was indeed as much of a dupe as Kaminski. The only difference was that he was being paid for his stupidity.

Fitzgerald had managed to pull up his bank records from back home and found that round about the same time Kaminski was following Randall round Huntsville, Randall had deposited a cheque for nearly thirty thousand dollars into his account.

The money came from a company run by Lucas Piper.

After he was persuaded of the seriousness of the situation, Randall's brother in Oklahoma confirmed the rest. Before he left Texas, Buck had told him that he'd been given the money by Piper in order to take a job with his electronics company. He didn't know what kind of job it was. Didn't know what it entailed. All Piper told him was that it would be well paid and that he would be back in Texas before the end of the summer.

Randall was in debt. He didn't feel like he was in any position to refuse. Besides, it seemed like easy money. All Piper asked of him was that he not reveal his whereabouts to anyone else, the police included, no matter what story they spun him.

Randall knew Kaminski was after him.

He knew why.

He was afraid.

Lucas Piper's offer represented a way out. If only he'd known that he was walking straight into Piper's trap. That in running away from Kaminski he was actually running straight toward him.

Randall's brother also confirmed that he'd spoken to Buck a couple times since he arrived in Dublin. Piper was acting strangely, Buck had told him. He'd been booked into some mean rooming house in a part of town far from the bright lights, big city atmosphere he'd been expecting, and he was being sent out around the city on pointless errands, buying flowers, turning up to meet people who turned out not to be there.

And Randall's drinking had also gotten out of control, his brother revealed. He could hear it in Buck's voice. He wasn't thinking clearly any more. Most likely that was Piper's plan too. To keep Randall so drunk that he didn't know what the hell was going on half the time.

Maybe he was drugging him too.

Randall certainly had no idea Kaminski was in the city, still pursuing him. He was just doing what Piper told him. Despite all that, he was getting suspicious.

He'd had enough, he'd told his brother in his last call.

He wanted to come home.

He didn't care about the money any more.

How he must've panicked when he saw that news report this morning and realized that he was still being hunted, not just by Kaminski this time, but by every cop in town. I guess he ran to Piper, looking for guidance, wanting to know what was happening. And how grateful he must've been when Piper said he knew someone who could help.

His brother told us that Randall had been twitchy around cops ever since he was questioned in New Mexico about the murder of a woman. They'd given him a hard time, apparently, which was why he'd been so nervous when he came across the same treatment in New York. Piper must've told him he could keep him away from the cops this time. Maybe he said he knew someone at the American Embassy who could clear up the misunderstanding.

By then it was too late. All the time, Piper had been laying the final pieces of the trail for Kaminski to follow, until finally he pulled the biggest rabbit of all out of the hat: himself.

He'd made contact with Kaminski.

Offered to help.

I recalled the book of matches Kaminski had in his pants the night he'd found the ring in Cecelia Corrigan's grave and been arrested. The Mountain House Lodge in Aspen, Colorado. I should have remembered this was where he and Piper had gone skiing together during their vacations. That had probably been Piper's sign to Kaminski that he was back in touch, that he'd forgiven him for taking Heather from him, and he wanted to help find the man who killed her. That was what Kaminski had been talking about that night. '*I'm making progress at last*,' he'd said. But his only progress had been right into Piper's hands.

And how would it end?

I thought I knew the answer to that, but I was almost afraid to form the thought in my head. Almost afraid that thinking it would make it true.

For now, only one thing mattered.

Finding Kaminski.

40

Shortly after midnight, a woman returning home late from work noticed that the wooden gates leading into Marsha Reed's house in the Liberties had been forced open.

She called the local police station, and the dispatcher sent out an order that the nearest patrol car was to go round to check it out. We heard the crackling message over the radio as we were returning to town along Morehampton Road from Becky Corrigan's house.

'It's probably just a coincidence,' said Walsh.

'Better check it out all the same,' said Fitzgerald, and she took the next left on to Marlborough Road, heading to Ranelagh, and from there to the Grand Canal.

The night still looked unfeasibly new, despite the lateness of the hour. No one was going to bed. The warm lights of the city kept them from wanting to go home. On the side of the canal, a group of young men, giddy from the evening's merrymaking, stood cheering round a lamp-post as one of their number shinnied up to place a traffic cone at the top like a hat.

Lovers embraced on bridges.

The streets were bleaker and more deserted once we crossed on to Clanbrassil Street, because here the city was less inviting, and there was less to stay outside for. The only other sign of life as we came to the place where Marsha Reed had lived was the patrol car, which was now arriving at her gate in answer to the radio's summons.

The uniformed cop looked almost startled to see us, until

Fitzgerald waved her badge at him. Then he looked relieved when she told him we'd be taking over.

'Just wait in the car in case we need you,' she said.

'See,' I said.

The gates had been forced with a crowbar. Splintered wood flowered from the wound. I pushed them open a fraction and peered into the shadowy alley, trying to make out movement, shapes, anything. The darkness wasn't co-operating.

It certainly didn't look so pleasant a spot as it had the other day when I came here to meet Marsha's friend Kim. The night may have been warm, but there was a harder edge now.

'Walsh, have you got a torch?'

'In the boot, Chief.'

'Go get it.'

Walsh walked to the car and returned quickly with a flashlight. He handed it to Fitzgerald, and she switched it on, pointing the beam down the alley, probing for any signs of movement, like a searchlight picking out enemy aircraft.

The beam was bright enough to reveal the whole scene ahead as luridly as though lit by a blast of lightning, only this lightning didn't burn itself out instantly. Way down the end of the lane, light reflected against a window and disturbed the bats in the trees. They squeaked in protest as they flapped out of the way of the light. Leaves were exposed like negatives.

'It's probably nothing,' said Fitzgerald. 'Kids. Or some drunk looking for a place to sleep. But there's only one way to find out for sure.'

She pushed the gate and we stepped inside and began to walk the path down to Marsha's house. The church loomed up in the darkness, more ominous now than it had seemed in the daytime. This must have been what it looked like that night Marsha Reed was murdered. This must have been what Lucas Piper saw as he approached.

Or maybe that night there'd been a light ahead, shining by the front door, forming some destination to aim at. Maybe the stained-glass windows had glowed from within.

Maybe Marsha had even been waiting at the door.

When we reached the end of the lane, where the grounds opened out around the church, Fitzgerald stopped and pointed the flashlight into the corners of the garden.

Just to be sure.

Emptiness gaped back.

That left only the church itself.

I heard Fitzgerald gasp as the light spread across the doorway.

The door was open.

'Should I get back-up?' whispered Walsh.

Fitzgerald took a moment, composing herself.

'I want to take a look first,' she answered.

We crossed quietly to the door and climbed the steps. Fitzgerald reached out a hand and pushed at the door. It opened smoothly, without a sound. The stone hallway behind it was cleared of furniture now. It looked more like a church again than a place to live.

'Let me go first, Chief.'

Fitzgerald raised her finger to her lips.

'Can you hear it?' she asked him.

I heard it too.

A whispering like her own, only this sound was continual, a voice talking to itself softly in the dark ahead, without any alteration in tone, as if in prayer. Someone else was still inside the church, and it sure didn't sound like kids or some drunk.

Only one more door to go.

My skin was taut with tension.

Fitzgerald's too, I realized, as her arm accidentally brushed against mine, and an electric shock passed between us. When did it suddenly get so cold? Wasn't it summer?

Her hand closed around the door handle.

Turned it.

Click.

The sound of the lock releasing was like a gun hammer cocking.

'Police,' warned Fitzgerald, raising her voice.

Then she entered.

The flashlight in her hand broke into the church first, bright as an angel appearing out of nowhere. But there was no angel standing ahead of us, only a man with his arms raised in front of his face to shield his eyes from the unexpected illumination, hands facing outwards.

His hands were stained red.

Behind him his shadow surged against the stone, huge as a monster.

He was standing on the altar where Marsha Reed's bed had stood.

The bed where she'd died.

And I saw now that the bed was still there. Her father must have wanted it left untouched, as though it was cursed somehow. Fitzgerald dipped the light so that the man standing there could lower his hands, and the beam of light spread across the bed – and found something else. Another figure, except this one was not standing, and would never stand again. Instead it was doubled over, arms clutched under a belly that must have been seared with agony at the moment of death but which was now far beyond the reach of pain. Blood pooled out on the mattress underneath the body, black as treacle in the flashlight's gaze.

A knife, coloured in the same black along the blade, lay discarded on the floor.

'JJ?' I said, because the figure standing in front of the bed had now lowered his arms, and I could see that it was Kaminski, and he was smiling, his lips still moving in whispers.

'Kaminski,' said Fitzgerald. 'What have you done?'

'I killed him,' he said, and the smile grew wider.

'Killed who?' she demanded. 'Who have you killed?'

'Randall,' he said, frowning like the question was so ridiculous as to not even deserve an answer. 'Buck Randall – he's dead. It's over. He thought he could get away with it. He thought he could kill Heather and I'd just let him get away with it.'

I couldn't speak.

Piper had told Randall he'd be back in Texas before the end of the summer.

What he hadn't told him was that he'd be returning in a casket.

I saw now that this had been the linchpin of his plan.

Our last hope – that Kaminski would learn the truth, and that Piper could take Randall's place, the place that should have been his – was gone.

Fitzgerald's voice was cold. 'You fool,' she said. 'Buck Randall didn't kill your wife.'

Kaminski started to laugh, and then the laugh became angry when he realized he was laughing on his own.

'What are you talking about?' he demanded. 'What are you – Are you fucking crazy or something? Do you think I don't know what this bastard did to me?'

'Buck Randall did not kill your wife,' repeated Fitzgerald.

Kaminski looked from her to me.

'Saxon?' he pleaded.

'She's right.'

'Then who – Who killed her?'

'It was Lucas,' I told him.

Kaminski began shaking his head violently 'No,' he said. 'He was helping me.'

'Kaminski, stop.'

'No.'

'He wanted you to suffer for taking Heather away from him.'

'No. He told me he'd find Randall. You know what Piper was like. He could find anyone. *You* wouldn't help me. He said we'd do it together for Heather. No,' he said. 'No.'

But the word wasn't a denial any more, and it wasn't disbelief. The word was the sound of a man who had just seen every reality on which he had built his life crumble.

A man who had suddenly woken up from a dream, and now understood that everything he had accepted as right was actually wrong. He was where Piper had wanted him. He was at the end of the line, with nowhere left to go. He'd crossed that invisible line and made himself a killer, for the sake of what he thought was justice, but it had all been in vain.

He had murdered an innocent man.

And now Kaminski knew it.

And he'd know it for ever.

His eyes were wild with strange truth.

'I'm sorry,' I said.

Kaminski didn't hear me. Instead he dropped to his knees. He was mumbling something under his breath as his hands felt around the floor.

A moment too late, I saw what he was looking for.

The knife.

Just as I realized what was happening, Kaminski's fingers

closed around the handle of the knife and he turned it round and pointed it to his chest. He closed his eyes.

He thrust the knifepoint toward him.

I watched it all as if in slow motion – but Walsh was quicker. He'd seen what Kaminski was about to do and had managed to make up the space between. As Kaminski's grip tightened on the knife, preparing himself for what was to come, the young detective threw himself forward to snatch at the handle. The knife still entered Kaminski, but not where he'd wanted it to go, not where the decision would have been irreversible.

Kaminski gave a low moan of pain that swiftly turned into a lower moan of despair as Walsh cheated him of the knife and stopped him finishing what he'd started.

'Let me die,' he begged. 'Please, let me die.'

I often wondered afterwards if it wouldn't have been kinder to let him do just that.

Epilogue

The following evening we repaired to Shanahan's on the Green. A restored Georgian town house now transformed into an American-style steakhouse, and best known, apart from the fact that the body of a young woman had been found in the foundations sometime in the eighteenth century, for the rocking chair behind the bar in the basement where we were now sitting.

The chair had once belonged to President Kennedy. He took it everywhere with him, including Air Force One. Now it presided over drinkers in the suitably named Oval Office Bar. It was Stella Carson who'd suggested we all meet up here – Fitzgerald, Healy, Walsh, herself and me – and I didn't complain. It was one of my favourite places in the whole city.

We were sitting now on red velvet armchairs around a table on which perched an antique lamp surrounded by champagne glasses, as though they were guarding it.

The champagne had been Fitzgerald's idea. She'd long been of the opinion that champagne was for celebrations and commiserations and all points in between. Me, I'd have preferred a beer, but when someone else is paying, you don't complain about that either.

So which was it? Celebration or commiseration? Two cases which I'd convinced myself were connected, and then been forced to admit might have nothing to do with one another, turned out to be connected after all, but neither in the way we expected, and the angle which had seemed to most of the investigating team like an absurd distraction turned out to be the heart of it all. Meanwhile the only person behind bars was Leon Kaminski. I didn't know what would happen to him. Even if a judge and jury took pity on him in the end for the murder of Buck Randall, he was locked now in a prison of his own making, and Piper had the key. As long as Piper was out there, Kaminski could never be free again, never be at peace.

As for Solomon, he'd been released earlier that day. There was no chance of pursuing a case against him for murder any more, not after all that had happened, and Ellen Forwood was refusing to press charges against him for the incident in which she'd been injured.

He was a free man, though I doubted his career would exactly flourish in future.

Mud sticks.

'If you close a case, then it's a celebration,' the Assistant Commissioner ruled in the end. 'Even if you feel utterly crap about it. That should be the first rule of detective work.'

'Hear, hear,' said Healy. 'I'll drink to that.'

And he reached out a hand and lightly touched the back of Stella Carson's own. It was a tiny gesture, scarcely noticeable. Walsh didn't even see it – though that could've been because he was eyeing up the waitress as she weaved her way slinkily among the tables.

I looked at Fitzgerald and saw her smiling.

Silently, I managed to ask if what I was seeing was what I thought it was.

Silently, she managed to answer that it was.

I couldn't have been more astonished. All this time, I'd been tormenting myself with the possibility that something might develop between Fitzgerald and Stella Carson, and all the while the one the Assistant Commissioner was getting close to was Healy. That was fast work for a week.

Othello should have taught me the dangers of jealousy.

It was like Fitzgerald said. You saw what you wanted to see, you made connections where your mind made them, making things appear that were not really there.

You started seeing the world through the wrong eyes.

'There's just one thing I don't understand,' said Fitzgerald.

'The necklace,' said Healy.

'Exactly. If Marsha really did inadvertently arrange her own murder, and Solomon had nothing to do with it, then how did the necklace end up hidden in a bag in his office? Piper never said anything about either of them. I'd swear he didn't know they existed.'

'I can answer that,' said a voice behind us, and we turned to find Todd Fleming standing close by, looking nervous and carrying a small holdall . . .

Fleming had followed us to Shanahan's that evening to make a confession. He wanted to tell us what really happened on the night of Marsha Reed's murder.

She'd called him at the internet café, he said, and told him what she planned to do. Told him about her arrangement with her anonymous caller. What he was going to do. He told her she was mad. Told her it was dangerous. Warned her about all the things that could go wrong, but she wouldn't listen. It was all an act, she assured him, nothing more.

Where was the harm in that?

She told him that she'd planned the whole thing to scare Solomon into thinking that he'd almost lost her. She'd tried everything. She'd tried begging and blackmail and a plentiful supply of easy sex and even the prospect of some of her father's money to try to lure him back to her, but Solomon was having none of it. He wanted out of their relationship once and for all. He was going to marry Ellen Forwood and nothing Marsha could do would change that. The only thing she could think of now to bring him back was to make him believe that she had almost been killed. Surely once he saw how close he had been to losing her for ever, he would realize that he loved her and had to be with her and how much she needed him?

She had it all worked out.

She was to be roughed up a little and tied to the bed. The bruises would make it look good afterwards. The cuts would heal. She didn't mind. Didn't she enjoy pain? Didn't it turn her on? She was happy as she told him what was in store. Excited.

She certainly wasn't afraid.

She just needed Todd's help to make the deception complete. His role was to call round later after work and let himself into the house. The story would be that he had disturbed the killer in the act and the monster had fled. Then he was to call the police. Marsha would take it from there. She was an actress, after all. She knew how to lie convincingly.

Todd Fleming was terrified, he was confused, he was angry that she was still thinking about getting back with Solomon after the way he'd treated her. But she managed to talk him round. He agreed to call at her house after he finished work. How could he refuse? He loved her. Whatever she asked of him, he had to do it. He couldn't help himself.

What he actually found when he got there and let himself

in with the spare key she'd left on the doorstep for him was Marsha's lifeless body lying on the bed.

A severed finger next to it.

The night had clearly not gone according to plan.

Fleming was distraught. For a time he couldn't think straight. All he could do was blame himself for allowing Marsha to talk him into taking part in her insane scheme. He should have walked out of work the moment she called, it didn't matter if he was fired, nothing else mattered except that he should have gone round to protect her.

He knew one thing.

It was his fault she was dead.

But then another, stronger thought began to gnaw at him. It wasn't his fault at all. Solomon was the one who was to blame. He'd driven Marsha to this last insane act. In a way, he *had* killed her. And Fleming wanted him to suffer for it. He longed for that more than anything he'd longed for in his life. *He* was the one who'd driven Marsha to put her life at risk, so he was the one who had to pay. Fleming already loathed Solomon because Marsha had wanted him so badly. Now he had even more reason to hate him. To want him punished.

Fleming even convinced himself that if it hadn't been for Solomon, maybe there'd have been a chance for him and Marsha to be together. That it was Solomon, rather than her own dark appetites, which had kept them apart. And he thought he knew exactly how to get his revenge on this man who had made him suffer so much.

He would frame him for her death.

He took the necklace, planning to plant it in Solomon's office when he had the chance, wearing the same shoes he was wearing that night so that the physical evidence traces would match. It wouldn't be difficult to get inside. Theatres are open places, like Zak Kirby said. So that's what he did, first covering her obscenely displayed dead naked body with a sheet because he couldn't bear to see what had been done to her. And then he took the tapes from the hidden camera at Marsha's door too, knowing they could clear Solomon's name. (Piper thought he had everything figured. He hadn't seen that one. The expert in surveillance had become the victim of it.)

His hurt at being denied kept him going for days, consumed him, sustained him, and then he stopped sleeping and lay awake remembering her brutalized body, and repeating to himself over and over that the man who did that to her, and would surely do it to other women too if he was not stopped, was still out there. He couldn't go through with it any more.

He didn't want to be the kind of man who crushed someone just because they'd had what he himself had wanted so badly. He wanted to be better than that. So he confessed – and brought along with him a holdall containing the missing surveillance tape.

Later, we sat in Fitzgerald's office, as Walsh took Fleming downstairs to make a statement, and watched the grainy black-and-white tape, seeing the clock ticking down and Marsha coming home, unsteady on her feet; the taxi driver helping her with her keys; and, once they had vanished from view, a cat, sleek and dark, out hunting, tiptoeing carefully across the path in front of the door before halting, startled by a new arrival, and fleeing.

Then there he was, Piper, strolling to the door like he was on some social call, entirely unaware that he was being filmed, and disappearing inside.

The surveillance footage told us nothing we didn't now know already, but there was still a grim fascination in watching the seconds tick by on the tape's own clock, while inside the church, in one of those seconds, Marsha Reed's life was snuffed out.

Was it that second?

Or this?

Eventually, Piper reappeared, and he walked down the path and out of sight. We fast-forwarded to see Todd Fleming himself arrive at 2 a.m., stepping nervously, not knowing what to expect, and finally there was only the cat again, tail raised, distrustful and alert, back to sniff the porch where these strangers had been, rubbing itself against the stone to replace their scent with its own. It sat on the path and looked up at the camera, as if it knew it was there, and its eyes glinted like mirrors in the dark. Then nothing, as the camera was switched out.

Case closed.

'More champagne?' said Fitzgerald.

She'd brought the half-empty bottle with her from the restaurant.

'I'd say there're about two glasses each left. We'll have to drink it out of paper cups from the coffee machine,' she added, 'but champagne's champagne. Just one condition.'

'Yeah?'

'Not a word about Marsha Reed. I've had quite enough of her for one night, the stupid girl. What do you say?'

'Consider it done,' I said with feeling. 'I don't know about you, but I'm in the mood for getting seriously drunk. When the world ceases to make sense, you might as well join it.'

It was only afterwards, when we'd gone back to my place to sit on the balcony and start on another bottle, and I was savouring a cigar and blowing the smoke defiantly across the rooftops of the piously non-smoking city below, that it occurred to me how similar Lucas Piper and Marsha Reed had been. What they had in common was that neither could cope with a situation most of us have to learn how to handle at least once in our lives: being dumped. Not being wanted. Their inability to cope with it had made one a killer and the other a victim.

It was on the tip of my tongue to share this nugget of dubious wisdom with Fitzgerald when I remembered what she'd said. Not a word about Marsha Reed.

A deal's a deal.

It could wait.

CHRIS MOONEY

THE MISSING

The woman missing for five years.

The Crime Scene Investigator who finds her.

And the serial killer who wants them both dead ...

When Boston CSI Darby McCormick finds a raving and emaciated
woman hiding at the scene of a violent kidnap, she runs a DNA search
to identify the Jane Doe. The result confirms she was abducted five
years earlier and has somehow managed to escape from the dungeon in
which she's been caged.

With a teenage couple also missing and Jane Doe seriously ill, the
clock is ticking for Darby as she hunts for the dungeon before anyone
else disappears or dies. And when the FBI takes over the investigation,
it becomes clear that a sadistic serial killer has been on the prowl for
decades – and is poised to strike again at any moment. A killer with
links to horrors that Darby has desperately tried to bury in her past ...

'The season's most unrelenting thriller ... will keep readers enthralled'
George Pelecanos

Jim Kelly

THE COLDEST BLOOD

Winner of the CWA Dagger in the Library Award

Mid-winter and Arctic temperatures grip the cathedral city of Ely, where a 39-year-old man is found frozen to death in his flat …

The police think that Declan McIlroy killed himself – perhaps accidentally, perhaps intentionally – but journalist Philip Dryden is less sure. He does what any good reporter should: he starts digging.

Dryden soon turns up another corpse – that of Declan's best friend, frozen in a shell of ice on the porch of his secluded home. And suddenly a routine suicide gives way to a shocking trail of cruelty and betrayal stretching back thirty years – towards a chilling mystery, barely remembered from Dryden's own childhood …

'Kelly writes with obvious affection about the Fens, which make an eerily atmospheric background' *Sunday Telegraph*

ELIZABETH RIGBEY

THE HUNTING SEASON

Dense woodland. Twisting paths.
It's easy to lose your way in the wilderness …

The rugged Rocky Mountains are a place some go to hide inside, some to escape into and others to hunt in. Dr Matt Seleckis has never been one for the woods: he remembers his childhood vacations there with his mother and father – and the looming threat of an unexplained death …

Now Matt lives in the mountains' shadow, in Utah with his wife and young son. Yet the prospect of a hunting trip alone with his father is bringing back dark, unwelcome memories – of a certain vacation, of his beloved parents. And of a hushed-up tragedy that he's sure concerns him.

But with the arrival of these unsettling memories comes the creeping realisation that in nature, death for the unwary lies around every corner. And in the woods, it's easy to take a wrong turn …

'The truth about what really happened one childhood summer vacation is tantalisingly revealed in this gripping tale' *Woman & Home*

NICK STONE

MR CLARINET

Winner of the CWA Ian Fleming Steel Dagger for Best Thriller of the Year

Winner of the International Thriller Writers' Best Debut Novel

The job: find a rich man's kidnapped son in Haiti

The reward: $10 million to bring the boy back alive

The man: Max Mingus, ex-cop, ex-PI and now ex-con

The stakes: his predecessors haven't just failed, they've been destroyed …

Max Mingus knows the price of a bad risk, but he takes the Haiti job because no one else will. A lawless island of voodoo and black magic where each man must face his personal demons, Haiti is also home to a monster they call Mr Clarinet – infamous for spiriting countless children away from their families.

In searching for the boy – alive or dead – Max has only his life to lose. But in Haiti, there are fates far worse than death …

'A triumphant debut' *Observer*

'An intriguing plot, believable characters and thrills and spills to keep you turning the pages eagerly. A rollicking read' *Big Issue*

He just wanted a decent book to read ...

Not too much to ask, is it? It was in 1935 when Allen Lane, Managing Director of Bodley Head Publishers, stood on a platform at Exeter railway station looking for something good to read on his journey back to London. His choice was limited to popular magazines and poor-quality paperbacks – the same choice faced every day by the vast majority of readers, few of whom could afford hardbacks. Lane's disappointment and subsequent anger at the range of books generally available led him to found a company – and change the world.

'We believed in the existence in this country of a vast reading public for intelligent books at a low price, and staked everything on it'
Sir Allen Lane, 1902–1970, founder of Penguin Books

The quality paperback had arrived – and not just in bookshops. Lane was adamant that his Penguins should appear in chain stores and tobacconists, and should cost no more than a packet of cigarettes.

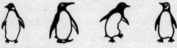

Reading habits (and cigarette prices) have changed since 1935, but Penguin still believes in publishing the best books for everybody to enjoy. We still believe that good design costs no more than bad design, and we still believe that quality books published passionately and responsibly make the world a better place.

So wherever you see the little bird – whether it's on a piece of prize-winning literary fiction or a celebrity autobiography, political tour de force or historical masterpiece, a serial-killer thriller, reference book, world classic or a piece of pure escapism – you can bet that it represents the very best that the genre has to offer.

Whatever you like to read – trust Penguin.